BECOMING THE ENIGMA

Loup-Garou Series Book 2

SHERITTA BITIKOFER

MOONSTRUCK WRITING

This story has been one that is near and dear to my heart. I have to thank everyone for helping me through the ordeal of writing, editing, revising, and countless reediting. I couldn't have done it without the support and love of my family and friends.

Also, a big thanks to my husband for rejoicing in my quirky obsessions. I can always count on you to be by safe harbor, someone I can speak freely with about my stories without fear of rejection. Your support has been invaluable.

CHAPTER 1

Darren rubbed at the back of his neck as he sat in one of the dining chairs he had brought into the sitting room, while Ben sat in another, elbows on knees and hands tightly folded together as if in prayer. Dustin sluggishly paced in the foyer just beyond the open French doors, and diligently watched the sleeping figures of Katey on one couch and Logan on its pair across from her.

The loups-garous had loosened their work attire, top buttons and ties undone. It'd been several hours since the attack and neither of them had shown any sign of consciousness. But, as long as the three men could still hear their gentle breathing and strong heartbeats, they knew that there was still hope.

Ben glanced to the clock on the wall, the pendulum swinging with each second that dragged. Dustin blew out a short breath and stopped just inside the French doors. Darren looked at his beta and his impatient, shifty gaze.

"Brooding won't make them wake up," he commented as he unbuttoned his cuffs and rolled up his sleeves. The air in the house was cool, but the sitting room took on a balmy, suffocating temperature.

Ben rolled his shoulders. "What else are we supposed to do? I can't just carry on with my evenin', knowin' that they're like this."

"I knew a loup-garou in Italy that tried to turn his girlfriend," Dustin said, brushing his fingertips underneath his chin with a distant look in his eye. "She was unconscious for nearly a day before she started fading."

"Katey won't fade." Darren had to stay strong for his pack. If he showed the slightest bit of panic, they would latch onto it and begin to doubt themselves and everything they secretly believed from the beginning. "She's strong. She'll pull through."

Ben hung his head and ran his hands through his hair, gripping at the roots. Dustin turned away, his arms crossed and shoulders rigid. Darren swallowed hard and turned his attention back to Katey, who looked to be sleeping soundly. At least she wasn't in any pain... yet.

Katey moaned as feeling finally returned to her body. Everything ached, from her muscles and bones to her skin, as if she had been stretched too thin and then pushed back together. She moved her head and pain shot down her spine. She hissed and struggled to open her eyes, but her eyelids felt bruised and swollen. The lights blinded her, and she squeezed her eyes shut again with a whimper. Bright dots danced in Katey's vision as her retinas tried to recover from the sudden assault.

Darren's voice whispered somewhere in the room. "Ben, turn off the lights."

She sensed some movement in the room, and assumed it was Ben obeying the alpha. Beyond her eyelids, she could tell the light directly above them had been cut off.

Katey sighed and blinked for a moment, trying to think, but that, too, made her hurt. She glanced between the three loups-garous and their anxious gazes.

Through the haze and chaos of alien sensations and pain, she could tell she lay on one of the sofas in the sitting room. She squinted around and recognized the old furniture and crystal chandelier in the dining room.

As her foggy mind reached into the past, another face appeared. One distorted with rage and the golden eyes of the wolf staring at her with hunger and distressed longing. Growls and harsh words hummed in her ears, and she remembered exactly what happened.

More pain streaked through her body, but it could do little to distract her from the memory of Logan bent over her with teeth bared in a snarl. Katey found the energy to push herself up, but Dustin gently pushed her back down onto the sofa, his touch like needles jabbing into her flesh. The prickly edges of the bandage tape bit into her skin as it shifted under her clothes.

"Just take it easy. Everything's okay. How do you feel?"

"Don't shout at me," she moaned, her own voice sounding like a clanging gong in her ears.

"I'm not."

"Give her ears a bit to get used to it," Darren whispered from behind Dustin.

Katey blinked hard and raised her hand to her throbbing head, the effort to move expending what little energy she had. "Where's Logan?"

"He's right here." Ben motioned toward the loveseat on the other side of the room.

Katey turned her head and her throat closed up. There lay Logan's limp and unconscious body. His face was blank, as if he were sleeping.

Dustin rubbed his thumb across her tender shoulder, a comforting gesture to her nerves. "Don't worry, we crammed meat down his throat after we brought you two home. He's just resting now."

Katey glanced down to her body, as if to make sure it was still in one piece. "Everything hurts."

Darren took a careful step forward. "It's going to hurt for a little while. But, once everything sets in, you'll feel relatively normal again."

Her thoughts were a tangled mess, searching for an explanation why everything was so sensitive and vivid. Her eyes widened as her mind slowly cleared.

"Am I..." She could barely voice the word, afraid that if she spoke it aloud, her hopes would be dashed to pieces.

The guys glanced to each other and Darren nodded solemnly. "We think so."

Katey took deep breaths and it was like each inhale was a new experience. Air passed in and out of her lungs, but it didn't quite feel the same as it had before. She glanced around the room. Everything from the fibers of the red carpet to the rough texture of the wallpaper was clear and vibrant. With her eyes wide open, she realized that colors were brighter, more distinct in their varying shades.

Not only that, but her nose was assailed with potent scents and smells she couldn't quite recognize. The guys' distinct scents from their cologne and deodorants, the metallic acrid scent of dried blood smeared all over her hoodie and jeans, the musty smell of old carpet, chemical odor of the paint and building materials, the earthy scent of the wood floors in the foyer and living room. She could even smell the food in the refrigerator all the way in the kitchen.

As the aching subsided, she began to feel something like shocks of static under her skin that made her muscles twitch. A tingly feeling in the back of her skull developed and slowly dissipated as the moments passed. She recognized it as a caffeine buzz, but like everything else, it wasn't quite the same.

There was another sensation. It was a visceral and emotional pull, like a loosely tethered rope between her and each of the men in the room, like a constant reminder that they were there. The connection pulsated as if strength and life were surging between all five of them.

"What time is it?" Katey strained her vocal cords to speak louder, though her ears protested.

"A little past ten o'clock," Ben replied. "You've been out for a while now."

Dustin's hand gripped her shoulder a little tighter. "We are so sorry this happened. We thought Logan knew better than to go behind our backs. This wasn't supposed to happen."

Katey could hear the sorrow in his voice, but what was more, she thought she could smell it. Like a predator smelled fear on an animal of prey, Katey smelled their worry, their regret, and guilt as clearly as if it were written on their faces.

"If we had known," Dustin continued, "we would have taken every measure to keep an eye on him. I... I wouldn't have left you alone in the classroom either."

"But... I asked for it."

Dustin sat back on his heels and withdrew his hand as if he had been burned. A ripple of shock filled the room.

"You asked for it?" Darren questioned, a tinge of anger making the words sharp and cutting. "I told you that you couldn't become a loup-garou. We told you the risks. You knew you would have died."

Katey felt the edges of her mouth twitch into a weak smile, straining against tired and sore facial muscles. "But, I didn't die. I'm still here and... it worked."

She was proud of Logan in a weird, morbid sort of way. He did what they thought he couldn't do, what they thought no loup-garou could do. It was worth the risk of death to give him such bragging rights, and worth the risk to know that now, nothing could come between them.

Darren shook his head, fury surging from him. "That's not the point. He could have killed you. If Dustin hadn't walked in, he probably would have. We don't know how long he had been holding onto you like that. He could have put way too much venom into you. You lost a lot of blood... We weren't sure if you were going to make it."

Katey turned pleading eyes to the pack. "Please, don't be hard on him about this. I wanted it, he turned me, and he didn't kill me. Everything turned out fine."

"Oh, rest assured, Logan will get his punishment for what he did." Dustin's Irish accent chose now to make an appearance. The anger flowed off him in buckets, threatening to drown Katey's delicate nerves. "He disobeyed us and he could have killed you. We can't let that slide."

Katey looked between their frustrated gazes and tried to push back the thickness that developed in her throat. She understood how much worse it could have been. She wasn't a fool. They all told her the dangers, but they also said she was special, that they already thought of her as one of the pack. If they didn't want her to try it, they shouldn't have encouraged her.

The guys' heads swiveled to Logan as he began to move.

Darren moved to sit in Katey's view of Logan. "Ben, take her to the kitchen and get her to eat something. The ground beef may be the easiest."

Katey grabbed at Dustin's sleeve. "No, I want to stay."

He pulled her hand away and stood to join Darren. "You don't need to be in here for this, and you need to get some meat on your stomach before something else happens."

Ben approached and in one slow, fluid motion, pulled her to her feet.

Katey felt more shocks and tingles in her muscles that caused her to tremble. Ben's hand gripped under her arm, and he platonically wrapped his arm around her waist to steady her. The room swayed in her vision and bile tried to push its way up her esophagus.

"Your strength will come to ya after a while," he told her. Katey took his word for it, knowing that he had been where she was over a century and a half ago.

As they hobbled through the dining room and into the kitchen, her eyes stayed fixed on Logan, apprehensive to leave him to his alpha's rage. She wanted to tell them everything, convince them to be gentle with Logan, but they were too determined and she was too weak.

Ben set her on one of the barstools, but she found she couldn't maintain her balance. After a couple of tries, he cursed under his breath and finally set her on the floor, leaning her against a cabinet. He left her to pull a package from the fridge and a plate from the clean rack of dishes by the sink. Katey watched with sudden eagerness as he unraveled the packaging and slapped the portion of ground beef on the plate. It had to be at least a pound, if not more, pink and glistening.

Her eyes suddenly felt cold, as if a winter wind blew straight in her face. The meat smelled incredible with no seasoning or preparation. Ben knelt by her and pinched a bit of the meat between his fingers to offer it to her as if she were a stray dog. Katey's mouth pulled in disgust, though everything in her told her that it was totally fine.

"Ya gotta eat," Ben chided. "If ya don't, the wolf's gonna come out and make ya eat and we don't want that just yet."

"Can't you cook it first?"

"Nope. It's better for ya this way. Just don't think about it."

A new feeling distracted Katey from the meal in front of her. That tether to Logan hummed to life and she looked to the dining room saloon door to listen. She heard some rustling, as if he shifted on the cushions.

"What the bloody hell were you thinking?" Darren growled.

"I'll tell you what he was thinking," Dustin rattled off in his thick accent. "The boyo wasn't thinkin' a damned thing. He just wanted to go and kill Katey, blatantly disobeying us."

A tremor of fear passed through the bond they shared, Logan's fear.

"Is she...?" Logan's scratchy throat managed to mutter.

Ben pinned her with only a look, warning her not to even think about going to him.

"She's alive, but that's beside the point. You could have killed her!" Darren roared, making everyone's ears ring. "Why would you do something so reckless and thoughtless?"

"I knew if I told any of you what I wanted to do, you'd just hold me back."

"Damn right we would have!" Dustin exclaimed. "Why in hell's blazes did you do this?"

"I ... I just wanted to be with her."

Katey's eyes blurred with tears as she listened and suffered along with Logan, even feeling Darren's crushing dominance.

Darren scoffed. "That's a lame excuse. You could have been with her in the way everyone else deals with having a mate."

"She was okay with it," Logan countered.

"Yeah, I'm sure she would be after being scared shitless!" Dustin cried. "I'd hate to have seen how you looked, your wolf completely unhinged like that."

"I didn't mean to scare her."

Darren snarled. "You pushed her into making that decision. This situation could have been a lot worse than it was. I've given you a lot of chances, Logan, but this takes the cake. I've taught you better than to go and do something like this."

Katey gave a begging look to Ben. She had to set the record straight, she had to tell them that Logan didn't push her, didn't manipulate her. He only coaxed her into asking for the very thing she knew she already wanted. The damned pros and cons listed didn't matter anymore, knowing that to be with Logan in the way they both wanted was to become a loup-garou like him.

"I'm sorry." Logan's whisper sounded just as loudly as if his lips had been pressed to her ears.

"You're sorry?" Dustin exploded. "What would you have said if you had killed her? Sorry?"

"I had to take that chance. You both have told me stories of how our kind mate with a human and have to watch them age and die. You've told me how it's the worst pain in the world... I didn't want that to happen to Katey and I... I thought I had it under control."

"She was bleeding all over my classroom floor, Logan!"

She heard Logan jump to his feet. "Then I'll clean it up if it'll make you happy!"

"What would make me happy is if you stop playing this 'Oh, pity me, I'm all alone in the world' act and get it together. You're not alone. You never have been and never will be, Katey or not. You have a pack and now you have your precious girlfriend."

Katey thought she heard Logan shoved Dustin. "I'd rather be human than a beast!"

"If you didn't change, you'd still be living with that dead-beat father instead of us!"

Katey pressed her hands into the cold tile floor, their negative and hateful words parading through her head like screaming ghouls.

"Enough!" Darren roared. "Logan, outside. Now!"

"Why?"

Dusting gave a huff of a laugh. "I think you know exactly why. You screwed up, and there's no way you're getting off with a slap on the wrist or a temporary lockdown."

Icy panic spread through her limbs.

"What do you mean?"

A scuffle ensued and Katey failed to scramble to her feet as the three loups-garous left the sitting room and tracked through the foyer, then the living room. By the sound of it, Logan struggled against them, his feet dragging and bumping into furniture. Logan gave some panicked protest as Darren and Dustin carted him out through the sliding glass doors and into the dark night beyond. The smell of the flowers from the garden and pine trees wafted through the house, and Katey was momentarily stunned by her awareness of it before understanding that Logan was gone.

"What are they going to do?" she asked Ben.

"Give him what he deserves."

A few moments of silence passed, both of them sitting still on the floor and waiting. When it came, Katey whimpered. They were hurting him. Badly.

"Why?" she cried out. "He only did what I asked him to do."

Ben stared at her, seemingly baffled by the tears that streamed down her cheeks. "Ya don't get it. He could have killed you." He drawled out the words slowly, a bit of his back-woods accent coming through. "You are under our protection. It doesn't matter if he didn't kill you. He could have. It's like murder with intent. He knew what he was doin'."

There was no point arguing anymore. None of them would understand. None of them knew what they shared, or why it was so important for her to be loup-garou with him. If only they could see that this was the only way, they wouldn't be so hard on him. Maybe she should have been the one out there, taking the beating that Logan didn't deserve.

Pain ripped through Logan's leg and hip as his femur snapped in two beneath Darren's heel. Lying prone on his stomach, he groaned into the blood-soaked soil of the forest floor and writhed with what limbs hadn't become completely useless.

Time passed in agonizing seconds as Logan's body was broken and then healed, only to be broken again. At the hands of his alpha and beta, bones were shattered, one by one. Claws tore through his flesh, slow and vengeful. With every piece of his punishment, Logan screamed in anguish, white hot pain blotting out all thought.

They had never done this to him, but he had never screwed up this badly. What happened in Chicago was different. He wasn't the target of their anger then. He hadn't been their responsibility during those months, so they didn't find it pertinent to punish him for what he did, and some good came out of his mistakes then.

The jury was still out whether what Logan did to Katey was good or not, but he knew that wasn't the point. He could have killed her. She could have died in his arms or on that couch in the sitting room. Those loups-garous in Chicago didn't matter to his pack, but Katey did. They were supposed to protect her. Logan was supposed to protect her, and he set her up to die at his hands. He made just the right decisions to let the wolf take over, because the wolf had the courage and fortitude to do what Logan couldn't.

They all had the suspicion that Katey may have been able to become loup-garou. She had some special spark in her, but that wasn't enough for Darren and the pack to take the plunge. There were no female loups-garous. They always died by the bite, no exceptions. Logan had another motive, one that he couldn't ignore.

He wanted to be with Katey. He wanted them to be mates. Not for her human, finite lifetime, but for centuries. He couldn't bear the thought of watching her grow old and die. Every loup-garou who dared to fall in love had to suffer such a loss, but Logan refused. His wolf refused.

That need for Katey to stay with him forever drove him to this, and now that Logan's wolf was back in its cage and human logic returned, he understood just how much he deserved this. Like Darren said when his punishment began, he needed to feel what he had done to Katey, as much as could be simulated. That way, he would understand how he hurt her, how much torture her body endured for his mistake.

After tonight, Logan knew one thing unquestionably. His wolf would never have control like that again. How could he have been so foolish to think it was a good idea? The wolf killed his parents. The wolf went on a rampage through Chicago. And now, it tried to kill the only good thing he had in his life. He'd never give it so much leash, never let it out of its cage to do something like that again. He and his wolf had only joined in agreement a few times in his lifetime to accomplish a goal, but this crossed the line. Ultimately, it was Logan's desire to turn Katey that let the wolf out, but that was no excuse. He used his wolf wrongly, and he paid dearly for it.

From that night on, Logan and his wolf were enemies again.

As his bones set and the pain ebbed, his raw and tender body quivered. His tattered clothes rubbing against his burning skin sent him into spasms. He couldn't move, could barely breathe, every action sending ripples of pain through his flesh again.

He heard his alpha stalk around him, likely picking the next body part to break. His ribs? His back? Maybe he'd crushed Logan's hands again. Or maybe his skull. How deep could a loup-garou's head cave in on itself and still mend back to a whole piece?

Moments passed, but Darren didn't assault him. Neither did Dustin.

"Think he's had enough?" The alpha asked his beta.

"I think he had enough a few bones back."

The crunch of footsteps on dead leaves approached and Logan cracked open his eyes to see Darren's shoes. The alpha squatted down and their stares met in the darkness.

"The next time you even think about defying me, or harming anyone under our protection, you remember this moment. You will remember the pain, and you had better change your mind."

Logan's throat worked, but his voice was lost in the slow healing process. Even if he could put some apology together, the words would mean nothing to Darren. Not when his hands were still caked in dark dried blood.

Darren got up and Logan listened to his alpha walk away, leaving him and Dustin amongst the trees. If they were to let him just lay here for the rest of the night, Logan wouldn't have minded. He wasn't sure he'd be ready to move for quite a few hours as his body tried to restore itself.

He closed his eyes and Dustin sat where Darren had been. He didn't need to look to see that the betas fingers were just as bloody.

For several minutes, Dustin said nothing. He let Logan get a little closer to being functional, waited for him to lay still and motionless besides the rise and fall of his back in time with his ragged breathing.

"Is your brain working yet?"

Logan cracked open his eyes and lowered his brows in a glare.

"Close enough... I need you to listen and listen good. You fucked up today, and you deserve more than what we just did to you. I get why you tried, but I don't have to like the fact that you did try... Now, you have a massive obligation. Not just to us, to earn our trust back, but to Katey."

The muscles in Logan's face went slack.

"You turned her. You two are going to share a tight bond. It's not as strong as a mating bond or pack bond, but it's going to be there. You won't be able to outrun it. You will also be in charge of her. She's your responsibility now. Her failures are your fault, and her successes are yours too. You will be her go-to as she figures all of this out. We will help when it's needed, but she's all yours. This is your chance to make up for what you did. You need to get your act together and show her that you're strong enough to take care of her now."

If any of them knew about the responsibilities of a loup-garou sire, it was Dustin. He had turned Ben into a loup-garou to save his life on the battlefield of Antietam during the Civil War. They tried to train, but had a falling out that drove Dustin to Europe and Ben into isolation. It messed up both of them, and it took years to track them down and reunite the pack as they were today.

Logan's eyes shifted away, thoughtful. He owed Katey not only an explanation, but a lifetime of atonement. He forced her into this, and now it was his job to help her adjust the transition from human to loup-garou.

His deranged thinking before that day had convinced him that Katey would like being a loup-garou, that she would take to it like a natural. Time would tell if she could cope and if he could take on the challenge of being everything short of her alpha for her.

CHAPTER 2

Katey sat on a barstool in the kitchen, hands folded in her lap, focusing on her breathing. Ben stood on the living room side of the counter, the empty plate between them. Red juices dried in the circular groove in the center, the remnants of the raw meat katey forced down her own throat. It was almost impossible to ignore the instinctual revulsion that told her not to eat what hadn't been fully cooked. In the end, Katey had to admit it tasted good. The sumptuous smells of the old juices tempted her to lick the plate clean.

Katey heard Darren's approach long before the sliding glass door opened. The tingling in her skull amplified, but she didn't need to see his face to know the alpha was still pissed. The metallic odor of blood assaulted her nose and she saw dark blood cover his hands and splattered across his forearms and clothes. She hunched her back to make herself small and non-threatening without thinking about it.

Darren came forward and let out a long sigh. Brown eyes fell on the plate, then Katey and he nodded. "Good. Do you want more?"

Katey felt her eyes go round and shook her head. The vibe Darren brought with him pounded her into submission for no reason. The blood didn't help matters.

Ben leaned his elbows on the counter. "Might wanna ease back a bit," he said to his alpha, jerking his chin at the bloody mess. He didn't seem bothered by it, as if seeing blood all over his alpha wasn't disturbing.

Darren blinked and the passive tension in the air left the room. "I apologize."

She felt the muscles in her shoulder loosen, but her mind was still troubled. "Is Logan... is he going to be okay?" She continued to glance toward the door, as if he'd come walking through at any moment.

"He will live. Don't expect him to come home before dawn."

A shrill, breathy whine emitted from her throat, much against her own conscious effort. Katey cleared her throat and flexed her jaw. "That's new."

Ben chuckled, but Darren took on a sympathetic expression.

"I'm sure you have many questions." Darren gestured toward the sofa and his recliner. "I know it's late, but I also know those questions will keep you awake all night anyway. Allow me to clean up a bit and I'll answer them all."

Darren didn't wait for consent before bounding up the stairs.

Katey slid from the stool, taking it easy as she settled her weight on her feet. She felt lighter, like her leg muscles could carry her more efficiently. Ben went to clean off the dish in the sink while Katey sat herself down on one of the sofas to wait.

Her new, keen ears picked up every little thing Darren did upstairs from his footsteps on the bathroom tile, turning on the faucet, washing off the blood that mingled with the hard water from the tap, his movements to his room, and changing his clothes. She found herself staring vacantly at the opposite sofa, fascinated by just how well she could hear and distinguish all of it as if she were in the same room. So engrossed in what Darren was doing, she hardly noticed when Ben slipped out the back door, perhaps to go check on Dustin and Logan.

Darren returned and must have seen the amazed sparkle in her eyes. "Now you understand why we have no secrets in this house."

"Is there any way to block it out?"

Darren dropped into his recliner next to her and let out a long breath like an older man getting comfortable after a long day of work. "In time, you'll learn to block out what isn't important. It'll become background information, but won't overwhelm you." He turned to her and flicked his fingers at her in a beckoning manner. "All right. Time for questions."

Katey glanced to the ceiling, searching for the words. "Where to start..." She touched the back of her head. "I don't know if it's some after effect of the bite or—"

"That tingling sensation? Like needles, but it doesn't hurt?"

"Yeah."

"That's how you know when one of us is near. An early warning system, courtesy of the wolf side of you."

Katey nodded. "What about this weird... I don't know, like I feel... connected to the four of you?"

Darren lifted his chin as if he had finally put two and two together. "Ah. I wondered if he tried that too. It's the pack bond. Normally, only an alpha can create it, but a preliminary bond can form between a loup-garou and his sire upon the turning. An alpha can choose to galvanize that bond and fully integrate them into the pack, or not. Dustin and Ben shared that bond for decades before we brought him in... The fact that it's not an exclusive bond between you and Logan, but connects all of us is interesting, to say the least." Darren rubbed at his jaw. "There may be many things about your anatomy that will be different from our own experiences."

That wasn't entirely a comfort. She was loup-garou, but a different flavor. "When will I first shift?"

"Likely not for another month, but it'll depend on a variety of factors. We'll mark the calendar to keep track and see if there's a distinctive pattern."

Katey put a hand to her stomach and felt less belly fat beneath her hoodie than there had been earlier that morning. Her eyes widened, but made a mental note to give her body a full check later once she was in front of a mirror.

"What... What happened to me, exactly? What happened when Logan bit me?"

Darren let out a long breath and let his stare go distant as if readying himself to give a long lecture. "From what I understand, the loup-garou venom is a chemical compound of radioactive elements that either hasn't been discovered yet or the compound is unique and hasn't been researched at all by human scientists. They still don't think we exist, after all. The venom is in the saliva, but it's voluntarily injected. It's not like I can spit in someone's eye and they'd change. It has to be administered through the bloodstream. Somewhat like a vaccine. The chemicals in the venom have unstable molecules and each one is biologically designed to go straight to some part of the body. When the compound finds its destination, it splits and gives off radiation to cause a mutation."

Darren gestured at his body and then hers. "Those mutations bring about all of our abilities, everything from cell regeneration and enlarging some organs to handle the stress of our lifestyle, to our eye color and ability to eat raw meat without getting sick. A friend of mine is a scientist who has been researching this for years.

"Before he shared his findings, we believed it was more of a spiritual transformation, a blending of two souls within one body. The spirit of the wolf would come upon the human and a symbiotic relationship formed between the two. I still know a lot of people that reject the scientific explanation and doggedly cling to the old myths. You can pick which you would prefer to believe."

Katey stared, engrossed. She didn't know which she wanted to accept. The scientific approach seemed much more rational and comforting in the sense that she knew exactly why and how her body worked.

However, the wolf spirit approach sounded more romantic and whimsical. It explained the new presence she felt deep within her that hadn't been there before, but it was also disturbing to think she shared her body with something else that she couldn't see or communicate with. She could only feel it and sense its yearnings. It was what convinced her to eat the meat and to react to Darren's dominance. She first chalked it up to her new wolfish instincts, but the idea that it was an actual wolf spirit telling her what to do made more sense.

"What do you believe?" she asked.

Darren thought for a moment, then replied, "The Science explains the physical manifestation of the condition in our bodies, but the spiritual explains many other things. Some people feel the wolf spirit and develop a strong bond with it over time. Do you feel anything like that?"

Katey paused before answering. "I think so." Her voice dwindled to little more than a whisper as she reached within herself to check for that wolf spirit. It was quiet for now, just as exhausted as she was from the long evening. They were both tired.

"In the beginning, it's best not to fight or ignore whatever your wolf is telling you to do. Eat the meat, obey the alpha and beta, whatever it may be. The wolf is trying to teach you. What it can't, we will fill in the blanks." Darren's expression darkened. "Logan, as angsty and foolish as he can be at times, will be your direct mentor when we're not around. Training you to master your new skills and abilities will take time. You have a distinct advantage that many didn't have in centuries past. We are all in your corner and will make sure that you do not harm others or yourself as you grow accustomed to this new life."

Katey tilted her head. "You make it sound like... so serious."

"It is serious. Every loup-garou has the capacity to do terrible things if they don't know what they're doing. A wild, feral thing lives inside you, whether it's a soul or a new psychological entity. Understanding it, working with it, and... taming it as much as possible is vital to living amongst other humans in this society. If you can't do that, then every loup-garou and human around you are put in danger."

Katey's mouth went dry. Up until that moment, she hadn't come to the full realization that she was no longer considered human. It was a part of her, but no longer her identity. She had more in common with this four-hundred-year-old loup-garou than her best friend.

"Did you have any more questions?"

Still rapt in her own revelation, Katey shook her head. More questions would come and she'd have the clarity of mind to ask them then, but not now. Not when she was dropped into the middle of an existential crisis.

Darren transplanted himself to the cushion beside Katey on the couch. "May I?" He motioned to her shoulder.

Again, she nodded and allowed the alpha to gently pull down the collar of her hoodie. The white bandages were still taped to her skin. With the utmost care, he peeled off the blood-soaked gauze. Katey peeked at her skin and saw it to be flawless. With a shaking hand, she touched the patch of skin that should have been torn to shreds. The only testament to Logan's bit was the dried blood smeared across her shoulder and down her chest. That stench had become a part of her sensory background, just like Darren said. Only fresh blood caught her attention when he came in from outside.

Darren wadded up the soiled bandages. "You should probably change clothes before going to bed. We'll take the blood stains out in the morning. "Are you going to shower tonight or in the morning?"

Katey blinked, and thought about wanting to check out her body in the bathroom. "Tonight... Do I have to go to school tomorrow?"

"I would suggest that you don't just because you're going to need time to recover and get an initial grasp of your new abilities. We don't want you pulling doors off hinges." A ghost of a smile crossed Darren's lips, as if he either had done such a thing as a young loup-garou or knew someone who did.

Katey cracked the tiniest of smirks at the thought of it. "I'd like to try. I feel pretty okay now, and maybe Logan can come with me to help if things get overwhelming?"

Darren seemed less than convinced and sighed before giving it some thought. "You have first and second period exams tomorrow. Dustin's second period isn't close to yours... But I'll be there for your exam in my class. I suppose as long as Logan will accompany you, and you take measures to keep yourself apart from the other students when it's not necessary, it could work. If something goes wrong or you no longer feel comfortable, you will come straight home. No exceptions. If that does happen, one of us will take off to escort you home and be a second help to Logan."

Part of that seemed like a challenge. If she behaved, if she maintained control on her first day as a loup-garou, then that would show them all that they didn't have to constantly watch her like she might explode at any moment. She'd make this work, one way or another.

"I promise, I won't be a burden."

Darren's hand settled on her shoulder. "You are not, and will never be a burden. We are here to take care of you. You're not alone in this, Katey. You're in the pack now and that will never change."

Such words would have made her cry like a baby if she wasn't so tired. Her nose burned with those unshed tears and she closed her eyes before any could seep out. Darren rubbed up and down her back in a bracing, comforting way that she wasn't quite used to, but it felt nice coming from him.

"Go wash up. We'll talk more in the morning before school if you think of anything else to ask."

Darren went across the house and turned off the lights, except for one in the kitchen for when Ben came back from the woods, and Katey made her way up the stairs. Her legs, as before, carried her easily up each tread as if she weighed nothing at all.

Once she arrived in the bathroom, she applied far more conscious effort to not grip the handle too tight or close it too firmly, just in case she used her loup-garou strength by mistake. She flicked on the light that she hardly needed, being able to see perfectly in the dark now, and gasped at her reflection in the mirror.

Katey was met by a pair of bright green eyes that didn't seem like hers at all. She leaned forward over the counter and touched just below her eyelid. Examining them closely, she saw bits of gold flecks across the irises, ringed by an even darker shade of green just around the outer edges. They were the same color she always had, but these were stunning and mystical, and certainly different from her human eyes. Part of the wolf bled into those eyes.

She leaned back from the mirror and ran her fingers through her hair. Each strand was as soft and thick as before, but she could see the subtle highlights of blonde streaked through the dark brown base. They reminded her of Logan's own hair. Clearly there was something more than just venom that translated through the bite. The contrast between her eyes and hair were striking and almost exotic.

Katey lifted her hoodie up, remembering what she had felt earlier. Her hand flew to her mouth in shock at what she saw. Underneath the ribbons of dried blood along one side of her torso, her stomach was now flat and the faint edges of hard muscle created shadows in the bathroom light. She couldn't help but let out a strained laugh.

She stripped off her hoodie to stand in just her jeans and underwear. Never had she looked so trim and fit. Turning in the mirror, she found that nearly every body part had changed in the same way. She had the figure of an athlete. No, she had the body of a loup-garou. If the change in her sensory perception and the feel of the wolf inside her hadn't confirmed the change, this obvious outward transformation was enough to finally convince her.

In a low, astonished whisper, she told herself, "I am... loup-garou."

Every stiff muscle in Logan's body screamed for the warmth and comfort of his bed. It was the only thing on his addled brain when he and Dustin stepped through the sliding glass door into the dark living room. The sun was an hour away from rising, and if he could make it up the stairs, Logan may have been able to snatch a couple of hours of sleep before breakfast. With any luck, Darren would let them stay home from school and he could get even more rest.

By the time he shuffled around the sofa, he heard Katey stir from her room. He hadn't seen her since he bit her, though he had been vaguely aware she was in the kitchen when he awoke earlier. He stopped and looked to Dustin. He gave a nod of consent. They'd be allowed to talk, but only for a little while.

He listened to her dart down the hall and crash into the wall at the landing, not having the chance to get a hold of her inhuman speed. He had done the same thing, only crashing into trees instead of walls. Dustin tried to hold in a chuckle. They had all done it. Underestimating their new abilities seemed like a rite of passage for all loups-garous.

When she came to the stairs, she went slower and more carefully. Katey stood in the living room, the lights off, but they could see one another as clearly as if it were daylight.

For a long moment, they stared at one another, gazes brimming with emotions neither of them could possibly understand. She knew what he had endured as his punishment, and he knew all too well what he had put her through. What could they possibly say to one another? How could they come back from this?

"You should be in bed," Dustin said to Katey as he moved toward the kitchen to give them some semblance of privacy.

Katey wrapped her arms around her stomach, as if suddenly self-conscious. She wore a pair of casual pajamas, but he could see the slight difference in her physique beneath her clothes. He had done that to her.

But one step forward from Logan made her rush forward, heedless of her speed. She collided into him and he didn't hesitate to catch her. The force of her run made him stumble backward, but his arms held her securely against him. Her warmth, the feel of her body pressed into his, all of that could have been taken from him because of one stupid, stupid mistake. He squeezed her a little tighter, despite the ache in his ribs, and wasn't afraid to crush her. She was so solid now. He could feel hard, lean muscle where soft flesh had been the day before. Katey wasn't so fragile anymore.

It worked. It actually worked. Katey is loup-garou.

Logan could have wept if he weren't so exhausted.

"Are you all right?" she mumbled against his torn and bloodied shirt.

He let out a breath and felt he could collapse. After everything he had done to her, she was worried for him?

"I'll be fine... Katey, I'm so sorry." He would have pulled away to look her in the eyes as he apologized, but relief that she was truly alive and loup-garou made him never want to let go.

"Don't be. Everything is going to be fine now."

With all the willpower he could muster, Logan took her by the shoulders and pulled her away so he could meet her gaze. He could see new golden flecks interspersed with the gorgeous green he loved so much. "That's just it... Everything is going to be very, very different." He dropped his voice, hopefully to convey the gravity of the situation. Neither of them had a right to be so happy in that moment.

Katey gave him a hopeful smile, her cheeks glistening with happy tears. "But in a good way. We can be together, just like we wanted. I know it'll be a lot to get used to, on my part at least, but now we can—"

"I think we need to take this slow." Logan had to cut her off before she got too excited. He knew what she would say. Yes, becoming true mates was a possibility now, but she wasn't even a day into her new loup-garou life. Mating should have been the last thing for either of them to consider.

Yet, the struck look on her face the minute he suggested they take it easy made him want to take it all back and form the mating bond right there in the living room.

"What do you mean?"

Logan steeled himself for the ultimate letdown. He had already come to this decision long before coming back to the house. "I think you need to focus on training and getting used to... everything. We need to be put on the back burner for a while."

Katey stepped away and out of his arms. He could sense her building indignation through the pack bond they now shared. "How long?"

"As long as it takes for you to be fully comfortable."

"I'm comfortable now!"

Dustin came back from the kitchen, two sticks of jerky in one hand and a half-eaten stick in the other. "Cool it. No loup-garou is going to be totally acclimated to this freak show for at least a few years."

Katey spun to face the beta, her thick hair whipping around her shoulders. "A few years?" She turned back to Logan, a frightening intensity in her eyes. "You're saying we need to wait a few years?"

Logan's lips tightened into a firm line, knowing there wasn't any easy way to say it, or put it in words that would make her understand just how her life would never be the same again. She would look like a teenager for decades. She would see her friends move away and start their own lives. She wouldn't have the kind of freedom they talked about in the cemetery the night they met. She would know what it was like to be like him, the good and the bad. It would take time for her to come to terms with that, and by then, she'd likely hate his guts for turning her. Mating may be completely off the table in a few months' time.

When he didn't say anything, Katey began to shake with suppressed anger, her face hardening and eyes flinty. Everything would feel so extreme now. What would be a mild nuisance before would send her into a flying fit of rage. They would have to watch out for that in the coming weeks. Though, telling her that they had to wait to be together was certainly more than a nuisance.

"If that's the way it has to be, then fine." Katey's clipped words cut him like a silver knife. She hurried back upstairs, leaving the room icy cold in her wake.

Logan didn't move, though his legs ached for rest. He stood rooted in place, hoping he hadn't just made another terrible mistake.

Dustin approached and handed him the beef stick. "You did the right thing."

"Tell me that in the morning when it doesn't hurt as much." He took the food and bit into the tough meat, though his jaw muscles protested against the act of chewing. The food tasted dry and dull in his mouth, and felt like a rock going down his throat. It may have been his body still trying to recover, or the dread that what he and Katey shared just became more complicated.

Katey glowered at her reflection in the mirror, her eyes darting from one new feature to the next. Her thoughts began to crowd in, tripping and stumbling over each.

Sleep was a torrid experience and afforded her no rest. Dreams of loups-garous flashed before her eyes in a tangled, snowy mess with no cohesive message. The faces of people that she didn't know or recognize spoke in foreign languages, some whispering and some shouting. In her dream, she traveled to places she had never been. Some seemed like visions of the past. As if taking a whirlwind tour of the world, she saw jungles, deserts, ancient ruins, dense forests, and barren prairies mixed in with the voices and people.

The woman in white was there, but not in the same fashion she had seen her before. The image of her was surrounded in flames as white as her dress, the fire charred her body. Katey awoke in a cold sweat as the rest of the pack began to leave their rooms for their morning routine. As she had done on other mornings, she listened from beneath her covers. Only now, their movements sounded loud in her sensitive ears, as if they were tramping around in her room.

She waited until everyone was downstairs, but Logan remained in his bedroom, dead asleep. He was the last person she wanted to see.

Earlier that morning, before dawn, he basically said that they couldn't be together, not until her training was finished. According to Dustin, that could have taken years. Years without Logan as her mate or boyfriend, or whatever it was they were supposed to be by now. Years of being so close, just on the other side of a glass wall from one another. When she agreed for the bite, years or waiting were not what she had in mind.

Perhaps, if she had fought back yesterday in the classroom, refused the bite and forced him to calm down, they could have talked it through. He wanted her so badly that he forced the issue on her before she was truly ready. Maybe if they had just talked about it like mature adults, they could have set aside the possibility of becoming a loup-garou herself and just formed the mating bond to make things more official. Turning could have come later, but Logan obviously didn't think so. He wanted her to be loup-garou immediately, not later. Upon reflection, if Katey didn't think the same, she wouldn't have felt the instinctual agreement slip between her lips. Before yesterday, she thought it'd be the ultimate solution to everything too.

Now she hated the sight of what she had become, but only because it caused so much friction between herself and Logan. If she were human, perhaps things would have stayed the same. In fact, she knew they would have. There was nothing wrong with where their relationship had been, besides the occasional moments of nearly losing themselves in one another. As far as she was concerned, things were going well before he turned her. In comparison, she would have gladly taken sneaking hugs and caresses behind the pack's back over absolutely nothing. She would have had Logan and the warm feeling of rightness in her soul. But all she felt was the wolf and a sense of displacement. Without Logan, what was the point?

The more Katey gazed in the mirror, the more she wanted to gouge out those new, bright green eyes tainted by the gold she couldn't give back to Logan. She didn't want it anymore, not the superhuman senses or trim, fit body, and especially not the wolf inside her. The only thing she wanted was Logan, and now she couldn't even have him.

She forced herself to stare longer, letting her anger grow, her body trembling from the power of it. A snarl rose up in her throat, her nose wrinkled, and her brows pinched into a glare as she felt the unadulterated hatred building up within. It was so intense, more intense than she had ever felt before and she finally understood why everyone had tried to warn her about a loup-garou's temper.

The more angry she became, the more gold spun into her irises, and the cold sensation she felt the night before was now linked with this physical manifestation of the wolf. After only half a minute, her eyes were no longer green, but a brilliant and vicious shade of amber. The wolf glared back at her, taunting her.

This is your life now.

She shrieked in fury, raised her fist, and smashed the mirror with every ounce of her loup-garou strength. Broken pieces clattered into the sink and fell to the floor. A dent in the drywall behind the mirror was a testament to just how strong she was. Her breath quickened, each exhale coming out gruff and growl-like as she sneered down at the shattered glass.

Before Katey could bring her fist down on the marble counter-top, two strong arms pulled her backward. She fell into Logan's warm body, one arm encircling her waist and the other crossing her chest, hand braced on her shoulder to hold her away from anything breakable.

Blind rage had her kicking and flailing, screaming like a mad woman as she fought against him, not unlike she had the day he chased her down in the senior hallway, the day her life changed forever.

"Easy, Katey. You're safe. Take a breath."

With his words, a surge of comforting dominance whirled around them like a tornado of calm. Along with being a tool to subdue insubordinate loups-garous, dominance could be used to sooth pack members who spun out of control. In that moment, Katey was out of control.

The dominance tightened like a warm blanket, enfolding them and restraining her wild limbs like an invisible straitjacket. Her hands gripped Logan's arms, feeling the ropey muscles beneath hot skin. Breaths slowed from harsh bursts out her nose to a gentle panting, her chest unclenched, the cold gold of the wolf left her eyes. A stillness settled over what used to be a warzone.

Her whole body felt as if it had deflated, the anger gone and little more than a memory, leaving her feeling embarrassed. Logan became like a rock in the middle of deadly rapids and Katey clung to him like her life depended on it. Her outburst left her exhausted and she sagged against him.

His face buried into her neck, his nose and lips pressed into her skin. The steady pressure of his expanding chest against her shoulder blades was both erotic and relaxing. It occurred to her that he only wore pajama pants, the upper half of his body completely bare. If she wasn't so emotionally spent, she might have felt something else other than relief and regret.

"That's it... Just calm down... Let it go." Logan's whispers were the last straw and silent tears rolled down her cheeks and curled around the edge of her jaw.

Why couldn't he have held her like this when she was human? Why did she have to lose her mind for him to give her this kind of attention?

A moment later, Dustin appeared in the doorway, but she couldn't take her eyes off the mess on the floor. Shards of mirror littered the floor and bathroom counter. In her peripheral, she saw thin streaks of blood down the length of her forearm and, rather delayed, she felt the sting of the jagged cuts across her hand and wrist.

Dustin nudged a big sliver of the broken glass with the tip of his shoe. "I didn't like that mirror anyway."

"Not now," Logan muttered, a half growl at the beta.

"All right, all right. I'll get a broom."

Katey blinked out more tears as Dustin walked away down the hall. They remained there, Katey blissfully trapped in his hold. She wished there was more to this embrace than just a way to get her under control. She wanted Logan to hold her like this because he wanted to, not because he had to. But, he was supposed to be her mentor, not her lover.

Logan lifted his head and tilted to look at the bathroom floor. They were both barefoot. If they took a step in any direction, the undersides of their feet could be sliced open.

"We need to move carefully." His breath tickled her skin. "I'm going to let go now."

Katey's fingertips squeezed his arms, a wordless protest to the idea.

"I know," he said, understanding perfectly. "It'll be all right. I'm not going to leave you."

She swallowed hard and took a moment to prepare herself, then nodded. With the utmost care, Logan released her body, but transferred his hold to her hands. They picked gaps between the broken mirror and were back in the hall.

Out of his arms and out of the bathroom, a knot of nausea clamped over her stomach and fresh adrenaline shot through her limbs, making her tremble. "I'm sorry. I didn't mean to. I'm so sorry," was all she could manage to say in a jumbled, blubbering way.

Logan stepped closer and cupped her face between his hands to shush her manic sobs. "It's fine. It happens. It's very normal, okay? We've all been through it."

That wasn't a consolation. Katey expected better from herself. She had to prove she could do this, that she could manage the wolf and her temper. But where did the wolf begin and Katey end? How much of that outburst was her and how much was the wolf? Did she instigate the rage and the wolf fanned it into a roaring flame? How was she supposed to get through a normal day without flying off the handle like that? The thought that perhaps she couldn't, made her want to cry even harder.

Dustin's approach with a broom had her tamping down the rest of her unshed tears as Logan wiped away the moisture on her cheeks.

"Might want to get her cleaned up," the beta said. "This will take me a while."

Logan forced her to meet his crystalline blue eyes. "Let's go downstairs to the other bathroom."

All the fight had gone out of her, and she let him lead her away. Katey refused to lift her stare as they made their way down the hall and across the house. She couldn't bear the looks the rest of the pack must have given her from the breakfast nook. Thankfully, they didn't say a word, but she sensed Darren rise from his chair and follow them down the hall to the half bathroom off the billiard room.

Like a helpless child, she let Logan turn on the faucet in the sink and wash away the blood. The water turned red against the white porcelain before swirling down the drain. She expected his strokes to hurt as he rubbed over the places where sharp edges carved into her skin. But his hands passed over her perfectly healed wrist and knuckles. Just like the spot on her shoulder where Logan had bitten her, there was no evidence of what she did.

"She's all right," Logan told Darren standing in the doorway.

Was she? Wasn't this some sign that she needed to be watched more closely? That she needed a guardian after all? That she couldn't be trusted around others?

"You two may be late for second period exams," Darren said. "I'll inform Lisa. This may be a good thing. Avoid the crowds."

Fighting weariness, Katey looked up to her alpha, a muted, panicked question in her eyes.

"Only if you feel up for it," he assured.

Katey gulped back the flash of anxiety and gratefulness. They were willing to give her another chance, but also a pass if she wanted to forfeit the challenge of going to school. Did that mean what she did was meaningless? That it was not as terrible as she thought it was? That made no sense.

Logan cut off the water and took up a towel to dry her hands. Again, he took care of her as if she couldn't do that herself. "Let's get some breakfast, then you can decide."

Katey snapped out of her daze. "No... I'll go."

She had to make up for what she did, to take the second chance she was given. Maybe this morning was a slip up, a temporary lapse in judgment brought on by an overflow of emotions. That was what they all acted like anyway. Katey knew she could do better and she had to show them.

Logan and Darren didn't seem too shocked, and the alpha gave a nod before pulling out his phone to make the call. "Take your time."

When Darren was out of the way, Logan turned Katey around and forced her to look up at him again. "Are you absolutely sure? No one will think less of you."

Checking herself, Katey realized she wasn't shaking as violently anymore, and a bit of her strength returned. "I'm sure."

Logan studied her, his stare devoid of affection and then let out a breath. "Next time you feel that mad again, close your eyes, clear your mind, and count. I know it sounds silly, but it can work. Count to ten or a hundred if you have to, but as long as you need until it goes away and you can think straight."

Katey listened and nodded, but she wondered just how effective it would be when the reason for her rage would never go away. Every time she looked at Logan, she'd be reminded that they couldn't be together until she got a handle on her loup-garou life. She needed that to happen sooner rather than later. She doubted any other loup-garou was as driven as she would be to earn that independence.

"It's also easier to deal with your anger when you've eaten. I know you're not big into breakfast, but it's going to be important that you try to eat three meals a day, if not more."

Katey's face wrinkled like she tasted something awful. "I don't know if I could eat anything right now. I'm... I'm too nervous about the exams. I studied a lot, but I don't know if I'll be able to focus enough." Right now, she couldn't remember a damned thing she learned over the last few months at school, besides what had happened just within the last week.

A corner of Logan's mouth tilted. "I think once you get into it, you'll find your information recall is much better than it used to be. If you're not going to eat, Darren will probably send us off with hunger suppressors."

"Hunger suppressors?"

"It's something a loup-garou scientist came up with. It holds back our hunger for a short time, but shouldn't be used all the time. He makes other things like pain killers specially formulated for our body chemistry. Darren keeps a stash of different little cures in his room."

Logan moved around her to the bathroom door, but then turned back. Either in her face or through the pack bond, he must have sensed her general apprehension. Today would probably be the hardest day of her life, if this morning was any indication of that. Hopping from one foster home to the next would be nothing compared to all of this, yet everyone had faith that she'd pull through. She had to have faith in herself, but all she felt was... overwhelmed.

"Don't worry about today. It hasn't been that long that I can't remember how rough this must be for you. I'll be right there the whole time to keep you on track if that's what you need."

She nodded and tried to take comfort in that. They may not have been an official couple, or whatever it was that they were before he turned her, but he was still here. It may have been out of obligation, or that he had much more patience to wait through the years, but he was still in her life. That was something.

CHAPTER 3

By Katey's estimation, they would end up arriving at school almost right on time. Instead of driving separately, Logan had suggested that he drive her to school instead of the other way around. With her new senses, her reflexes may have been better, but driving, like everything else, would be a brand new experience. Katey gave in, but not without some eye rolling. She didn't like the idea of letting someone else drive her car, but there was logic in what Logan said. That became clear once they were on the road and Katey's eardrums felt as if they would vibrate out of her head from just the road noise.

Before they left the house, Darren had entrusted Logan with their lunches, an exorbitant amount of deer steak and sliced roast beef, most of which would be for Katey. She may have taken some hunger suppressors, but there was no telling how the pills would affect her. New loups-garous were not supposed to go too long without eating, especially within the first twenty-four hours.

For the first half of the commute, they sat in silence. Through their bond, Katey could tell that Logan was just as conflicted as she was, though she wasn't sure why. With one elbow propped against the edge of the driver's side door and fingers thoughtfully grazing across his chin and cheek, Katey wondered what was on his mind.

In an effort to sneak the truth out of him, she said, "I'm sorry Darren's making you go with me. I'm sure you would rather be sleeping off what... what happened last night."

He shook his head, gaze still fixed on the road. "It's fine. I'd rather go and make sure you're all right."

Katey shifted against the seat and sucked in a breath. "What about that whole sleep deprivation thing?"

"I'll be all right. I'll probably sleep during the exams anyway. Mrs. Kimbrough won't like it, but Darren will understand... Unless he decides to be a sadistic ass about it."

That made her smile a little, but her thoughts trailed back to exactly why he was tired, and why he walked a little stiffly around the house that morning. "Did you know that they would do that to you?"

He blinked slowly, as if the memory of his punishment caused him pain. "No, I didn't."

Katey couldn't stop herself. "If you knew what they would do, would you still have... you know."

His blue eyes darted in her direction and he sighed. "I don't know... I wasn't thinking clearly yesterday. I... I let my wolf take control of the situation and I shouldn't have done that."

"Why did you?"

"The wolf is braver than I am, but also more reckless. It didn't care that I could have killed you, but we... we agreed so strongly on one thing that I made the logic work when I should have left it alone."

Katey tried to follow what he meant. "So, you regret it?"

Logan finally looked at her dead-on, but he froze before he could answer, then turned back to the road. After some thought, he said, "I regret putting you in that position to make a life or death decision, and swaying that decision in my own favor without regard to your safety."

That sounded so rehearsed, as if he had been thinking about it ever since he woke up in the sitting room the evening before, or like it came out of Darren's mouth instead of his own.

Then, came the hardest question of all, the one Katey wasn't sure she wanted to ask, but knew she had to. "If I had said no... would you have turned me anyway, since you wanted it that badly?"

Logan rubbed his face as they entered the city limits. They had a couple of stoplights before reaching the school and Katey would not let him get out of the car before answering her.

"I don't know what I would have done." At the first red light, he stared at her. "Would you have still said yes if you were facing the real me instead of the wolf?"

Katey's mouth twitched into a tiny smile. She had been thinking about that too. "I would have. You didn't scare me into saying yes. I already knew it was what I wanted, but Darren said it wouldn't happen, so I wasn't going to push for it... I wanted this, Logan. Please don't let them convince you that this is bad."

A line formed between Logan's brows. "Katey, I could have killed you. Nothing about that is a good thing. I don't care if it was for a good reason, if you wanted it, or that it all turned out fine in the end... I could have killed you."

He talked slowly at that last part, biting out each word as if they were driving the nails into his own coffin. Katey heard him, acknowledged the pain, but she would be the last person in the world to condemn him.

"I would have preferred death over a future without you in it."

The light turned green and Logan said nothing as he eased into the intersection, but a wealth of emotion passed through their bond to tell her that what she said meant a great deal to him. They may have had to wait, but that didn't mean Katey loved him any less. It was less that made her say yes, not the wolf, and not logic. Even if she said as much, could he have accepted it?

The next light was green, and they slowed through the school zone before turning onto the campus. Right about then, Katey realized they wouldn't speak any more about it. Not that morning, anyway. Whenever, or if ever, he wanted to return to the subject, she'd be ready.

The campus still hummed with activity by the time Logan pulled Katey's jeep into a parking stall.

Logan turned to her after he shut off the engine. "Do you want to wait in here for a little while?"

She stared out the window, already overwhelmed by all the sounds inside the building that somehow reached her within the safety of her own jeep. Was this what they all heard on a daily basis? No wonder they wanted to live out in the middle of nowhere. If she had enough courage to take back her choice to go to school, she would have demanded they go back to the house where it was quiet.

"No, I can do this."

Logan gave her hand a reassuring squeeze and they made their way across the parking lot. Katey kept her head down and stayed close to Logan's side, merely following his scent to stay with him. Through the harsh scents of the city and parking lot, she was amazed that she could recognize anything. When they entered the school, Katey ran into a wall of smells and sounds that left her reeling as if she were hit by a sledgehammer.

They all mingled together in a discord that made her head swim. For a moment, all she could do was stagger and grope for something stable to cling to.

Logan was there in an instant to steady her. "Are you all right?"

Stunned into silence, she couldn't answer and squeezed her eyes shut in an attempt to block it all out somehow. Shuffling feet, whispers down the hall, the roar of copy machines, and odors that were indistinguishable from one another, but still familiar all crowded around her.

After a moment, Logan pulled Katey back outside to recover. "If it's too much for you, Darren said you don't have to be here. We can leave now and go back home."

She opened her watering eyes and stretched out her sinus cavities with her facial muscles. "No, I'm fine," she said through a sniffle and cough.

He sighed in a way that made her think he pitied her struggle. "Try to block it out. Just focus only on what you want to hear and nothing else. It'll take a while, but all of it can become just background noise without even trying."

That was what Darren said before, but she wasn't going to snap at Logan that she already knew that. Katey nodded and steeled herself before they walked back in. This time, she tried as Logan suggested and tuned out much of the chaos, letting it become white noise. It worked for the most part, but Katey couldn't wait to get into a quiet classroom where students would be silently testing instead of screaming.

Logan edged closer to Katey and took her hand in his, gripping it firmly. She jumped and turned her inquisitive eyes up to him. They had never held hands like this in front of so many people. Was it to comfort her, or to claim her? With the way teenagers noticed stuff like that, rumors were bound to make their rounds through the grapevine before the end of the day. Did Logan realize that? Did he not care?

His eyes were fixed upon the crowd, keeping a sharp eye for anything and everything as if he were her bodyguard, as if ready to jump in and intercept her from danger or any minor inconvenience. His hand was rough and a little damp with sweat, as was hers, but she held on tightly despite her jittery nerves.

As they were halfway to Mrs. Kimbrough's room for their English semester exam, and the initial shock of sensory overload began to subside, she realized she could sense something else entirely new.

Emotions.

They passed by students filled with joy and anxiety over the coming exams, which was to be expected. She felt it all so keenly, like invisible auras around their bodies that only her wolf could sense. She knew dogs could sometimes read the energy in humans, but she hadn't thought wolves could do the same. Their main method of communication was body language, and humans could be masters of putting off one emotion while feeling another. She knew that all too well.

Grouped around a set of lockers were several girls, all happy and giggling amongst themselves about some juicy gossip. Amongst them was a girl that Katey knew. She was top of their class, beautiful, easy going with all the students, envied by the freshmen girls for her grace, and a prize to be won by the senior studs. But Katey was thrown off guard by something she hadn't expected to see. The girl was smiling and laughing, but Katey could sense a deep sadness within her. She recognized that sadness.

She froze in the middle of the hallway and stared at the girl who wore a mask just like Katey had only weeks ago to hide how she truly felt from the rest of the world. The depression this girl gave off was so consuming that Katey could feel it thicken around her like mud, even from across the hall.

How could this girl, who seemed totally different from Katey, suffer the same way that she had? What did this girl have to be so sad about? This extra sense for emotions could have been a blessing, but Katey could only see it as a burden. She knew that this girl was struggling, and yet, there was little she could do to help.

Logan must have seen the distraught look in Katey's face and followed her gaze to the girl. He sighed heavily and wrapped his arm around her waist to lead her out of the way of student traffic.

"Logan..." Katey managed to whisper. The swell of emotions tightened around her throat and threatened to choke her.

He continued to lead her toward the senior hallway. "I know. Just keep going."

"But, can't we—"

"I already asked Darren about her. There's not much we can do unless she asks for help."

Katey didn't want to accept that. Her wolf, too, couldn't accept it. She wanted to heal that hurt somehow, just like the pack had tried to help her when she suffered behind the mask.

She tried to put it out of her mind as they entered the classroom. An effective distraction looked up from her phone and gasped at the two of them.

Lily gawked at her friend's new body and Katey forced a weak smile as she wondered how many layers of perfume Lily had sprayed on before leaving the house that morning. She smelled more like a walking chemical factory than the usual flowery perfume Katey knew.

The blonde jumped to her feet and rushed to meet them at the door, stepping aside so other students could enter.

"Oh... my god," Lily whispered, taking Katey's jacket sleeves and forcing her to spread her arms. Her blue eyes skimmed over every new and altered feature before her hands flew to her mouth. "You're not..."

"She is," Logan replied. "Don't have an aneurism."

Lily shot a scowl at Logan and smacked his arm. "Oh, shut up. When did it happen?"

"Yesterday," Katey winced. "Is it that obvious?" She looked down at her body and clutched a fistful of her thick hair. She hoped that no one would notice anything, given how well she could fly under everyone's radar.

"Oh. My. God." Lily's shock morphed into a kind of giddiness that Katey rarely saw outside a shopping mall. "I have to tell Forrest. Does he know yet? Does anyone know? Oh, Katey! How do you feel? What the hell are you doing at school if it just happened yesterday? You should be at home resting or something."

Logan bent to get Lily's attention and stop her hyper string of questions. "No one outside of my pack knows. Don't tell Forrest yet. We don't need the whole town freaking out."

"But this is a huge deal," Lily hissed.

He gave her a sardonic grin. "We know it is, which is why we need you to keep your loud mouth shut until Darren can figure out a way to break the news."

"Who did it?" Lily asked Katey, undaunted by Logan's intimidation. "How did it happen? I want all the details."

"She can tell you later. Right now, she needs to sit down."

Logan was right. A sudden dizziness struck Katey and she didn't feel sure on her feet. She attributed it to Lily's perfume.

"Oh, right. Sorry. Promise you'll call me later?"

Katey gave her a nod and they took to their seats as Mrs. Kimbrough entered the classroom. She gave Logan a questioning look, likely not expecting them to be on time for the bell. The dizziness didn't go away, even when she covered her nose with the sleeve of her jacket to block out Lily's perfume.

The shrill alarm bell to announce the start of the period rang in her ears like a piercing gong that continued to buzz in her brain for an extra few long seconds after the alarm died away. Katey's face twisted with the pain and was sure her eardrums would finally burst, but she resisted the impulse to cover her ears, lest someone watched her.

Logan put a comforting hand on her shoulder, to at least communicate that he understood what she just experienced. When it rang next, she'd have to be prepared somehow.

Mrs. Kimbrough passed out the exams and the noise in the classroom, and throughout the building settled into a dull rumble of activity and murmur of voices. For a while, Katey began to believe she'd be okay. The exam was not as difficult as she thought it would be, the information flooding back to her almost instantly, just like Logan said.

However, about halfway through, she began to take notice of a throbbing pain behind her eyes and across her forehead. She pinched the bridge of her nose, but the ache reached through her temples to encircle her head. She had a migraine a few times in her life, but this was different. It came on too suddenly and spread too violently to be anything normal.

As calmly as she could manage, she set down her pen and pressed the heel of her palms into her eyes, then took deep breaths through her nose as if that would make a difference. Logan's hand settled on her shoulder, more as a show of support than a need to get her attention. If she said the word, they'd be out of that classroom in a heartbeat, but he wouldn't force her.

The pain intensified, bringing on a gut-churning nausea, and she couldn't bear it any more.

"I can't," was all she could whisper, dropping her voice so low that only Logan would be able to hear her breathe the words.

Logan jumped to action and went straight to Mrs. Kimbrough's desk. They exchanged some heated words about getting Katey out of the classroom and the woman agreed. Her husband was loup-garou, part of Forrest's pack.

The world around her dissolved into a blur by the time Logan snatched up their bags, took her arm, and escorted her out of the classroom. Katey lost her footing a number of times as they tried to make it down the empty hallway.

"What are you feeling?"

Katey blinked and shook her head until everything came back into focus. She found a little more strength to lock her knees so she could stand without Logan's help. But, there was something else rising to the surface and it startled her.

"Headache... Feel sick," she mumbled, her lips barely letting her speak at all. She pressed her palm against her forehead, willing her world to stop whirling as she forced whatever was pushing up to stay down.

Logan's arm fell around her waist as he led her out onto the bus ramp. The cold December winds chilled the droplets of sweat developing on her forehead and eased some of her queasiness.

"You probably need to eat something. We'll go to the wrestling gym. No one will be there."

She summoned every ounce of composure she had left and walked with him down the covered walkway, only occasionally using Logan as a crutch when her strength failed her. She despised this feeling of helplessness as if her body were fighting against her.

They soon ducked into the spacious, gym-like room where she and Logan had eaten lunch and listened to music. That stolen half-hour seemed like a lifetime away. The rolled up mats were still pyramided against the far wall, and the well-worn, dated couch still sat to one side of the room.

"I'm not hungry," Katey insisted as Logan led her to the sofa. "I just need to lay down for a little while." Her voice was barely louder than a sigh.

Logan let Katey's body sink into the squeaky cushion and knelt down to his bag. She sprawled herself across the length of the sofa and pressed her fingers into her temples as the sickness grew stronger.

He pulled out his lunch box and she smelled the meat instantly. Her chest was set ablaze and burning eyes widened as drool leaked from the corners of her lips. She wiped it away and covered her mouth and nose with her jacket sleeve. The aroma was almost intoxicating.

"Katey, don't fight it. You have to eat," Logan barked. They were completely alone in the wrestling gym and with all the students and faculty still in exams for the next hour, no one was likely to bother them here.

"I feel too sick. I'll just throw it all up."

She fiercely shook her head and clamped her eyes shut. She didn't want to see the thick cuts of juicy steak in the containers he withdrew from the lunch bag. He popped the lid off one and held it closer to her face. The smell seeped past the fabric and her hand, enticing her to take the meat and give into the animalistic instincts that raged against her human mind.

She felt that cooling sensation wash over her eyes, and she knew the wolf was there at her doorstep again. She cracked open her eyes, but her vision was clouded over and she knew this was different. Something wasn't right at all.

Logan's eyes narrowed and he leaned in closer with the meat. "I know it doesn't make sense, but you will feel better if you eat."

Katey felt her lungs convulse. It was like she couldn't take a breath. Bile rose in the back of her throat and her body rattled violently. "I'm gonna... I can't..." She retched as she felt something warm travel up her esophagus. She moved her hand and leaned over the edge of the sofa, letting blood gush from her mouth and puddle on the floor.

"Katey!" Logan tossed the meat aside and put a comforting hand on her back. More blood flowed from her lips, tainting her tongue with the metallic flavor that she oddly enough, was not repulsed by.

He cursed under his breath and pulled out his phone to speed-dial one of the pack, likely the one who was closest.

"Dustin, something's wrong with Katey. She's vomiting blood. I don't know what to do... Out at the wrestler's gym off the bus ramp..." Logan hung up the call and turned back to Katey. "Dustin's coming to help. It'll be okay."

An unbelievable anger rose within her, the same anger she'd felt that morning staring into the mirror. She didn't have the sense to do what Logan suggested and count to ten. They were well past that point.

Katey paused in her vomiting and scowled at Logan. She could feel blood dripping down her chin. "I'm not hungry! Leave me alone!" Every breath came out as a guttural growl and her irritation only magnified, creeping through her veins like a poison.

"Katey, just calm down. You need to eat. This is what happens when you resist the hunger."

She turned her face away and gripped the edges of the sofa cushions, her nails, or maybe claws, ripping into the upholstery. She could feel the last bit of control slip away as she shook even more powerfully in spurts of seizure-like episodes.

Something had possessed her and Katey knew she wouldn't win the battle. The wolf was taking over, and it was furious with her. She thought for a fleeting moment that it was going to kill her, devour her from the inside out.

With one more throaty growl, she was no longer in control of her own body. The wolf was. She retained her human form, but the spirit within her solely governed her mind. Katey became a mere backseat observer to the chaos she created.

Dustin rushed through the metal doors and over to the sofa. What he saw on the couch startled him. Katey, eyes gold, fangs and claws extended, animal in everything but bodily form. Logan knelt in front of her, his shoes in a small pool of blood. He hadn't seen another loup-garou this wild since the first days of Ben's transition.

Katey roared, jumped off the couch, and in two long bounds, tackled the beta to the ground. She snarled at Dustin, ready to lash out at his exposed neck with her bared canine fangs, now grown long and sharp. Her hot breath reeked of blood and bile. Dustin launched her over his shoulder and sent her rolling across the concrete floor to the other side of the gym near the rolled-up mats.

Katey sprung onto her hands and knees and growled at her two packmates, blood and saliva glistening on her lips. He knew they should have forced her to eat this morning before they left the house. The hunger suppressors could only do so much. Now, Katey would be out for flesh and she wouldn't care where it came from.

With Logan's eyes still trained on Katey, he edged closer to the beta. "Any ideas?"

Dustin recovered to his feet and sighed, wishing it hadn't come to this. Katey had allowed herself to soar past the point of no return. There was no talking her down from this beastly high. From his experience with Ben, only brutal force would get through to her. They had to speak the wolf's language.

They braced themselves for a fight. Their main goal was to get Katey fed, but just as important, they couldn't let her out of this gym. If she bolted into the school, or if anyone saw her like this, it was game over.

Dustin mutely communicated to Logan for them to split up and circle around. They did, never turning their backs to Katey. They gave her a wide berth, but they knew if she wanted to, she could be on either of them in an instant. The wolf might have had control, but she was still young and didn't know her own strength and speed. It could prove deadly, yet they could use her greenness to their advantage. She didn't know how to fight as they did.

Katey continued to snarl and tried to keep her eyes on both of them as they came around to either side of her, her head snapping in each direction with a frenzied, wide-eyed gaze.

"Hey! Wolf girl! Look over here!" Dustin shouted, waving his arms.

She turned her body completely toward him and roared again, completely distracted. Logan pounced on Katey from behind and pinned her down onto her stomach. She struggled and tried to break free of his grasp, but he had her trapped in a tight bear hug with his legs forcing her own to keep still. Logan wouldn't be afraid to hurt her. She'd recover quickly.

Her growl slowly turned into a whine with her cheek flattened against the cold concrete, admitting defeat against the dominant wolf. That was easier than Dustin expected it would be, but that was a fortunate thing. A day when they could all walk away from a slip-up like this was a good day.

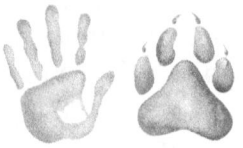

"Katey, just take it easy," Logan whispered.

His words were like a balm to her chaotic mind and Katey felt her true self drift back to the surface, but the wolf still lingered beneath, impatient and foaming at the mouth with hunger.

Logan leaned his head against Katey's temple and continued to whisper sweet endearments in her ear. "Everything's going to be okay. We're taking care of you. It's all right."

Ben ran in, a lunch box in his hand. Inside, she could smell the raw meat. Katey squirmed a little as the aroma of the food came to her nostrils, but Logan tightened his grip. She only leered at Ben as he brought it closer and popped the lid off the container.

"I see you brought the good stuff," Dustin remarked.

"Always got an emergency stash," Ben replied. "Did I miss the fun?"

"Not yet. This is the fun part." Dustin squatted near Katey and took the container of meat from Ben's hand. He pinched out a bit of the pink ground beef and held it in front of her nose.

She snorted and wiggled her head away from the meat, fighting the animal that was telling her to devour it with reckless abandon.

Dustin pushed the meat in her face. "Come on, you stubborn girl. Eat." Katey's lips curled back into a snarl, baring her teeth angrily. "Yeah, go on. I don't care if you're pissed."

Logan twisted Katey's hands around so he could grip her wrists with one hand. "Here, Dustin, let me try." He took a pinch of the meat from Dustin's fingers.

While still straddling himself over her back, Logan held the meat just a few inches from her nose. He simply held the meat to tempt her instead of forcing it upon her.

The coppery smell of the blood and the familiar scent of meat lingered, taunting her rumbling stomach. Katey winced and tried not to give in. Logan slowly brought it closer to her mouth and she snapped.

Katey struck at his hand, taking all the meat between her teeth, and snatching it away.

Logan jerked back his hand and hissed out a curse.

"What?" Dustin asked.

"She snipped my finger."

The two older loups-garous chuckled.

Katey chewed on the meat and felt peace wash over her once more. It was the best thing she had ever tasted. Better than the world's best fries, better than the meat she had the night before. Maybe it tasted better now because she had needed it so badly. Then the thought suddenly occurred to her that she might never be able to have fries again. That didn't bother her as much as it would have ten minutes ago. The beast within was satisfied.

She moaned in contentment and rested her feverish forehead on the cool ground. Katey chewed to savor the flavor before swallowing. Every muscle in her body went slack.

"Better?" Dustin asked, a playful tilt to his voice.

"I'll get the blood cleaned up," Ben said. "She can't stay in school like this. Someone could get hurt if she lapses like that again."

"I'll take her home and get her exams on the way out," Logan said as he took another pinch from the container in Dustin's hand. "I'll get mine, too, and stay there with her to make sure she keeps eating."

Dustin bent his head so he and Katey could see eye-to-eye. "Can you hear me in there?" She nodded. "You're going to take all this food home with you and I want this container and your steaks completely empty before we get home. Understood?"

She nodded again.

The loups-garous watched over their two youngest packmates as Logan hand-fed Katey the meat until the humanity had returned to her eyes. He slowly slid off of Katey and she propped herself up on her forearms. She rested for a moment with her head held in her hands. A mountain of tension had been released, similar to how Logan's dominance soothed her earlier that morning.

"I'm sorry," she managed to mutter.

Dustin huffed a laugh. "You should have seen Ben just before he came to after his transition. Nearly killed me. What you just did was nothing."

The beta handed Logan the container after he took a pinch for himself. Ben did the same as they made their way toward the exit, confident that Logan could handle her so they could return to their classes.

From the way her facial muscles ached, Katey imagined she must have looked as grotesque as a gargoyle with a twisted, contorted expression of hate and rage. Katey promised herself that she would never let it get that bad again. Like Logan said, three meals a day, if not more. She never wanted to be that out of control again, but by now, she began to wonder if she made herself an empty promise. How often did seasoned loups-garous lose it like that?

To say she was humiliated was an understatement. Though her stomach was full, it twisted into nervous knots, knowing that the others had watched her disgraceful episode. Still on the floor, she crossed her arms around her face to hide her shame from Logan. She wondered when would be an appropriate time to cry. His hand rubbed soothingly down her back, petting her as if she were a frightened animal.

As if to answer her unspoken question, Logan said, "That was your loup-garou side. When it doesn't get fed, it forces its way out to get the food it needs... You're just not used to this yet."

Logan took her arm and lifted her up off the floor. Her knees wobbled at first, but his arm steadied her, the other hand holding the container still full of meat she had been ordered to eat. He gathered up their things and stuffed all the food into his lunchbox before they walked out of the gym. Katey was numb to it all, like walking in a dream.

They stepped onto the bus ramp and Katey blinked at the harsh sunlight. Logan pulled out a bandana rag from his back pocket and gently wiped her lips and chin to clean her up. The taste of blood remained in her mouth, and likely would until she brushed her teeth or gargled something a little stronger. She couldn't stop herself from letting out her shrill whine once again, thinking of how much trouble she had caused them simply by being stupid and proud.

Perhaps the others could go about the rest of their day like it hadn't happened, like she wasn't screwing up at every turn, but Katey would never forget the way the wolf snarled and snapped at her fellow pack members. It was as if the wolf didn't even know them or care about them like she did. It was one thing to smash a mirror in rage, but another to harm another loup-garou. Yet, they seemed to understand that her wolf was not the same as her. It was part of her, but Katey couldn't think of the wolf as an extension of herself. Not yet.

"Come on now. Everything's okay." Logan put his hand under her chin and lifted her head for their eyes to meet. A small tear trickled down her cheek and he gently stroked it away with his thumb.

Somehow, gazing into his eyes, so full of warm affection and sympathy for her struggles, Katey believed him. She would get the hang of being loup-garou one day. That day, she vowed, she'd be in such control of herself that she and Logan could be mated and everything really would be okay again.

Until then, Katey knew she had to listen to them. If they told her to eat, she would eat even if she wasn't hungry. It would be a hard habit to break, to do everything she was told without question, but she knew she couldn't be irresponsible like that anymore. Ben was right. Someone could have gotten hurt. What if it was Lily or Beth? Or another teacher? Or, heaven forbid, if she hurt Logan? She'd never be able to forgive herself.

CHAPTER 4

Logan felt as if he were improvising every step of the way. He had never mentored anyone, never had to deal with a new loup-garou personally as he did with Katey. There was always another alpha around to handle any crisis. Now, he had to pull on his own memories of how Darren guided him in those first several years. Still, that didn't keep him from feeling as if he were the blind leading the blind.

He took comfort in the fact that nothing major or irreparable occurred. Mirrors could be replaced. Katey left the classroom in enough time to avoid a scene. She sat silently in the passenger's seat on the way home, taking tiny bites of the raw ground beef every mile or so as they made their way back home.

When he spoke with Darren before leaving the school, the alpha theorized Katey's sudden sickness was a bad reaction to the hunger suppressors, coupled with her own empty stomach. He had never heard of a new loup-garou crashing the way she had.

They arrived home and through their pack bond, Logan could tell something was not all right with Katey. Since her wolf receded and she took control over her body again, a despondence hung over her. How he wished he could have saved her from all this trouble and pain.

"Now, I want you to lay here and take it easy," Logan instructed Katey as she made her way to one of the sofas.

Katey slowly lowered herself to the sofa to lie on her side, her body stiff and unsteady in the action. Logan took the lunch bag into the kitchen and transferred all the remaining meat into a single bowl. When he brought it back, he took the container from Katey's hands and added it to the bowl.

He handed it back to her, now brimming with steak and beef. "Keep eating. Darren said to have the exams finished by tonight. I'm going to be in the kitchen if you need me."

Logan pulled out the two unfinished exam packets from his backpack and felt her bloodshot eyes fix on him, but he wouldn't meet her gaze.

"Did you ever get like that?" she asked.

He was silent for a moment, remembering the days he had spent wandering in the woods with no food and refusing to eat anything but berries between South Carolina and Alabama where he found Darren. The insatiable hunger had frightened him into preferring starvation as opposed to debasing himself. In the end, the berries weren't enough to curb the hunger, and the wolf took over to gorge itself on a fawn it caught when Logan fell unconscious.

"Yeah, I did the same thing." The memory stole away much of his voice.

From the corner of his eye, he saw Katey smile a bit. "Then I don't feel so bad."

Logan exhaled deeply and went to the kitchen to fetch her a pencil. "I'm sure everyone has done it at some point just to test their limits."

"I didn't do it for that."

He stopped and turned to see uneasiness etched in her expression. "Then why?"

Katey's face wrinkled with painful disdain. "I wanted to prove that... that I could control it, but I just... I lost it so easily. It was like I could barely put up a fight against the wolf in that moment. It was like this morning when I smashed the mirror. I just couldn't stop myself. I've never felt so out of control and I hated it."

Logan didn't know whether to take comfort in the fact that they were alike in so many ways, or to feel another pang of remorse for what he had done to her. "It'll be like that for a long time. Every emotion will feel so... amplified. I remember the morning after my second shift, after I knew what I had turned into. I don't even know what emotion it was, but it was like I tried to just will myself to die at that very moment. I was so disgusted and horrified by what I had become that I didn't want to live anymore... I'm just lucky I had Darren and another loup-garou there to pull me out of it."

Sympathy welled in Katey's eyes and he looked away. He didn't tell her that story to be pitied, but to give her consolation. She wasn't alone. That was the point.

"Is that why everyone's so forgiving of how much I've screwed up today? Because you all expected me to be like this?"

Logan opened a drawer and rifled through it to find a pencil that didn't need sharpening. "Pretty much. I wouldn't call what you've done today 'screwing up'. You're learning. Everyone makes mistakes when they're learning. We don't expect you to be perfect in the first twenty-four hours. Hell, they don't expect perfection from me half the time."

He found a mechanical pencil. Close enough. He brought it to her and saw her distraught look.

"Is it ever going to get easier?" she asked.

If only he could lie to her. "You just need to stay on top of the eating thing. It won't keep you from getting a little crazy sometimes, but it'll help. Make sure that you eat more than enough at each meal. If you ever start feeling that dizziness again, that's a sign you need to eat and you better listen to it."

He couldn't count the times that it had happened to himself. Every time, it terrified him beyond words could say. There were periods where he pushed his limits, but he never wanted to feel that hunger, that sense of total loss of his humanity.

A feeling of unrest settled in his gut and he knew it wasn't his own. When Katey took the pencil from him, he didn't let go. "What is it?" he asked, giving her a steady look that demanded honesty.

Katey's throat worked and jaw tightened as she mustered the courage to say it. "Are we okay?"

"What do you mean?"

Her gaze searched his face, as if her answer would be written there. "Last night, what you said about having to wait. It... And with today how I told you I basically agreed to be bitten because I wanted to be with you, and you told the guys something similar last night, but... Are you just done with me now after all that? Are you done with us?" Her voice grew high-pitched as she became flustered by her lack of articulation.

Logan let out a long breath as he stared down at her. He couldn't help but see her as beautiful, even as a loup-garou and a hot mess as a result of her episode. The way her slightly tangled hair fell around her face, her eyes glimmering brightly, still a little red with restrained tears. He couldn't help but love her. Didn't she see that?

"Done with you? Done with us? You talk like you're just something to throw away."

Katey turned sheepish. "That's just how it seemed... Like this was all for nothing."

Perhaps he began to understand her a little better. She was afraid of losing him just as much as he was afraid of losing her. "It wasn't for nothing. I know it's hard to think about it now, but have patience." He bent down and pulled the pencil closer to him, forcing her to lean his way. He touched his forehead to hers. "Our story isn't over until you say it's over. I'm not backing out."

Her eyes closed and he heard the escape of a short breath. Perhaps now, as a loup-garou, she could understand why he did this. When she was human, the meaning behind this nearness, this simple act of intimacy, went straight over her head. Their souls touched where skin touched, a pinpoint of heat that snaked through his chest and core down to the soles of his feet. Now, she could feel that same connection.

Katey tugged back on the pencil and her lips tilted in an effort to find his.

Logan released the pencil and let her fall away. "Not yet," he whispered.

Katey pouted and did that cute puppy whine, but he wouldn't cave.

"If you need help with your exams, let me know. I won't be far."

Everything was still so raw, so unbridled. One kiss, one tender touch could send them both over the edge. In a house by themselves, with no chaperone, and knowing what they felt for one another, Logan knew exactly where it would lead.

Katey had finished her exams and her meat long before the rest of the pack came home. Full and contented with a feeling of accomplishment, she settled in for a nap on the sofa. Her senses, as sharp as they were, continued to track Logan throughout the house, making the act of falling asleep take much longer than she anticipated.

She wasn't sure how long she had been in dreamland before an ear-piercing whistle threw her back into the waking world. Katey screamed and sat up with a start to cover her ears. Her face warped with agony from the harsh assault on her senses. Wild eyes turned to the source of the whistle behind the sofa. She stared at Dustin in disbelief that he would try to wake her like that, knowing how it would affect her.

"Time for your first training session, Katey Kat!" he yelled loud enough for her to hear through the momentary deafness that the whistle had caused.

Katey glared after Dustin as he walked out the glass doors with a smug expression.

After calming her thundering heart, she stood up and followed him outside, driven by curiosity. All the pack and Logan stood near the gazebo, watching her walk through the garden toward them. She noticed that they were no longer wearing their formal school attire but were dressed in dirty, torn jeans and t-shirts that were tight across their muscular frames, much like what they wore to the paintball trip last Sunday, or they were prepared for a day of yard work.

"Feeling better?" Darren asked. She nodded. "You know better now that you need to eat, right?"

Katey stole a glance to Logan. "Yes, sir." The words she spoke surprised her. She had never addressed anyone with that much respect before. None of her numerous foster families could teach her manners or any esteem for authority. It must have been an alpha thing.

"Very good. Your first and most important lesson about food is behind us, but now we need to make sure you can function with your new strength and agility." Darren laid his heavy hand upon her shoulder and pointed across the open field behind their house, and toward the tree line that was well over one hundred yards away. "I want you to run from here to that very far oak tree marked by the red marker ribbon over there as fast as you can. Don't go past the tree."

It seemed simple enough. Katey looked between the guys, wondering if this was a joke. Running from one point to another was child's play. Why did it matter? Then, she saw Ben pull out a stopwatch.

Darren took a step back to give her space. "Ready... Set... Go!"

Katey took off toward the tree at the fastest speed she could manage, the world blurred around her and she closed the distance in mere seconds. When she realized that she had passed it, she skidded to the stop, but slid on dead leaves and toppled onto her side. Dirt and twigs found their way up her shirt and felt like sandpaper against her skin.

"Are you all right?" Dustin asked. She noticed that he didn't have to raise his voice at all, and she still heard him perfectly at this distance.

She pushed herself to her feet and dusted off the debris. When she looked up, she realized that she had passed the tree by nearly five yards. She slumped her shoulders in disbelief that something so simple suddenly became something almost unattainable.

"Yeah, I'm fine," she grumbled.

"Okay, come back and try again."

Katey shook out her legs a bit and took off for the gazebo. She did her best to stop before she reached it, but once again her shoes made her slide on the smooth grass blades.

Logan whipped his arm out to catch her around the waist, the force of the catch making them spin. She let out a breathless giggle as she steadied herself against him.

"How does that feel?" Darren asked, a smile curving his lips.

"I'm not even tired! Before, I wouldn't be able to get half as far without losing my breath. It's kind of cool."

"Good, because we're going to keep you running until you have enough control to stop on a dime. Get ready."

Katey eagerly did so and flew off once again. This went on and on, running back and forth, back and forth. Each time she missed the tree, she made her frustration known. She stomped, punched nearby trees that got in her way, and screamed in fury.

Katey knew she was the only loup-garou female on the planet, but she was determined to be the best student as well. How sad would it be if she was a loup-garou, but failed miserably in her basic training? More than proving herself to her pack, she wanted to prove herself to their world, once she was allowed to be part of it.

Back at the gazebo, the guys watched her and each time Ben clocked her on the stopwatch, keeping record of her time.

Once, she heard Ben tease Dustin, "She's beatin' your time, by the way."

Dustin shoved Ben. "Knock it off."

Each time Katey came closer and closer to reaching her target, Logan gave his best encouragement and tips of advice. It occurred to her that all of them had to do this at some point in their training, and were comparing her success to theirs. That drove her even more to nail this challenge.

Then, her labors paid off and she was able to stop right at the tree, not an inch too shy. Katey could express her elation in no other way besides giving a loud "whoop" of victory and ripping off the flag tape wrapped around the trunk of the tree.

She ran back and stopped right in front of Darren with the ribbon. Likely thinking that she would crash into him, he staggered back a few steps.

"I got it! I got it!"

The others laughed at her childlike giddiness.

"Good job," Darren said heartily. "It takes some young loups-garous a long time to do that. But, you're not done yet. Have you ever climbed a tree?"

Katey's face fell as they led her over to the tree line. She didn't expect any more training for that afternoon. "I climbed little trees when I was a kid."

"Well, it's time to take it a step up. I want you to climb this tree, to just over halfway to the top and wait for further instructions."

Darren placed his hand on the rough bark of a pine tree that must have been over one hundred feet high. Katey craned her head back to stare up at the daunting task ahead. The nearest branch was nearly ten feet above her head and no one was running to fetch her a ladder.

"How am I supposed to get to the first branch?"

Dustin stepped forward and leaned against the trunk. "You can either grow wings, jump, or eject those claws you have hidden in your fingers and climb straight on the bark."

Judging by the broad grin on his face, Katey wondered if he was teasing her about the claws. Then, he glanced at her empty hands, as if waiting for her to whip them out just like he suggested. He was completely serious and she heard a light snicker from Ben behind her.

Katey laughed. "Growing wings sounds easier."

"Let's try a jump first," Darren suggested as they all took a few steps back from the tree. "Get a fast start and try running up the tree after you've jumped as far and as high as you can."

Katey took a deep breath and paced herself back a few yards. Her eyes traveled up to her target branch. The idea of the claws began to sound easier than the jump.

She ran, leapt, and managed to latch onto the trunk just a few feet below the branch. Her hands tried to grapple and claw at the bark, but gravity became her enemy. She dropped to the bottom, cracking a few fingernails on the way.

Logan rushed forward and caught Katey up into his arms before she hit the ground. "You okay?" He looked her over for any serious damage as he set her right on her feet.

She followed his roaming eyes and shook her head. "I'm fine. Didn't hurt that much." Then she looked at her nails and let out a cry. The edges were jagged and broken down to the quick. Normally not a vain girl to begin with, Katey nonetheless, liked her nails and how evenly trimmed she had been able to keep them up to this point.

Darren approached and inspected her nails and the scars in the bark. "At least we know your limit for jumping. Let's try the climbing approach. For the sake of time, give me your hands."

Katey eyed him curiously, brushed off her dirty palms onto her jeans and held them out for Darren. He took one and began massaging on a few pressure points. She hissed in pain as she felt her nail beds tingle and sting. Soon, her broken nails grew long, sharp, and hard with a tinge of tawny yellow, like an animal's claws. She stared at them in amazement as Darren repeated the process with the other hand. Now, she didn't feel so bad about a few cracked human nails when she knew she had such vicious loup-garou claws at her disposal.

"We'll teach you how to make them come out on demand later. They won't stay like that for long, so get to climbing."

Darren turned her shoulders and gave her a guiding push toward the tree. Katey took a deep breath and then jammed her claws into the bark of the tree with all the strength she had. They sank nearly all the way to her fingertips. Finding that they were firmly in the wood, she reached up and planted her other set in.

Gradually, she managed to climb her way up the tree without much difficulty, though she could feel the strain of her weight against her claws. She was amazed that they didn't break off or rip from her fingers completely.

She made it to the first branch just in time before her claws retracted back to normal. Inspecting them once more, the broken human nails had healed themselves and regenerated along the rough edges. She nodded in approval.

"Great, now just climb to that halfway mark," Darren said.

Below, she saw the pack fan out to act as a safety net in case she fell in any direction.

Katey searched for the best way to climb and took it, pulling herself up to each branch with ease. Her muscles tensed and pulled beneath her skin, but they wouldn't give out on her like they would have if she were human.

A fiery determination drove her to climb higher and faster, knowing that they were all watching her. Over and over in her head, she told herself that she had to make them proud. She had to impress them and show them after her episodes from earlier that day, that she could handle her new body. They may not have expected much from her, but she expected it of herself. The wolf within her seemed to approve and helped her along the way, keeping that desire burning in her chest.

With a final grunt and pull, she was over fifty feet in the air. A few birds were startled by her presence and fluttered away at the sight of the new threat. Katey gazed around and found she could see for miles and miles into the forest ahead. It gave her heart an unexpected thrill to see the endless sea of woodlands. How many people could say they had reached such a height without the aid of tools and pulleys? Katey had gotten there by her own capabilities and for a moment, she realized how amazing it was to be a loup-garou.

She breathed in deeply, relishing the pure uncivilized scent of the forest and pines that surrounded her. She appreciated its splendor more now than as a human. She much preferred these sounds and smells to that of the school. Out here, there was only nature. The chattering of woodland creatures, the gentle grazing of a deer half a mile away, the cool breeze ruffling her hair. Yes, this was what it meant to be loup-garou, part of the wild and yet, not wholly one with it. Not yet. But one day, she'd shed her human skin and run through these trees. The wolf within her rejoiced at the idea.

Realizing she had gotten caught up in her own thoughts, she called down, "What now?"

"I want you to practice jumping from tree to tree. This will hone your dexterity and balance. If you fall, one of us will catch you."

Katey wasn't worried about falling or being caught as much as she was concerned about successfully completing the challenge. She looked to an adjacent tree a few yards away. She balanced herself to stand on her branch and leapt.

She caught herself upon it and hung from her hands like she did on the monkey bars at the playground as a child. The branch shook and creaked from the new weight it acquired, but it didn't break. Katey pulled herself up and crawled up to squat in place.

"Don't just grab for the branch, land straight on it as if you were jumpin' on stones in a creek," Ben coached.

Katey had to laugh at the comparison. Stones were easy to jump to and from because they were safely lodged in the ground. The worst that would happen if she missed was that she could twist an ankle. These branches were high above the ground and there was nothing but a pair of strong arms to catch her if she slipped. She'd break more than an ankle.

She steadied herself onto the branch and sighted her next target. She jumped, but fell short. She waved her hands frantically for any branch and caught it by the tips of her fingers.

"You got this, Katey!" Logan urged. "Just pull yourself up and try again!"

"It's not as easy as you made it seem," she groused under her breath as she pulled herself up onto the branch.

"Get used to it!" Dustin replied. "Nothing's going to be easy."

Katey let out a low, short growl at his comment and crouched down again, now much lower than the upper canopy where she had been.

She wasn't tired, but she grew aggravated with her own inability to get this right, just as she had with the agility exercise. Even though she was completely new to the body and her abilities, somehow she thought she should have been able to nail these tasks perfectly without too much effort. Something in her said that she was better than that. She could succeed and she would, even if it killed her. They depended on her to get this right and she was resolute not to waste their time.

She took a few calming breaths and focused. She was going to beat this one way or another.

Katey jumped for the next branch and nailed it perfectly.

She leapt like a frog from one branch to the other, growing more and more precise with each jump.

The guys below did their best to follow her into the woods, keeping their eyes fixed upon her in case she missed again.

"Much better, Katey! Try doing it standing up, not crouched down."

Katey stopped and stood up straight on the branch, balancing herself like a tightrope walker. She bounded for the next branch. It wobbled a little underneath her, but she resisted the urge to stoop down to stabilize herself. She continued her course, wholly concentrated on the next branch, the next leap. Yet, her ears continued to pick up their remarks on her progress.

"She's doin' good," Ben said.

"Better than you did the first time," Dustin quipped.

"Shut up," Ben grumbled, pushing him playfully into the trunk of a nearby tree.

"You're doing great, Katey!" Darren called up to her. "Just a few more times and we'll be done with the exercise for now."

Katey nodded and made a few final jumps perfectly before shimmying herself down to the lowest branch on the last tree. Now, she just had to get back on the ground.

"How do I get down?" she asked, peering over the edge to the pack congregated around the base of the tree.

"Listen closely," Darren said. "You're going to jump and roll across your shoulders. Did you ever learn how to roll like that?"

Katey scoffed. "No!" Where in her life would she have needed to learn how to leap from such heights and roll?

Darren stepped back a few paces. "Just do the best you can. We're right here."

Katey looked between them all, but only found true comfort in Logan as he braced himself to run to her aid. She inhaled and jumped from the branch. Wind roared past her ears and she endured the tickling sensation of falling.

She knew it wasn't a well-executed tumble and her body felt jarred by the impact. Her feet touched the ground first and crumbled beneath her at an awkward angle as she tucked herself and rolled long-ways across the leaf-littered ground.

Pain instantly shot through her arm and elbow. She let out a shrill whine and clutched her arm tightly to her chest as the pack rushed forward. Logan was the first to her side and hurriedly inspected her for injuries.

"I think I broke my arm." She had never broken anything in her life, but she also knew that she had never felt this kind of pain before.

Ben leaned forward and took her wrist. "Quick, let me see."

Katey extended her arm for him as she sniffled back the urge to cry. The broken bone was threatening to puncture through the skin on her forearm. Bile rose up in her throat at the sight of it and she quickly looked away.

Ben skillfully took her arm in his hands and set it back into place with the flick of his wrist. She whimpered at the second volley of pain, and he laid her arm back across her chest.

"Okay, just give that a second to heal and you should be fine."

"Just like that?" But Katey already felt the bone begin to mend itself within her arm, the pain fading away as the seconds ticked by. Logan sat her up and began picking out the twigs and bits of crumbled leaves from her hair, smoothing back the strands.

Ben smiled and nodded. "Just like that."

"Where did you learn that from?"

"I was in a few wars, remember? It pays to know how to set a broken bone when the medic's takin' forever to get to ya."

"We'll work on the rolling later from a safer height." Darren stood and stuck his hands in his pockets. "You did better than Logan's first time, though. He broke his neck."

Dustin laughed and sat back on his heels. "I wish I could have been there to see that."

Ben kept his attention fixed on Katey. "Can ya wiggle your fingers for me?" She flexed her fingers. "Hurt at all?" She shook her head.

"How do you feel? Tired yet?" Darren asked.

Logan gently took Katey in his arms and hoisted her to her feet. She extended her injured arm, twisting it around and felt absolutely no pain in it anymore. It was like the fall had never happened and Katey was confident that she could get used to this new invincibility.

She beamed at her alpha. "I'm not tired at all. What's next?"

CHAPTER 5

The sky was alive with shades of bright orange and purple twilight by the time the pack came back to the gazebo behind the house. Ben ran inside to flip on the exterior lights so they could continue training. Spotlights installed on the rooftop eaves illuminated the grassy field around the gazebo.

Darren turned to Katey. "One more bit of training and then we'll go inside and get some dinner. We know you're a big girl and can take care of yourself, but if you're going up against another loup-garou, you're going to need to know how to fight and disable one. Let me show you a trick." He stepped up to Dustin. "If you ever have the advantage over an opponent, there is a specific hold that you can use to incapacitate them."

Dustin eyed his alpha warily, but added, "It comes in handy, especially if you ever cross the paths with a rouger."

"Rouger?" Katey asked.

Ben folded his arms. "Kind of a nickname we use for a rougarou."

"What's a rougarou?"

A shameful look dawned in Darren's face. "I believe I neglected to mention them before. It's a term we use for those loups-garous who prefer the taste of human flesh over animal."

Katey slowly nodded in understanding. They had mentioned rougarous, though not necessarily by name, when they first told her about the existence of loups-garous.

"Rougarous can be stronger, faster, and meaner than the garden variety of loup-garou," Dustin said. "If you ever find yourself on their bad side, it's best to run the other way."

Darren raised his hand and wrapped his fingers around a specific spot on Dustin's shoulder. "But, if you can't run, squeeze this spot as hard as you can."

"Oh, no, not me! Do it on Ben or—"

Too late. Darren squeezed the nerve and Dustin yowled in pain, seizing Darren's wrist, but unable to tear the alpha's hand away.

"This is putting pressure on a particular nerve that only loups-garous have in their shoulder. If you just gently squeeze on it, they'll be nearly paralyzed with the pain and can't fight back. If you squeeze even harder, you can end up making them change involuntarily. So, be very careful to never give your shoulder to your enemy like that. It'll turn the course of a fight."

Darren let go and Dustin dropped to his knees to catch his breath. Katey watched as the beta flexed and rubbed at his sore shoulder. At his expense, it was a good demonstration.

"However, a loup-garou may not leave their shoulder un-guarded so easily. If you can't run or disable them, you'll have to fight them." The alpha then turned to Logan and inclined his head to Katey. "You're the best to teach this lesson. Go on."

The pack looked to Darren as if he had just told them to put a silver bullet to Katey's head.

Logan narrowed his eyes. "What?"

"You heard me. You two fight and give her tips as you go along. Don't worry about hurting each other. It's not like you won't heal from it."

Dustin, who had fully recovered, shook his head and made a gesture as if he were pointless to argue. "Okay you two, get to it. I'm getting hungry."

Katey looked to Logan, dumbfounded. She didn't want to fight him and didn't know the first thing about combat. Logan seemed less inclined to fight her either, but it was for the sake of training. He began to circle her and she did the same, not turning her back to him. She pulled up memories of how wolves initiated combat and wasn't sure how it compared to loup-garou fighting.

She leapt forward with a punch, but Logan dodged it and twisted her into an arm lock from behind. The hold was light and painless, but Katey couldn't budge.

He leaned his head down over her shoulder and breathed on her neck, sending chills down her spine. "Your first mistake was to attack first. You gave me the advantage. I have you right where I want you and there's nothing you could do about it."

It was the first bit of flirting they had exchanged since she turned and Katey bit her lips together to keep herself from smiling.

Logan released Katey and she whipped around to face him, staggering back a bit to give herself room. They circled once more, and Katey kept her eyes trained on him. Her attention on his body language constantly deviated to his dazzling, intense blue eyes. Without even trying, he effectively distracted her.

In a blur, he leapt forward and tackled her around the waist, spinning her in such a way that she landed hard on the ground, trapped in his hold. Katey struggled against him, but found she was no match for him. Not only did he outweigh her in size and build, but he was able to channel his strength to do as he willed while Katey couldn't figure out how to flip the switch and activate her loup-garou instincts for survival.

She managed to wiggle her knee up and pushed against his hip to roll him over. Something cracked in the process and Logan let out a grunt of pain. Katey straddled his tight abs and pinned his arms to the side. The sight of him beneath her made her deeply aware of her own body and the way their pulses raced together. Logan smirked and countered, rolling her onto her back.

Before she knew it, they were rolling across the grass. After a few turns, Katey started to laugh. It had turned into a game and neither of them made even a half-hearted attempt to fight anymore.

"What are you two doing?" Dustin yelled from the sidelines. "This isn't time for play!"

Darren laughed heartily. "Dustin's right. Come on, now."

The two stopped rolling as Logan pressed his full weight on top of Katey, their noses just inches from each other. Katey caught her breath, but once they settled down and she realized how close they were, her nerve endings stirred with the need to be closer. Through their pack bond, she knew Logan wanted the same.

Katey could feel Logan's tense muscles against hers, the solidness of his thighs on either side of her hips, and the heat that chased away the chilly evening. She gripped Logan's arms and let out a sigh of pleasure as a shiver zipped through her. They were in the perfect position to kiss and Katey's body ached for it. Insatiable passion roiled around them, filling her senses with a musky, hot aroma, which only fueled the longing. What was that smell? She could see the same desire in Logan's eyes, but neither of them moved to take the opportunity.

As they locked gazes, Logan's irises began to slowly fade to red. Katey gasped and Logan blinked hard as if he knew what change had just occurred. He quickly crawled off to put a few yards of distance between them. Cold rushed in and squelched that carnal need before it could consume her.

"Oh, come on!" Dustin groaned. "None of that!"

Katey, half dazed, sat up on her hands and looked at the pack. Logan paced and rubbed and smacked his cheeks as if trying to knock away some drowsiness. The other three stared in agitation, as if they had just broken some rule she didn't know about.

"His eyes," Katey muttered. "What does red mean?"

Darren sighed. "Not just his eyes, but yours as well. Red is... Well, it's nothing you two need to be feeling in a moment like this."

Now that Logan's masculine scent wasn't pounding the sense out of her, Katey was able to think clearly enough to realize how turned on a loup-garou could become. Was red like another warning sign? She rubbed at her eyes to rid herself of the embarrassing evidence. She couldn't believe all of that could be so plainly telegraphed in front of the pack.

"Forget who you're fightin'," Ben chided.

Katey looked back at Logan and his whole attitude seemed to suddenly shift. He hunched his shoulders and crouched down like he was about to pounce. Now free of any lustful thoughts, Katey mimicked the stance and waited, tensing every muscle like a wound-up spring.

Once she ducked into that stance, she felt her wolf side reemerge. This time, it wasn't hungry, but bent on defending itself against Logan by whatever means necessary. Katey didn't fight it this time, because she needed all the help she could get. Logan had been fighting for money for nearly a century. She didn't have a chance in a no-holds-barred fight. She needed the instincts of the wolf. Katey took a backseat, watching the show as the wolf dictated every move.

Logan came running and tried to tackle her as before, but Katey rolled out of the way and leapt upon his back. She wrapped her legs and arms around him in an effort to grapple him to the ground. He gripped her around her shoulders, and threw her over to pin her onto her back. She was sure his claws had come out, because she felt the sting as they punctured her skin.

Katey raised her hand, her own claws suddenly extended and slashed at his throat. Logan recoiled just in time. In doing so, he momentarily lost his balance and sacrificed the upper hand of the fight. Katey pushed him off and pinned him down, digging her forearm into his throat.

Logan choked and sputtered for a moment, but then grabbed her by the hair and yanked hard. She shrieked, and turned her head enough to sink her fangs into his arm. Logan kicked her in the stomach to throw her off and wiped the blood on his shirt.

They retreated a short distance and glared at each other, wolf against wolf, gold meeting gold.

From the sidelines, Dustin commented, "Wouldn't want to get on her bad side."

Katey pounced on Logan, too fast for him to dodge. He grabbed her waist and flipped her around to pin her again, the same move he had done before. His hand went quickly for her shoulder nerve and squeezed. Katey cried out as fire shot through her blood vessels. She could barely think past the arresting pain and each breath was a gasp for oxygen. She had done what they told her not to do, exposed her weakness.

"Not too hard, Logan," Darren warned.

Katey's eyes went wide as they glowed their loup-garou gold. Tawny claws slashed at Logan's throat again. This time, she didn't miss and found purchase in tight flesh.

Logan immediately released and staggered to his feet. He held his neck, blood seeping between his fingers as he choked and gulped for breath. She likely cut into his windpipe. It would have been a mortal wound if their rapid healing didn't stitch him back together. Katey, however, wouldn't give him the luxury of a break. The wolf within her roared, fangs bared and claws extended, and charged, swiping and snapping at him with wild savagery. No strategy, only the single-minded goal to disable or kill.

From the recesses of Katey's mind, her human side began to pound at the walls, demanding to be given the reins again. Her wolf refused.

Logan dodged and ducked through each strike and slipped behind her. With his neck wound healed enough that he could breathe, he hooked his arms around hers and positioned his hands

just behind her neck in a full nelson hold. Katey kicked and struggled madly against him, her heels beating against his shins. Bones
cracked, but Logan fought the need to fall or let go until she
surrendered.

Katey suddenly dropped, loosening Logan's hold on her, then
forced herself upwards and back to throw him off balance. Logan
stumbled and finally let go. As she began to fall back with him, she
twisted and pushed herself away before spinning to kick him in the
face. Logan fell and his hand fled to his bloodied face. That was the
second time she broke his nose.

Katey fell upon all fours as she had in the wrestling gym, readying herself for another attack. She had lost control of herself and
succumbed to the might of her inner wolf. At the sight of Logan's
busted face, Katey grappled with her subconscious, begging for
her human side to be released again and take the place of the beast
that fought for her protection. Just as before, the wolf wouldn't
listen and gave a deep, gruff growl.

"A little help here would be nice!" Logan shouted to the pack.

Heeding his plea for help, Katey somehow took hold of her wolf
and forced it to be still, her body stuck in that tensed, crouched
position in the grass. She wasn't sure how long she could hold it,
but she'd try until someone could permanently stop her.

Darren and Dustin didn't need to be asked twice.

Dustin lifted Katey to her feet, wrapping his arms around hers
to keep her claws out of the way and Logan rushed forward to
envelope his arms around her legs. Darren sandwiched her head
between his two powerful hands and forced her to look him in the
eyes.

Katey let go and the wolf surged forth to growl at her alpha.
She struggled and thrashed, but she couldn't break their hold.
Dominance blasted from the alpha and beta, cocooning her and
restraining her better than their own strength could.

"Katey! Katey, look at me!" Through the haze and dominance,
Katey slowly came back to herself and looked deep into Darren's
chocolate brown eyes. "Calm down! You're okay. No one here is
going to hurt you. It was just training. Take deep breaths. You're
safe."

Her body went limp and all will to fight left her at the prompting
of her alpha. His dominance was the only thing the wolf would
listen to, but it was a begrudging submission.

The men slowly loosened their grip on her and Katey collapsed into Logan's embrace. He cradled her in his lap and held her close as she became frantic and confused. The wolf had slunk back into its hole, leaving Katey to deal with the mess. Somehow, Logan seemed to understand that it wasn't her who fought so hard to hurt him, to kill him. He hugged her tight, even though her hands had shed his blood, the blood that stained the front of his shirt and filled Katey's senses. It was a reminder that she had done what she never wanted to do.

"I'm sorry, Logan. I'm so sorry. I didn't mean to hurt you. I couldn't control it." She became hysterical, sobbing into his blood-soaked shirt.

"I know. It's all right." Logan smoothed back her hair, dampened with sweat.

Katey leaned her head onto his chest as if to hide from the world, while Logan shushed her whimpering and rocked her gently back and forth, treating her like a frightened child. In many ways, she was.

She didn't mind as Logan enclosed his legs around her. Burrowing into him, she felt safe, whole, and like nothing could harm her, not even what lurked inside, waiting for another chance to come out. Her eyes returned to their normal green and her fangs and claws reduced to a safe length. Yet, she couldn't stop herself from trembling, remembering the complete vulnerability of knowing that she was not in command of her own body, and she had let it happen.

Darren stroked his beard, deep in thought. "We're going to have to watch out for that."

"I never remember getting set off that easy," Dustin said, "She broke out of that shoulder grab like it was nothing."

Katey heard their words and cringed, disappointed in herself.

"I don't think any of us did, not even Ben."

Dustin sighed and looked to Darren wearily. "Are we going to have to teach her that meditation Zen crap that you learned?"

The alpha shook his head. "I'm not sure yet. We'll wait until after she changes for the first time and see how she is after that."

Katey could hear their low voices, deep in conversation about what they would do with her. If she was good enough, if she had more control, they wouldn't have had to waste so much time and effort in training her. Her body felt heavy under the realization that there was no way she could expedite her training just by trying harder. The years she'd have to wait became more and more like a reality she had to accept. So much could happen in those years.

"Logan, I'm scared," she whispered.

"Don't be," Logan said softly, "we're going to take care of you." He squeezed her tighter and kissed the top of her head.

As the midnight oil burned, the senior members of the pack were still awake, restless and troubled by the day that seemed hardly over yet. In the back billiard room, the loups-garous played the tenth game of pool since the two younger loups-garous had gone upstairs to bed.

The room was covered in a low-pile green carpet and the walls were lined with dark tongue-and-groove panels, resembling the inside of a bar, which was just what they had intended when they designed the home. In the middle of the room sat the billiard table, the colored balls scattered across its felt surface. Dustin lined up for a shot while the others waited, their intense gazes fixed on the game.

Billiards had been their pastime of choice for decades, the perfect form of entertainment that doubled as training. Precision aim and careful gaging of shots helped to hone their control and fine motor skills. In the early days, one strong hit would send balls flying about the pool hall, knocking holes into the wall. The wood panels proved more resilient than drywall. By now, their accuracy had improved, and they could carry on dozens of rounds without damaging the house any further.

"So, how are we going to do this?" Dustin asked as he slid the stick back and forth between his fingers, aiming at the cue ball. He was the first to bring up the topic in the last two hours since they first entered the billiard room, but everyone had been stewing on their predicament for just as long. He took his shot and pocketed a solid.

Darren sat in one of the barstools by the cocktail table and absently tapped the heavy base of the pool stick between his legs against the floor. "I don't know. This is new to all of us."

Ben gave him a curious look. "Y'all trained loups-garous with John in France for decades. How is this new to you?"

Out of the three, Darren was the most experienced in teaching young loups-garous. When he had graduated from his own training, he stayed on with John for a number of years at the chateau to manage the other orphaned teens who had no father or mentor to explain what they were and what they could do. Though there was no need for the chateau anymore, the place bombed out by the Germans during the second World War, John's work had been invaluable to hundreds, if not thousands of loups-garous who went on to become part of their own packs. Those years he had spent under John's tutelage inspired Darren to the vocation of teacher and educator.

But this... This was different.

"Katey isn't the same. Today was proof enough of that."

Ben took aim as Dustin moved around the table to assess the field. "How so? Ain't this normal? I know I wasn't the best student, but I figured that was more Dustin's fault than mine." He pocketed his striped ball with a clatter.

Dustin gave him a derisive laugh. "Very funny. But no. Katey's skill is... incredible to say the least."

Darren stood to evaluate the field. "She nailed her training faster than any fresh loup-garou I've ever known. It's as if she has years of experience and innate control already." He bent down and eased the end of his stick toward the cue ball. "Yet, she doesn't have a handle on her wolf in the same way." He struck the ball, sending it barreling toward a solid. He missed.

"It's almost like her wolf is too strong," Dustin added as he readied for his turn. "Strong enough to tear the house down if we let her."

Two balls in the corner pocket.

Darren took his seat again and bowed his head to tap the upright pool stick against his forehead. Dustin was right. He could sense that plainly enough through their pack bond and it startled him. Katey sat on a wealth of untapped dominance, like an underground reservoir and they were just one strike away from unleashing an insurmountable torrent. If she ever tried to use it, they would all be in trouble, including Darren.

"Do y'all think it's because she's a girl?"

Dustin shrugged. "Maybe. Or it may have something to do with the fact that Logan was the one who bit her. Pieces of the sire transfer in the bite sometimes. Have you noticed those highlights in her hair?"

Ben guffawed. "If she's gonna take after Logan, we're all in for it."

Darren lifted his head and regarded a spot on the opposite wall where a ball had dented the wooden panel years back. "Logan's training was much worse than this. He didn't want to have any-thing to do with the wolf. But Katey... She's eager."

He remembered how she continued to insist that she wanted to be turned, that she wanted the bite. Perhaps they had been wrong all along and Logan's efforts to intimidate her into the decision was utterly wrong. Despite everything she knew about them, despite all of their warnings, Katey had been willing to take the bite and turn into a loup-garou, even if it would kill her.

Dustin propped a hand on his hip and laughed. "Eager is putting it lightly."

"Talented and untamed," Ben said with a shake of his head. "Bad combination."

Darren frowned. "Not bad. Simply... uncommon."

"Everything about Katey has been uncommon from day one," Dustin reminded them. "We all knew it. Maybe our wolves saw that."

It was possible. Katey had that special spark, something that drew them to her like a starved horse to lush green pastures. Their wolves already saw her as part of the pack and the bond established so easily without trying, as if the groundwork was there from the very beginning.

Everything about this situation seemed more complicated, more delicate. Did they have a ticking time bomb or the next loup-garou prodigy?

"I wonder if John would have any advice."

Ben's question reminded Darren that he had forgotten all about the coming weekend.

He groaned and covered his eyes. "Bloody hell... Alaska."

It seemed to have slipped everyone's mind as well and they mumbled their own curses.

"How the hell are we going to manage Katey in Alaska?" Dustin exclaimed, a hint of his Irish roots shining through.

Darren's head spun with all the fresh complexities. "John will be there. Perhaps he will know."

"We need to call and warn him what we're bringing with us."

He nodded in agreement with his beta. "We need to prepare Katey as well... The poor girl will be so overwhelmed. The noise, the attention—"

"The shift."

Darren and Dustin snapped toward Ben.

"The shift?" Dustin bawled. "She hasn't had her loup-garou legs for even a week. There's no way she'll be able to shift at will."

A startling thought came to Darren's mind. "Maybe she will." Now it was their turn to stare in disbelief at their alpha. "She's already come so far in her own training. It may be possible that with the right coaching, she could shift with the rest of us for that night."

Dustin came a few steps closer. "You realize she'd be the only unclaimed female amongst potentially hundreds of other shifted loups-garous. If they don't try to kill her, they'll try to—"

Ben slapped his hands over his ears. "I don't wanna think about it! Don't even say it!"

Dustin raised his voice. "But it's true. She'll be vulnerable. There will be plenty of alphas there to keep her safe from the younger loups-garous, but that's no guarantee. The only guarantee is..." He gave Darren a pointed look, the one that taunted him with the reminder of a conversation they never got to finish. The day before, Dustin had warned him about Logan's love for Katey and that it may indicate some trouble ahead. None of them could have known that it would have been him turning her, but their initial theory was that he would try to form a mating bond with Katey far too soon.

Darren let out a long breath. "Well, Logan would certainly be happy about that."

"Mating?" Ben exclaimed. "The girl has been through enough." He ticked off the points on his fingers. "She finds out werewolves exist, her foster mother dies in a car accident that she somehow walked away from, she moves in with us, and Logan scared the shit out of her to make her agree to the bite. Now we'd be askin' her to fly across the country to a gatherin' of dozens of packs and, oh yeah, she has to make a lifelong commitment to an angsty loup-garou that can't even shift at will, or else she may get ravaged by her own kind."

Darren grimaced. Ben wasn't wrong, but it could have been said in a nicer manner. It was a lot to ask. All of those things had occurred within just a few weeks' time. How Katey hadn't lost her mind already, he couldn't understand.

The billiard room went dead quiet. How could things have gotten so out of hand so quickly?

Dustin looked back at the abandoned game. "Maybe we shouldn't go to Alaska under the circumstances?"

"We won't be able to return the tickets so late," Darren said, voice low. "Besides, John will be there. He should be able to help. Katey won't need to shift, so mating will not be necessary. We're delving into mere speculation."

Ben huffed. "What're the odds she'll twist our arms into lettin' her try to shift anyway?"

"Pretty high," Dustin returned. "You know we're wrapped around her finger."

A knowing smile cracked across Darren's mouth. "Well, we'll just have to resist her charms somehow... Whose turn was it?"

Dustin thought for a minute and then pointed to Ben, but he didn't seem too sure.

After consideration, Darren told his pack. "We will continue to do our best for Katey. We'll train her like any other loup-garou and get John to weigh in on the matter when we get to Alaska."

They agreed and the topic was closed... for now.

Their game continued, but Darren's thoughts tripped and tangled over this new challenge. Katey came into their lives like a subtle, intriguing mystery. She had been someone to protect, but from a distance. They knew better than to become too attached. Such boundaries were obliterated when Logan finally met her and saw what they all saw in her. He had latched on with a dangerous intensity, straining their carefully balanced world to spend more time with her. He became too invested and careless, falling in love along the way. He disregarded their rules and before they knew it, Katey was in too deep to claw her way out.

Now, she was part of their lives in a way that none of them could have imagined. None of them could fathom that a female could become a loup-garou. It was impossible. It had never been done before, and when it was attempted, every convert died in the process. While Darren couldn't regret the turn of events, he knew it all happened too fast. It was as if the hands of destiny hastened them all toward some final end beyond the mists of their own ignorance. They couldn't see beyond the next day, couldn't predict what would happen. All they could do was tread carefully and keep Katey alive in the process.

Katey moaned and kicked at the comforter that constricted around her legs. She couldn't bring herself out of the nightmare, couldn't grab for reality through the darkness.

Her powerful loup-garou heart pounded against her rib cage, rapidly beating like a sledgehammer. A cold sweat broke out over every inch of her skin, dampening her pajamas and sheets. Even the wolf seemed scared.

She realized one thing had not changed since Logan bit her. The dreams about the woman in white still plagued her sleeping hours. This was the first time she had dreamed exclusively about the woman since she was bitten, but everything had been magnified by her new senses.

Even in her nightmares, she could smell, hear, and sense everything with a heightened intensity. Not only could she hear the woman calling to her, but she could hear the whisper of fabric as her white dress bellowed in the wind. She could smell the musty scent of wood and torn upholstery. The stench of coppery blood was prevalent, wrapping around her mind in a vice grip. Even more startling was the odor of sulfur in the air, and she couldn't find where it was coming from.

As vivid as her dream was, she wasn't able to see it through to the end, not even close. Katey had taken one step outside the cabin to run after the woman when Dustin rushed in and shook her awake.

Her golden eyes snapped open, she looked around and saw that she wasn't in the ransacked cabin of her dreams. The familiar sight of her blue canopy bed and cozy room, brilliantly lit by the early morning sun streaming through the windows, set her a little more at ease.

Katey looked to Dustin, who bore a look of confusion and worry. After taking a few deep, soothing breaths, she sat up and ran her fingers through her slept-in hair.

"I thought it was Ben having the bad dream," Dustin said. "Imagine my surprise when it was you."

She blinked back the grogginess. "What are you talking about?"

Dustin sat on the edge of the bed, the mattress bowing under his weight. "We could feel your fear through the pack bond. Ben has nightmares about the wars and he doesn't trust anyone else to wake him, so I thought it was him, but he was fine. You're the only one who hadn't woken up yet."

Katey had heard somewhere about soldiers who came back from wars with psychological problems. If they were startled in the wrong way, it could snap them into combat mode. If Ben trusted Dustin enough to wake him from a nightmare, they must have had a closer relationship than she originally presumed.

But if they could sense her nightmares through the pack bond, they would sense her fear pretty often. These dreams about the woman in white came too frequently these days. A ransacked cabin, blood and debris everywhere, and the woman with the long blonde hair in the doorway beckoning her to follow into a white void. Katey could never catch her.

Silence reigned between them as Katey took hold of her senses and Dustin watched her with expectant eyes.

"Are you going to tell me what the dream was about?"

Her dreams were an intimate thing. She'd never told anyone about the woman in white or the relentless repetitiveness of the nightmare. In the back of her mind, she believed that if she told anyone, they would try to analyze its meaning and she was afraid to know. The woman's appearance in other dreams may have been a coincidence. She was there the night before, after she had been turned, and she was there to comfort her when she dreamed about the pack as wolves before she even knew what they were. Part of Katey wondered if she had anything to do with the miracle of turning into a loup-garou without dying.

Yet, if she told Dustin, if the rest of the pack knew, how might they interpret the dream? Would they think it had any meaning or disregard it as some obsessive vision?

"I don't want to talk about it," she croaked out, her voice still a little hoarse from sleep.

"Talking about it might help."

Katey passed a hand over her face and then through her hair in frustration. "I'm not ready to talk about it."

Dustin leveled a look at her and then nodded in surrender. "All right. If you want to talk about it, let us know."

Katey waited until he left her bedroom before snatching up her stuffed dog toy, Captain Jack, from the foot of the bed. She collapsed back into bed, landing hard on her pillows. Closing her eyes, she reached out beyond her bedroom with her senses to find the pack elsewhere in the house.

They were all awake and moving around in their bedrooms. She listened closely as they migrated down the stairs for breakfast. Their voices were low, and she couldn't hear much of what they were saying, likely a conscious effort to keep their conversation private.

She could smell the savory aromas of bacon and sausage wafting down the hall, tempting her to rise out of bed and face the world. She wasn't quite ready.

Thankfully, she completed the last of her semester exams through the madness and all that was left were two days until winter break. The trip to Alaska hadn't been brought up, so she assumed nothing had changed. She'd go with the pack to the gathering of loups-garous. The thought knotted her stomach with anxiety, but came unraveled when she remembered what Logan had said the day before. They would take care of her.

She snoozed for what seemed only moments before she heard the slow procession of footfalls back up the stairs and down the hallway. Checking the clock on her nightstand, the pack would be leaving soon. None of them pushed her to come out or for a decision whether she would go to school or not. In truth, she wasn't sure if she wanted to after yesterday's disaster. But, despite all of that, she wanted another try, another chance to do things the right way. Eat plenty, keep a handle on her emotions, and forbid her wolf from making any unscheduled appearances.

Katey scooted herself out of bed and dressed for the day, wearing a rather snug-fitting shirt that she hardly ever wore. She had the body to pull it off now, but slipped on a jacket that hid her curves. She then made her way to the bathroom, just as the rest of the pack were coming out to wrap up their own morning routines.

They greeted her in turn, but asked no questions apart from the polite, "How did you sleep?" and, "How are you feeling? Any trouble?" Katey wondered if she should expect such a custom every morning, and if they would accept her monosyllabic answers.

After her time in the bathroom, she ventured downstairs. Her packmates were already in the midst of packing their things for work when she came in and set her bag down on one of the sofas. She didn't have to look to know that Logan was in the kitchen with a half-eaten plate of breakfast meats. Another plate, fully prepared for her, sat on the counter near where he leaned.

Dressed in a pair of drawstring pajama pants and a large band shirt, Logan still looked hot as hell. Katey crossed her arms over her skittering stomach, fighting a storm of feelings. The last thing she needed was her eyes going red again.

Logan looked up and smiled. "Good morning."

Katey shyly wandered over to him and took up the plate of breakfast. In any other circumstance, with all her bundle of nerves, she might have refused any food. Since she was making an effort to behave and play by the new rules that dictated her body. She took up the plate, leaned against the counter beside Logan and dug in. The cooked bacon and eggs were not as satisfying as the raw meat from before, but it eased her roiling tummy.

"Darren thinks that the reason you crashed so hard yesterday in the gym was because of the pills. Normal hunger wouldn't make you vomit blood like that. So, he's given me strict orders to make sure you eat something before each period."

"Why do I have to eat so much? Wouldn't three meals do?" Katey asked, glancing up to him from her plate.

"You may have a higher metabolism and get set off easily, like yesterday during training. It's just a theory, but we need to take every effort to make sure you don't wolf-out in class on someone."

Katey turned her eyes away as she remembered the evening before. "But, I wasn't set off. I just let it happen."

Logan went still and looked up to her in mid-chew. "What do you mean?" he asked with his mouth full.

"Darren was telling me about the whole 'wolf spirit symbiosis' thing. So, yesterday during training, they wanted me to get rough, so I simply let it take over to help. I thought listening to the wolf was better than fighting it like I did when I resisted eating."

His eyes narrowed and swallowed what was in his mouth. "That's very dangerous, Katey. Don't do that."

Logan's tone frightened her and she bowed her head in shame. "I didn't think it would turn out the way it did though... I'm sorry."

He set down his plate and slipped a comforting hand just behind her ear, his fingers weaving into her hair. Katey lifted her eyes to meet his, the breath stolen from her lungs. "Don't fight the hunger, but don't let the wolf tell you what to do all the time. That's how people get hurt. That's what happened when I bit you. Bad things can happen when the wolf is given too much leash... Promise me you won't do that again?"

"I'll try," she said with a nod and tiny, unsure smile.

Logan dragged his thumb across the bottom of her jaw and her breathing became ragged as parts of her body tingled and others warmed to his caresses.

"We're heading out, guys," Dustin called from the living room.

Logan dropped his hand and took a step back. If she didn't have so much respect for the beta, she would have growled at the interruption.

They turned just in time to see the pack walk toward the foyer. Logan settled in the space next to her again and shoveled the last of the sausage pieces into his mouth.

Katey tried to push aside the hollow feeling of unsatisfied hunger for Logan's touch as she continued eating, but found it hard to put out of her mind. They were alone again, but clearly the pack wasn't as concerned about that, even after yesterday's training and all the little hints before then that they shouldn't be unchaperoned.

Logan set his plate in the sink and went upstairs to get ready while Katey finished her breakfast.

After disposing of her plate, she willed away the fluttering sensations in her core and wandered into the living room. Her feet automatically guided her to the sliding glass door, and she mechanically opened it to step outside. She had no previous inclination to go outside, but it was as if something else prompted her to seek fresh air.

She breathed in the soft scent of pine from the forest, the nectar from the flowers in the free-range garden, and dew that lingered on the blades of grass in the yard. Katey smiled and sat herself in one of the wrought iron patio chairs as she basked in the crisp winter morning.

Her thoughts darted from one fretful thing to another. School, Logan, the pack, her training, Alaska, the endless years and decades that stretched in front of her like a highway through a barren desert. No clear end and no clear roadmap for her to follow. All she had was the loups-garous and the wolf within her that now seemed more of an enemy than an ally.

She hadn't allowed herself to drown in the reality of it all, that she wasn't human, that nothing would ever be the same. All she wanted to do was focus on one day at a time and forget the day before. Stay present, stay grounded. But the more she tried, the more unstable it all felt beneath her feet.

Out here, nature silenced her thoughts, beckoning her to relax and forget it all.

She stretched out her legs, leaned her head back, and closed her eyes to listen and give into the call. Birdsongs of all varieties drifted through the air. Small critters scurried through brush in the distance. If she listened carefully, she could almost hear the rumble of car engines on the far away highway that edged the expansive property shared by the loups-garous of Crestucky.

She felt something familiar pulling her to go out and run with no destination in mind. It wanted her to just run and be a part of the wild. The urge was undeniable, accompanied by a complete lack of contentment to just sit and observe. She needed to experience it, to taste it and savor it first-hand.

Katey could tell it was the wolf telling her to run away, but she resisted. She could hear it weave lies to her already, tempting her.

Just for a little while, not too long. You can be back before it is time to leave. Just one run, please?

Logan came downstairs and it didn't take him long to find Katey. She was outside, looking as if she were taking a nap in one of the patio chairs. As he stepped out to join her, the aura of nature and peace floated around the porch like a heady perfume. He likened it to what he felt when they first met. It was that utter serenity that charmed his wolf into submission before they ever said a word. Katey emitted that gentling force that made him fall in love with her.

The longer he stood there, the more he realized that she was completely oblivious to his presence. She let out a soft, pleasant sigh and he could have watched her all day. Too bad they didn't have that luxury.

"Katey?"

She jerked and looked up at him with a golden stare. His smile faded at the sight of her eyes, but grew easier when they began to fade back to their stunning emerald.

"Were you just fighting it?"

Her lips parted a bit in shock. "How did you know?"

"Your eyes."

She groaned and gently smacked her forehead. "I swear nothing was going to happen."

One corner tilted up in an understanding smile. "It's fine. It's easy to get lost out here." He glanced to the garden.

It was Darren's own project, a remnant of the years they spent with John at the chateau in France. Gardening, as stupid as it sounded, was part of their early training. Loups-garous could be strong and fierce, but tending to flowers and other living things required gentleness and a softness of touch that did not come easy to new loups-garous.

Katey stood up and took another look out over the garden and forest beyond the gazebo. "You felt the pull too?"

Logan stepped aside as a cue that they needed to get back inside. "We all do when we stay out here too long. Are you ready to go? Or did you want to stay home today?"

Katey lifted her chin. "I'm going to school. I want to give it another shot."

He didn't know whether to be proud or concerned by her determination. "All right. The minute you don't feel well or think you need to leave, you let me know."

She nodded and they proceeded back inside. Logan cast another glance to nature. How he wished he could fast forward even a year from now. He could see them running together as wolves, forsaking society and all its constraints. But even that daydream was poisoned. He couldn't shift at will and had never been able to. It'd take a miracle for him to join her in wolf form. Yet, plenty of miracles had happened over the last couple of weeks. Maybe fate would work another in his favor.

CHAPTER 6

Dustin rounded the corner in the hall on his way to Darren's classroom. The pack was to meet there for lunch and assess Katey's stability to stay in school for the rest of the day. To his surprise, he sensed no trouble from the new loup-garou during his third period class and Logan reported no issues either. According to her, and by their own observations, Katey had gained some control over her sensory filter, even in the crowded hallways of the high school. She only gagged when they passed the gym, the stench of the locker rooms a little too strong, but other than that, she was adjusting just fine.

Logan bypassed their alpha completely when he asked Dustin if he and Katey could have lunch with the younger loups-garous of the Devian pack, rather than sit through any of Darren's lectures. Perhaps they placed too much confidence in Katey's ability to handle a packed lunch room, but it would be a true test of her control. Dustin approved and assured that he'd take the alpha's wrath if it was the wrong decision.

He arrived to the classroom, Ben and Darren already digging into their portions of steak and sliced beef. Dustin closed the door and received the alpha's hard stare.

"Where are Logan and Katey?"

As calm as could be, Dustin pulled out his lunch and hopped onto one of the tables. "Off to lunch."

The trickle of dominance didn't faze him. "They were to have lunch here."

Dustin pointed his fork at Ben. "Did they have trouble in your class?"

The old soldier merely shook his head, mouth full of meat.

He then pointed at Darren. "What about you?"

"That's not the point," the alpha snapped. "We know how well Katey can hide things."

Dustin jabbed at a piece of his rare steak. "I feel nothing in the pack bond to suggest she's struggling and she'll be with Logan and some of the Devian kids. She'll be all right. If she isn't, blame me. I let them go."

The alpha let out a low, nearly imperceptible growl. "You know how I feel about you overstepping my authority."

"Indeed, I do," Dustin replied, almost cheerfully. "What's the worst that could happen if she's surrounded by other loups-garous who will help her at the drop of a hat?"

Darren went silent, knowing he had been defeated. "I want you to go check on them after we're done and make certain she's all right."

Dustin rolled his eyes as he began to eat. "Aye, Captain. Have you let Jacob know about Katey yet?"

Darren set his container in his lap. "No. I wasn't sure if it would be wise, this soon, to spread the news. Though, if Logan's going to expose her to that bunch, our little secret will be all over town by the end of the day."

Ben swallowed back a mouthful. "You think Logan knows that?"

"Likely," Dustin replied. "It would come out eventually, especially when we go to Alaska."

Darren sighed. "Yes, I know. It would be impossible to hide it there."

"Are we going to come up with a script to explain what happened?"

"We will tell them the truth," Darren said. "If they ask deeper questions, we'll be honest and tell them we simply don't know how it happened."

Ben waved his fork at them. "Ya know every loup-garou and his brother's gonna try to turn their women after they see that Katey survived."

Darren winced. "Let's hope it doesn't come to that."

A buzzing noise broke the temporary quiet between the pack-mates. Darren pulled out his phone and checked the caller ID. He answered, "Hey, Jacob. We were just talking about you."

Dustin heard on the other end of the line. "Are you with your pack?"

The stiff, serious tone told them all something was up. "Yes."

"One of my betas spotted some evidence of vamps in town last night. We don't know if they're still around and waiting for dark or if they've left already. Keep your pack inside tonight if you can help it."

Darren looked up to Dustin, both understanding the significance of the situation.

"We will. Thank you for warning me."

"Can we hijack Ben this evening to do some recon around the city limits? He has the sort of military experience we need to do a thorough sweep."

Darren looked to Ben for approval. When he gave it, Darren replied, "Yes, he's all yours."

"Thanks. If you guys see anything, let us know."

The alpha agreed and disconnected the call. "We'll postpone Katey's training for the night until it can be confirmed that the vamps have passed on."

A tension knotted between Dustin's shoulder blades, as if the threat were there in the room. "Do you want me to tell her next period?"

"No need to alarm her this soon. We'll tell her when she gets home. Just inform her that she shouldn't dally too long after the final bell. I believe they rode together this morning, so if any of you see Logan, fill him in on what Jacob told us."

Dustin suddenly had no appetite, but continued eating. Vampires may match them in strength and speed, and had an added weakness to sunlight, but their presence in Crestucky couldn't be disregarded. Just like hunters, vampires had perfected the art of killing loups-garous over the centuries. They hadn't told Katey about the cold war between their races. It didn't seem important until now. It did make him realize how much they still had to tell her, how much she needed to know before it was too late.

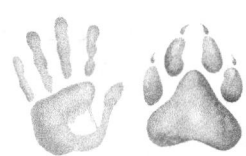

"You know, you're spoiling me."

The hallway may have been crowded with students, but with Katey's hand securely nestled in Logan's, they might as well have been the only people on the planet. They may not have been mates or an official couple, but she wouldn't question these sweet moments as they made their way toward the lunchroom.

Logan inquiringly looked down to her. "What?" Katey squeezed his hand and grinned. "Oh, is it bothering you?"

"No, not at all," Katey replied with a shake of her head. A bit of her hair tumbled over her shoulders. "I like it. I liked it yesterday and this morning, and between every class."

Logan gave her a smug look. "I figured you would, but I also wanted to make sure you didn't feel too overwhelmed. How are you feeling?"

She rolled her eyes. "I feel fine, just like I did the last thousand times you've asked me."

"I just want to make sure."

"I know. Doesn't make me resent the harassment any less."

They arrived at the cafeteria, and all manner of scents and noises bombarded her like a tidal wave. Logan pulled her aside and allowed her to adjust. As before, she took calming breaths and set a thicker filter in place before it became too much. It took several moments, but Katey finally nodded and they continued toward one side of the lunch room.

Logan had told her he wanted her to meet some people, but wouldn't explain any more than that.

They approached one large round table, populated by a handful of guys she had seen around the school before, but didn't know personally. The tingling in the back of her skull exploded as they drew closer, the sign that other loups-garous were near. It was then she understood.

Katey edged nearer to Logan for security as all eyes turned toward them. They seemed curious, but not hostile.

"Who are they?" she asked in a whisper.

"A few of the Deviant pack, Forrest's pack. They're second or third generation descendants. A couple are newly turned, and the rest turned in the last couple of years. Darren and the others try to keep an eye on them as well."

The Deviants, she remembered, belonged to the community further north of Crestucky. Back a century ago, shortly after Logan turned into a loup-garou, hunters raided the community.

The bloodbath scattered the loups-garous across the country, but their alpha, Jacob, recently reunited them in Crestucky, not a hundred miles from the place of so much tragedy. It was like flipping the bird to the hunters who tried to wipe them out. They survived and thrived, though they'd never be the same. From what she gathered, Forrest had some connection to the Deviant's former alpha, Robert, but Logan hadn't told her that story yet. She only knew that Forrest may have been a big man in his pack because of his father, but not everyone agreed on that.

The closer she came, the tingling sensation in her skull began to dull, growing acclimated to their signature. The group cleared a couple of spots at the table for them and they took their seats, though Katey couldn't help but feel awkward and suddenly the center of attention.

"Hey, Logan. I didn't think you'd be enrolling until next year." one with dark hair and green eyes said. He wore an ACDC t-shirt that was a little too tight for him across the chest.

Logan retrieved his lunch bag from his backpack and pulled out their containers of steak and sausage. "Plans changed pretty quickly. Guys, this is Katey."

Katey shrank herself nearly an inch as Logan pointed out each of the loups-garous by name, still unsure of how to act around them. She understood her place in Darren's pack, but where did she fall on the hierarchy with these guys?

None appeared more dominant than any other, except perhaps Logan, who glowed with pride for the new addition to his pack. If what he said was true about their age, he was also the most experienced at the table.

Any two wolf packs who happened to clash might have created a territorial conflict, but she realized early that was not the case for loup-garou packs. Darren and Jacob's packs seemed to be on good terms, sharing territory and forming friendships as if there was no competition at all.

They all gave her enthusiastic and sincere greetings, while she replied with a nervous smile and a nod. A loup-garou on the other side of Logan leaned in, the one named Kenneth. He had blonde hair, dazzling brown eyes, and wore a turtleneck sweater and dark jeans.

"Logan, is she what I think she is?"

"Yeah, but don't make a big deal of it."

Another loup-garou from across the table who had brownish hair, dark blue eyes, and a muscle shirt spoke up, the one named Parker. "How can we not make a big deal out of it? How'd it happen? My dad said it wasn't possible."

Logan handed Katey her food. "It isn't. Katey's the exception. Don't get too excited."

"Did you do it or Darren?" the first loup-garou with the ACDC shirt, Allen, asked.

"I did."

Katey ate maybe three bites, not feeling near as hungry because she sneaked pinches of dried beef jerky between each class period throughout the day. They all had similar lunches of meat, some raw and some cooked, and water with the occasional side of berries or some other fruit.

Getting in on the conversation was another loup-garou with black hair, brown eyes, and wore a red long-sleeved shirt that was pushed up to his elbows. His name, Katey recalled, was Jared. "What? You're joking!"

"Nope," Logan replied through a mouthful of deer meat. "Did it on Tuesday."

"Who else knows about her?" Kenneth asked. "Can we tell Jacob?"

"We're trying to keep it quiet for a while. Darren doesn't want all the attention too soon."

"Are you going to talk like I'm not here all lunch period?" Katey muttered amusedly. Some of the guys chuckled and she felt a little more at ease.

Parker leaned over his lunch and cupped his hand around his mouth, as if wishing his comment was supposed to be a secret. "Hey, Logan, can I get me some of that or is she taken?"

Katey was taken aback by such a comment, but she was glad to hear Logan's response. "She's taken, don't even think about it."

She looked to Logan and hid her shock well. They weren't mated, weren't boyfriend-girlfriend, but she was, indeed, taken. That was a comfort. Was "taken" a step below "mated,"? If it was, why didn't he tell her that before when she demanded that they somehow label their relationship?

Jared chimed in laughingly, "With the way he kicked your ass a few years back, I'd take his advice."

The group laughed over some inside story, and even Katey cracked a smile. Her eyes drifted over to the rest of the cafeteria and her heart lurched in her chest. Unable to pull her attention back to the pack, Katey watched the other students. Some ate their lunches, some talked and told stories. A few were sitting alone and silently slumped over their meals. All of them human, as she was just days ago.

She wondered how her life could have changed so suddenly. She went from being one of them; a human with flaws. Now, she sat amongst a group of supernatural creatures and she wasn't afraid because she was part of them.

Yet, something drew her back to the mundane world of humans. Life was simpler, or as simple as it could be for a foster kid that had just aged out of the system with no plans for the future. She could do simple things like eat what she wanted, go where she wanted, feel what she wanted, without having to consider the ramifications of her actions. She could socialize with her friends and never worry about hurting them or exposing her secret.

Now she understood what Logan had once told her about freedom. Though she was part of a global community of loups-garous, that would have her back, there was a freedom in human life that she would never experience again. Katey looked back to her lunch and wondered if all the perks of superhuman strength and speed could make up for the limitations of being loup-garou.

"Katey!" she heard a voice cry from across the cafeteria.

She looked up to see Lily, blonde hair bouncing with each step as she rushed for the table. The tightness in Katey's chest eased. At least she had Lily. As Forrest's mate, she knew all about loups-garous. They wouldn't have to walk on eggshells around one another or give veiled excuses for not explaining themselves. Lily had done an amazing job of hiding the truth of her relationship with Forrest and the Deviant pack up to now.

When the other loups-garous around the table lifted their gazes, she saw the glint of recognition in their faces. They greeted Lily in their own ways, all cordial and openhearted. It was clear that they all knew one another.

"Hey, sugar!" Parker said, standing to hug her around the shoulders.

Katey's eyes went wide as Lily hugged back. Was Lily cheating on Forrest? Impossible. Lily and Forrest were as good as mated.

The Deviants would know that. Or, was there some odd threesome going on between them?

Parker sat down and resumed his meal as Lily moved around the table. Logan gave her a tiny gesture of a wave when she passed behind him. Katey could tell there was a sort of little-sister bond between Logan and Lily, which came out in their biting banter from time to time.

"Hey guys, how's it going?" Lily moved around the table and shot a perturbed look at Allen on the other side of Katey. "Aren't you gonna move?"

He wrinkled his nose and stuck out his tongue in a teasing manner and scooted over to make room for the petite blonde.

Lily bumped shoulders with Katey and winked. "So, this is the crowd you're hanging out with these days?" She leaned in as if to whisper. "Watch out for that one." She pointed at Parker. "Never turn your butt to him or he'll pinch it."

Parker crossed his arms over the table. "You know you like it," he replied, wiggling his brows at her.

Katey held up her hands. "Hold on, I'm confused." She turned to Lily. "You're with Forrest and you're flirting with him?"

Some at the table laughed, including Parker.

"No, no. I dated Parker back in freshman year before I ever met Forrest. He wasn't... you know what back then. We're just friends now, but he seems to think otherwise." Lily passed a playful, but scathing look his way.

"Yeah, yeah, whatever." Parker waved her off. "I've still got time. You're not mated yet."

Lily fished out a chain necklace from her shirt and held up the little gold band. "You know very well we've got the preliminary bond laid, Parker. Forrest halfway demanded it because of you and your roaming hands."

The other loups-garous at the table made impressed noises the way boys did when one of their own were called out.

"Preliminary mating bond?" Katey asked Logan.

Logan swallowed back the meat in his mouth and donned a look like he was caught in a lie. "Yeah, it's... Okay, it's like declaring an engagement, if you want to get technical."

Katey folded her arms. "You said there wasn't anything like that for us."

"It's complicated."

"Oh, don't give me any of that crap." Katey felt her insides boil. "I'm in on the jokes now. You better start explaining."

Now it was Logan's turn to endure the mocking of his peers.

Logan set down his fork and angled in her direction, as if he were being inconvenienced. "A preliminary mating bond is like a precursor to the official mating bond. It's all a spiritual thing. It's not necessarily legally binding, but it's not as easy as just declaring it verbally. It takes an act of will in both parties to form it and hold it until a true mating bond can be formed. I can't really explain it because I've never tried it and I don't know exactly how to do it, which is why I can't give you a real answer on how it works. That's all I know... Satisfied?"

Katey stared at him, believing that she understood, but definitely wanted to know more of the complexities of how the bonds worked. Logan had laid the pack bond with her, but Darren didn't explain the science behind it. Then again, maybe there was no science or hard, discernable evidence of what a mating bond was or how it formed. Maybe like love, it was a feeling and a connection.

Halfway lying, Katey answered, "I guess," then turned back to her lunch as the table resumed its conversations. She listened to their stories, laughed at the jokes and tried to understand the little insider bits that only packmates shared.

Suddenly, those at the table grew silent and they all turned toward the double doors that led into the cafeteria. Katey saw the change and directed her attention that way as well. She saw only one person coming in from the halls.

Tall, broad-shouldered, with a mass of dark curly hair and equally black eyes, the star football player strode in. Erik was one of the most popular jocks in school, adored by girls and worshiped like a god by some boys. Katey couldn't see what all the fuss was about, until his eyes locked on their table and her skull nearly vibrated with the intensity of his presence.

Erik was loup-garou.

However, by the way he was received by the rest at the table, she could tell that he wasn't part of Forrest's pack. A shiver of mild fear passed through each of them, stinking up the area with that potent, peppery odor. But no fear emanated from Logan. Instead, he pulsated with such red-hot hate that Katey could feel it in her bones.

Erik had an arrogant look on his face as he walked straight for their table. Instinctively, Katey shrunk into Logan. The Deviants turned their backs on Erik, but all had anxious expressions as they continued eating their lunches in silence. Lily sighed and watched Erik closely, just as Logan and Katey did.

As Erik stopped on the opposite side of the table from them, Logan's hand shot underneath Katey's chair and pulled her in close. Their chairs bumped together with a crack of finality, as if the gesture were a warning that she was claimed and under his protection.

Logan kept his chin high in defiance as he hung his arm around her shoulder and let his hand dangle in front of her chest. She could tell that he was showing this as a sign to Erik that Katey was Logan's territory and to distinguish his dominance between them. This surprised her, but she went along with it and leaned into Logan, glad that he was finally expressing his possession over her in some way.

"May I join you fine gentlemen?" Erik asked cordially, putting on his best impressive smile.

"No," Logan growled.

Erik didn't seem concerned at all. Then, his eyes turned toward Katey and Lily. She needed to find her poker face at a time like this. She knew that if she smiled, Logan would scold her later for encouraging him, but she knew that if she glared, Erik would take offense and cause trouble. Not knowing what kind of conflict was between them, she didn't want to risk upsetting either.

"Why, what a couple of pretty dolls amongst a bunch of ugly mugs," Erik said, slowly moving around the table to get closer to the girls.

"Fuck off, Erik." Lily snapped. "This isn't your table."

Erik slid a resentful glance her way, but continued moving as if she hadn't spoken. Katey could hear Logan growl in his throat, but Erik still persisted, taking step after bold step.

When Erik placed his hand on the back of an empty chair, Logan bolted out of his seat and stood defiantly between her and the offender.

Katey watched with piqued interest as the two sized each other up, both standing tall as if squaring off for a fight. A spark of dominance flared between the two, clashing like two swordsmen who were equally matched and the sparks sizzled around the pack. They could all feel the dominance, and none dared to move. Even Katey lowered herself closer to the table as if it would save her from whatever was about to happen. At least she had the surety that these loups-garous would back Logan up one hundred percent.

Erik grinned, something wicked in his eyes. "You need something, Logan?"

"You're not welcome here," Logan snarled.

Another long hard moment passed as a silent play for dominance unfolded that Katey felt, but could barely describe. All that existed was the premonitory sensation that she was standing in the middle of a war zone.

Finally, Erik bent his knees a bit and lowered his head by the tiniest degree, likely a move that no human in the cafeteria would ever notice, but all loups-garous at the table knew instinctively as a show of submission. Logan won this time.

"If that's the way it is, fine." Erik looked directly at Katey and icy shards pierced her core. "I'll see you around."

Logan stood still until he knew Erik was out of sight and sat down. He replaced his arm around Katey, but nothing was the same after that moment. She snuggled herself into him and held the hand that was around her, hoping something in her show of affection would ease the trembling anger that coursed through their bond.

It took such a traumatic event for Shane, a guy she recognized from her sophomore year of Spanish class, to finally speak up. "Man, I wish I had your balls, Logan. I could never stand up to Erik like that."

Parker nodded in agreement. "Yeah, he could tear any of us apart without breaking a sweat."

A light bulb went off in Katey's mind. The way they shunned him, the power in his presence, the way he and Logan clashed. "Wait... Erik's a—"

"A rougarou," Logan finished.

"No!" Katey gasped. She frantically tried to wrap her head around the concept that Erik had been a rougarou the whole time, and no one in the school, save for those at this table, knew it. That explained his unerring confidence and athletic talents.

Allen nodded. "Afraid so. Him and a couple of others attend school. They're kind of the bullies around here. I heard he's only enrolled in school just to torment us and get all the accolades of star football players. Dude's got some superiority complex. He's nearly Logan's age and doesn't need to be here at all."

Lily grumped and propped her chin in her hand on the table. "He's a jerk to everyone, loups-garous and humans. He tried to convince me to go out with him a week after I hooked up with Forrest, but I knew better by then. He's bad news and a total ass."

"I had no idea," Katey mumbled, blinking down at her half-eaten lunch. She suddenly lost her appetite. When they had told her about rougarous the evening before, she didn't want to think that any were living in Crestucky, but there may have been a whole pack of them.

"Why did he look at you that way?" Logan demanded.

Katey stammered. "I... I don't know. I've never talked to the guy before. I just know who he is."

Logan's gaze went hard. "Don't talk to him. Don't have anything to do with him. He's dangerous... I don't want you getting hurt." His voice turned warm and calming and she took heart in it.

There was a reason for Logan's protectiveness, she knew that now, but there was something more in the way they faced one another down just moments ago. It might have been because they were nearly equal in age, or that Logan felt responsible for their safety. But she felt there was something more. There was a deep, personal offense against Erik apart from just being a rougarou and Katey couldn't quite place it. The others felt an obvious disdain for Erik, but none more so than Logan. If they were about the same age, had they known one another for a while? Did something happen between them in another decade that he wasn't ready to tell her?

CHAPTER 7

Katey couldn't help but feel a sense of new comradery with the Deviants. Despite being a female, they welcomed her and talked freely about pack business or their personal lives as loups-garous. It was more than she had heard out of Logan and the others, and closer to what she expected a pack to talk about when they gathered together.

She heard stories of their daily struggles and Katey no longer felt embarrassed for her hunger episode the day before. The others, like Allen and Parker who nearly changed during their weightlifting class, had suffered greater challenges and overcame them. It gave her hope.

After lunch, Logan escorted Katey to Dustin's classroom. Her fifth period was spent as his assistant, usually grading papers and assignments to help with his workload, or running errands across the school.

Before they parted ways, Dustin took Logan into the hall to discuss something with him. By the grave, concerned look in the beta, she knew it must have been serious, but when she asked about it upon his return, he shrugged her off. All he would say was that she needed to be home as soon as possible after school let out, and to meet Logan at her jeep, since they rode together that day. They spoke no more about it the rest of the period while she worked through the mountain of semester exams.

She wished Logan could have stayed with her, or that perhaps she could have ditched her sixth period study hall in favor of leaving for home early. If her study hall supervisor didn't take attendance, she would have.

Once she left Dustin's classroom and wandered the halls alone, she couldn't help but feel a little adrift. It was like her tether to the pack had been temporarily untied. The pack bond was still there, but this was the first time she truly distanced herself from any of them since she was turned. A sense of loneliness made her chest tight and body shake as if she were on the verge of tears.

She was halfway to her sixth period when her skull tingled and her head swiveled, searching for the loup-garou who triggered it. Jared, the Devian she met at lunch, came alongside her.

"You all right?" he asked.

She let out a breath and she didn't feel so lost anymore. One of her own kind was near. It was as if she had somehow summoned him to her without realizing it.

"I am now. Are you going in this direction?"

"Sure. Toward the Language Hall for French class. You?"

"Auditorium. Study Hall."

"I'll walk with you."

Katey gave him a grateful smile. "Thanks... I feel a little silly. This is the first time Logan hasn't been right beside me and it's..."

"I get it," he said with a nod. "Kind of felt the same way for the first few weeks. Just didn't feel right to be walking by myself anymore. There are plenty of us around and we'd be glad to have company."

His smile, so understanding and compassionate made Katey want to cry. "It's so weird for me though. I've never really cared about having company and now, it's like I need it to breathe."

Jared leaned closer. "That's the wolf, for ya. A bit of that pack mentality is hard to shake."

It was like Katey wasn't the same person anymore. She enjoyed her privacy, a bit of solitude every once and awhile. It was what drove her to be at the cemetery the night she and Logan met. Was it that pack mentality that made him seek her out to talk to her? But he had gone out there to be alone as well. Then, she remembered how he said they could be "alone together" and something of that made a little more sense. Katey and Jared were loups-garous in a sea of humans, alone but also together.

They chatted a little about one of the Spanish teachers and some disastrous toupee incident three years prior, then came upon the auditorium.

"This is my stop," Katey said.

"I wish I could say there'd be someone for you to hang out with in there, but I don't think so."

She gave him an "Oh well" look and shrugged. "I appreciate you walking with me."

He gave a little bow. "Anytime." Then, he was off down the hall and around the corner.

She braved the next hour of study hall, occupying herself with homework assignments so she wouldn't have to worry about them that evening. She wanted all of her free time available for training.

The final bell rang and Katey had to watch her speed as she hurried out the auditorium doors and into the hall. Logan parked on the other side of the building, and she still had to drop off some books at her locker before meeting him. The thought that she'd be in his presence, under his protection, and have him all to herself for the drive home made her quicken her steps.

A few things happened so quickly that Katey didn't register them until it was far too late. The loup-garou radar in her head sounded, alerting her to the nearness of one of her kind. A door to her left that led outside onto an outdoor picnic area suddenly opened, allowing a gust of cold wind to sweep through the hall. A hand, big and strong, grabbed her arm and yanked her out that door, nearly throwing her off her feet.

Katey gasped and froze as someone pinned her to the brick exterior wall. The hand that grabbed her squeezed with bruising force on her arm. She looked up into dark eyes that almost appeared black in the shadows of his face.

Erik leered down at her, his lips curled into a victorious grin that sent a shiver down her back and legs. She tried to rip her arm from his clutches, feeling the dread of a coming storm swell around them, but Erik's grip was too strong.

His hot breath, tinged with the smell of old blood and meat nearly made her gag. "Hey, hey, hold on now. I just want to talk."

She struggled harder, remembering Logan's warning, but Erik's solid body eased closer, trapping her against the wall. The need to panic rose up, but she tamped it down. Instead, she pulled her lips into a tight, grim line and slanted her brows over the fierce glare. Her wolf growled and snapped, recognizing that this loup-garou was a dangerous threat. If she weren't in public, she might have done the same.

"Logan told me to stay away from you."

"I wouldn't listen to much of what he says. He has a tendency to twist things to his advantage." Erik reached out and let the back of his fingers glide across her cheek.

Katey managed to swat his hand away, defiled by his touch. He only chuckled and seized that wrist, effectively trapping her.

The tip of Erik's tongue slid across his lips like a starving man presented with a buffet spread. "I thought you'd be a feisty one."

"I know what you are," she hissed.

"And I know what you are, too. I'm impressed." Erik studied her face, gaze raking up and down the length of her body as if he were inspecting her. "I didn't know Logan had it in him."

For a moment, Katey wondered how long it would take for Logan to realize she took too long to meet him and went to look for her. She needed to get out of his compromising situation and to someplace safe before this got out of hand. Just because students could see them through the glass of the exterior door didn't mean she was safe.

"What do you want, Erik?"

He lifted her hand to the level of her eyes and slammed it against the brick, the prickly surface rubbing against her skin. She gave a short whimper, but refused to give him the satisfaction of any whiff of fear. One of his legs wedged between hers, forcing her knees apart. Her nostrils flared and breaths came quick and gruff. She wondered how long she could hold back her wolf before it made an untimely appearance in the form of golden eyes or long fangs.

"I wanted to see what you were up to tonight." He flashed a toothy grin and she could see his sharp canines gleam back at her.

"Why?"

"Well, I was wondering if you'd like to go and see a movie... with me?" Erik asked with a smug shrug.

He was asking her on a date? They hardly knew each other. It was likely he didn't even know her name. She wondered if this was related to when Erik asked out Lily shortly after she got involved with Forrest. Erik targeted the women of other loups-garous that he couldn't have. Why? To test them? To steal them away?

"Get lost," she spat and refreshed her struggle. Erik only pressed in tighter and she could feel his muscled torso tight against her chest, restricting her breathing.

"Come on, don't be difficult."

"Let me go," she growled and her eyes finally turned gold. If she didn't break away from the situation soon, Katey knew the wolf would rise up to take care of Erik one way or another.

"Are you turning me down because Logan says to stay away from me or because you two are an item?"

Katey's lips turned up in bewilderment. "Who uses that term anymore?"

"Well, are you?" Erik pushed, his patience growing thin and grip on her arm tightening to the point she wondered if her arm would break.

Katey wished she knew the answer. She wished she could have said they were going to be mated, that they were definitely dating, but it would be a lie and Darren said their kind could detect lies easily. Yet, Logan had demonstrated his claim on her and said she was taken in front of the Deviants. She was his, but in what unmistakable way? They hadn't even kissed, but they turned on each other as easily as a light switch. Those forehead touches were like heaven, but all they had was the sire and pack bond to connect them. Old wounds opened at the reality that she didn't have a name for what they were, and it pissed her off.

"I don't know," she muttered, her head spinning as Erik hogged the air around her.

"So, then you're single. I'm single. We're the same species and there's no reason not to give me a shot. If you don't like me after one date, we never have to associate again." Erik bent his mouth to her ear and whispered, "All I ask is for a chance."

Katey didn't need more than a few minutes alone with him to figure out that she didn't like him. Even if he wasn't a rougarou, Katey didn't want to have anything to do with him. Still, if she didn't go out, Erik would never leave her alone. If she did, Logan would be furious and Darren wouldn't condone it anyway, not when she was still so new to this.

But, then again, maybe this would be the trick to get Logan to finally tell her the truth about how he felt. This date could be a way to get him jealous enough to admit it to her face, to decide once and for all what exactly they were. She had seen the petty tricks of some girlfriends who purposefully flirted with other men to make their boyfriends jealous. Up until then, Katey thought they were immature and pointless tactics that would yield no good result. Now, she wondered if that was the key to her problems.

If she could get Logan so desperate to claim her, maybe he'd talk Darren into letting them make a preliminary mating bond, like what Lily and Forrest had. With that, Katey would be off limits and she could have the satisfaction of knowing they were going somewhere with this relationship. If she went out with Erik, maybe she wouldn't have to wait after years of training to have Logan the way she wanted. Did the ends justify the means? Was it a safe gamble? Likely not, but something reckless in her told her that she had to try.

"You promise you'll leave me alone?"

"I'll avoid you like the plague if you want me to."

The wolf inside roared against her plan, but Katey wouldn't listen. "Fine. What time?"

"Seven o'clock. I'll see you at the movie theater."

Erik gave her a wolfish grin and in one liberating move, released both her arms and stepped away to release her from the wall. She almost collapsed with the relief and took several fortifying breaths as he walked away and around the corner of the building, out of sight. She wouldn't rest easy until the sensation in her skull was completely gone, ensuring that Erik was far away.

Her eyes had returned to normal and she rushed back inside. With each step toward her locker, the little voice of conscience inside her head blared out the alarm sirens. A date with Erik could never end well. If he was as dangerous as the others suggested, then Katey could have been putting herself under the guillotine.

Not only that, but going out with Erik would destroy Logan's trust in her and possibly damage her relationship with the pack. She already knew she'd have to go off in secret somehow, and so far, she hadn't a clue how to go about it.

When Katey came into view, Logan's heart leapt and it took too much control not to rush forward and sweep her into his arms. Two hours was too long to be apart. Maybe, if Katey's credits allowed it, she could drop her last two classes for the next semester and they wouldn't have to endure any separation.

Yet, as she came closer, he noticed two things. She wasn't smiling, and she didn't smell right. The breeze shifted in just the right way to bring her scent directly to him. Every muscle tensed and his jaw clenched so hard he thought he'd crack a tooth. His heartbeat thudded loud in his ears, drowning out the rumble of the bus engines nearby. This couldn't be right. Erik's scent was all over her.

By the time she stood in front of him, he and his wolf wanted to pitch her jeep across the parking lot. He told her to stay away from him, and she had the audacity to come to him, smelling like she had just been rolling around with him.

"What's wrong?" she asked, a note of worry in her words.

It was then Logan realized his eyes were gold and face rigid with repressed anger. "Get in the car," he growled.

He turned on his feet and marched to the driver's side. With all the control he could muster past his rage, he slammed the car door and started the engine. Katey slid in beside him, fear telegraphed in every move from how softly she closed her door to how she fumbled with her seatbelt.

They tore out of the parking lot and onto the highway, giving him time to find the right words.

"Are you going to tell me why you're so pissed?"

Logan gripped the wheel so hard the leather creaked in his palms. "You were with Erik."

It took her too long to reply and he forced his mouth shut to keep himself from screaming at her.

"Yeah, but he cornered me. I couldn't get away."

"That's a bullshit excuse."

"Would you rather have me wolf out and attack him?"

The edge of sarcasm didn't help. "Would have been better than letting him have his damned hands all over you." When she didn't reply, he beat his hand on the steering wheel in an effort to dispel the anger before it spilled onto her. "Why didn't you fight him?" he roared.

"Don't yell at me!" she roared back.

They passed a speed limit sign that gave Logan permission to gun it, so he did. His foot pressed on the gas pedal, forcing the engine into high gear.

"I told you he was dangerous. I told you to stay away from him. You deliberately disobeyed me. Why would you risk yourself that way?"

"I didn't disobey you. I told you that he ambushed me. I didn't have a choice."

"You had the goddamn choice to fight back and you didn't!"

"Logan, someone could have seen me. Isn't that the first big rule not to draw too much suspicion? Would you want me to blow everyone's cover?"

"I want you to protect yourself!"

"He didn't hurt me!"

"Then what the hell did he want?"

The car went dead quiet. He looked at Katey, who glared out the window, face set in a scowl and red with the anger they shared through their bond.

Logan strained to soften his voice. "Tell me what he wanted."

"Nothing. He just wanted to intimidate me."

Quickened pulse, the salty scent of sweat, shifty gaze.

"Now you're lying to me? Katey, what happened?"

"I'm not going to tell you what will only make you mad enough to wolf-out and wreck the car."

Logan went quiet and looked at Katey in the passenger seat. A second or two of clear thought made him realize what he had done. Speeding up, showing his anger, it scared her. Everything in her body language proclaimed her own frustration, but the way her hands gripped the seat, and the little glint of unshed tears told him enough.

They had never talked about what happened in the car that night when her foster mother wrecked the car. All he knew was what Katey told the cops in the hospital. Mary was drunk and swerved into the oncoming traffic. Only Katey's interference saved them from hitting the semi-truck head-on. But she never mentioned anything about what happened in the minutes before that, or the unspoken trauma that developed after.

The last thing Logan wanted to do was bring back that night like a pursuing nightmare. He eased up on the gas pedal and let the jeep drop to the speed limit again. As urgently as he wanted them to get home and the safe privacy of four walls, it wasn't worth destroying her peace of mind, even though she had destroyed his own.

How could she have done this to him? Did she even realize what she had done? Likely not. They never talked about Erik or Chicago. He knew that Lily had cautioned against bringing it up. Maybe it was time to make her understand just how dangerous Erik was, how the mere act of talking to the bastard might as well have been like stabbing him in the back with a silver dagger. Yet, in the same breath of Erik's sins, Logan would have to confess his own. If she knew what he had done, what the wolf helped him do...

Shame stifled his rage to the slightest degree, but it couldn't extinguish that burning in his chest. Once upon a time, he believed Katey could have been the only one to put out that fire and make him forget the past. Now, she was the one dusting off those terrible memories and shoving them in his face.

Erik already stole from him before. He wouldn't have Katey. *His* Katey.

When they finally made it back to the house, Katey saw Logan's eyes had lost much of their golden hue. Only tiny flecks of the wolf remained, telling her she was not out of the woods yet. She jumped out of the jeep and fled quickly into the house, thinking that if she could outrun him, they wouldn't have to finish their conversation.

Logan ran after her and slammed the door behind them, making the whole house shake from the force of it. She tried to run toward the stairs, but he blocked her way with his body, driving her back into the living room.

"Tell me what happened."

Katey dropped her bag and folded her arms over her chest, mouth set. Two choices lay before her. She could continue to stonewall him and dance around the issue, or she could dive into the whole reason why she agreed to go out with Erik in the first place. Perhaps, if she could drive Logan to that desperation before the date, she wouldn't have to go out in the end.

"Erik ambushed me after study hall to ask me out to the movies."

Logan's expression evolved in the span of just a few seconds. A once halfway coolness soured into disbelief. "What did you tell him?"

She squared her shoulders and readied herself for the eruption that was soon to follow. "I said I would."

A long, pregnant moment passed and Katey watched the change in Logan. Hands balled into tight fists at his sides as his face flashed white in shock and then a deep red with rage. Through their bond, she felt his anger mount and build, a steadily strengthening earthquake that made them both tremble.

"Why would you say that?"

Katey shivered at the deep and throaty change in his voice. "So he'd leave me alone. He said if I go out with him, then I'd never have to see him again."

"And you believe him?" Logan charged a step forward, driving her a step back in return.

"Wouldn't it be a good thing for him to leave me alone? It's only one night, one date. It's not like he can hurt me in a public place like a movie theater."

Logan huffed a mocking laugh. "Oh no, he can still hurt you. Didn't any of that training mean something to you yesterday?"

Kate gave a nod. "Yes, and what happened should have told you that I can handle myself against a rougarou."

Logan stalked so close, as if he were about to grab her, but Katey scuttled away deeper into the living room to escape him. "You think because you lost control of your wolf that you'd be any match for someone like Erik?"

That was a low blow. He knew how much it broke her not to have that same level of control as the rest of them. "Wasn't that the whole point? Teaching me to fight so I could go up against a rougarou?"

"Not one like Erik." Logan's lips curled just enough to show his fangs were out.

So much rage and hate shined through Logan's now golden wolf eyes. "Besides him being a rougarou, I still don't get why you hate him so much."

Logan opened his mouth as if to answer, but then clenched his jaw shut and turned away to stride the living room. She watched his eyes dart about the space, unable to fix on any point as he searched for the best way to explain it.

"What? Is this too complicated?" she snarked. "Do you know Erik from someplace else? The way you two sized one another up at lunch looked pretty personal."

"Yes, I know him."

Katey waited for more than his impassioned growling, but when nothing came, she pushed again. "What'd he do? Step on your tail?"

That, too, was a low blow. Logan couldn't shift at will like other loups-garous, meaning he had never found his purest wolf form. He could only shift once a month when the more monster-like loup-garou form commandeered his body for the night.

Apparently, those were the right words to bring his restless feet back to her in a storm of fury. "He killed one of my best friends!"

Katey was tempted to recoil at his outburst, but the wolf inside her reared its ugly head once more and she felt the courage to thunder back. "Don't yell at me like that! How was I supposed to know?"

"Do I have to explain every damn thing to you? If I tell you to stay away from him, then you stay the fuck away from him!"

Katey's eyes flashed to their loup-garou gold in challenge to his own. "I told you I didn't have a choice! You try being pinned to a wall and half the size of whoever is holding you there."

"He had you pinned to a wall?" The words came out so harsh, like two heavy stones grinding against one another.

"All of me." Katey took a step closer, their bodies nearly touching. "I couldn't fucking move, Logan! I thought I could feel his damn hardon against my hip!"

That was the wrong thing to say. Logan turned away and let out a thunderous roar that shook the house and made her ears ring. That was enough to make Katey's wolf prod her to run for cover.

She dashed for the stairs, but Logan grabbed her wrist and spun her around to pin her against the stairwell, not unlike how Erik had her trapped. In the shadows of the tight space, she witnessed the peak of Logan's wrath.

"We're not done here!" he bellowed.

"Well, I am. Let go of me!"

"No, not until you learn to listen."

Senseless indignation rose up in Katey, regardless of how Logan's body completely pressed into hers. She couldn't feel anything past the anger and fear. "You're not the boss of me! Darren is! I don't have to listen to anything you say!"

"What we ask you to do is for your own safety. Why can't you see that?"

Katey's mouth curved back into a snarl. "That's all any of you ever think about! Safety, safety, safety! I thought I had to be safe being human around you, but now I have to be safe about everything else that was totally fine before! I can't even hang out with my friends or go see a movie without someone having a conniption fit!"

Logan slammed his hand into her shoulder, the very spot where he bit her. "You asked for this and you knew what you were getting into. It's your own fault!"

"No, it's yours!" Katey hardly knew what she was saying until it came spilling out of her mouth like vomit. It was too late to take any of it back and her wolf wasn't done. "If you had just given me a little more time, maybe I wouldn't have chosen this at all!"

Inside, she wanted to scream back that she didn't mean any of it. It was a complete contradiction to everything she had confessed to him before, but she couldn't stop herself, just like she couldn't stop the wolf from slashing into his throat the day before.

"Well, tough shit! You're in this pack now. Being a loup-garou isn't some license to go off and do as you please."

"Well maybe I don't want to be in your pack!"

Logan jerked back as if she had spat in his face, but it abated none of his ire. "If you don't want to be in this pack, then fine." His voice dropped so low that it rumbled in his chest. "Leave for all I care. Go be with Erik's pack and be his whore."

Katey had enough. She screeched and slashed her claws at his face, leaving behind long, deep gashes from his forehead to his jaw. He roared, let go of her, and stumbled a few steps down. His hand pressed into his cheek and nose. Katey turned and bounded upstairs before he had a chance to catch her again.

She slammed her bedroom door, locked it tight, and half expected Logan to break down the door. Her whole body shook with anger as the wolf inside continued to froth at the mouth. No thought could take hold in her mind, other than the glaring, irrational rage that consumed her like a fire.

She grabbed one of her heavy hardback textbooks from a shelf and chunked it at the far wall with a shriek of rage. The corner of the book made contact with the wall and left a dent in the sheetrock.

Her vicious words to Logan echoed in her mind, taunting her and condemning her for the way she had spoken to him. He was completely right, but she refused to admit it. She chose this life, and now she was paying for it. Tears of regret and anger streamed down her cheeks as she paced and tried to push back the wolf so she could form some coherent train of thought.

As time passed, and through her tears and seething, a peculiar awareness pierced to her core. Logan didn't come to force her back into the argument, he didn't come to apologize. If anything, Logan felt more distant through their bond, like an elastic band stretched to its limits just before snapping apart.

Katey stood still in the middle of her room and held her breath, waiting for the bond to settle back. It didn't.

After a moment of panic, Katey went back downstairs, but her fear was confirmed. She desperately searched the house and found it empty, hoping foolishly that she might have been mistaken, but the bond didn't lie. Logan was gone and she was alone in the house. His bike and her jeep remained under the carport, so he had to be in the woods.

Guilt and loneliness arrested her rabbiting heart as she dropped on the sofa. She dumbly stared down at the dark blood under her nails, Logan's blood.

Once more, she screwed up. Her anger went unchecked, but so did his. She said things she didn't mean and disregarded his feelings.

She wasn't too far gone to understand how he could decipher the decisions she made. It wasn't just that she had agreed to go out with a rougarou. It was because it was Erik, the man who killed his friend. She thought of how she'd feel if someone killed Lily and expected her to just get over it. This was worse than betrayal. Katey didn't really know what to call it, but it was definitely worse.

That's why he left. Why stick around for her? Why stay in a house shared by a girl like her? Why try to make her understand when she seemed so determined not to?

Thoughtless of the mess on her fingers, she buried her face in her hands and wept. The strain of the bond, the grief of pushing Logan away, the sense of finality in her offense, it all collapsed around her ears as violently as if the house caved in on her.

What could she do? Should she stay and wait for Logan to come back so she could beg for forgiveness? Should she seize the opportunity and sneak out now before the pack came home and asked questions she couldn't answer? Where could she go? Would she still meet Erik for the movies?

The only reason she would consider it would be to ensure Erik wouldn't continue to harass her at school. If Erik left her alone, he would leave Logan alone too. If she just went through with it, maybe that would be the end of it and they could somehow get past this. It could show Logan that not only could she handle herself against a rougarou, but that she still chose him over Erik.

She doubted Logan would be back anytime soon, and she only had an hour, maybe two, before the pack came home.

Fresh determination fought away the last of her tears and she marched upstairs. She washed up, and shed the clothes stained with Erik's scent to change into a new outfit suitable for a date night. She could kill a couple of hours in a coffee shop while she waited for seven o'clock. Tea would have to be her beverage of choice, and she would have to find another place to eat, but a plan gradually took shape. Logan would never understand why she would keep her word to Erik, and explaining herself would be pointless. This may dig a deeper hole for herself, but if she had lost Logan by now, nothing would bring him back anyway. At least doing this, she could force Erik out of her life long enough to try and fix things. It had all backfired so quickly and Katey tried not to think about how impossible mating was now, as she climbed into her jeep and left for town.

"You've reached the voicemail box of—"

Darren ended the call before leaving any message. The curse exploded from his mouth, and he was prepared to smash his own phone.

Dustin came back inside through the glass doors. "Logan's trail goes into the woods and Katey's scent is the freshest out by the carport." He looked up into his alpha's golden eyes. "No luck?"

"Neither of them are answering," he growled. "After two calls to Katey's phone, I believe she turned it off. It stopped ringing. Logan's never rang at all."

"They've both gone dark," Dustin spoke the obvious. "Orders?"

Darren stormed the length of the living room. "You said there was blood. Whose?"

"Logan's."

"Vamps?"

"Not a trace."

That should have been a comfort, but they still had two missing pack members. One was totally unaware of the vamp threat and the other likely didn't care if he was so willing to abandon Katey.

Darren passed a hand over his eyes. "What the bloody hell happened?"

Dustin crossed his arms and let his alpha pace. "They seemed fine after lunch."

Darren took up his phone one more time to call the one person he knew would answer.

Ben picked up after the second ring. "Yeah?"

"Logan and Katey are missing. Logan's on foot and Katey took her jeep. Where are you?"

"With Jacob and his betas. We're goin' over the plans."

Darren knew he had to be vague. Jacob would likely hear him. "Katey doesn't know about the vamps. We doubt Logan told her. Work them into your plans. Dustin will look for Logan and I'll stay home in case one of them comes back."

"We'll keep an eye out for both of them... Any idea why they took off."

"None. If you find either of them, call me immediately."

"You do the same."

He ended the call and gave one more desperate call to each of the young loups-garous. Same results. This time, he left a message for Katey.

"I don't know why you thought it was such a brilliant idea to go off on your own, but you better have a damn good explanation." Darren sucked in a breath. "Please come home, Katey. We're worried."

He hung up and looked to his beta, worry in every line of his body. They both knew the risks at hand. Once night fell, if there were any vamps in town, Katey and Logan could easily become targets. If they were in the wrong place at the wrong time...

"We will find them," Darren said, forcing calm authority into the words as if it were a certainty. "Alive."

CHAPTER 8

When Katey arrived at the theater, she instantly spotted Erik leaning against the wall by the advertisement posters with his hands slung casually in his jean pockets. Their only theater featured three movies at a time. One was usually some kids film, one suitable for any age, usually a chick-flick, and another for those over eighteen. This week featured *Alvin and the Chipmunks*, *Sweeny Todd*, and *P.S. I Love You*. Katey had absolutely no interest in any of them, but she wasn't there to enjoy a film.

The minute Erik saw her jeep park near the front, he shot her a wicked grin and went to meet her. Every muscle and nerve in her body went on alert. Knowing what she knew now, Katey wasn't going to let herself be put in another dangerous situation.

"Glad you could make it," Erik greeted as she opened her door.

Katey gave him a brief, forced smile and angled out. "Let's just get this over with."

"What's the hurry?" Erik reached up to hang his arm around her shoulders, but she quickly ducked out of it and hopped onto the covered walkway in front of the theater. He spat a laugh. "What's stuck up your ass?"

She didn't think that deserved a response, but she narrowed her eyes into slits. "Listen, I'm breaking all sorts of rules to be here, so be grateful that I showed up at all."

Erik loomed over her. "Alpha got you on a tight leash, little pup?"

Katey looked around to make sure no one was within earshot. A family some distance away argued about what movie to see, and the couple at the ticket booth were too busy paying for their fares.

"Or is it because of the vamp warning out tonight?"

Katey's head whipped around, eyes wide. "What?"

A pleased look crossed his face. "Oh, they didn't tell you?"

Her face reddened at her unaccountable embarrassment. "I kind of snuck out of the house before anyone knew I was gone... Vamp, as in vampire?"

"Yep. Half of the wolves in town are out lookin' for them." Erik leaned closer. "But, don't worry. I won't let any vamp harm a hair on your pretty head."

His hand lifted to stroke the hair he spoke of, but Katey darted away again. "I can take care of myself."

He chuckled. "Sure you can, Katey. Just like you did today, right?"

She blinked. "You actually know my name?"

Erik moved toward the ticket booth as the couple made their way inside. "I've had my eye on you since last year. You're a foster kid, just turned eighteen, are best friends with Forrest Croxen's girl, and are now part of Darren Dubose's pack of misfits."

Katey swallowed hard. He had been watching her? For what purpose? Was she just next on some list or did he have other intentions with her, now that she was loup-garou? "And here I thought you were just trying to mess with Logan's head."

"Oh, that too. But, that's easy enough to do." Erik turned to the teen behind the glass. "Two for *Sweeney Todd*."

At least he wouldn't make her sit through some sappy love story or watch talking chipmunks. He paid for the tickets and passed one stub to her.

"Question is, how did you ever get mixed up with Logan?" he asked as he opened the door to the theater lobby.

Katey walked through and lifted her chin just enough to tell him that she wasn't going to give up any information so easily. "I don't think that's any of your business."

"Probably not, but I'm sure he's told you all about me by now."

They passed by the concession stand. Besides beef sticks, they'd have little that could suit the diet of a loup-garou.

"Only that you killed his best friend," she whispered as they neared the double doors that led into the showing room. The cartoon down the hall had already begun and she could hear the squeaky voices of the chipmunks. Watching a movie may have been an excellent practice in sensory control.

"Wow. Jumped right to the good part." Erik gave her an appraising look. "And yet, here you are, breaking his heart by going out with his second most hated enemy."

She passed him a curious glance. "Second?"

"Logan hates himself way more than he will ever dare to hate anyone else, even me." Erik opened one of the thick doors and made a sweeping gesture to invite her in before himself.

Katey didn't walk through, but stayed rooted in place. "For what he did to his parents?"

A dark, cunning look came over Erik. "That, and so much more he'd probably never tell you. Don't worry, I have all the juicy details."

With cautious, slow steps, Katey entered the dark theater room. Local advertisements shown on the big screen at the end of the room. Only a handful of people were seated throughout. Katey picked two seats in the very back row against the felt-lined wall. Erik settled in next to her and draped his arm across the back of her chair. He smelled of cigarette smoke masked by expensive cologne.

"Now, where to start," he mused.

"I don't want to hear it," she whispered, keeping her eyes fixed forward, even though she could have cared less about the tire shop ad on the screen.

"What? Afraid it'll hurt your opinion of the bastard if you knew all the crazy things he's done?"

"Don't call him that, and no. I'm not afraid, I just don't want to hear it coming from you. He'd tell me if it was important."

Katey wanted to believe that, but her mind drifted back to what Erik said before about vampires. It shouldn't have surprised her that vampires existed alongside werewolves. Witches and all sorts of other magical creatures may very well have been hiding in plain sight, but that didn't bother her so much. The fact that neither Logan, Darren, or any of the rest of the pack told her about vampires had her suddenly second-guessing their honesty. If vampires were dangerous, wouldn't they have told her that there were some prowling around Crestucky that night? It made her wonder what else they kept from her, and why they'd choose to withhold that information.

"Logan's funny that way," Erik said. "It could be terribly important for you to know something, but he won't tell you unless it pays dividends to let you in on the secret, he won't say a thing. Did it to me. I thought he was some greenhorn pup hanging out with some big men in Chicago. Then, I find out later he's got one of the bosses wrapped around his finger, and the guy could rip apart a warehouse of bootleggers like they were tissue paper." Katey turned to see Erik shaking his head and grinning at the memory. "Damn, it was a beautiful thing he did. Like freakin' poetry. Oh, it scared the shit out of me at first, but man, it was just..." Erik made that weird kissing the fingertips move chefs did. "Inspiring."

Her lips parted and a flash of heat washed through her. What was she supposed to do with that? Was it even true, or was Erik spinning a yarn just to mess with her? Was that why no one would talk about Chicago? Because Logan was involved with the mafia? Back in her freshman year, she watched some gangster movie. She couldn't remember the name, but it was epically violent and dramatic. Did Logan live that life, once upon a time?

Erik glanced her way and the satisfied glimmer in his dark eyes told her that she may not be able to take him seriously. She looked away and said nothing. What could be said?

"Aw, but you can't blame him too much. You know, Forrest's family dragged him into all of that. Forrest's uncle was called Billy 'The Butcher', after all. You wanna hear some gritty stories, that's the man to talk about. I know what they call us. Rougarous. Like we're some whole other species. Well, that guy was a rougarou. It probably runs in Forrest's blood too. His old man was ruthless, just abandoning that whole community to the hunters the way he did."

Now she knew Erik had to be lying. Katey closed her eyes and let out a breath. "I told you I didn't want to hear about it."

"Ah, so you did." Erik shifted as if trying to get comfortable. His fingertips brushed her shoulder, tracing little circles. "My bad."

"Stop touching me," Katey hissed through her teeth. When Erik didn't stop, she grabbed his fingers and twisted. Tiny bones snapped in her grip and he gave a little grunt of pain before withdrawing his arm.

"You could have just said, 'please.'"

"Didn't figure an asshole like you would listen."

Little pops from beside her told her Erik's fingers were well on their way to mending themselves. If only she could have done more permanent damage. She wondered if loups-garous could regrow severed limbs, and just how much strength she'd need to rip off a hand at the wrist.

The ambient lights around the room dimmed and the true previews for the movie began, but Katey's mind was on anything but what new film was coming to theaters that spring. Her mind drifted back to Logan, their big fight, the pack, the vampires, and Erik's ridiculous stories. She couldn't take any of it seriously, yet the niggling, haunting doubt would not leave her alone.

What if Logan had killed people in cold blood? What if he did work with the mafia? What if Forrest was somehow responsible for all of that? But then, how did Erik fit in and what friend had been killed? Too many questions, and Katey wasn't sure she'd be brave enough to ask. Confronting Logan about any of it may have been like admitting she believed Erik, even on a microscopic level. How insulting would it be to ask if he had been some murdering gunslinger and Forrest descended from a rougarou bloodline.

Before the movie could ever begin, Katey felt a stirring in her chest. The bond with Logan wasn't so strained anymore, like he was nearby. She braced against the armrests, as if ready to stand, but she hesitated, waiting. When she felt the tingle in the back of her head, she knew it had to be him.

The theater doors behind them opened, letting in the bright lights of the lobby to blur the images on the screen. With the light came the scent of pine and forest, of the home she missed and the man she loved.

Katey abruptly stood and saw Logan stand at the end of the row of seats. Without thinking, she stepped over Erik's long legs and rushed for him. But, there was no welcoming embrace, no kind word or sensation of relief in their bond. Logan's glare, obscured by the dark, was reserved for her and Erik alike.

He grabbed her arm and pulled her toward the exit, Erik trailing after them through the lobby and out into the parking lot. Now with the aid of the parking lot lights, she noticed the evidence of the wilderness on his clothes. Dirt and mud covered his shoes and the pant legs of his jeans. Katey hadn't planned for Logan to come after her, but now they had an entirely new conflict on their hands.

Erik caught up with them and the three stood just on the edge of the light near Katey's jeep. "If you wanted a threesome, all you had to do was ask."

Logan pushed Katey behind him and turned to face Erik, his eyes glowing their fierce gold. "Stay away from her!"

The rougarou laughed and crossed his arms. "Why should I? Is she your property?"

"She's under pack protection. You had no right to ask her to go anywhere with you!" Logan shouted.

Looking around, there was no one in the parking lot to watch, except for the ticket booth attendant who looked too absorbed in browsing social media on his phone.

"Your pack shouldn't have all the fun. Can't I get in on some of the action? I'm sure a female werewolf is a lot better than any human girl." Erik moved to the side to leer at Katey with hungry, sadistic eyes.

Katey slyly reached up and clung to the back of Logan's leather jacket in an effort to seek some shelter. He didn't push her away.

Logan growled through clenched teeth, dominance seeping from him like a thickening fog. "You touch her and I'll kill you."

Erik was unfazed. "If she meant anything to you, she wouldn't have agreed to come out with me in the first place. So, since you don't want her, why can't I have her?"

"She doesn't belong to you or anyone else."

"Is that all she is? Something to covet and keep hidden? I heard Jacob doesn't even know about her yet. How selfish that you and Darren seem committed to keeping this little miracle a secret. Or, how insecure you must be. The minute word gets out that there's a female wolf walking around, unmated males will be lined up at your door for a chance at her. Wanna keep your little pet all to yourself before she gets passed around?" Erik's voice turned taunting, as if he were trying to goad Logan into doing something stupid in view of the public. Of course, his words were anything but true.

"Shut your fucking mouth, Erik, before I shut it for you."

Erik chuckled. "Oh, no. I made the big bad wolf mad, didn't I? Why don't you do something about it?"

Logan took one step closer, but Katey reflexively pulled him back as if to keep him at bay. "Don't," she whispered.

"Better listen to your little pet and run along home with your tail between your legs."

Katey's hold slipped on his jacket and Logan bounded forward. In movements too quick for her to follow, he grabbed Erik by the throat and slammed him against a nearby SUV. Both snarled, eyes golden and fangs bared as if they were more than ready to fight as wolves in the theater parking lot.

"You wanna know how long I've waited to have you right here, just like this?" Logan's voice took on a sinister key that had Katey backing up against her jeep. "Way... way too long."

"Still mad about that old hit?" Erik's voice came out hoarse and choked. "Can't seem to recall his name."

Logan lifted the rougarou half a foot off the ground. "You remember his name. Don't think I won't gut you like you gutted him."

Erik snickered. "You won't kill me. Not out here. Not in front of her."

"You think this is a game? You think I'm just pulling a laugh?" Logan lifted his other hand to reveal his wolfish claws. "Let's see how well you laugh with your spine hanging out of your back."

Katey leapt forward and grabbed his arm before it had the chance to carry out the threat. "Logan, people could be watching. Please, let's just go home."

Gold eyes fell on her and she tried to maintain her courage in the face of a wolf out for blood, his dominance so dense she could barely breathe. It took a few moments, but Logan slowly lowered Erik until his boots touched the blacktop, and a bit of the bristly beast gave way to human reasoning.

With his hand still wrapped around Erik's throat, he leaned in so his words could not be mistaken. "You tried to steal something I love tonight. You will pay for it, one way or another."

What he said was not lost on Katey, and her whole world began to tilt. Only her hold on Logan's arm kept her from losing her own equilibrium completely.

A mischievous smile crossed Erik's lips. "How about we settle this the old fashioned way? I seem to remember you like going a round or two in the ring. Bare knuckles? No holds barred? You against me." He looked right at Katey. "For her."

Struck dumb by the challenge, Katey forgot to tell Logan that he didn't need to fight for her. He could have her, totally and absolutely. No contest necessary.

But he was too quick. "Deal. Tomorrow night."

"I'll be there."

Logan let go of Erik's throat and stormed away. "Get in the jeep," he ordered Katey.

Without a second thought, she put as much distance between herself and Erik as quickly as possible and ran to the passenger side. She didn't dare look for Erik in the mirrors or look at Logan until they were on the highway and headed home. Only then could she let out the breath she had been holding. Even with Logan still seething, and a trickling of residual dominance filling the car like a noxious gas, she felt much safer.

When she finally looked at Logan, she noticed the way his arm muscles flexed and chest heaved with a deep sigh. For a moment, she wondered if it was her turn to be yelled at, but he said nothing. She had anticipated a continuation of their fight from earlier that day. She predicted golden eyes, some screaming, maybe more hateful words, but there was practically nothing beyond the obvious signs that he was pissed, and that scared her the most.

Yet, she got what she wanted, or at least part of it. He admitted that Erik tried to steal something he loved. He tried to steal Katey out from underneath him. Katey wished it could have been confessed hours before so she would have never had to be out after dark, so he would have never had to come after her like this.

They were halfway home when Katey finally decided to break the heavy silence.

"Are we going to talk?"

"Wasn't planning on it." Logan's voice was gruff and agitated.

"Can we?"

"I'd rather not... I don't want to say something I'll regret later."

Katey was shocked by his lucid honesty. It gave her hope. "Does... Does Darren know about all of this?"

"Not unless you told him. I turned my phone off. Haven't been home."

Oh, they were both going to get in so much trouble. Katey bit her lips together, thinking of how bad her punishment might be. "Are there really vamps out?"

Logan snapped a look her way. "Who told you?"

"So it's true?"

"Who told you," he repeated more urgently.

"Erik did... He told me a lot of other stuff too."

Logan looked back to the road. "Don't believe everything he says."

"What about the vamps?"

He nodded. "That's true. They didn't want me to tell you until after they got home, but..."

"Then you left me."

A hint of pain snaked through their bond and Katey knew she had wounded him.

"I... I didn't want to stay and do something we'd regret... I'm sorry for the things I said."

Katey jumped at the opening. "I'm sorry too. I wish I could take back everything. I know you're just trying to keep me safe and I should have listened."

"But you didn't." Logan hardened again.

"Because I... I wanted to get something out of you. Something I could hold onto. Something to hope for."

His face wrinkled with confusion. "What are you talking about?"

Katey sighed. "I know it's super petty and totally a player move, but I was trying to make you jealous and push you to... do something about us."

Logan's expression went slack. "Are you happy with yourself now?"

"Not really... Are you two actually going to fight over me?"

"Yes, but don't think this is just about you. It's overdue... Long overdue."

Her heart lodged in her throat. Didn't Darren say that fights between them and the rougarou never turned out in their favor? Why would he make such a deal when he knew it would end badly? Or was he too confident in himself? Katey wished she had known that this would happen. If she had thought they would try to challenge each other, she would have never gone in the first place. It was never her intention for Logan to risk his life or threaten Erik's.

"Please don't fight... I don't want you to get hurt."

"I can't go back on it now. Even if I did, it wouldn't resolve anything. He'd likely keep hounding after you just to get at me... I showed my cards a little too obviously tonight and he'll take every advantage he can."

Katey turned her gaze out the window, knowing that he was right. She didn't want him to be, but he was. Their date was interrupted and the way Erik looked at her in the parking lot spoke volumes about his intentions for her. But Logan's words spoke louder, so loud they continued to play on loop in her mind even as he continued to drive a little too fast down the highway toward the house.

Bracing herself for the worst question she could ever ask at a time like this, she whispered, "Do... Do you love me?"

Logan was silent as he stared back to the road, gritting his teeth at the question. Suddenly, the jeep slowed down and Logan flipped on the blinker to alert the cars behind him that he intended to pull onto the shoulder of the road. Once safely there and out of traffic, he parked and turned to face her and placed a hand on the back of her seat.

"Yes."

One word, but it felt like a burst of cannon fire. Katey's mouth twitched, as if trying to smile, but the grave look on Logan's face prevented her from feeling the full joy of the moment. What did he have to sacrifice in that few seconds in order to tell her how he truly felt? What courage did it take to admit something so profound and terrifying?

When she said nothing, Logan filled the silence with more confessions that never needed to be said. "I don't want to ruin what we have, Katey. I never have. I know I haven't made it easy for you either. I suck at this whole thing. I show that I care for you and I want to make a better life for you, but I could have killed you for a selfish purpose. I say I want to keep you safe, but then I abandoned you. I never gave this a name. I couldn't be honest with you about the options of what we could have together because I was too lazy to try and explain it... And the moment I finally say how I feel out loud, I couldn't even say it to your face. I said it to the man I should have killed over eighty years ago."

The injured look in his eye would have made her forgive everything. She couldn't bear to see him suffering in his own guilt like that. She would have promised anything, given him anything, just to make all the pain go away.

All she could do was cup his hand between hers and try to show him through their pack bond that he had never been more wrong. "You haven't ruined anything. Not from the very beginning."

She knew he didn't believe her, but it didn't matter. It was the truth, and she'd continue to speak that truth until they were a thousand years old, if they lived for that long.

"But, please..." Katey threw every ounce of dignity aside to plead with him. "Please, if you care anything for me, do not fight Erik tomorrow.

Logan shook his head. "I can't do that because I do care about you. I know Erik. He won't stop until he gets what he wants. And right now, he wants you. He can't have you."

In another circumstance, Katey would have thought that utterly romantic. Her voice became choked with threatening tears. "But what if you get hurt? I couldn't stand the thought of you getting hurt because of me."

Logan reached out and brushed his thumb against her cheek to wipe away the tears that had snaked down her face. "That's a risk I'm willing to take... for you."

She gripped his hand in hers and clasped it tightly as if their joined hands would somehow translate how she felt without having to say it.

Her phone, which she had turned back on before arriving at the movie theater, suddenly buzzed with an incoming call. Knowing what deep shit they were in with Darren, she broke away to check the caller ID. It was their alpha.

"I wouldn't answer that just yet," Logan warned.

She let the call pass and saw the list of missed calls, voicemails, and texts. All of them were from the pack. "They must be worried."

"If you had packed a change of clothes, I would have suggested we stay at a hotel for the night."

She cracked a smile and tasted the salt from her tears on her lips. "That would just be putting off the inevitable."

Logan sighed and rotated in his seat to face the steering wheel again. "I guess we should get it over with then." He pulled back onto the highway, but didn't drive so fast now that they knew what waited for them at the end of the journey.

The moment was gone, but the crisis was hardly over. He'd still fight Erik, and there was the real possibility that he may not walk away from it in one piece. Yet, Katey did get what she wanted. He didn't say those three words in that specific order, and she didn't admit it in the same way, but they came to some understanding, even if it was a vague one.

CHAPTER 9

Logan was still caught in a tempest of feeling by the time they pulled up to the house. His wolf refused to be still, coming so close to having a piece of Erik and denied the satisfaction at the last minute. For decades, he tried to heal from what Erik did to him, and to Forrest. Until that day, he thought he could finally move on. The acceptance that Erik and his pack of rougarous were likely thousands of miles away and far out of his reach helped tremendously. Now that he knew different, now that he was in Crestucky, the pain and rage came back a hundredfold.

In the hours he disappeared from the pack, his mind took him back to that apartment room in Chicago. The stench of blood, drugs, and death haunted his senses. He jerked at the ghostly echoes of machine gun fire and the shouts of Forrest and Mitch taking cover behind furniture.

He should have done something. He knew he could have done something, but fear of losing control stopped him cold and he hid like a coward. They all tried to tell him that there was no way he could have saved Mitch or any of the other loups-garous of Chicago. His wolf knew differently and took the lead in trying to make things right. If the pack hadn't come back to take him away, Logan wasn't sure what would have happened in the end.

Back then, he failed to take his revenge on Erik, but he had a second chance.

"Do we want to come up with a story to tell them?"

Katey's voice launched him back into the present, leaving behind Chicago for the time being.

He blinked and looked up to the house as he shut off the engine. "Probably best to stick to the truth."

"What will they do to you?"

He knew what she was thinking and smirked. "Nothing so bad as they've done before, I think."

They climbed out of the car and Katey walked ahead down the gravel walkway to the front porch. The door swung open, spilling light onto the concrete. In an uncharacteristic move, the alpha rushed forward and wrapped Katey in a tight hug of relief.

"Thank God, you're safe," the burly alpha murmured against her hair.

Katey went stiff, likely not expecting the hug either. With jerky hesitance, she raised her arms and returned the hug before melting into it. A twinge of envy sparked in Logan's chest, but it couldn't catch into anything more than a mild annoyance.

"Don't I get a hug for bringing her back?"

Dustin appeared from the foyer and charged for him. "Oh, no. You're mine, kid." He grabbed the lapel of Logan's jacket and dragged him into the house. "What the hell were you thinking leaving her alone?"

Logan pushed him off when they came to the living room. "I didn't plan on her taking off. She was safer alone than with me at the time."

Darren and Katey joined them, the alpha's heavy hand on her shoulder. Unshed tears shone in her eyes, aftermath of a hug that probably meant a great deal to her.

"I think it's best if someone starts explaining what exactly happened before we go any further."

A beat of silence passed before Katey took the initiative and began with Erik cornering her after school, hurried through the vicious argument between her and Logan, and concluded with the challenge. She graciously left out his confession of love and the conversation on the way home. That was irrelevant compared to everything else, though only to the rest of the pack.

By the end of her story, Darren and Dustin looked torn over who to be more mad at, Katey for going off with Erik, or Logan for threatening to kill him out in the open and for leaving Katey alone after dark while they were still under a vamp-alert.

Logan beat all of them to the punch. "Why didn't any of you tell me Erik was in Crestucky?"

Dustin gave a wild gesture toward the front door. "For this exact reason! We knew if you knew, there'd be no stopping you from going after him and doing something stupid."

"I had a right to know!"

Darren gripped him with dominance to remind him who was in charge. "Erik is none of your concern. Your first priority is to take care of Katey."

"And I did. I got her back from Erik."

Dustin crossed his arms. "She might not have run off if you had been home to keep an eye on her."

"So, you would have rathered I stayed close to her when I was mad enough to kill?"

Katey stepped forward. "You know you wouldn't have killed me."

Logan spun on her, his tone a little harsher than he meant to express. "I almost did once. I could have done it again."

She retreated toward Darren as if to take shelter in the alpha. It seemed a contradiction to all he told her in the car, but not really. Logan loved her. He had known that for a while now, but he had a funny way of showing it. No matter how hard he tried, he couldn't convey it in the way she needed. He wondered if he was even capable of it. He hadn't known this sort of love his whole life, and he didn't know how to act anymore.

"I think we all need to take a breath and get something to eat," Darren said firmly. "We can at least be thankful that both of you are safe. We will discuss this issue with Erik in the morning."

Logan wasn't so ignorant to think that this was over. He'd be punished eventually, but the details remained unknown. One thing was for sure. He wouldn't give them the chance to take away this fight with Erik. He'd disappear again if he had to, but he would get his retribution, even if it was the last thing he'd ever do.

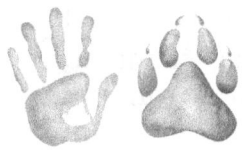

Katey knew the moment she woke up that Logan was gone. Again. The steely gray of dawn barely touched the sky, and she could tell he was not in the house. The strain in their bond was what jolted her from her deep, dreamless sleep.

The night before, after Darren filled her in on the vamp situation and she ate enough meat to compensate for her impromptu and inadequate dinner at a fast-food joint, Logan made himself scarce. Ben came home soon after to give the good news that he and the Devian betas found no fresh sign of the vampires, declaring Crestucky safe for loups-garous again. That didn't make her little escapade any less of an offense. In consequence, Darren made a call to Jacob and discussed the possibility of attaching one of the high school loups-garous as a bodyguard to follow her between her last two classes of the day. When she specifically requested Jared, Darren may have guessed he made a mistake. He might have seen this punishment as a way to keep tabs on her, but she enjoyed the idea of never having to revisit that lonely, pack-less feeling again. Additionally, it may deter Erik from approaching her again.

However, with Logan MIA, she wondered if she would need an escort between every class that day, not just toward the end.

She went downstairs and found Darren seated at the dining table with a cup of hot tea in one hand and his forehead resting in the other. Dustin and Ben were still in bed. Most of the lights in the house were still off, casting everything in dark blue shadows, but she could see just fine with her loup-garou eyes.

"Where's—"

"Out." Darren interrupted with a flippant wave. "He says he needs to get ready for the fight tonight. He won't be back until it's over." He looked up and gave her a sympathetic smile. "At least he warned someone this time."

Katey's heart fractured. She hoped a good night's sleep and a hefty meal would have convinced him to call off the fight. It seemed so much like a guy-thing to try and settle everything with violence, and she couldn't understand it.

She wrapped her arms around her stomach and let her stare wander as the worry for Logan's safety hit her hard again.

Darren stood and slid past her into the kitchen. "Take a seat. I'll fix you a cup." He probably knew there wasn't a chance in hell she'd go back to bed.

She did as he said and absently listened to his movements in the kitchen, but mostly went over every word she and Logan shared the night before. Maybe something in what he told her could be used to talk him out of it. Then again, it was likely she would never be able to reach him, just like they couldn't get him yesterday when he disappeared.

Darren came back and set the steeping mug of chamomile in front of her before taking his seat again.

Karey wrapped her hands around the porcelain to warm her fingers. "Why is he so determined to do this? I know Erik killed his friend, but that was a long time ago, wasn't it?"

Darren took a sip before answering. "Something you'll come to realize, Katey. Last week and last century tend to feel the same after a while. We have a keen memory, and grudges are easier to hold than forget. For Logan... the loss of his family and friends has shaped who he is today. Those events are imprinted upon his soul. It's not something he can just get over."

Katey could understand. Whether she admitted it or not, every foster home she got kicked out of left a mark. Each time she picked up her bag or suitcase to follow the social worker out the door, a little piece of her crumbled like a wadded up note, forever wrinkled.

"What happened in Chicago?" she asked, her voice hardly above a whisper. She needed the truth, all of it, and not whatever scattered details she could glean from Erik's mind games.

Darren's face scrunched. "It's not an easy story to hear."

"I want to know. I need to understand why this is so terrible that no one wants to talk about it."

The alpha leveled a penetrating stare on her, but she wouldn't waver. "After we came back to the states from Europe to find Ben, the opportunity came for Logan to stay with Forrest's family in Chicago. Forrest was his first friend in Devia and they corresponded some over the years they spent apart, but it had been decades since they saw one another. Forrest's great-uncle, Will, owned a butcher shop. He, Forrest, and Forrest's cousin on his mother's side, lived together. What we didn't know was that they were involved with the mafia in Chicago. This was during the height of the Prohibition, and plenty of people were making money on the side running illegal operations like distilleries or bars. Will owned a bar himself, and they did odds and ends jobs for the local bosses."

Katey's lips tightened. She didn't want Erik to be right, but it seemed to be working out that way.

"Logan got mixed up in the whole thing, and from what we were told, earned himself a reputation. It drew too much attention to himself and Forrest's family. Erik and his father were also in the Chicago circuit, leading a gang, or pack, of rougarous with the intent to take over the city. To do that, they had to take out the loups-garous who stood in their way."

Katey propped her chin in her hand. It was like some blockbuster gangster movie, but with werewolves.

Darren took a breath and eased back in his chair. "They were lured into a trap and ambushed by rougarous under Erik's command. The guns had silver bullets. Forrest's cousin was killed... Logan took it hard, blaming himself. So, he went on a killing spree. We don't know how many, but he specifically targeted the rougarous, trying to find where Erik was hiding. By the time we found Ben and came back to get Logan, he had gotten himself into a real fix. He nearly went up in flames inside a warehouse along with at least a dozen other mauled corpses. We pulled him out in time, and that's when we found out about what had been going on."

The blood drained from Katey's face. Yes, Erik had been completely right. Damn it.

"We took him out of Chicago, but it took years to work through the damage. Last night likely undid nearly a century's worth of healing."

And it was her fault. Katey hung her head in her hands, letting the steam of her tea condense on her face.

"Fighting Erik may bring closure, which is the only reason I didn't stop him from leaving this morning."

Katey looked back up, despair laced in her voice. "But what about that whole thing of rougarous being stronger and meaner? How is Logan supposed to come out of the fight alive?"

Darren smirked. "Did you miss the part about Logan killing the rougarous in Chicago? He can handle himself."

"Isn't that dangerous? What about exposure? What if Logan gets too out of control?"

"Oh, yes, all of that is a great possibility." Darren paused to take another sip. "But there's no use stopping him. This matters far too much to him. All we can do is hope for the best and get all the details in the morning."

Her ears snagged on that last word. "Morning? Why not tonight if... when he comes home?"

"It's Ben's night to shift. The three of us will be... occupied until morning." He made a noise of remembrance and reached behind him to the buffet table against the wall. He grabbed up an envelope and showed it to her. "Speaking of which. Today is the last day before winter break. We fly to Alaska tomorrow morning. These are our ticket confirmations. We leave at seven o'clock. It won't be an easy trip, but we will do our best to make the journey bearable for you."

In all the hysteria, Katey forgot what day it was, and all that the Alaska trip would mean. Crowded airports, loud plane engines, and the gathering of loups-garous that would ogle at her. Her mind raced. So much would happen within the next forty-eight hours. Logan was to fight his arch enemy from the Prohibition, and she would be the only female loup-garou amongst a huge national gathering of their kind. She still couldn't believe how much her life had changed since she turned eighteen.

Darren slid the envelope back on the buffet. "You should stay home tonight. You'll be alone, but I want you to get plenty of rest before the trip. That means no running off to watch Logan fight. The last thing he needs is for you to be there and watch whatever happens."

The idea had crossed her thoughts. She looked down to her tea growing cold.

"Listen." Darren's voice deepened. "Logan is still the same man you first met. Knowing what he's done doesn't change who he is. He would argue on this point, but he is not a monster. He was put in a difficult situation and made poor choices. We have lived long enough to build our own mountains of guilt. Logan is no different, but he is much harder on himself than any of us will ever be..." Darren's eyes softened. "I know you two care deeply for each other. Have patience with yourselves and remember you both are still half-human."

What Katey learned should have changed everything. Logan committed murder, lots of murders. Yet, she couldn't bring herself to be afraid of him or think less of him and the choices he made. She wasn't there. There's no way she could pass judgment on what he did or why he did it and say there could have been a better way. And just like Darren said, Logan was the same man she loved. It's not as if he had done these things just days before they met. He was a different Logan, a different loup-garou than he had been in Chicago. At his core, Katey knew he was a good person, even if he didn't think so himself.

The heavy thud of Logan's fists meeting the punching bag echoed off the walls of the workout room. Forrest stood on the other side of the bag, struggling to keep it stable as Logan sent blow after blow sailing into the padding.

"If you keep this up, you're going to owe me another bag," Forrest said over the heavy rock music blaring from the wireless speakers.

Logan wasn't paying attention. Eyes blazing gold and face streaming with sweat, he could only think of how it would feel to have the bones of Erik's face crunch beneath his knuckles. He threw more force behind his punches, Forrest grunting in time with his jabs and hooks. If his friend had a hard time staying on his feet, he knew Erik would likely go soaring across the ring. Good.

"Logan! Take a powder, man! Slow down!"

Breaths quickened and power surged into his muscles, compliments of the wolf.

Suddenly, the bag exploded, stuffing rippling from long, deep gashes in the softened leather.

Forrest let out a curse and shoved Logan away to assess the damage. "No claws! Didn't we agree on that?"

Logan looked down and saw his tawny claws were indeed out. "Sorry," he managed to say between pants.

He paced back and brought up the bottom of his sleeveless shirt to wipe away the sweat from his mouth. They had been at this for hours, only breaking for water and meals. Logan wanted to be thoroughly conditioned for the fight that evening, but he wouldn't let the wolf have control. He'd stay fed, stay balanced.

Forrest reached up to unhook the bag from its chain. "I know how pissed you are, but save some for Erik."

"I'm surprised you're not taking your fair share of shots on the bag. You look way too calm."

When Logan came to him looking for a workout partner for the fight, he had to break the news about Erik's presence in town.

Apparently, Jacob and the Deviants agreed to keep it a secret from Forrest just like his own pack had. Forrest, of all people, should have been furious, but the redhead only simmered with mild irritation, mostly that Jacob neglected to tell him.

"I made peace with the past, Logan. If I held onto all the anger I have a right to, I wouldn't be able to function."

Peace with the past? How could they make peace with what happened? Forrest was in the room. He was there when Mitch breathed his last, body riddled with bullets. How could Forrest move on from that?

Logan looked at himself in the floor-to-ceiling mirror mounted to the wall. Sweat glistened across his arms and forehead, a lock of black hair loosened from the tie at the nape of his neck, and the wolf stared back at him, reminding Logan that it wanted in on the fight just as much as he did.

"Are you doing this for Katey or Mitch?"

Logan turned to Forrest as he offered a bottle of water. "Why does it have to be 'or'?"

Forrest shrugged. "Guess I wanted to know which one was more important to you."

Logan's lips pulled into a snarl. "And what is that supposed to mean?"

By now, Forrest was used to Logan's temper and didn't flinch away from his dominance. "If you love Katey like I know you do, you're fighting for her, not for my dead cousin. Just wanted to make sure you understood that."

Of course, Logan was doing this for Katey. The fight was to decide who would have a right to her, wasn't it? But the more Logan reflected, the more he realized Forrest was partially right. Since the night before, his thoughts were stuck in Chicago. He thought about Mitch and his murder more than the goal of keeping Erik's paws off Katey. That was of more immediate importance than settling old grudges.

While he wanted to deny it, Logan couldn't lie to his friend. He took a breath and pushed the wolf back one more time. "Thanks. I needed the reminder."

Forrest shook Logan's shoulder. "That's what I'm here for... But sock Erik in the nose for me."

He snorted a laugh. "Yeah, I'll do that."

Katey's head sagged against the cool wall of the billiard room, her gaze following the game, but her heart miles away wherever Logan was. Besides her steady breathing, Katey had barely moved since she took her seat in the barstool maybe an hour or two ago. At any other time, she might have isolated herself instead of seeking company, but her wolf drove her to stay in the vicinity of her pack.

That day without Logan was pure hell. Before, she only had to endure a few hours away from him, but this was too much. An aching emptiness within her refused to leave her in peace. It nagged and gnawed, eating her from the inside out. It was like her lungs had no air, like the light had been stolen from her, leaving her in total darkness without him. It started to creep in slowly at first, starting early that morning during breakfast. Then as the day dragged on, it grew worse, until she was almost completely gone. This full-blown, mind and body numbing sadness was more devastating than the darkness that haunted her before Logan came into her life.

The wolf within her could feel it too and didn't make the situation any easier. Her wolf missed the peace and comfort that Logan brought, and Katey occasionally felt the sudden urge to howl, but she at least had the sense to stifle it. The wolf wanted to call out to the world in search of the one who could complete them and chase away the agonizing sadness.

There was no doubt that the rest of the pack sensed her misery, if not through the pack bond, then through plain common sense and observation. Katey saw their occasional glances her way, so full of sympathy. They tried to comfort her, telling her that Logan would be all right and he'd come back in one piece. Katey wanted to believe it, but that didn't stop her from missing him. Being with the pack lessened the pain, but it was only a matter of time before they would have to leave for the woods. By the way Ben looked, it wouldn't be too much longer.

"Are you sure you don't want to play a game or two?" Dustin asked before lining up his shot on a solid. "It'd even out the teams"

Katey wagged her head lazily. "I'm good."

The beta's mouth pulled into a thin line and he struck the cue ball, nailing the ball into a corner pocket after it bounced off the felted edge of the pool table. One thing she realized quickly, was that they were all incredibly adept at this game.

"Are ya excited for the trip to Alaska?" Ben asked from the opposite wall. He had a favorite spot to rest as the tension of the coming shift became harder to ignore.

"A little."

"It'll be fun," Dustin said. "The plane ride always sucks, but once we're there it's a nice vacation."

Katey found it ironic that she had never had the opportunity to go on vacations as a human foster kid. She'd only seen Alaska in pictures and on television. That thought made her wonder about the photos in Darren's classroom, the ones from all over the world, places that looked straight out of a National Geographic program.

She looked to her alpha as he took his turn and shot for two striped balls. "Those pictures on the door in your classroom, where are they from?"

Darren gave a hint of a smile. "Many places. We take a trip to Europe during the summer every so often. We visit other packs and loups-garous we've come to know over the centuries."

"You'll like those trips too," Dustin added. "We rack up a lot of frequent flyer miles."

Ben pushed himself off the wall to approach the table for his turn, but one knee buckled and he had to use the pool stick to keep himself from collapsing.

The other three loups-garous in the room straightened with alarm.

"You good or—"

"I'm fine," Ben snapped at Dustin. "I can go a few more rounds."

"Don't push yourself," Darren reproved. "If you need to go, we're ready."

Ben lifted his light brown eyes to Katey, as if he were checking her first before responding. "I can go a little longer."

Shame singed her insides. "Please don't push yourself on my account. I'll be okay."

Katey wasn't convinced of that. The only reason she wasn't a sobbing mess was because of her nearness to the pack. But the last thing she ever wanted to be was a burden.

Instead of giving in, Ben leaned over the table for his turn. Despite whatever stress he suffered, he sent two solids, one after another, into one of the middle holes. "See, I'm fine."

Dustin made a choking noise that may have been a laugh. "Yeah, sure you are."

"What does it feel like?" Katey asked, in an effort to distract herself as much out of curiosity. She knew she only had a few weeks until her own first shift. Part of her knew she should have been terrified by the prospect of morphing into some creature straight out of a horror movie, but like everything else, a twinge of enthusiasm at becoming just a little more loup-garou fought away any fear she may have felt.

Ben took the stick in both hands and leaned heavily, looking like a weary traveler using a staff to keep them upright. "Muscles burnin', bones vibratin', headache, skin flashin' hot and cold... other than that it's a breeze."

His self-deprecating smile made her shiver. "It's going to hurt a lot, isn't it?"

Dustin took his turn and scored the last of the solids. "Worst pain imaginable."

"Don't scare her," Darren frowned. "Yes, it will hurt, but you won't be alone in it. We'll be shifting right along with you. And no matter what you think in the moment, you won't die."

Katey dropped her gaze and wondered what it had been like for them. From what she was told, all of the pack except for Ben had turned alone. They had no one to help, no one to guide them through that much pain and fear, or explain what was happening to their bodies. Maybe Darren's comment came from personal experience. It made her that much more grateful to have them.

By the time it was Ben's turn again, he knocked in the eight ball, winning the game for him and Dustin.

Darren set his pool stick on the rack on the wall. "I think it'd be best to wrap this up and get ready to leave."

No one argued and hung up their sticks as well. The pack moved to leave the billiard room and she stiffly slid from the barstool. Dustin fell back to stop her in the hall between the billiard room and the kitchen. To their right was a set of folding doors that hid the laundry room, and to the left was a stretch of counter below a wide window that looked out over the back patio and garden. Night was just on the verge of completely consuming the evening, leaving the hall dark.

He glanced over his shoulder and waited for Ben and Darren to disappear up the stairs. "I know you're worried about Logan," he whispered so low there was no way the others would hear. "I am too... a little." Dustin pulled out a piece of paper and handed it to her. "Here's the address and directions to the fight club. Wait about an hour after we leave. I'll take us in the opposite direction of the driveway to make sure you've got a clear escape."

When Katey took hold of the folded up paper, he cupped her hand between his. "Whatever you do, don't interfere. Just watch. Even if Logan looks like he's about to get his ass handed to him, you are just a spectator. Got it?"

The serious glint in his eyes startled her. There must have been a reason for what he said, but Katey was too excited for the pass to go see Logan to care about reasons. She felt like an eager puppy who heard the word "walk" after spending a long boring day inside.

She nodded in agreement and Dustin gave her a light slap on the back to get her moving down the hall. "Don't tell anyone I let you go. Darren will skin me alive."

"Our secret," Katey affirmed, her face splitting in a grin.

She slipped the directions into her back pocket, thrilled that she'd get the chance to at least be in the same room with Logan sooner rather than later. She didn't care if he was in the middle of a bloody showdown with Erik. Any sight of him, any chance to catch his scent, any unlikely opportunity to feel his arms around her, was worth whatever she'd witness in the ring that night.

CHAPTER 10

Katey followed Dustin's directions south and then west toward a smaller community just outside of Crestucky. The community was mostly residential with one gas station, a convenience store and a restaurant, but just on the edge of that was an old warehouse or factory that had been renovated into a fight club and bar. The dirt parking lot was packed, cars overflowing into a nearby field and across the street. She hadn't expected it to be this crowded. Light beamed out from the few high windows on the front and Katey could hear the thumping music and general noise of people coming from inside as she pulled up in her jeep.

She stepped out and realized she, Logan, and Erik were likely not the only loups-garous there. Scattered amongst the humans, they came to watch the fight as well. The odors of cigarette smoke, sweat, all manner of colognes and perfumes, piss, drugs, and alcohol assaulted her nose. Some patrons loitered around the outside, talking and laughing with friends. They didn't pay her any mind as she hurried toward the entrance.

Once inside, the stench of the place hit her even harder. Her hand reflexively shot up to her nose as she felt the need to puke, but held it in and did her best to block it out the way Logan taught her.

The room vibrated with the music and shouts. Among the noise, she could just barely make out snippets of conversations, almost all of them about the coming fight. Somewhere, a man was taking bets on the combatants and the pool was a hefty size. In the middle of the warehouse was a square stage that was raised three feet with four poles on each corner that held up barriers of elastic ropes on every side. It made her think of the wrestling rings on television.

Her first instinct was to find where the fighters would prepare for a fight. Maybe a locker room or dressing room. But, then she remembered Dustin's warning not to interfere. If she saw Logan, or had the chance to talk with him, she'd likely try to talk him out of it again. All she could do was wander, listen, and wait, as much as it killed her not to know where he was.

Just when she was ready to give up and look for that back room, the lights began to flicker and strobe lights danced along the walls and ceiling. The room erupted in shouts, screams, and cheers.

The music faded and the voice of an announcer shouted from an intercom speaker high in the rafters above their heads to announce the commencement of the fight. The room exploded with more shouts and hollers, as Katey shoved her way closer to the stage. She made it as far as the secondary perimeter around the ring itself to keep back spectators. Off to the side, she saw burly men in black polo shirts clear a path from the fighting ring to an entryway from which the fighters would arrive.

The lights came back on, but they were tinted a devilish red. Katey felt her heart pounding as heavy metal music blared over the speakers. A few seconds into the song, she saw a darkened figure emerge from down the hallway. As it came into focus and her bond surged back to life, she recognized it as Logan. Katey leaned over as far as she could to get a better look or catch his eye.

He wore black, baggy pants and a tight, black muscle shirt, but his feet were bare. His hair was wet and dripping over his shoulders, gleaming in the harsh light. There was a menacing, bloodthirsty look in his eyes as he stormed down the path toward the ring.

At first, he seemed completely oblivious to her presence, but she saw the change in him as he came closer to the ring. He must have felt her through their bond, just as she felt him. His steps slowed, the tension in his shoulders eased, and the tightness in his brows released as he searched for her face in the crowd.

The minute their eyes locked, Logan froze in his tracks and every rigid line in his body softened at the sight of her. The chaos around them faded and Katey wished she could have vaulted the low fence around the ring to run into his arms. But she was only there for support. She gave him the best encouraging smile that she could muster in the moment. It wasn't approval or forgiveness, but an armistice. She accepted that for whatever stupid loup-garou reason, he had to do this.

Logan's chin dipped in acknowledgement and turned to hoist himself onto the stage and slip under the bottom rope. Once back on his feet, he stretched and bounced like a boxer ready for the brawl. He had a concentrated look about him, as if getting his head into the fight already.

The heavy metal faded out and displaced by a rap song Katey didn't recognize. The lights strobed quickly, giving out a frenzied sort of feeling that made it hard to focus.

Katey kept her eyes fixed on Logan, knowing fully well that Erik was about to come onto the stage, but she didn't expect it so suddenly. She blinked and Erik was up in the ring, standing in front of Logan, already in his battle position, ready to kill. He wore something that looked like jean shorts torn at the knees and was bare-chested to show off his toned muscles.

The lights came back on and everyone shouted for their favorite fighter. Katey stood on her toes to get a better look. Logan and Erik glared at each other and stalked around the ring, circling each other like real wolves would in a fight in the wild. A near-century's worth of brooding and festering anger pitched between them and created a thickening cloud of loup-garou dominance that suffocated Katey even more than the cigarette smoke.

The announcer came on once more to remind spectators that all bets would be accepted at the bar.

Then, a mesh cage, suspended high in the building rafters, descended upon the ring, trapping the fighters inside. Bouncers came up and strapped the walls of the cage together with chains and padlocks. Only the top remained open, and a door on one side as a means of escape.

Logan snarled at the cage and charged at Erik, fire burning in his eyes. "We didn't agree to a cage match, Erik!"

Erik held out his arms, as if satisfied that he riled Logan with just one change of the plans. "Does this change anything?"

A referee pushed his way through the crowd and entered the ring to give the rules. Just as they agreed the night before. No holds barred. The match stops when one of the fighters falls unconscious or forfeits. Katey knew well enough that neither Logan nor Erik would give up, but it did make her wonder if Logan had any intentions to take the fight even further. A life for a life?

It was then, Katey finally realized why Logan liked that movie, *The Maltese Falcon*. Toward the end, the main character said something like, "When a man's partner is killed, he's supposed to do something about it." Logan's friend had been killed, and this was his way of doing something about it. The fight had as much to do with her and Logan's claim over her, as it did with doing some justice to the memory of the friend he lost.

Once the referee was out of the ring and the door locked tight, they growled and circled each other once again, ready to strike as their muscles tensed and bunched.

Shocking the crowd, Logan straightened from his hunched pose and offered his fist out to Erik as a sign of friendly sportsmanship. Erik paused, and then took the invitation, but as soon as he bumped fists with Logan, Erik sent that same fist straight into his jaw. Katey gasped at the suddenness of the attack. She was sure that she heard the crack of bone on impact.

Logan was thrown backwards and seemed to be in real pain for a moment as Erik paced around him, waiting for his old enemy to get up. When he did, Erik sent a fist flying straight for Logan's face again. Logan ducked just in time and hooked his arm under Erik's arm and around his neck with their backs against each other. Logan dropped to his knees to use that tension in an attempt to snap Erik's neck.

But just as quickly as Logan had put him upside down, Erik slid out and pushed Logan to his feet to receive another hook punch that fell short on his chest instead of his face.

Katey winced as Logan cringed and held his chest. Bones would break and fracture throughout the fight, but would also heal within mere seconds or minutes.

Erik took advantage of Logan's moment to heal from the broken chest bone, and grabbed a fistful of Logan's hair to throw him into one of the corner poles.

Logan caught himself before he had the chance to hit the turnbuckle, but Erik ran full speed in Logan's direction. Logan turned around, lifted himself up with the help of the ropes and slammed his feet into Erik's chest, causing Erik to double over. Logan took the opportunity, grabbed at Erik's short hair and continually punched and kicked him in the gut until it looked like Erik was going to puke his own intestines. It looked even more brutal than the few clips Katey had seen of MMA fighters going at one another in championship matches.

After a short break from the volley of punches, Logan tossed Erik into the opposite ropes. But instead of falling down, Erik used the ropes to propel himself back toward Logan to plant his boot into Logan's face. Katey squeaked in terror and waited for Logan's counterattack, but she waited in vain.

Logan fell to the mat and held his nose for a moment, wiping some blood onto the back of his arm. Erik denied him any reprieve and began kicking him in the gut, just as Logan had done to him a moment ago. Katey didn't want to watch, but couldn't look away as Logan struggled to keep himself together.

Erik dragged Logan's limp, sick body into one of the corners and laid him against the pole. But, as Erik was ready to charge and body slam his opponent, Logan maneuvered to the side and Erik collided into the metal pole, probably cracking a couple of ribs in the process.

Logan quickly came back to the center of the ring and bounced around on his toes, all injuries healed with only the traces of blood on his face and arms. When it took too long for his rival to recover, Logan charged at Erik and sent a flying roundhouse kick to Erik's ear, further disorienting him. Erik cried out in pain as Logan pummeled him with more kicks, his shin smashing into Erik's chest and stomach. Katey could have sworn she heard more cracking and breaking of Erik's ribcage. She cringed at every stomach-turning snap.

Suddenly, Erik grabbed Logan's foot to try and stop the attack. This didn't keep Logan from spinning up with his other foot and kicking Erik in the jaw, which sent his enemy soaring into the ropes.

Logan landed with a loud thud onto the stage, but hopped right back up, ready for more. Katey could hear people around her start to rush to the bar to place more bets on Logan, predicting that he would certainly win. She, however, knew that the fight was far from over. They could go like this all night.

Just as Erik came back from the ropes, he charged toward Logan and slammed his elbow into Logan's sternum, knocking him down. Katey covered her mouth and watched as Logan struggled to get up and breathe, but Erik was too fast and within the blink of an eye, had his shoulder in a tight squeeze. Katey screamed out, knowing exactly what Erik was trying to do.

They were facing her on the edge of the ring so she could see every agonized, twisted expression in Logan's face as Erik gripped tighter and tighter into that tendon between the shoulder and neck, that dangerous spot for any loup-garou. Logan roared in pain, a bit of the wolf coming out in his cry.

"No! Stop it!" Katey shouted over the crowd. Erik looked up and locked glares with her. Logan lifted his eyes, full of anguish and rage. She felt tears swelling up in her eyes, but Erik had no mercy and gripped tighter. Katey could hardly stand to hear Logan's screams as Erik dug claws into his shoulder, blood trickling down the front of his black shirt.

If Erik kept up that hold, Logan may shift in front of all these people. His loup-garou side would be unleashed and go on a rampage through the club. Erik had to be doing this on purpose, but why?

Logan suffered for what seemed like an eternity, holding himself together for much longer than Katey expected. Once his strength was spent, golden eyes shot open and looked deep into Katey's, emanating regret, defeat, and pain.

"I'm sorry," she saw Logan mouth to her. Katey hysterically shook her head and pleaded that he couldn't do it, he couldn't let go, not now.

Logan took his claws and dragged them across Erik's arm that held his shoulder. Erik roared and released Logan, turning his back and covering his injury until it had a chance to heal. Logan breathed heavily through his nostrils and helped himself up with the aid of the ropes. He hadn't changed completely, but she could tell he was about to let the animal out of its cage, just as he had done before, just as he hated to do. What stood in the ring was the Logan that turned her, the one that was prepared to kill Mary in defense of Katey, the one that nearly killed Erik the night before. A part of Logan's wolf took control once again.

Logan rushed up and began to punch Erik at blinding speed, lashing at him with his claws. Erik dodged as many as he could, but every time Logan made contact, it was like a train had crashed into his jaw instead of a fist. Logan dug his claws into Erik's shoulder, grabbed him by the seat of his shorts and threw Erik against the ropes with astonishing strength.

Erik countered this by bouncing off the ropes and attempting to ram into Logan. But, Logan didn't so much as budge against this attack. He stood as stiff and sturdy as a brick wall against Erik's assault, knocking him to the ground.

Logan grabbed him up by the neck and pinned him where he lay. He roared in Erik's face with everything he had and Erik didn't hesitate to do the same, fangs bared and both sets of eyes glowing gold.

Katey glanced around to the crowd, but no one seemed shocked or perplexed by their bestial behavior. The loups-garous in the crowd would understand, but the humans seemed to enjoy the animalistic carnage. Did they know about loups-garous? Or did they think it was all for show? Maybe some weird special effect? There was no way the sounds these two made in the ring were anything resembling human.

Finally, Erik managed to shove Logan off, grabbed him by his shirt and hurled Logan into one of the corner poles.

Logan countered by climbing up onto the top of the pole, blindly jumped backwards and spun in mid-air to nail Erik in the chest once more, leaving Erik gasping and wincing on the floor.

Then, Logan did something completely unexpected. Katey watched breathlessly as he jumped over the ropes, onto the cage that had them trapped in the ring, and climbed to the very top. Logan pulled his shirt up over his head, threw it off to the side and roared to the ceiling. The crowd cheered him on, but all Katey could do was watch in pure horror as he leapt from the cage and flipped down all the way to the stage, planning to snap Erik in two. Katey wished he had, but Erik had moved at the last second and Logan landed flat on his own back with a loud crash.

Logan cried out in pain, but it was short lived because he immediately jumped up as Erik began to climb the cage as well, more so in a desperate attempt to escape than to do a spectacular move like Logan had just performed. Logan rushed over, gripped Erik by his back flesh and threw him off the cage wall and into the middle of the ring.

Katey couldn't help but notice the regret on Erik's face as he pushed himself up from the floor. Logan used a stealthy, swift move and flipped Erik completely over his shoulder, making Erik land hard on the stage again. The fight seemed to be leaning in his favor.

The crowd shouted and placed more bets on Logan. Logan stepped off to the side, pacing back and forth and shouting insults as Erik recovered and stood up on shaky legs.

Logan was on him in an instant and they locked arms, their hands on each other's shoulders and heads bent down, pushing and pulling against each other, trying to make the other fall over. They resembled two mighty deer that had locked antlers, tussling over the mating rights to a doe.

Erik managed to get Logan into a position with his arm around Logan's neck, the other around his back and body slammed Logan into the mat.

Logan countered this with a headlock as Erik managed to lift them both to their feet.

Erik pushed Logan aggressively into the ropes, but Logan came straight back and elbowed Erik in the chest, making him fall flat onto his back.

This didn't keep Erik down for long. When Logan bounced off the ropes again, Erik lifted himself up and placed Logan into a tight headlock. Logan maneuvered to the side and kicked Erik's calf out from underneath him, sending him down onto his back.

All of these attacks were so insanely fast that Katey could hardly follow everything. All she could tell was that they seemed to be evenly matched again. Logan had the experience, but Erik had enough endurance to last through everything that Logan could throw at him.

Then, Katey sensed a distinct change in the atmosphere. A heaviness dropped onto her chest, a suffocating, choking feeling like the air became suddenly toxic. There was nothing obvious to suggest it, but she knew it came from Logan, through their bond. Something was wrong. The wolf continued to fight for him, but something new and dangerous rose up from within him. A darkness, foreboding and murderous, seeped into Logan's golden eyes. The color didn't change, but she could still see the difference somehow. That darkness, that evil, became more evident in each blow, in each growl and vicious attack. Even Erik saw it and she smelled his fear from where she stood.

She couldn't stand this. She hated fighting. She hated violence. She couldn't stand the pain and hate that emitted from each other's eyes and what residual pain filtered through their bond. Even her wolf fidgeted nervously at the sight of their battle, pleading with her to stop the madness somehow, to stop it before Logan unleashed whatever it was that could tear the place down.

Fuck Dustin's orders. She couldn't take it anymore.

Katey desperately looked around the cage and forced her way through the crowd, vaulted over the perimeter and made her way to the door on the cage. She ripped the padlock from the door. Pieces of the lock and hinges clamored to the floor as she yanked the door open and charged inside.

Katey put herself right between the two feuding loups-garous, standing solid, shoulders back and eyes glowing gold in the bright fluorescent lights. All at once, she felt her wolf surge forward, emanating a force of will in Erik's direction. She didn't know what it was, only that it made him stop dead in his tracks and stare dumbly at her. Behind her, she could sense equal surprise in Logan, the coming shift smothered by her energy.

The crowd gushed in shouts of anger as Katey interrupted their sport. She didn't care. They didn't know that Erik would stop at nothing until Logan was dead and Katey wasn't about to let that happen. No matter the cost to herself, she couldn't just watch them tear each other apart. She would have rather given the last breath in her lungs.

Erik growled, and Katey returned the threat, showing him that she was like no other woman he'd tried to intimidate in the past. She had fangs and claws the same as he did.

"Move!" he commanded, a thread of dominance trying to break through the force she emanated. It only bounced off like a Ping-Pong ball.

"Never."

"Back away," Erik snarled, as if her answer would change.

"No! I chose Logan!" Katey roared, knowing very well that if her presence didn't end the conflict, her words would.

Logan tried to push her aside, but she shot him a likewise fierce glare. That darkness was gone now, leaving only the wolf to contend with her. It took some exchange of will through their bond to force her to yield and let him face Erik.

Erik's golden eyes darted between Katey and his rival, a whole other battle taking place in his mind that they couldn't control. In a move that shocked the assembly, Erik lifted his hands, palms out and backed away, ending the fight and giving Logan the victory.

The gamblers that had put their money on Logan hooted their own victory and went to the bar to collect their earnings.

Before Erik turned toward the cage door, he pointed to Logan. "Don't think this is over."

Neither of them expected it. It wouldn't be over until one of them was dead, and Katey realized that far too late.

Once the rougarou disappeared into the crowd, Logan turned to Katey, but there was little joy in his expression. "Why did you do that?" Logan's voice was hoarse and gruff with pain and fatigue.

"That fight was getting way out of hand. You two were about to kill each other."

"I had everything—" He paused in his retort to wince and grip his side, apparently not fully healed yet. It was then she realized how much sweat and blood streaked across his arms and down his smooth chest.

She knew he was going to lie and say he had everything under control. The match was spiraling into chaos and they all knew it. It might have gotten worse if Katey hadn't stopped the cascade of violence. Did he even realize what was about to happen? Did he feel that beast rise up in him at all?

"Let's just get you out of here before someone calls a paramedic." Katey eased into place beside him to serve as a crutch if he needed it. She didn't even care if he got blood all over her hoodie. As proud as he could be, he accepted her help and they left the cage via the busted door.

"There's already someone waiting in the locker room," Logan grumbled. "But he's one of us."

"Thought of everything, didn't you?" A loup-garou medic would easily sign off that Logan was fine, and no one would question it, unless they heard the snapping of bones the way Katey did from the sidelines.

"If it were up to me, we wouldn't need a medic."

Katey gave him a hard look. "I know. You males and your damn pride."

Logan emitted a soft growl. "This isn't about pride and you know it."

She rolled her eyes. "Sure it isn't."

Two bouncers came up alongside them, both loups-garous, to save them from being accosted by the gamblers who lost money in the fight. They were more pissed at Katey than Logan. If she hadn't stepped in and ended the fight, maybe Erik would have won. Their insults rolled off of her like water off a duck's back. They didn't know if she let the fight carry on to its inevitable end, they'd be giving testimonies to crime scene investigators or something.

A third loup-garou came out of the crowd, one more familiar and welcome presence in the madness. Forrest fell in on the other side of Logan and made a show of helping him.

"Got that out of your system?" he asked Logan, brows furrowed.

"Hardly."

They passed through the wide entryway into the back hall-way. The bouncers dropped off to guard their exit, but Forrest continued with them down the hall toward the locker rooms. Recessed lighting spaced rather far apart, lit the path down the hall, casting an orange glow against the cinder block walls. The strong scents of soiled clothes, body spray, and soap mixed in the air. The sounds of the fight club lowered into a dull rumble in the background, the main event over and done.

Logan gave a cue for them to stop just outside the locker rooms and the three of them waited as he braced himself on his knees.

"Aren't you healing?" she asked, mildly worried that Erik had done some irreparable damage.

"A single wound or broken bone is one thing, but several takes a little longer." Forrest finally settled his attention on Katey and realization lit up his face. "Katey... What the hell?"

Right. He didn't know yet. She gave a helpless shrug.

Forrest shoved Logan, nearly throwing him off his feet. "You didn't tell me!"

A cough sputtered into a laugh and he smiled back at his friend. "I'm shocked Lily actually kept her mouth shut."

Forrest's eyes widened. "You told Lily?"

"She figured it out on her own the morning after," Katey replied. "We're not telling many people yet."

"Jacob?"

Logan shook his head and straightened up with great effort. "Not unless Darren told him." He turned to Forrest, all serious again. "Watch her while I get cleaned up. I don't want Erik sneaking in."

"You got it. Go shower. You look like you slaughtered a hog."

Logan glanced down at his body, as if finally noticing the results of the battle. "At least I don't smell like I did." He looked at Katey, an apology in his eyes that didn't need to be there. "Stay with For-rest. I won't be long."

He lifted his hand as if to touch her face, but curled his fingers away at the last minute and hurried through the locker room door. She had to stop herself from following. Just a door sepa-rated them, and it was too much.

"He's going to be fine," Forrest told her. "He's come out of worse."

She knew he had. The beating Darren and Dustin gave him earlier that week as punishment for turning her nearly destroyed him. The aftermath was much more devastating. But part of Katey still didn't believe him. The fight was brutal, and his body would definitely heal, but what about the wounds no one else could see?

"What's the likelihood that they're going to fight again?"

"Who knows. If Erik doesn't leave town, Darren may have a hard time keeping Logan from tracking him down."

Katey grimaced. "Did I... Did I do the wrong thing by stopping the fight?"

Forrest let out a long breath, lips drawing into a thin white line. The beats of silence that followed may have been the most honest answer. "We both would rather see Erik in pieces in a shallow hole somewhere... but you did the right thing."

It took Katey until this moment to remember what this fight would have meant to Forrest too. "Darren told me about Chicago... I'm so sorry about your cousin."

The hard lines softened, and he gave her a disarming smile. "Thank you... It was a long time ago."

Katey wrapped her arms around her stomach and felt the slick residue of blood on her sleeves where Logan had touched. "And your dad. Devia and all."

Forrest let out a light, disbelieving laugh. "They really told you everything, huh?"

"There's still a lot I don't know about."

"I don't think anyone knows absolutely everything about every-one's stories. We are entitled to some privacy."

Katey smirked, knowing he was completely right. "I just can't believe after all these years, it feels like I hardly knew you."

Forrest leaned against the wall and propped up one foot, some-thing she had seen him do a thousand times at the ballroom dance studio. "You knew what you needed to know at the time."

"Yes, nothing about being a mafia hitman from the 1920s, or the son of some big heroic martyr."

Forrest laughed, such a familiar sound. Just like Logan, he was the same man she knew before. Nothing changed. "Yeah, you still don't know much."

"What should I know?"

His smile reached his blue eyes. "That I'm still your friend, and that I'm here for both of you, no matter what."

Katey refused to cry in front of him, or show the full force of her gratitude. Even knowing what little she apparently knew, she couldn't change the way she felt about him, one of her oldest friends and her best friend's boyfriend... mate... whatever.

From the other side of the locker room door, Katey heard Logan in conversation with the loup-garou medic about what all he injured, what was healed, and what wasn't. The list was long, longer than Katey would have guessed.

"Logan rode with me, so I assume he's riding back with you?"

Katey leaned against the wall next to Forrest. "That would make sense."

They waited in silence, listening to the conversation wrap up and Logan turn on the shower faucet to wash away the blood and sweat. The medic exited the locker room a moment later.

"Where's the other guy?" he asked.

Forrest shrugged. "He took off. Haven't seen him."

The medic gave a nod, and glanced Katey's way, but gave a quick shake of his head as if he didn't trust his senses, then walked away with his unused medical bag.

"Am I going to get a lot of looks like that?" she asked Forrest.

"They did tell you how big of a deal you are, right?"

Katey snorted. "They hardly let me forget it."

Forrest gestured in the direction the medic walked. "That's why you will get looks like that from every new werewolf you meet for the rest of your life. Get used to it. Maybe come up with some one or two sentence explanation to cover the important details and move on."

"Right, I'll just say, 'My boyfriend didn't want to live without me, so here I am!'"

Forrest chuckled. "Something like that..." He regarded her with newfound amazement. "You know, I knew there was something special about you, but I didn't think it was this."

Katey cocked her head. "That's what the other guys said, too. Everyone sees something in me, and I just... don't. I never did. I don't get it."

He shrugged. "Maybe you're not supposed to 'get it' and just go with it."

The shower water cut off and Katey took a deep breath. "I don't know if I can. You know about all the shit I've been through. It's hard to think some sad little orphan girl could become... this." She swept a hand down her body as if revealing its existence for the first time. "It's like something out of a corny teen novel or something."

"Heroes come out of the most unlikely places." He thumbed toward the locker room door. "Take Logan for example. He's got balls for fighting Erik like that. Few of us are brave enough to do it."

"And he almost killed him."

"If he did, that's one less problem in the world."

The locker door opened and Logan stepped back into the hall, a duffle bag over one shoulder and dressed in a fresh pair of torn jeans and black shirt. His hair was damp, but pulled back at the nape of his neck as usual. He looked right at Katey, a hint of something contrite in his stare that made her wonder how much of their conversation he heard.

"Feel better?" Forrest asked.

Logan only nodded and stood in front of Katey. "Thanks for staying behind."

"Anything for you, man." Forrest gave his shoulder a friendly slap and moved around them to take his leave. "I'll catch up with you later. Are y'all still going to Alaska?"

Logan tilted his head back in aggravation. "Damn, I forgot... Yeah, we'll be there. We fly out in the morning."

Forrest grinned. "I bet you're going to sleep like a baby. I'll see you up there then."

With that, the redhead walked down the hall and back into the club, leaving Katey and Logan completely alone. Katey gave into every insistent urge in her body and threw her arms around Logan, squeezing him tight against her. He dropped his bag and didn't hesitate to envelope her in an equally tight embrace.

"I was so worried he was going to kill you." Katey buried her face in the place where his neck and shoulder met and listened to his thrumming heartbeat. She breathed in his fresh, clean scent, letting it seep into her, reassuring her that he was safe and alive.

"Not much can kill me." One hand came up to cup the back of her head, weaving his fingers through her hair. The other stayed fastened around her waist, entrapping her against him.

"I know, but I was still scared."

"I never meant to scare you."

"I know that too."

She pulled away to meet his gaze. In the dim light of the hall, she could see his bright blue eyes focused on her and only her, eyes full of longing and a touch of sadness. Katey felt his body press against hers and every contour of his muscles beneath his skin. She shivered, knowing he was so close and completely hers. No pack around to interrupt. Nothing outside of them existed and for a breathless moment, Katey forgot everything.

"I'm sorry for stopping the fight," she whispered. "I know it probably didn't resolve anything."

Logan smirked. "The fight was for you, not my friend."

She blinked. "But... doesn't me stopping it make it a draw or something?"

"Two things." Logan walked her backward until the wall stopped them. "Erik forfeited, and you made your choice. That ended the fight." He touched his forehead with hers and that spark of spiritual awareness zapped through her. "I win. You're mine."

Hot breath cascaded over her face as he bent lower, their noses nearly touching. Electricity, so intense and overpowering, surged through her, threatening to make her legs buckle. Her fingertips on his shoulders pressed into his flesh until she could feel the quivering of his muscles. Even if she went boneless, Logan was there to catch her. He'd always be there.

Logan's mouth came down upon hers and the universe exploded. She had never been kissed, never knew the consuming intimacy of anything beyond Logan's tender touches and embrace. If she had known that such powerful magic existed, she would have kissed him the first day they met in the cemetery.

As the kiss deepened with slow, careful exploration, Katey's soul soared as her body fell apart. Their hearts beat wildly against their chests as they melted into one another, unwilling to tear away. The ache, low in her belly, grew to a magnitude that she could barely contain as it spread down her legs and into her core to warm her blood. His hands gripped at her like his life depended on it, pulling her harder against him as her own fingers traveled the forbidden curves of his muscles, places she had only ever daydreamed about.

When Katey met Logan, he stitched back together the pieces of her that had been ripped apart. The dysfunctional families, the depression, the feelings of total abandonment and worthlessness was nothing to her once he came into her life. But in this kiss, their first, she felt the stitches come undone to reveal that she was truly whole once more. No more brokenness, no more despair. All that existed was the need for more of Logan, more of his loving touch that set her spirit on fire.

A tiny, almost imperceptible moan found its way out of her mouth and Logan's lips moved more urgently as if he were trying to consume every piece of her that she'd let him have. His hand spread across her back, then with frustrating slowness made its way to her hip, then her thigh, then the back of her knee, leaving a trail of stardust in his wake. With one easy, graceful pull, her leg was up and hooked over his hip, his heat radiating into hers. Katey let out a pleased sigh and he broke the kiss only long enough to descend upon her neck. The way he teased his tongue and teeth across her skin had her shuddering and gathering fistfuls of his shirt in her hands.

The hand in her hair snapped closed, thick locks caught between his fingers. She had to bite her lips together to keep silent as his other roaming hand swept up her thigh, drawing dangerously close to the seat of her jeans.

"Logan, we..."

Her hushed words got his attention, and he lifted his head from her neck. Crimson gazes locked, and the world came back into focus, despite her eyelids feeling heavy. If things kept going on this trajectory, they were liable to sneak away to the empty locker room.

As if waking up from a dream, the fire cooled in Logan's expression, and he made a concentrated effort to slow his breathing. "I'm sorry, I... You should probably slap me now."

Katey huffed a laugh and shook her head, "Never." She leaned forward to kiss him again, a sign that all was right, all was perfect. She kept it short and tame, feeling far more confident in the act than she would have been moments before.

Logan let down her leg and let his hands slide to places less dangerous. He slid his thumb across her jaw to settle on her chin. "We should probably go home."

Her body warmed again at the idea of it. Home. Their home. A place where she'd forever be safe, forever be loved by him.

CHAPTER 11

The drive home was considerably more tame. Logan held Katey's hand over the gear shift, fingers laced, while she filled him in on what happened that day at school. She guessed that he asked for the sole purpose to avoid talking about the fight and the kiss, because he seemed unfocused and only half-listening.

"And then Jared, that other Devian loup-garou, he did a cartwheel in the middle of the hallway and walked me the rest of the way to class on his hands."

Logan's brows bunched. "What?"

Katey smiled. "Just making sure you were paying attention."

"I am, I'm just... thinking about other things too."

"Like where Erik is likely hiding out in Crestucky?"

She heard the creak of the steering wheel leather and knew she just probed too deep. "Forget I said it," she followed up quickly.

"No, it's okay... You know me too well. That is what I was thinking about. I was going over in my head where he might be living and how best to do a search."

Katey squeezed his hand. "How about we not think or talk about that scumbag for the rest of the night, huh?"

Logan lifted her fingers to his lips to kiss her knuckles. "I can try... Jared didn't really do a handstand, right?"

She giggled. "No handstand. But he did keep me company between classes. It was nice of him."

"I'm sorry I left you the way I did. I didn't mean to make you worry or feel like I was abandoning you or something."

"You did make me feel that way, but I sort of get it. You needed to get your head in the right space to fight... you know who."

One corner of his mouth twitched upward, as if he were trying to smile. "Yeah, but that's no excuse for making you lonely."

They approached the house, every light downstairs still on to cover her escape.

"How did you get out of the house anyway?" he asked as they parked.

Katey then explained how Dustin gave her the directions before they left for Ben's shift.

"Remind me to thank him. When I saw you in the crowd, I..." Logan opened the front door for her. "Well, okay, I'll admit I was a little upset to see you there, but more relieved than upset."

"Everyone kept telling me that I didn't need to be there," she said as she entered the foyer. "Like I wouldn't be able to handle it or something."

Logan dropped her keys on the sideboard. "They likely knew you'd pull a stunt like you did and didn't want you to get hurt. I doubt any of them would have guessed you'd throw up enough dominance to stop a rougarou like... you know who."

Katey froze. "I did what?"

He gave her a puzzled look. "You used dominance on Erik... Isn't that what you intended to do?"

Her eyes went round at the thought of it. Maybe she did use dominance. "I don't know what I was doing. All I knew was I had to get you two to stop fighting and I just... thought really hard about it, I guess."

"There's a lot more to dominance than just thinking. It's a sheer act of willpower, and you've got a ton of it." Logan smirked and gave her a once-over. "Though, that shouldn't be a surprise to anyone who knows you."

"What's that supposed to mean?" She propped a hand on her hip.

Logan pointed at her. "That's what I mean. The attitude, the stubbornness, it's all there."

Katey gave him a drole look. "Who would have thought the thing that gets me kicked out of every foster home is what makes me a decent loup-garou."

Logan strode forward and caught her chin to plant a tender, sweet kiss on her lips. "Just as long as you don't abuse that fire. Darren will snuff it out in a heartbeat if you try to use it on him."

She melted into his touch and parted her lips, a silent beg for more.

"We should probably both get something to eat and head to bed. It's getting late and we've got that early flight in the morning."

Katey groaned and her shoulders slumped. "Don't remind me. I've never flown before. I'm really not looking forward to it."

He chuckled as they made their way toward the kitchen. "Don't tell me you're afraid of heights."

"Not the height, but the falling part."

Logan dropped his bag by the stairs. "Bright side is, if we crash, we'll be the only survivors."

"Not funny."

"You're right. It'd be a little hard to explain how we could walk away without a scratch while all the other passengers were torn to bits."

Katey smacked the back of her hand against his rock-hard abs and he chuckled. "Still not funny."

"All right, all right." He saddled up to the refrigerator. "My point is, you won't die, so there's nothing to worry about. "So, what do you feel like having? Deer? Cow? Chicken? Fish? I think we have some squirrel in here if you're interested in trying it. Too chewy for my taste, but Ben loves it."

Katey hopped up on the stretch of counter that separated the kitchen from the living room and swung her legs. She enjoyed this part of Logan, the funny, sarcastic, gentle Logan. She hadn't seen this side of him in so long she almost forgot it existed beneath all the angsty loup-garou rage.

"I'll have whatever you're having."

"Deer it is, then."

She watched him take out two frozen steaks of deer meat and thaw them in the microwave.

"We both will need to pack, too." Logan pulled down two glasses from the cabinet to fill with water. "Last time I waited until the morning to pack, I made us late and Darren was not a happy alpha."

"How long will we be up there?"

"Probably a week. At least through Christmas."

Katey went silent, wondering what Christmas with loups-garous would be like. Did they even celebrate it? Did they exchange gifts? If they did, she was slap out of money with no time to get anyone anything.

The microwave chimed and Logan fixed them their plates. He joined her on the counter and handed her plate to her without utensils.

"Uh... Fork and—" Before she could finish her sentence, the sight of Logan picking up his steak and tearing into it with his fangs made her stop.

It took him a few seconds to realize she was staring and then smiled, the slab of meat between his lips. "Too much?"

Katey rolled her eyes and hopped down to fetch utensils for herself. "Men are such animals," she teased.

"Maybe that's why only loups-garous are males. We're already wired the right way."

"And what does that say about me?"

Logan gave her another appraising look. "Maybe your feral side shows up in a different way."

As if that was an invitation, Katey turned on her best, simpering, hip-swaying look and moved to ease between his knees against the counter, leaving her dinner to the side. "Oh, and what's your theory of where that shows up?"

Instead of playing along, Logan sent a pulse of dominance, just enough to snap her out of the game and back to reality.

"Too much?" Katey stepped back and sagged against the kitchen island across from him.

"I walked into that one. My fault."

She turned her attention back to her late-night dinner and began to cut up the raw steak into bite size pieces. "Are we still being careful for the next few years, or did tonight change anything?"

Logan didn't respond right away as he thoughtfully chewed on his mouthful, half of the steak gone already. "I don't know. I haven't decided."

"You haven't decided? Do I get a say?"

"Well, what do you want?"

Katey met his blue, heartfelt gaze. "I want whatever is going to make sense, not piss everyone off, and give us what we want too."

Logan laughed. "Much easier said than done. All of those things likely contradict each other."

"A preliminary mating bond, maybe?"

He sighed. "How did I know that was stewing around in your head since Lily mentioned it."

"Wouldn't that be better than nothing?"

Logan's gaze went distant. "What we have right now is better than nothing, but if we keep pushing it, we might end up with nothing." He turned back to her. "I know you like labels and explanations for everything, but I'm way too tired to think of any better answer than, 'You're mine and I'm yours'.'... Is that enough for now?"

Katey felt a blush rise to her cheeks. It was more than enough to know she belonged to him. "Yeah, I guess so." But her girlish grin was anything but a placid reply.

They finished their food and made their way upstairs, a fresh wave of something dangerously close to the passion between them in the hallway at the fight club threatening to wash over her.

Logan turned to enter his room and paused, hand on the doorknob. Katey waited, holding her breath. They were completely and utterly alone in the house. The pack wouldn't be back until the morning. No one would know.

She shook her head to erase the thought. Her body may have wanted that, but she still had some common sense left to know it'd be reckless to have sex with Logan. There was a time when she thought that sort of casualness was what he wanted, but she knew better now. They needed to take it slow, and Logan was far more respectful than she thought she deserved.

That showed when he gave her one last look over his shoulder. "Good night, Katey." He entered and closed the door before either of them had a chance to change her mind.

Again, separation by a door was just as agonizing as if they were a thousand miles apart. It took every ounce of courage and strength to walk down the hall to her own room and put one more slab of wood between them.

After packing for Alaska and changing into her pajamas, Katey climbed into bed, under the covers and turned her back toward the door. She knew very well that if she watched the door, she would be tempted to walk out of it and back into his arms. Through their bond, she knew he felt the same.

She could hear every little movement from within his room. She could hear him taking clothes out of his drawers to stuff them in his luggage, his undressing, and then redressing for bed. She heard the rustle of bed sheets, the soft compression of springs in his mattress, his deep sigh as he settled against his pillow. All of it drove her imagination mad.

For the better part of an hour, Katey debated whether she should stay in bed and be miserable or go to Logan and at least sleep on his floor for the night. Just to be close, nearer than she was now, could have afforded her some relief.

Katey checked her phone and it was almost midnight. She sighed once more, admitted defeat and carefully tiptoed down the hall to Logan's door. Staring at his initials that were etched into the wood, she tried to summon the courage to knock. What if he turned her away? What if he let her in and they did something they would regret in the morning? Calling on her wolf for the bravery she needed most dearly, she sucked in a breath and tapped on the door with her fingernail.

It took a while, but soon she heard him rise from his bed to answer her call.

Logan stood there in only a pair of flannel pajamas, his torso bare and hot as ever, but he didn't even look remotely tired. Maybe he had been just as awake as she was, missing her just as she missed him.

"You okay?" Logan leaned against the doorframe in such a way that made heat rise up her neck.

Katey felt her breath seize in her lungs. She hadn't prepared anything to say. All she could think was that it was stupid for them to spend another moment apart in separate rooms. "Can I stay with you tonight?"

If there was a rejection coming, it fell dead in his chest. They stared at one another, Logan clearly calculating the risks. Whether he shared in her own sentiments, or if he just didn't have the heart to turn her away, he let her into his room anyway.

It was like walking into a cloud of his scent, so heady, warm, and comforting. In the dark, she could still see every detail as clear as day. The floor was clear of dirty clothes or other clutter, so unlike her own room.

Off to the left in the corner was a desk scattered with sketching materials and a lamp. Sketches covered the space above the desk, but her attention was drawn elsewhere for the moment. The furniture in the room was drastically different from everything else in the house. Every piece was masterfully crafted with various carvings.

Depictions of old feather quills, ink bottles, scrolls, parchment paper, and books spiraled down along the surface of the wooden legs on the desk. The tall headboard behind the bed portrayed a remarkable nature collage. In it were all kinds of predatory animals like wolves, bears, lions, tigers, and foxes. Katey thought she even saw a leopard. Every detail down to the tiny hairs along their faces and the contour of muscles were finely sculpted into the wood, giving the images a life of their own. The bedposts matched the headboard with the same type of animals, only on a smaller scale, climbing up the posts with their razor claws.

Logan let her wander about the room, his territory, and closed the door, plunging them into a thick, murky blackness. He turned on the overhead light and Katey could appreciate the subtle details of everything that much more.

She turned to the collage of sketches above his desk and her jaw went slack. Most of them were of a single woman. Some of them were portraits of her doing things like writing and staring aimlessly into the distance, some of her walking and talking with friends whose faces were shadowed out. It was clear Logan didn't want them to be the focal point of the sketch.

A special one that was featured in the center of the collage depicted her sitting with a pack of wolves lying on either side of her. Katey examined her features more carefully. She had long, dark, wavy hair and gentle, light-colored eyes. In every picture, she looked graceful, and her features were almost angelic.

It took her much longer than she cared to admit, to realize that the woman in every one of these sketches was her. The open sketchbook on the table showed his most recent work-in-progress. It was a sketch of three wolves. Two were growling and ready to leap onto the other, but the third was standing between them, as if trying to make peace. Had he predicted what would happen that night, or was it just a coincidence?

"Well, I guess we know who your muse is," she quipped.

Logan didn't respond, but sat on the edge of the bed and watched her.

Another piece of art caught her attention. At the base of his lamp sat a little wooden figurine of a howling wolf. She carefully reached over and picked it up to examine it. The smoothness of the wood surprised her. Not a single jagged edge or protruding splinter. It also looked old, as if it had been carved many years before.

"Did you make this?" she asked, fascinated by the details, from the wolf's fur to the realistic contour of the eyes.

"I did." Logan's voice heavy with something that Katey couldn't recognize. It had a tinge of nostalgia hidden beneath layers of desolation that sparked her interest.

"It's beautiful." She looked to the bed. "And the furniture?"

"I made it. I've made most of the bedroom furniture for the pack."

"Really? That must have taken forever."

Logan angled away to look at the headboard. "Not really. I think the whole room took only two weeks of my time."

"How did you get to become such an artist?" Katey asked, tracing her fingers along the edges of the desk.

"When I was younger... before I turned, I was a carpenter's assistant for a few years. When I turned, the skills became master level somehow, as did a lot of other things... I can make the same furniture for you if you'd like?"

"That'd be cool." Katey turned back to the sketches, mesmerized by how stunning and beautiful he made her seem. "Is this how you see me?"

"It is," he replied, voice carefully even.

"Before or after you turned me?"

"Before."

She huffed. "You just make me look so... perfect."

"You are."

Katey looked over her shoulder at Logan, who stared back with such intensity that she wondered just how far they would push their limits for one night. "I'm not perfect. Not even close."

Logan stood and came closer. "You are to me."

She had nothing to say to that, and even if she did, she didn't trust herself to say it. She wrapped her arms around her middle, willing her stomach to stop flipping for just a minute so she could think straight.

The way he walked to her, the way he looked at her, all of it screamed that he was about to take her up, throw her on the bed, and have his way with her. But something stopped him, and forced a step backward. Katey didn't dare move.

He cleared his throat. "Um... So, I'll sleep on the floor and you can sleep in my bed." He retreated back to the bed and grabbed up one of the pillows.

Katey sharply shook her head to snap her out of the daze he had put her in. "No, it's okay... um..." She paused in indecision and looked from the ground to his bed. Logan turned to Katey, alert to her next words. "The floor is really hard and that's not fair to you... We can both stay in the bed."

"Katey," Logan groaned. "I can't—"

"We don't have to do anything," she said quickly. "I'm not suggesting that we... I just can't stand to not be close to you. All I ask is to be near you and know you're there."

Katey had never dared to be this vulnerable to anyone, and she hoped Logan understood that.

He didn't say a word, but he put the pillow back in its place at the head of the bed and pulled the comforter out a bit so they could both slide in.

The fluttering in Katey's stomach doubled and she felt as if she'd come completely undone. She had never done this before, never dared to even think of it except with Logan. Now that it was actually happening, she couldn't chicken out.

Katey climbed under the warm covers, letting her bare feet brush against the crisp sheets and waited for Logan as he turned off the lights. She watched him glide through the darkness and slip into the bed next to her. She wondered if he could hear her pounding heart within her chest as he lowered himself down onto the mattress.

They faced each other, both anxious to get closer. All she could think about was how his eyes reminded her of the wide open sky, and that his familiar scent was the closest thing to home she knew. Nothing about this seemed wrong to her. It only scared her that it seemed too right.

Logan was the first to move as he shifted a little closer to close the gap between them. Katey scooted herself in as well and before long, their bodies were just barely touching one another. She silently willed herself to be still, but calm was nearly impossible while he was so dangerously close.

Logan's arm carefully wrapped around her waist. Katey pushed herself in closer and Logan's leg entwined itself around hers, drawing her into him. She couldn't help but inwardly remark that they fit together so snug, like two puzzle pieces perfectly meant for each other.

"Is this okay?" he whispered, his breath hot on her face and engulfing her senses.

"Yes." Every bit of tension and unease vanished against the feeling of total perfection. This was more than enough.

Their foreheads touched and Logan's nose faintly brushed with hers, breathing deeply as his eyes drifted shut. Katey knew that he could sense the same thing that she did, that grand sense of completeness that only existed when they were with one another. It thrilled her and yet, soothed her spirit all at the same time. Even her wolf felt like this was right and glowed with gladness.

Katey watched as he breathed in and out in a deep steady rhythm. It was dark, but not too dark that she couldn't search every detail of his face.

"I'm so... so tired of fighting," he said. Words spilled out in a grand confession. "I feel like I've been fighting since the day I was born. Fighting my father, fighting the wolf, Darren, myself, the past, my future... I'm just so tired." Every word dripped with that bone-deep weariness he must have suffered all his life.

Logan opened his eyes, burning bright in the darkness. His hand found its way to her hair and his fingers weaved through the wavy locks. "But with you, I don't have to. In you, I can finally rest and breathe, and just exist without struggling for every damn second. I know it sounds so selfish, but I can't imagine losing you. Not to death, not to Erik, not to anything... I'd do anything to keep you... because I love you."

Since the day they met, she wondered why Logan would waste his time on her. With every compliment he gave, every kind gesture he performed, Katey asked herself why he would take the time for a person like her. Why would he choose to be with a girl like her when he could have had any girl on the planet. She was an orphan, a nobody, but now she understood. His love slowly made her into somebody, and he deserved to know it.

"You have been the closest thing to home I have ever felt. All my life, I've just been passed around from one family to the next, never belonging anywhere or to anyone. Here, with you, this is where I fit, where I want to stay. You make me feel seen and heard. When it feels like no one gives two shits about me or what I do, you show me every day that you care." Katey let the back of her hand rest against his chest, feeling his rapid heartbeat against her bones. "I guess I'm a little selfish too, because I never want to lose this feeling of being yours and only yours..." She took a breath to say the words her soul had been screaming for what seemed like an eternity. "I love you, too."

Finally, she knew what this was. She had a word to call it by, and she understood the whys behind it. He was right when he said that she wanted labels, she needed a clear definition, and she had it. They were in love, and that was finally enough. Everything else could wait.

Logan's eyes drifted shut and he pulled her in, so their foreheads touched. That sparkle of soulful harmony languidly poured through her, a welcome release after weeks of chaos and struggle. They rested in one another, and peace finally came to settle over Katey's troubled heart in a spectacular moment of bliss. She prayed it would last forever. There were many more years to live and many more challenges to face, but they had each other. That would never change.

CHAPTER 12

Logan couldn't remember the last time he slept so deeply. No tossing, no turning, no tangling the blanket, or soaking the sheets with fevered dreams. There was only Katey, safe in his arms, and a comatose wolf tucked away in the back corner of his mind. He wasn't sure he could ever go back to sleeping alone after that night.

A sliver of gray dawn fell across his bed through the partially closed curtains. He cracked open his eyes and studied the serene look on Katey's face. In sleep, nothing was complicated, nothing troubling. Through their bond, he knew she had never slept better either.

From outside, he heard the quiet sounds of the coming morning, and the approach of the pack from the woods. He should have been worried when they came inside through the sliding glass doors off the back patio, but nothing could touch the peace Katey gave him. Not even when they made their way upstairs and realized Katey and Logan were sharing a bed.

Beneath his arm, Katey stirred, her brows pinched as if she were about to wake. Logan pulled her closer and shushed her like she was a baby ready to let out a cry. He wanted this for just a little longer and they weren't going to take it away from him.

"Logan. Out here. Now." Darren's hushed voice might as well have been like a gunshot.

Katey's eyes shot open, and a tremor of panic sizzled between them. Logan knotted the back of her shirt in his fist to keep her still.

In the hall, Dustin and Ben went about cleaning up from the night before. Ben was in the shower first. Only Darren remained like a sentinel outside Logan's room, waiting. The alpha gave his order again, this time a little louder and with more authority behind the words.

Katey tried to push up on her elbow, but Logan's hold kept her against the mattress.

"Logan, you have to go."

He shook his head and pulled her tight against him like a child unwilling to give up their favorite toy. "No." The rumbled answer was directed to both her and their alpha.

Darren let out a low growl and, as predicted, dominance rolled under the bedroom door like asphyxiating smoke. Logan wanted to be mad, but under Katey's beseeching gaze, he couldn't bring himself to growl back or assert his right over this moment with Katey.

He gave it one more moment, then admitted defeat. They would have to leave the room eventually. He pushed back the comforter and gave Katey a muted command to stay put.

He closed the bedroom door behind him to face his alpha. Darren's arms were folded, disappointment written in the stern lines of his face. Dustin came out of his own room with a spare set of clothes in his hand, but he seemed unruffled by the whole affair.

"Would you mind explaining yourself?"

He knew what Darren meant, but Logan only shook his head. "Nothing happened."

Dustin came closer and took a sniff. "He's telling the truth. I don't smell it on him."

Logan gave the beta a wry look. "I guess I should be thankful you can tell the difference."

Darren inspected the both of them, then visibly relaxed. Perhaps it was too much to assume he would understand their need to be together and that sex didn't have to be involved. "Good. Are you both packed?"

"Packed last night."

"We leave in a couple of hours. Make sure she's ready." A new wave of concern came over Darren. "The fight?"

Logan remembered that they didn't know Katey had gone to the club. He had to be careful how much he told them. "Erik forfeited."

"Looks like you came out of it all right," Dustin said, looking him up and down. "Was it rough?"

Logan's memory was a little spotty. The wolf took over for the majority of the fight and only Katey's interference pulled him back from the brink of losing himself completely. The shoulder hold Erik had subjected him to had changed his plans to keep the wolf away, and everything spun out of control from there. When they were alone, he would have to thank Dustin for letting Katey sneak out. If she hadn't come, there was no telling how the fight would have ended. He wasn't concerned for Erik, but for the innocent bystanders that would have been caught in the crossfire.

"There were a few close calls."

"But you won?"

Logan smirked. "Yeah. Not the way I wanted, but I won."

Darren's brow lifted. "Let's be glad it didn't end the way you wanted. Not so easy to hide murder in a warehouse full of spectators."

"He could have claimed self-defense." Dustin shrugged as the patter of water on the shower floor abruptly cut off and metal hooks squealed against he curtain rod.

"Unlikely. How was Katey when you came home?"

Logan didn't have the energy to lie, but thankfully Dustin cut in to do the job for him.

"Oh, I'm sure she was thrilled to see him after the hell of a day she had." He looked at Logan. "I don't recommend you do that to her again."

That comment had a double edge. Don't leave her again, and don't make her worry like that again. If she suffered even half as much as he did because of their distance, she was definitely in hell. Logan had the luxury of pouring himself into a punching bag, but she had no one.

"I don't plan to."

After last night, after all they said to one another, Logan had plenty of new plans for him and Katey. It would only be a matter of time before they could have one another in every way they wanted. For the first time in a long time, Logan actually looked forward to the future, because all he saw in it was Katey.

Logan gave his pack a sly look. "Now, if you'll excuse me, I have a beautiful woman waiting in my bed."

Dustin let out a great belly laugh, but Darren was not amused.

He grabbed Logan's loose ponytail and yanked him away from the door. "You two need to get ready to go. That means getting dressed, eating breakfast, and being downstairs with your luggage. Do you understand?"

Logan allowed the rough treatment but sneered over his shoulder at his alpha. "Yes, sir."

Once released, Logan returned to his room and locked the door behind him. Katey was already sitting up, arms wrapped around her knees and giving him a "You should know better" look, eyes bright and brown hair messed from sleep. He ignored the silent reprimand and pounced onto the mattress. With one arm, he pulled her down onto her back and smothered her giggle with a kiss.

Her lips parted, inviting him in for a deeper experience, and he gladly accepted. Gentle hands settled on his biceps, fingertips soft against his bare skin. Never in the last century would he have dreamed that a woman as beautiful and amazing as Katey would touch him like that.

Logan paused when she lightly pushed against him. He eased back to let his nose affectionately brush against hers, a smile permanently fixed on his face.

"We should probably get up," she whispered, breath sweet and hot.

"They can wait a few more minutes." Logan supported himself on one elbow as his free hand savored the landscape of her body. He knew his eyes were blood red by now and so were hers.

"I don't want you to get in trouble." Katey's voice held an almost dreamily quality, and she emitted her own potent scent of arousal to tell him he hit all the right places from her shoulder to her thigh.

"You wanna know what I told the pack when I asked about turning you?" Logan leaned down so his lips brushed the shell of her ear in an intimate whisper. "I reminded them that they all had the chance for something good in their lives, and they had no right to deny me my own happiness. Therefore..." His mouth lowered to the sensitive skin just under her jaw, "they can wait while I take my moment of happiness."

Katey arched against him and bit back a moan that vibrated against his cheek. There was no way she wouldn't be able to feel what that little sound did to him, with only the thin, soft fabric of their pajama pants between them. He knew this couldn't progress into dangerous territory with the pack within earshot, but they could get close.

Her hands traveled down the slope of his back as he kissed and licked paths down her jaw, across her neck and to her collarbone, savoring the taste of her, letting her scent swallow him whole. When his hand gripped her ass to pull her tight against him, her claws suddenly came out and sunk into the flesh around his ribs.

Logan jerked away and gave a stifled growl of pain.

Katey instantly shrank beneath him, every inch of her recoiled. "Oh my God, I'm so sorry!"

From somewhere downstairs, he heard Dustin burst into a peel of vulgar laughter and Ben mumbled, "Serves him right."

Logan bit his tongue to hold back the curses Katey didn't deserve. It wasn't her fault, and maybe Ben was a little right. The holes she made in his skin and muscles closed up quickly, leaving behind ten rolling droplets of blood on his back.

"It's all right. No harm done." He stayed there, suspended over Katey to give her plenty of space. "That may be our cue to stop."

He hated the subtle odor of fear supplanting her passion. "Is that the reason we need to wait until after my training is done?"

Logan breathed away the last of the red in his eyes. "One of them." He rolled to the side, being careful not to let the blood smear on the sheets. "I'd be just as likely to do something like that, though. Don't feel bad."

Katey sat up and he felt her gaze follow him as he looked for something to wipe away the blood. She didn't have to say a word to convey the blend of feelings that pumped through their bond. She didn't believe him that it was all right, just like she didn't believe him all the other times she lost control. She took her inexperience so personal, like she was a failure because of just one slipup. After a couple of decades, hopefully she'd get used to it. If she continually beat herself up for accidentally letting her wolf off its leash, she'd never have the confidence to wield that outstanding dominance he witnessed in her the night before.

Once he found a rag in his desk drawer and cleaned up his blood, he came back to Katey's side. With one swift move, he slid his hand behind her neck and tilted her into a tender kiss to convince her that there was nothing she could do to deter him. She could break his nose, slash open her throat, mar his face, and stab him with her claws, and he would never love her any less.

Just in case she still needed it, he murmured, "I still love you." He knew she would need that constant encouragement, and he was all right with that. Whatever she needed to feel safe and loved, he'd do it. She was worth it.

Katey grinned, high on their kiss. "I still love you too."

Logan stroked the tiny hairs along the back of her neck, making her shiver. "However, we do have a plane to catch."

They arrived at the airport with enough time to make their way through the security checkpoints. They parked Dustin's red truck in the extended stay parking garage and each of the loups-garous took their own luggage while Logan grabbed both his and Katey's.

"I can get my own bag," Katey protested as they made their way inside the local airport.

"No, I've got it." Logan slid her a wink that made her blush. She let it go and followed him through the automatic doors to the ticket counter to check in their luggage.

Katey stayed close to her pack, looking around at the other flyers that were heading out that morning and hoping no one would notice a teenager traveling with four men and assume things. She hugged against her stomach the thick white coat Darren had given her before they left the house. The alpha had guessed correctly that she'd have nothing that could stand up to the extreme cold of Alaska, so earlier that week, he purchased the coat, a matching pair of gloves, and a thick knitted stocking cap for her to keep.

When Darren finished checking in all five suitcases and made sure they were under the poundage limit, he led them toward the security check-in. Each of them had carry-on luggage that would need to be inspected. Katey and Logan shared a bag packed with things to keep them busy on the long flight.

Darren distributed their boarding passes. "We've got a layover in Dallas, then Phoenix, and it's straight on to Alaska from there. We should arrive at about nine o'clock Alaskan time."

Katey quickly did the math and figured that meant a six-teen-hour flight.

"Are we staying in a hotel or something once we get there?" she asked.

"Sort of," Logan replied. "It's a lodge resort that's maintained by the pack that hosts the gathering. It's just outside the national park. Most of the attending packs and their families will be staying in that lodge." He took her hand in his as they waited in line.

She glanced to the pack to see if they noticed Logan holding her hand. If they did, they didn't seem to mind. Breakfast had been far less awkward than she anticipated. No one asked her why she had stayed the night in Logan's room and they didn't treat her any differently. She wanted to interpret it as a sign of approval, but she knew better than to assume it. For all she knew, Darren was just itching to give her a lecture about the dangers of intimacy as a loup-garou.

"Sounds like a big place if it can hold that many packs and their families."

"It is," Darren replied, turning to face them. "We'll be sharing a suite with an old friend and his sons. We'll all be sharing rooms, so it may be a tight fit, but comfortable."

Katey blanched at the idea of sharing a room with a stranger, but Logan squeezed her fingers to draw her out of the thought.

"If it's the same room we had last year," Dustin commented as they inched forward in the line. "They'll have a game room, kitchen, and a fireplace. Very cozy."

Ben, who had looked half-dead all morning, sat on his heels and rubbed at his face and bloodshot eyes. Dustin stepped closer and watched him, but offered no words or gestures. Katey half expected him to knock Ben off his balance, but the beta only stood, as if guarding his packmate.

"You okay?" Katey asked.

Ben let out a heavy breath and nodded. "Just tired."

Logan bent his head low so their conversation was private to any human ears. "Shifts take a lot out of us. He'll be better if he can catch some sleep on the plane."

The group passed through security without any trouble. After they re-stuffed their pockets, slipped on their shoes, and fastened their belts, the pack exited security to find their gate. Along the way, Katey listened to their exchange of stories from previous trips and harrowing experiences through other airports across the country.

The closer they came to the terminals, the louder the plane engines roared in her ears. It only became worse when they boarded and the only thing that separated them from the plane was the gangway tunnel that connected the terminal doors to the plane itself. Her head throbbed and after a while, she couldn't even hear anything above the jet engines.

The plane was more cramped than she had imagined, but big enough to accommodate four passengers in a row. Darren and Dustin sat together in one set of double seats near the front, while Ben sat next to them in the opposite row with a businessman who was busy tapping away at his laptop keyboard. Logan and Katey sat next to each other near the back.

Katey thought the combination of the noise and confined space would send her wolf into a frenzy, but surprisingly, she hadn't heard a peep out of the beast since they left the house. It might have worried her, but at a time like this, she was glad for a little peace.

She was vaguely aware that Logan had said something to her, but over the deafening roar of the engines, she only saw his lips move. He turned to her, waiting, and she only pointed to her ear and shook her head. Her pained expression was enough and he nodded in understanding. Instead of trying to repeat his question louder, he motioned to her then the window seat.

The thought of looking to her left and seeing an immeasurable drop to the ground below made her stomach clench. She shook her head and tried to remind him of her fear of heights through the pack bond. He understood, smirked, and then moved in to take the window seat instead, so she could have the aisle seat.

As they settled in and Katey fastened her seatbelt a smidge too tight across her lap for good measure, Logan pulled out a cloth pouch from his jacket pocket and uncinched the cord that kept it closed. He shook out two pairs of foam pellets and handed one pair to Katey. She wasn't sure earplugs would do a damned thing against the earsplitting noise, but she humored him.

The difference was remarkable and Katey almost likened it to her human level of hearing, something she didn't expect to miss so dearly. She let out a long sigh as if she had just slipped into a hot, relaxing bath.

"These were made by the same guy that made the hunger suppressors." Logan slipped in his own pair. "They're designed just for us for situations like this. I figured you'd need them."

"Thank you." Katey leaned over and kissed his cheek.

It felt like it took forever before all passengers were on board, the flight attendants did their safety spiel, and the plane began taxiing out to the runway. As the plane began to take off, Katey gripped the edges of her armrests so tightly that she could feel the metal bend beneath her fingers. She squeezed her eyes shut and tried to breathe normally as she felt the plane lift off the tarmac.

Sensing her distress, Logan carefully pried her hand away from the armrest closest to him. "Hold my hand. Can't risk damaging the plane."

So, Katey transferred her hand eagerly into his, and she instantly felt his bones crack beneath her grip.

He winced and Katey quickly let go. "Oh! Sorry!"

Logan grunted and flexed his fingers. "It's fine... Already healed. See?" He took hold of her hand once more and this time, Katey tried not to grab too hard. "Just relax and it'll be over before you know it. I tend to sleep on long flights. Ben is nervous about flying, too, and normally takes something to knock himself out, but I think he's so exhausted from last night he won't need anything. I think Darren has them in his bag if you want to try it."

For a moment, Katey considered it. If the drug was powerful enough to render a strong loup-garou unconscious, then it might have been potent enough to keep her nerves under control.

She shook her head, eyes fixed upon the seat in front of her as she took her deep soothing breaths. "No, I'll be all right."

Logan was dubious. He lifted up the armrest that separated them before wrapping his arm securely around her waist. The edge of the seatbelt bit in her hips as he pulled her close. "Would this help?"

A substantial chunk of her anxiety melted away in his embrace and she nodded. "A little."

She leaned her head against his shoulder and closed her eyes to try and rest as the turbulence of the flight tickled at her stomach.

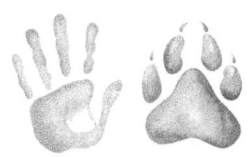

When they landed in Dallas, they exited the plane and Darren told the others that they had an hour layover. Darren read a magazine at their next gate as they waited, Dustin went off to shop in the convenience stores, and Ben was in charge of getting food from a restaurant inside the terminal in hopes of finding one that employed a loup-garou.

Within sight of their alpha, Logan and Katey settled themselves at the boarding gate. He sat with his back to the wall and Katey settled herself between his legs, nestled safely in his arms like two puzzle pieces joined together. Logan pulled out the book he had been reading during the flight and opened it up in front of Katey, his head hovering just over her shoulder so he could continue reading. She read along, mostly out of boredom and lack of anything else to do.

When Ben came back with five takeout boxes from a Chinese restaurant and a plastic bag from a convenience store weighted heavily by bottles of water.

After dropping off two boxes and three drinks with Darren, he approached and handed one box to Logan that smelled distinctly of pork and spice, along with the last of the water bottles.

"Chicken or steak?" Ben asked Katey, holding up the remaining two Styrofoam boxes.

Katey wasn't a fan of Chinese in general, but wouldn't complain when she was already hungry. "Chicken."

He passed off the box filled with teriyaki chicken and took the steak for himself back to sit beside Darren.

Katey and Logan didn't get up to join them. It was amusing trying to coordinate their arms and movements, so they didn't hit or spill the contents of the boxes on each other as they attempted to eat. Occasionally, Logan would share a bit of his black pepper pork to Katey, and she'd do the same with her chicken. She remembered how she'd see couples doing similar mushy stuff and roll her eyes. Lily and Forrest were that way, and she had always been glad for them, but would often walk away or make herself scarce when they got too effusive. Now, she finally got it. Doing these little silly things with Logan was fun. Wasn't that the point of being in love?

Dustin had come back from his window shopping some time after Ben returned with food. Katey saw that he ate some, but soon got up and came over to sit on the armrest of the bench in front of them. He pushed his meat around in the Styrofoam tray with his plastic fork. "So, I guess you two are serious now, huh?"

Katey didn't want to speak for them, so she stayed quiet and took another forkful of teriyaki chicken into her mouth.

"Yeah," Logan replied. "Any problem with that?"

The challenging tone and the way he leaned forward, his chest pressing into her back, all screamed unwarranted protectiveness. Dustin, despite looking like he was in his early thirties, was Logan's grandfather. He wasn't making a move, so there was no need to be so territorial, but maybe Logan braced for a similar lecture about rules and safety that Katey expected from Darren.

Dustin didn't appear offended. "Oh, no. I'm the last person that'll have an issue with all this." He twirled his fork at them. "Probably a good thing you two are finally hooking up in time for this trip. It'll make things less... tense."

Katey's brows puckered. "What do you mean?"

Dustin waited to swallow the bit of orange chicken before answering. "It's going to sound sick, but unclaimed females at gatherings like this can make unmated loups-garous a little rowdy. You'll see plenty of wives and girlfriends wandering around, and probably some younger girls, but no one of mate-able age. They get left at home."

Imagination conjured a scene of young loup-garou boys like the ones she met at school, brawling over a single girl for mating rights. Part of that seemed comical, but Katey knew such fights must have been serious and could very well end in death if they weren't careful.

"So, we don't need a preliminary mating bond for people to know I'm Logan's?"

Dustin nearly choked on his next bite and gave a fierce look at Logan. "How does she know about that?"

"Lily and Forrest."

The beta rolled his eyes. "Figures. Don't worry about any of that, Katey. If Logan keeps hanging all over you, that'll be enough for most."

"But not all?"

He wagged his head. "It's complicated. We can talk about that part later. Finish your lunch."

Oh, how she hated to be brushed off like that. Logan used to throw her that line so often that she was sure she'd never learn anything. She wanted to get up and take Dustin's food from him until he explained exactly what he meant, but Logan likely sensed her irritation and hooked his legs over top of hers to keep her seated. His thighs hugged her own and she was sure she'd burn up from the heat of his body.

"It's probably nothing to worry about," Logan murmured in her ear. "I'll make sure someone explains it later."

Alarm streaked through her. That told her that not even Logan knew what Dustin was talking about. This was too far out of the realm of his own expertise. She tried not to let it bother her as she kept eating.

Dustin then proceeded to go over some rules of basic etiquette, most of which she felt was common sense and didn't need explaining. Don't talk to a loup-garou she didn't know, do what she's told without question, especially when in a serious situation, and don't start a fight she couldn't finish.

"That means don't start any fights," Logan added as he set aside his empty tray.

Katey bristled. "I could probably hold my own in a fight if I really put my mind to it."

Dustin closed his container. "We aren't worried about you. That first day of training proved that enough. We'd be worried about the other guy. So, finishing a fight is when both combatants walk away of their own strength and something is resolved."

"What if someone tries to pick a fight with me?"

Logan wrapped his arms around her waist and pulled her back against him. "Then they'll have me to deal with."

The mock-sinister cadence of his answer made her smile, but the furious nuzzle of his face against her neck, growling like he was devouring her, coaxed it into a giggle.

When she looked up to Dustin, she noticed a sudden change. A dull, haunted, vacant stare transformed his face. She had only ever seen him mad or in some permanent attitude like all life was one humorous game. This was different, and startling.

"You okay?"

Dustin snapped out of it and a piece of his old self came back into place. "Yeah. You too are making me nauseous with all that gushy stuff." He gave a flippant wave, his smile perfectly crafted to throw them off the truth, but Katey knew better.

He stood and went to join Darren and Ben on the other side of the gate waiting area after throwing away his empty tray.

"What was that?" she whispered to Logan.

"What was what?"

Katey watched Dustin settle next to Darren in a chair and lean over to talk to the alpha in low, imperceptible tones. That dark emotion was completely gone now, but it made her wonder if they needed to settle down.

Not once did she ever consider how a relationship with Logan would affect the pack. What Logan said that morning came back to her. They all had their happiness, they all had their chance at love. They must have all had mates or wives at some point, but what happened to them? Clearly, they had been human, and they were no longer in the picture, but what was their story? Was it something so tragic that the love Katey and Logan shared would make the rest of the pack sad?

Katey sat up straight, putting some distance between herself and Logan. It might as well have been like a canyon suddenly severing the earth apart.

"Maybe we should be careful about the PDA."

Logan almost looked wounded by her suggestion. Then, his gaze darted to their packmates, and he seemed to understand.

The tension in his face softened. "I see... Have I ever told you that I love how much you care?"

Katey smiled. "I probably care too much."

Logan leaned closer to kiss the edge of her jaw. "No. Just enough. You're right." He rubbed her arms and shifted out from behind her to sit next to her instead.

A chill swept down her back at his absence and she felt like whining. He compensated by hanging his arm around her shoulders and planted another kiss on her temple.

"I can be respectful to their pasts, but don't think I'll go easy if I see one young pup make eyes at you in Alaska. You're mine and everyone's going to know it."

Katey grinned and squirmed at the delicious way his possessiveness made her feel. To be his in every way was all she wanted, all she could think about for weeks. She finally had it, and she was determined to never let anyone take that from her.

CHAPTER 13

Katey couldn't express her relief enough when they finally landed in Fairbanks. It was dark outside the airplane windows, but she could see the subtle moonlit glow off the banks of snow around the tarmac as they taxied in.

It finally hit her how far she was from home. Katey had never seen snow before since she had never traveled any farther north than Alabama and farther west then Mississippi. She wondered how different Alaska would be compared to Florida, besides the snow and bitter cold.

With Katey's hand firmly clasped in Logan's, they all exited the plane and made their way to the baggage claim.

Through her sleepy haze, Katey got that familiar twinge in the back of her skull that was so intense she could hardly think straight. She looked up as they entered the place where row upon row of conveyor belts continuously rotated luggage for passengers to claim and saw that she was surrounded.

Everywhere, she could feel eyes turn and fix on her, the eyes of loups-garous from all over the country. She saw some were alone, some with their wives and kids, and some were traveling strictly with their own pack, indicative of the way groups of men walked together and gathered up their luggage. Some appeared rather young, just in their teen years. Others sported shocks of gray and silver and were much older than Darren. The only common trait amongst them, was their solid builds, just like her own pack. She remembered how she heard rumors float around that Darren must have worked out after school to get so buff, for a teacher. Now, she knew it had more to do with his loup-garou genes than any workout routine, and the same went for every loup-garou she had come across so far.

Katey stared blankly at the awesome sight, feeling a general uneasiness rise up in her. Never had she seen so many of them in one place. The biggest crowd she had seen was the other day at lunch when she and Logan sat with the Deviants. It seemed like not one soul in that baggage claim was a lone human that had no connection with the loups-garous.

As her pack made their way through the crowd, the other loups-garous did doubletakes with curious stares. She tried not to meet their gazes, but found it difficult. It was like they instinctively knew what she was without having to ask. Part of her thought that if they all felt that prickling feeling to tell them another loup-garou was near, they may not be able to pinpoint it to her, if she were enveloped by her pack on all sides. Forrest warned her that she'd get this sort of attention, but now that she was in the midst of it, she hated it. Katey wanted nothing more than to turn around and get back on a flight to Crestucky, fear of heights or not.

Katey clung to Logan like a shy child as they waited for their bags to show up on the carousel, her eyes gawking at all of the loups-garous that started to mutter and whisper about her to their travel companions. Some voices portrayed heavy accents from around the country and others spoke in foreign languages like French and Italian. She wanted them to have good opinions, but she had no clue what they could have truly been thinking. She felt as if she were on display, like a freak of nature, there for everyone to stare and point at.

Logan settled his arm around her waist and tried to get her attention as Katey nervously scanned the room. "Hey, you're shaking. It's all right."

She pressed herself into Logan's side to seek comfort, her nerves in tangled knots. "I feel like a sheep among wolves."

"Don't worry. You're a wolf in sheep's clothing just like the rest of us," he whispered and pulled her closer to kiss her forehead.

"You sound so sad when you say it like that."

"Well, it's true. Besides, you have nothing to fear from them. You're one of the pack now, remember?" he said softly into her hair.

It was then she realized that she and Logan stood in the center of the pack, with Darren, Dustin, and Ben around them like a bodyguard detail. Did they mean to do that, or was it instinctual?

Ben got the pack's attention that their luggage was making its way on the conveyor belt. The guys swiftly grabbed theirs and easily hauled them onto the floor as other loups-garous shuffled in to grab up their own.

Logan guided her over to the carousel and pulled out their luggage before hurrying after the rest of the pack making their way to the exit. Katey never let herself be more than a foot away from him, unnecessarily afraid that she would lose him in the crowd or that one of the other loups-garous would snatch her away.

"Let's go, kids," Darren called from the glass doors that led out to the carpool lane.

Logan opened up the flap of his carryon where they had stashed Katey's new coat. "You might want to slip this on now. It's pretty cold out there."

Katey gently took it from his hands and shrugged it on over her hoodie, zipping it closed. She then slipped on the gloves and the hat, feeling entirely overdressed already. Logan carried her bag for her as they stepped outside to join the others on the slightly crowded sidewalk to wait for their shuttle bus. It was an hour's drive to the lodge, but Darren told them a fleet of vans were making the circuit to pick up loups-garous that flew in that evening.

It was colder than anything Katey had ever experienced before. The coat just kept out the wintry weather that stung her cheeks as the wind whipped through the carpool lane. Her bones felt as if they would freeze and break at any moment. Katey noticed that no one else in her pack seemed the least bit fazed, even though they were wearing even less than she was.

Logan glanced over to Katey. "Something wrong?"

"Why am I so cold? No one else looks cold." She tried her best to keep her teeth from chattering as they walked a little further down the covered walkway.

"I don't know. Maybe you're just not acclimating quickly enough. Darren said you may not adapt as well to the weather as we would since you've never been to some place this cold before.

It then occurred to her that she still didn't feel her wolf. She had gone almost the entire day without feeling the smallest stirring or impulse from the wolf, not through two whole plane flights, or after hurrying through busy airports. All that stress should have done something. She could still feel the wolf inside her, but it was like it was sleeping or dormant. It was just there, not doing anything, or feeling anything with her as it once did.

Maybe it was just a byproduct of being with Logan. He was a force of calm and peace to her. Maybe being so close and spending a whole night in his bed had sedated her wolf, and therefore suppressed some of her abilities. Then again, what if it was a sign of something else. Anxiety rose up like acid in her throat. Katey didn't like the idea that her loup-garou abilities could have been diminishing. It meant that maybe she wasn't a full loup-garou somehow.

"What if it's starting to fade?" she asked, keeping her voice low so only Logan would hear her.

"I'm sure you're fine. Don't worry about it."

"But what if—"

Logan turned on her suddenly and she saw his eyes flash gold. "Don't worry about it," he growled. She could tell that he didn't like the idea either.

Katey took a cautious step back but didn't let her gaze drop. He took a deep breath and blinked hard to crush his flair of temper.

"I'm sorry. I'm just a little hungry. Come here." Logan dropped their bags and pulled Katey into a tight, apologetic hug. In his arms, he projected more warmth that she gratefully accepted as the tips of her fingers went numb beneath her gloves.

Dustin stood not too far away and must have sensed the trouble. "We'll get some food as soon as we get to the lodge."

They didn't have to wait too much longer for the next shuttle bus to pull up along the curb. The bus had enough seats for at least two dozen passengers, three seats per row on both sides of the bus, and a rack for just as many pieces of luggage.

Before Katey and Logan could board the shuttle bus, Darren held them back. "Sit in the back row. Don't make eye contact."

His whispered warnings made Katey's stomach flip. She wanted to ask why, but the alpha broke away before she had the chance. The pack loaded up, tossed up their luggage on the rack, and occupied the second to the last row on one side. Behind them, Katey took the window seat with Logan beside her, and their carry-on in the open seat. She was perfectly buffered from the rest of the loups-garous, but that didn't keep them from ogling at the elephant on the bus.

Katey reflexively slunk in her chair as the bus lurched and rocked on the way to the resort. As Logan had done long ago in Darren's classroom, he leaned in such a way that most of his body hovered close to hers. She recognized it now as declaring his claim over her, letting them all know that she was under his protection. Then, she noticed Darren, Dustin, and Ben also made shows if some possessiveness by leaning elbows on knees as if ready to bolt up at the first sign of trouble or draping theirs arms across the back of their chairs, and shooting daggers with their eyes at the wandering gazes of the loups-garous. A touch of dominance shielded them. Just like at baggage claim, they surrounded her. No one would dare make a move without going head-to-head with her pack.

As soon as they all settled, the other loups-garous didn't look their way again, and their conversations switched to anything but the female loup-garou. Katey was the safest person on the bus, but she still felt so out of place.

Instead of stressing herself over how much worse it'll be at the resort lodge, Katey stared out the window, watching the fields of snow and veils of trees rush past her view. Only a sheet of glass separated her from a winter wonderland of pristine nature, and still, the wolf in her did nothing. She tried not to worry, as Logan so adamantly insisted, but it was nearly impossible. Maybe it was normal. Maybe the wolf wasn't constantly tangible, or this was a good sign that her control was improving. Yet, the voices came back to taunt her.

Not good enough. Don't belong. Waste of time. Burden.

Katey squeezed her eyes shut against the urge to cry. Not here. Not in front of everyone.

Logan's arm settled around her waist and leaned his forehead against her temple, likely sensing her growing anxiety. She let herself relax in his embrace and hoped that whatever this was, it'd resolve itself before she had to ask for help.

They arrived at the resort lodge an hour later, and everyone piled out of the van onto the walkway, freshly cleared of snow. Katey gaped up at what looked like a massive cabin-like hotel. The front was long and she could hardly get the whole image in one sweeping look.

Two giant oak doors opened up into an expansive circular lobby area with dark mahogany flooring, and the ceiling was a beautiful emerald shade that reminded her of a canopy of leaves. Great rustic chandeliers decorated with deer antlers hung from beams that intersected the space above the lobby, and cast an amber glow on the hall. In the middle of the lobby was a grand redwood that towered from the floor to the ceiling, its trunk disappearing into the green to ascend through the numerous floors above.

Several stories of mezzanines, accessible by open stairs and a few elevators, followed the curve of the lobby, hallways and doors breaking off from the space like spokes on a wheel. On the opposite side of the entrance was another set of doors that led to a dining hall or restaurant, where Katey could smell fresh meat being served.

The lobby buzzed with activity as loups-garous, their families, and packs were trying to find their rooms, check in at the front desk, and hunt down meals. Katey thought her spinal cord and brain would explode with so many different sensations.

Darren led his pack into the lobby and toward the desk where a frantic attendant handed out room keys. He smiled warmly and waited patiently to give his name and reservation information.

Almost everyone's attention had turned to Logan and Katey by the time they crossed the room to the desk. Their behavior and puzzlement wasn't much different from the other loups-garous at the airport.

Katey took deep soothing breaths through her nose, willing herself not to care what they said. Still, their words fluttered around her ears like annoying flies that couldn't be wished away.

"Who the hell is she?"

"Is that her alpha?"

"That can't be right. It's impossible."

"How did they do it?"

Darren procured their room keys and the pack made their way, luggage in hand, out of the lobby, leaving behind the other guests and their flurry of unanswered questions. Logan tightened his grip on her hand as they maneuvered past the crowd of onlookers.

Once in a quiet hallway that led toward a set of elevators, Katey let out a long breath. "I don't know how much more of that I can stand."

Dustin turned back to her with a reassuring grin. "It won't last. Tomorrow, you'll be old news."

"Don't lie to the kid," Ben groused.

"Don't mind what they say," Darren advised as they approached the elevator doors. "They don't mean any ill by it."

"I know, but..." Katey scrunched up her shoulders as if chilled. "I can't stand being the center of attention like that."

Dustin barked a laugh. "Get used to it, Katey Kay. You're way more special than you were before. Every new loup-garou you meet is going to have the same questions. Might as well get used to answering them."

The elevator dinged and opened to let out a pack of four loups-garous of mid-ranking onto the ground level. Their gazes fell straight on her and, once more, she ducked against Logan like a frightened child. They blinked in confusion, but after a bit of nonverbal convincing from Darren, they exited the elevator and passed them by. Still, they stole peeks over their shoulder and began talking about her the minute she disappeared into the elevator.

"See, not so bad when Darren's around," Dustin said as the doors closed on them and Ben hit the button for the fourth floor.

Katey passed him a cutting look that only made him chuckle.

They arrived to their floor and traveled down more hallways and deeper into the resort. They knew exactly where they were going.

Down each corridor, Katey could hear voices from behind the many doors they passed, but was grateful to find the halls mostly empty and not nearly as congested as the lobby or stairs. They came to a door marked with antique brass letters that read "Suite 410".

"Here we are." Darren pulled out one of the vintage skeleton keys that the attendant had issued him. He attempted to open the door, but it refused to give way to him. "Blast these keys. I can never get this right... Dustin?"

Darren admitted defeat and handed the keys to Dustin, who smiled with pride. He had plenty of experience with pesky locks from having to deal with his classroom door on a daily basis. It only took him a few seconds before the door popped open.

Inside, it was a similar setup Katey would have pictured for a mountain cabin. On the far left wall was a roaring fireplace, with several upholstered armchairs centered around the hearth and a few plush couches alongside them. Some of the furniture pieces were already occupied by the other loups-garous that would be staying in the suite with them. Three closed doors lined the far wall past the living area that must have led into bedrooms.

A staircase hugged the wall across from the fireplace and led up to a loft that overlooked the living room. Three more doors led to more bedrooms on the second level. A cased opening lined with raw wood beams just before the stairs led to a game room with a billiard table and some free-standing weights.

To the immediate left of the entry door was a kitchenette complete with cupboards and the modern conveniences of a kitchen, though Katey wondered how often the stove and microwave were really used when the resort had its own restaurant.

A man stood from one of the armchairs and made his way to the pack. "Darren! It's so good to see you all could make it! It's been a long time!"

Katey detected a British accent in his greeting, not unlike Darren's. He was a strong-built man like all the other loups-garous, wearing a white button-up dress shirt tucked into faded jeans. Prominent streaks of silver cut through his dark hair and thick beard, giving him a dignified appearance. His eyes gleamed a bright brown, similar to Darren's, and held an element of authority that shouldn't be questioned.

Katey's wolf suddenly came awake and immediately picked up on the subtle dominance. It instilled a sense of meekness before him. Without even knowing who he was, Katey somehow knew this man was important. She supposed he was also an alpha in his pack. She could find no other explanation, but how much more dominant was he amongst other alphas to make her wolf perk up like that?

When he came over, he embraced Darren like he was an equal, which contradicted what her instincts presumed.

"Good to see you, too, John. You brought the usual motley crew with you, I see." Darren motioned to the other four loups-garous around the fireplace.

Logan tried to herd Katey toward the stairs, but her presence, like everywhere else, wouldn't go unnoticed. They almost made it before John spoke up.

"I see you have a new member to your party."

Katey turned at the foot of the stairs and Logan's fingers pressed into her ribs a little tighter as if she would blow away at any moment.

John had pinned her with an intrigued, but peculiar gaze that made her core and chest tighten with dread. Logan stepped in front of her, as if to protect her from the powerful alpha and the others around the fire.

"She's... She's different," John's gaze raked over her, but didn't venture for a closer look, though she sensed he wanted to.

Logan grew tense and she saw a muscle jump in his jaw at John's words.

"This is Katey... She's been loup-garou since Tuesday," Darren announced. "We felt it best that she came with us so she wouldn't be home by herself, and so she may benefit from your guidance, John."

Everyone's faces lit up with excitement that electrified the room, and Katey wanted nothing more than to dash upstairs to any of the unlocked rooms and barricade herself inside.

"How is that possible?" one man asked from the couch. "Did you change her, Darren?"

Darren shook his head and motioned to Logan. "No. Logan did. Not exactly how we would have wanted, but he did."

"You're joking. A kid? I don't believe it," another loup-garou stated bitterly from his armchair with a flippant gesture.

"Oh, believe it," Dustin interjected as he leaned casually against the breakfast bar in the kitchenette. "She's one of us and has got all the perks, too. Nearly tore up Logan during a bit of her training the day after."

Katey winced at the reminder of when she lost control. It wasn't a proud moment, but maybe it was the kind of story that needed to be told to assure them that she was loup-garou.

"She's quite tired right now," Logan said with a strand of resentment. "We've had a long day of traveling. She can talk more tomorrow."

Darren nodded in approval and they continued their way up-stairs as the others discussed matters about the meeting, charity luncheon, and of course, Katey.

Logan ushered her down the loft above the common room to a door on the far end, marked room 410-D. He let her in first and followed with their luggage. They had told her ahead of time that they would be sharing a room with Dustin, while Darren and Ben roomed with one of the other loups-garous next door.

It resembled a hotel room in nearly every way. There were two queen-sized beds with crimson spreads and a small wooden end table between them where an alarm clock sat, blinking the time in bright red digital letters. To the left of the entrance was an open closet and to the right was the door that led to a standard bathroom. The beds faced a desk and a tall cabinet that housed a television set with a selection of DVD cases below it and a channel guide brochure.

Logan dropped their luggage to the floor in front of the beds as Katey let herself collapse onto one of the plush mattresses. The pillows were filled with downy feathers and extremely soft as she hugged one tightly to her chest. But no matter how deeply she breathed in the fresh scent of detergent, she couldn't will away the persistent restlessness in her chest.

The words of that one loup-garou bounced around in her head. A joke? Did they think she was a joke? That somehow she could fake giving off the loup-garou aura and she was just playing pretend?

Logan sat down on the edge of the bed just in front of her, and gently pushed her hair from her face to tuck behind her ear. "Talk to me."

Katey wouldn't meet his gaze, but stared at the space of pat-terned carpet between the beds. "I just feel like such a freak. Everyone's staring at me and talking about me. It's worse than high school."

He leaned down and hugged her tightly around the waist, his comforting weight pressing her into the mattress. "We're all freaks here, Katey... If there was any way I could make this easier, you know I would do it in a heartbeat."

Katey slipped one hand out to rest against his arm. "I know. Just you being here helps."

Logan nuzzled his head against hers, then pulled away to sit up on the bed. "I bet you're hungry." She nodded and gave him a faint smile. "Let me go grab you something to eat and I'll bring it right back up, okay? You just rest." Logan leaned down to kiss her lips in a brief, but not unpassionate way, then stood up to leave.

When he shut the door, Katey sighed and snuggled into the covers, sliding off her shoes and heavy winter-wear before slipping her feet under the comforter. The cozy warmth of the empty room untangled her nerves enough that she could let herself calm down, at least for a little while.

Logan bounded down the stairs toward his pack members, his face twisted into a scowl and his hands balled into fists. Dustin was the first to notice, then John who had been casually talking with Darren up until this point. Ben sat on the couch with the other loups-garous, John's four sons.

"What's wrong with you?" Dustin snapped.

"You're all making her nervous," Logan growled.

Blake, the youngest of John's sons, looked up from where he stood by the fireplace. "She has a right to be nervous."

"No," Logan barked. "She needs to feel welcomed, and everyone in this resort is treating her like some damn pariah."

Darren glowered and snapped out a pulse of dominance. "Mind your tongue, Logan."

"No, he's right, Darren." John stepped forward to face Logan. "I admit we didn't give her the warmest greeting, and I didn't help the situation by calling her 'different.'" John placed his hand upon his chest and respectfully bowed his head to Logan. "I apologize, Logan. We will do better to make her more comfortable."

Logan gave him an angry snort and stormed out of the room to find food for Katey. He had expected much more from the loups-garous he had grown to trust over the years. Now, he wanted her to be as far away from Alaska as possible, simply so she would be spared from such humiliation.

When Logan slammed the door, Darren rubbed at his face. "Sometimes, I don't know what to do with that boy."

John chuckled and slapped Dustin on the back heartily. "He takes after his grandfather," he said with a toothy grin.

"Hey, I don't remember being that rebellious."

"Not rebellious. Spirited," John corrected good-naturedly.

Darren shook his head. "But he had no right to speak to you in that way."

John was unmoved. "He's only defending her. I would do the same for any of my own."

Darren grimaced. "You're just saying that because you don't have to live with him."

John erupted with a cheerful laugh of agreement. Darren was glad for John's understanding. His many years of training other loups-garous had turned him into an considerate alpha who tolerated the quirks of his pupils. Yet, he remembered many times when he had ignited his mentor's temper and paid the price. John, benevolent as he was, was not the loup-garou to cross.

"What I don't understand, Darren," John's eldest living son, Noah, said from one of the armchairs, "is why you didn't warn us about Katey sooner."

Darren looked to the blonde loup-garou who was closer to Dustin's age. "I wasn't sure what to make of Katey at first. I apologize for not giving any warning." He wandered to the blazing fire where the others had congregated. "She shows all the signs of being loup-garou. She had no complications in the turning, and besides a little struggle with controlling her wolf, she excelled in what little training we could give. But I hoped..." Darren swallowed his pride hard, "that you'd have some advice or guidance. I'm out of my element here. I've never seen anything like it."

"I've never seen anything like her," Aiden remarked, an insinuation in his tone that rankled Darren. He was John's second youngest and the wiliest of the four men who had come along with the old loup-garou. He sat in his own armchair near the hearth next to his brother.

"Don't cross Logan, Aiden," Dustin warned. "He nearly beat a rougarou to a pulp last night for taking a shot at his girl."

John's brows furrowed. "His girl? Do they have an understanding?"

All eyes turned on Darren as the more crucial offense was made known.

Darren combed his fingers through his hair, feeling the long day of travel begin to catch up with him. "It's not as clean cut as we'd like." He looked to John's intense gaze and felt like a newly turned pup again. "No, sir. They don't have a preliminary mating bond, as you can tell, but they are very attached to one another. Logan has expressed a desire to mate but only to us, but we haven't explained the procedure to Katey. It's so soon in her training that we didn't see the need for it... until now."

John gave a heavy sigh and looked to his four sons. "Until something can be confirmed, no one is to make advances upon Katey. If she's in your company without her pack, you will protect her from anyone who wishes her harm. Do you understand?"

Liam, the second oldest and the epitome of a beta with his broad chest and mountain-of-a-man frame, laughed from where he perched on the arm of the sofa. "You don't have to worry about me, dad. My tastes don't run that young."

All the while, Darren inwardly scolded himself for not preparing Katey for this possibility. Between the training, the vampire threat, and the affair with Erik, there seemed no time to sit her down in private to discuss these things. Dustin explained some of it during their layover, but not enough.

He knew he would have to talk to them first thing in the morning. They were all too tired from their journey to bother with it now. At least Katey would be safe within their suite, and he could entrust her into the hands of the Croxen loups-garous, should the worst happen.

John turned to Darren and gave him that sage look he always gave before administering advice that was needed, though not always wanted. "Katey is an anomaly, not unlike Logan. I remember what you told me about the nature of his birth, and how the gift of the wolf was passed down through his mother, rather than his father." He slid a glance to Dustin in the kitchen. "To my understanding, there has never been a woman loup-garou. It was considered impossible, but you seem to attract impossible cases. As with Logan, tread carefully. We don't know what she's capable of, but I'll help in any way that I can."

CHAPTER 14

Logan gaped at John. "Why the fuck would you ask Gregory Jennings to join us at the charity luncheon?"

"Watch your tongue, Logan." Darren gripped the pool stick between his powerful hands and gave a stern look to his packmate.

It was late morning and everyone in the suite but Katey was awake, most of them already dressed in their suits and formal wear for the charity luncheon. Dustin, Darren, John, and Noah stood around the billiard table, their two teams in the middle of the second game that morning.

Aiden and Liam would not be attending the luncheon and intended to spend their day in Fairbanks. Only Blake remained, sitting with Ben on the other side of the room and in the heat of a personal chess tournament that began the night before and looked like it would continue well into the afternoon at their rate. Blake, the youngest of John's sons, was similar to Ben in his quiet demeanor and brilliant mind for strategy.

Logan stood off to the side, the odd man out, watching the game in his white button-down shirt that he neglected to tuck into his black slacks. All the others had their ties pinned down and suit jackets draped over the backs of barstools against the wall. To wear anything less formal would have been an insult to the loup-garou who founded The Global Association for the Conservation of Wolves.

"I didn't invite him." John watched his son take a shot at a solid. "He is coming of his own free will and asked to sit with me at my table. Naturally, I accepted."

Dustin's face wrinkled as if he caught a whiff of some terrible smell. "I can't believe after all this time the rougarou wants to have anything to do with you."

It was common knowledge to all of them that Gregory, the alpha of the rougarou pack in the southern part of the country, had once been an instructor for young loups-garous under John's tutelage in France. From what Darren had told Logan, he was not a compassionate teacher, and pushed the orphans ruthlessly in their training. At the time, he hadn't turned rougarou, but after a difference of morals, Gregory broke away from the pack and set out on his own. As far as Darren's pack knew, John and the rougarou were still on bad terms and refused to associate with one another.

John took a deep breath, his barrel chest rising. "Gregory and I have been in contact for some time now. I believe he's grown wiser in his old age, now that his son is starting to follow in his misplaced footsteps."

Noah knocked his target into a corner pocket and straightened to allow Darren to make his shot.

"Will Erik be with him?" Logan asked with his arms crossed and hands balled into tight fists.

John nodded an affirmative and propped out his pool stick as if it were a proud weapon. "Yes, Gregory's son is coming. I trust that won't be a problem for you or Forrest?"

Logan remained silent and averted his eyes, sure that the elder alpha in the room would demand his vow of peace that he was not inclined to give.

"Where is Forrest, anyway?" Ben asked from his seat, his eyes focused on the chessboard as Blake finally moved his rook. "I imagined that all of your kin would be stayin' with ya in the same suite."

"Forrest is with his pack in another wing of the resort," Noah replied. "We met with him yesterday and he'll be joining us at the table as well."

Dustin guffawed. "And you really think Erik and Forrest can sit at the same table without a fight breaking out?"

Darren took his shot and at two stripes, but only one made it into a pocket. "As long as Erik doesn't try to start something, they should be fine. I'm not worried about Forrest. He's not naturally dominant or aggressive."

John approached the table and assessed the field. "It's a shame his father couldn't have been the same."

A muscle in Logan's jaw jumped as he looked to the graying loup-garou. "You weren't there. How would you know?"

"Enough," Darren snapped.

Forrest and John were distantly linked through paternal relations, but the dominant streak was consistent throughout their line. Forrest was not inclined to take over as alpha of the Deviants, though some thought it only right. He was content to stay a midranking pack member without the burden of responsibilities. He knew what such a weight could do to a man. Robert, his father, had made a poor decision not to evacuate Devia as hunters targeted their community. He waited until the last possible moment, and sacrificed his life, as well as the lives of many other alphas and betas to save a lost cause. To this day, the Deviants were split on whether to worship Robert as a martyr or a villain that destroyed their families. Logan and Darren, who saw the destruction first-hand, were of the latter opinion.

Logan slumped and abandoned the tirade he had planned for Forrest's great-great-grandfather. Knowing that he would face Erik again in a matter of hours only made him more irritable. When they left Florida, he had hoped that he would leave behind his problems for a short while. Now, it seemed that the trouble had followed them.

A repentant look crossed John's face and he nodded to Logan's words. "This is true. My point is, Forrest is not a fighter, which we can be thankful for."

Dustin leaned on his pool stick. "Why do you say that?"

John's stare became unfocused, and a silent moment filled the room as all waited. "I feel the time is coming for those who have been fighting to put down their guns and take up the banner of peace. Don't ask me why I feel this way, because I don't know. But I've felt it in my spirit for the last few months. My wolf feels the same." He looked to Darren. "Our world is about to change."

An ominous air settled over the pack. Even Ben and Blake paused in their game to regard the old man with questioning eyes.

"Are you talking about Katey?" A mix of fear and excitement shot through Logan.

His mind raced with the implications. Perhaps the females of the human race were strong enough to withstand the change? Then again, what if Katey was a fluke? What if she would be the only one for the rest of eternity with no hope of duplicating the conditions of her change in another human female? More alarmingly, what would her children be like, if she were to have children? Would they be full-blooded loups-garous or humans? The thought of Katey having children startled Logan more than he liked to admit, because if she had any children, he wanted them to be his as well.

Katey could have been the change that John had premonitions about, but what did the old alpha think of her after their brief meeting the night before?

John blinked and pursed his lips in thought. "May I be honest with you, Darren?"

"By all means."

John shifted the pool stick between his palms and looked hard at Darren. "I'm not sure if she will change. I think it might have been unwise for you to bring her to the gathering."

"Bullshit!" Dustin exploded, eyes going gold. "She almost changed nearly twice since Logan bit her."

Darren completely agreed and pointed a cautious finger. "Watch it, Dustin. He's entitled to his opinions."

"And this is not meant to insult you, Logan, or your abilities to change a human... Darren has told me of those instances, but I'm still not convinced. There has never been a female loup-garou in all of known history. She is a miracle to have survived the bite at all... If she does manage to change, she may not survive that." John paused in thought as Logan grew even more agitated. "I just don't sense a strong wolf in her."

Logan understood that he had to respect John, but the thought of Katey not being a loup-garou, that both of them had failed in some way, inspired a rage in him. The previous day's conflict at the airport came back to him. Katey mentioned fading, that her abilities were waning in some way. He didn't want to think about it, didn't want to even entertain the idea of it. Yet, he tried to think back over the last couple of days. The last time he saw her wolf manifest was at the fight club and then the morning after in bed when her claws came out accidentally. Apart from that, she retained her senses, but that was all. Was her wolf weakening somehow that John couldn't sense it in her?

"I have to disagree with you," Darren said, squaring his shoulders. "Her wolf is very strong. The last couple of days have been rather trying for her."

Logan straightened, hoping this would help to validate Katey's wolf, though it may have been a mistake to bring it up, since the pack wasn't supposed to know about the fight. "I felt Katey use her dominance. Few loups-garous can tap their dominance so early. That should be proof enough that her wolf is strong, right?"

All eyes turned to Logan as if he had just confessed to murder.

"When did this happen?" Darren demanded.

Logan lost some of his boldness and rubbed the back of his neck. "When we had that fight. Nearly knocked me off my feet."

Dustin's gaze narrowed on him, as if mutedly asking for the truth, but Darren and John seemed to accept the quick lie without question.

"That is remarkable," John said in a reverent tone. "I may stand corrected, but to use dominance and to shift are two very different matters. The shift is incredibly taxing on the body, especially the first one." John bent over the edge of the billiard table and lined up his shot.

Across the room, the loups-garous telegraphed their own feelings on the subject. From his peripheral, Logan saw Blake and Ben resumed their game, but exchanged private glances as if to say that they were concerned for Katey just as much as the others were. Darren turned and paced away from the table, deep in thought, while Dustin watched John take his shot and execute it perfectly. Noah kept his eyes trained on Darren, studying his agitated movements.

"You're saying she can't come with us tonight?" Logan asked John, breaking the silence.

"I would not recommend it."

"Just for the sake of hypothetical situations, if she comes with us tonight and doesn't change, what do we do?" Dustin asked the alphas. "Being around seasoned loups-garous who can control themselves is one thing, but there will be many newbies there. She'd be in some serious danger if she stays human."

"I haven't talked about the gathering much with her," Darren turned back to the table. "I don't know what she expects. I told her about it before she turned, before she had the potential to be included. At the time, the other details seemed unnecessary."

John nodded. "If she went with us tonight and didn't change, then we would have to get her out of the park and back here where it's safer. I personally think it would be less of a hassle to keep her here at the lodge."

Darren smirked. "Unless something has changed in the last forty-eight hours, I doubt she'll appreciate being left behind."

"If she's going to try and shift tonight, who's going to talk to her about mating?" Noah gave a direct look at Logan. The almost challenging flash in his eyes nettled Logan's wolf.

What was that about? Did Noah have hidden schemes for Katey? He looked almost twice her age, but that wasn't always a deal breaker for loups-garous. Age differences, when they could live for centuries, mattered less.

Logan was too busy locking stares with Noah that he forgot to answer.

"I will. I'm the most logical one to do it. I'll speak with her after the luncheon," Darren said. "We know if Katey elects to shift tonight, she won't be safe among the unmated loups-garous in attendance. I'll bring up the possibility of the shift at that time as well."

A low growl sounded in the back of Logan's throat at the thought of it. He hadn't considered it before now. In human form, he could protect her from unwanted attention. As loups-garous, feral instincts would dominate. Anything could happen. If they had a preliminary mating bond, she'd be spared. Their connection would be more obvious. Yet, how safe was it to make that connection so soon in her training? Logan was perfectly ready for it, and he was sure Katey was too. But was it smart? Should they continue to wait?

Two options were before them. They could make her stay behind, he would not form the preliminary mating bond, and the question of her legitimacy as a loup-garou would remain open-ended. Or, they could throw caution to the wind, form the bond so she would be safe at the gathering, and let her attempt a willful shift, despite being so new in her loup-garou skin, in order for her to prove herself.

What John said next threw Logan out of his thoughts. "We will be flying back home next week. If all parties agree and Katey proves she is capable of shifting at will, I could perform the official mating ceremony before we leave."

Logan's eyes went wide as his body flushed white hot then frigid cold. "What?"

Darren stammered, just as thrown by the suggestion, his gaze jumping between his old mentor and Logan. "John, I... That may not be possible. We would need more time."

More time and a miracle. Logan knew what the mating ceremony entailed. That was another critical reason it was too soon to mate that hadn't come to mind until just then. Even if Katey could shift at will, Logan couldn't hold up his end of the deal. Shame and soul-crushing regret hit him square in the chest like a wrecking ball.

John appeared confused, then looked to Logan with understanding. "Oh... I didn't realize that was still... I apologize."

Noah propped a hand on his hip. "Then how are you going to attend the gathering?"

"Tonight is Logan's night to shift," Dustin answered, quiet and sympathetic to this sore spot in Logan's history. "The timing worked out well this year so we won't have to force a shift on him."

John nodded. "I see. It'd be unconventional, but we could force the shift for the—"

"I can't control myself either."

That also sent ripples of shock through the Croxen loups-garous. Yes, he was over a century old, and he couldn't break through the veil that dropped between himself and his wolf during the shift, whether it was voluntary or not, and he couldn't shift of his own volition.

A mating ceremony was off the table, an impossibility until Logan could fix himself. All this time, he had led Katey to believe that she was the only one preventing them from taking the next step in their relationship. First, she was human, then she was too inexperienced in her loup-garou skin. Now, even if she managed to shift on her own and shock them all, he was the final roadblock to mated bliss. Preliminary mating bond, however, was completely doable for now. It would have to be enough, but how long would Katey wait for him?

Darren glanced to the clock on the wall. "You may want to go make sure Katey is up and ready for the luncheon. We need to leave soon."

Logan nodded and eagerly left the game room, feeling uncomfortable under their scrutiny. He knew Darren and John would talk about his problem as soon as he was out of earshot in the soundproof bedroom.

Upstairs, Katey was still sleeping in bed, curled and wrapped up tight in the plush comforter. Logan cautiously walked in and saw her peaceful face half buried in the pillow she hugged so tightly. He wanted to be that pillow. He pushed aside all of the pestering fears and thoughts that gnawed at his mind and sat down on the edge of the bed.

Katey stirred under the covers and her unconcealed eye cracked open.

"Good morning, beautiful." Logan rubbed her back through the blankets and gave her a tender smile.

Katey grunted in response and hid her face entirely in the pillow. Logan chuckled and pulled back her soft, dark hair to loop it affectionately behind her ear, revealing her smooth cheek.

"How'd you sleep?"

"Good." The pillows and sheets muffled her voice, but he could hear her well just the same.

Logan trailed his fingertips along the top of her head to smooth down the little tendrils of hair that curled against the silky pillowcase. "If you don't get up soon, we're going to be late for the luncheon."

Katey grunted again and rolled over to stretch out her stiff arms above her head, arching like a cat basking in the warm sun. She turned her sleepy gaze up to him and exhaled deeply. Even half-asleep, hair a mess, and bed clothes crooked, she was beautiful beyond words.

"Today is your birthday, isn't it?" Her voice cracked with sleepiness.

He had completely forgotten. Logan smirked and nodded as he loomed over her, his weight supported on his hands. Driven by the mad forces within him, he kissed her and cherished the taste of her lips. Kissing her would never get old, not for a thousand years.

When he pulled away, he brushed his nose against hers to incite a tiny giggle. "What are we going to do today then?" she asked with a smile.

Logan shrugged. "I wasn't planning on doing much of anything except spending time with you."

Birthdays were not a big thing in the loup-garou community. Many of them lost track of what day they were born altogether, especially those like Darren and John who had been around for centuries. Keeping count of their years was no longer a priority or an achievement for them, as it was for humans.

Katey snuggled deeper under the covers and Logan lowered himself down on his elbows, their bodies pressing into each other. Her breath heated his neck, stirring warm feelings down his core and thighs.

"Then can we go into town and do stuff?" Katey grinned like a mischievous child under his loving gaze.

"After we get through this luncheon, we'll go anywhere you want."

Katey pouted. "That's not the point of celebrating *your* birthday."

"The best present I have is you. What more could I want?"

She beamed under his endearment and reached up to wrap her arms around his neck. As her fingers played in his hair, Logan felt his core tighten with expectation. He leaned down once more to kiss her. Lips parted and his tongue swept over hers, tasting with appreciation.

A low, pleased sound rumbled in the back of his throat and his hands came up to caress the arms still stretched across her pillow. As the kiss deepened, his hands ventured down, stroking down her ribs, the tips of his thumbs just grazing the edge of forbidden places with only the fabric of her sleeping shirt separating their skin. Katey bucked and arched against him with a gasp. The scent of her arousal encouraged him and his kiss turned possessive, demanding.

Completely distracted by the beautiful creature beneath him, Logan didn't sense Dustin's approach until the bedroom door was open and he stepped inside.

"Ah, for fuck's sake," the beta groaned. "Knock it off!"

Logan was willing to avoid the interruption, but Katey pulled back and shrunk into the mattress as if to hide from Dustin. He opened his eyes to see that hers were wide and red, filled with mortification. With one last peck on the lips, Logan sat up and let the covers fall back across her chest.

"Did the game end that quickly?" Logan asked.

Dustin stood in front of the closet, his back to them. "Noah got the last of the solids and the eight-ball in one shot. That guy's pretty good with a pool stick." He pulled out a formal black jacket and two ties. He finally turned and threw the jacket across the bed and tossed the tie at Logan, hitting him in the chest. "Finish getting dressed." He pointed at Katey. "And you, little miss, need to get up."

Katey stiffly sat up and combed out her tangled hair with her fingers. "When do we leave?"

"In fifteen minutes."

That got Katey moving. She whispered a curse under her breath and threw back the covers to race to her suitcase sitting at the foot of the bed. She had passed out before having the chance to unpack it the night before.

"You did bring something suitable, right?" Dustin asked, saddling up to the full-length mirror on the wall next to the television cabinet in order to put on his tie.

Katey fished out a skirt and blouse, not unlike the one she wore to the ballroom dance party last weekend. "Is this fine?"

Dustin turned and made a face. "It'll have to do. We probably should have told you it was going to be pretty formal."

"Am I going to stand out?"

Logan took up his tie and knotted it without sliding it over his collar, a trick Darren had taught him. "Probably, but at least you won't look like a sequined mermaid or something."

Katey sighed and rushed to the bathroom after grabbing her toiletries and shut the door behind her.

"Is Erik and Gregory going to be a problem?" Dustin asked in a low tone as he finished with his tie.

Logan grimaced. "I can behave in public, but if the bastard provokes me, I won't be held liable." He gave a considerate look to the beta. "By the way, thanks for sending Katey to the club. If it wasn't for her, it would have ended badly."

A wrinkle formed between Dustin's brows. "How so?"

In as few words, and as vaguely as possible, Logan explained just how chaotic the fight had become, and how Katey's interference won the day.

"Damn... I'm sorry I missed that." Dustin seemed more impressed than disturbed by the fact that Logan nearly lost control in the ring. "Rematch?"

"We didn't get a chance to discuss it... Do you think that's why Erik's here? To get another shot at us?"

Dustin shrugged. "Who knows. Plates for that dinner are expensive and they can't be bought at the last minute. We barely got a spot for Katey in time before the RSVP deadline. It's more likely that Erik and Gregory planned to be here, whether or not you two duked it out in the ring or not. Just be on your best behavior."

"Again, not promising anything."

At this point, he'd be mad enough to ambush Erik in a dark, snowy alley, and gut him. He didn't want that threat hanging over their happiness any longer.

The bathroom door opened and Katey stepped out in a long, silky black skirt and white blouse. Her wavy brown hair hung from a high ponytail and bobbed as she tried to slip on a pair of high heels in mid-stride.

"Sit down and do that before you fall and break your neck," Dustin chided playfully.

Katey dropped on the edge of the bed next to Logan and fastened the side buckles on her ankle straps. Logan breathed deeply her perfume, his nose gravitating to her neck like a moth to a flame. She went still and looked at him sideways, a slow smile spreading over the lips he needed to kiss again.

"What're you doing?"

Logan grinned and opened his mouth as if to take a chunk out of her neck, then he remembered his grandfather stood not far away, watching with his arms folded. He withdrew and let out a breath, disappointed.

Dustin must have gotten the hint and rolled his eyes before heading toward the door. "Meet us downstairs when you're ready."

He waited until the door latched, then tackled Katey to the bed. She let out a squeal and let herself be assaulted by a barrage of kisses across her face and neck.

"Logan! We're going to make everyone late!"

"Then you shouldn't have come out of the bathroom looking like that."

Katey easily overpowered him, since Logan wasn't truly trying to retrain her, and skipped away from the bed and out of his reach. He stuck out his lower lip in an exaggerated pout, but loved to see that little sparkle of mischief in her eyes.

"We'll have plenty of time for that this afternoon," she said, grabbing up a little black purse from her luggage that matched her skirt.

Then, Logan remembered the gathering and everything they discussed in the billiard room. All playfulness left him and he wished they could just freeze time. They could stay in this room all day, forget about the pack, the gathering, and all the little things that threatened to make their world more complicated.

CHAPTER 15

As Katey and Logan descended the stairs, only Darren and Dustin waited for them near the kitchenette. Both were in their formal attire, ready to go, but she noticed Ben was not among them. When they came to the bottom of the stairs, she peeked into the game room to find him and another loup-garou playing chess.

"You're not going?" she asked Ben, shifting her hold on her big white coat.

He didn't look up from the board, but waved her off. "Nah. I never go to these fancy shin-digs."

While Katey was tempted to feel a little crestfallen that he wouldn't be there with the rest of the pack, he seemed content enough in his game.

With his hand on the small of her back, Logan guided Katey toward the door to join the alpha and beta in the hall. The noontime resort activity blended together into a dull roar, the many scents of loups-garous and their families nearly indistinguishable from one another.

"Anyone else we know going to be at the luncheon?" Katey asked as they made their way to the nearest elevator.

Each of them looked to the other, as if waiting for someone else to answer.

Darren broke the stalemate. "John and one of his sons, along with Forrest."

At the mention of Forrest, Katey perked up. She knew she'd see him, but at such a large gathering, she wasn't so sure just when that would be.

"And Erik and his dad," Dustin added gravely.

Her body went rigid and a cold sweat broke over the back of her neck. "What?"

"I know," Logan mumbled. "I'm not happy either. It's only for a couple of hours."

If they weren't already in the elevator and headed down to the lobby, she would have bolted for the suite. As it was, there seemed little chance to turn back now.

"Game plan?"

"Not kill each other," Dustin answered wryly.

"Everyone will be civil," Darren said in a reproving tone. "Either myself or John will handle the situation if anyone decides not to be civil."

Katey frowned. "Fantastic."

The lobby was not nearly as bustling as it had been the evening before, but some late arriving guests and their families trickled through the front door. Once again, loups-garous across the room turned their heads to look her way. She took comfort in knowing it had more to do with her very existence, than for what she wore or how she looked.

Darren fell in next to her, on the other side from Logan while Dustin walked ahead toward the doors that led outside. "We'll be riding with John to the convention center where the luncheon is being held. You two wait inside until the van arrives." Then, he broke away to follow Dustin onto the covered walkway just outside the front doors.

Katey took that moment to slip on her coat, just as a familiar scent drifted toward her from somewhere behind them. Both she and Logan turned to see Forrest hustling across the lobby, a big grin on his face that she soon mirrored. He too, wore a suit and tie for the luncheon.

Forrest stopped in front of them and clasped arms with Logan in greeting. "Glad to see you've recovered well. Where's John?"

"He went to get the van."

"You know John?" Katey asked.

Forrest looked to Logan with mock surprise. "Wow, something you haven't told her."

"We haven't talked about John much." Logan turned to Katey. "You'll meet him formally, but John is the older loup-garou from last night. The one that said you were... different."

"I remember him." How could she forget the appraising look he gave her?

"He was the alpha that trained up Darren after he turned, and helped to train Dustin. I spent several years with him in France, too." Logan thumbed toward Forrest. "He's one of John's distant descendants."

"My great-great-grandfather to be exact," Forrest said with a smile.

Katey's brows arched. "That's a lot of 'greats' for people who live forever."

Forrest shrugged. "It's a few centuries' worth of family history. We'll have to tell you about it some other time."

"Van's here," Dustin called to them.

Logan claimed Katey once more by her arm and they made their way to the carpool area. Fastening the last of her buttons on her coat, Katey slid on her gloves. Her pack and Forrest piled into the warm van. One of the loups-garous from their suite sat in the driver's seat, while John sat beside him.

"All ready?" The driver looked over his shoulder and briefly met Katey's stare. He must have been John's son, but she saw only a slight resemblance in his facial features. The dark blonde hair and blue eyes were definitely from his mothers side. Given how old he looked, his mother was long passed.

It then occurred to her that if this was John's son, then he and Forrest were distantly related. Just how, she didn't know, and to try and puzzle it out made her head hurt.

Darren gave him the affirmative and shut the sliding door once he took his seat. Logan nudged for her to fasten her seatbelt. Dustin and Forrest sat in the far back and started a conversation about news from the Devian pack. Darren, Katey, and Logan occupied the first row just behind the driver and passenger, but the van could have easily accommodated half a dozen more loups-garous.

"I understand we got off on the wrong foot last night," John spoke up as the van rolled away from the lodge. "I hope you weren't offended, Katey."

The great alpha looked to her and gave a friendly smile that loosened her tongue. "I wasn't."

"I'm glad to hear it." Katey was entranced by his British accent that was slightly heavier than Darren's. It also held a slight twist that she couldn't place, as if he maybe came from a different part of England than Darren. "This is Noah, my eldest son. I have three others that will not be attending with us, but you saw them last night."

Katey recalled the other three from the night before, one of which was with Ben in the game room that morning. Again, she saw only a partial likeness that tied them back to John, but none of them had blonde hair like Noah. Did they all have different mothers? The thought made her dizzy. John must have been pretty old to have so many wives.

"Nice to meet you, Katey," Noah greeted as he directed the van down the road.

"Same." Katey hated this first phase of awkward small talk. She always came across as impersonal or standoffish.

A beat of silence passed before John started in again. "You are fortunate to be part of Darren's pack. He's a good alpha."

"And a good teacher." Katey slid a glance Darren's way and he beamed under the compliment.

"Indeed, he is. Everything he knows, he learned from me." John passed a sly wink to the younger alpha.

"He and Logan told me that you've trained a lot of loups-garous."

John nodded. "I have. Around the sixteenth century, I began taking in orphaned loups-garous or newly turned loups-garous who had no pack support. I trained them until they were strong enough to find their own packs. Darren was one of my first pupils."

The edges of Katey's lips twitched, willing her to smile at her next thought. "So, you were kind of like a foster father?"

"I suppose you could say that."

Katey knew a tiny piece of what it must have been like for the young loups-garous. They were alone in the world before finding their way into his care. She saw the parallels between herself and those orphans who had no place to belong. Yet, John gave them a home and a family, just like Logan and Darren had.

If John was such a renown alpha within the loup-garou society, she felt even more privileged to have met him, and to be indirectly connected to him through Darren.

"Tell me something about yourself," the alpha requested, shifting in his seat to face her more completely.

Katey tried to hold in her wince. She was never good with questions like that. Logan snorted a laugh, because he knew that too. "What do you want to know?"

John chuckled. "Anything you're willing to tell me."

"She's a wonderful student," Darren helped.

"I'm glad her training is going well."

Dustin leaned forward from the back seat. "I think he means academically."

"She's been doing fine in her loup-garou training, too," Logan remarked.

"Academic training?" John questioned.

"Yes, sir," Darren said. "Before she met Logan, she was a student of ours. She had classes with Dustin, Ben, and I."

John laughed. "What a story. A girl finds out her teachers are loups-garous and becomes a loup-garou herself."

"Stranger than fiction," Noah quipped.

Katey smirked. She had to admit it was a weird story. "Add in that Logan and I met in a cemetery, and that I was a foster kid, too."

"Is that right?" John asked with an amused smile.

Logan slipped his arm around her shoulders. "Every word."

Katey reached up and laced her fingers between his, enjoying the freedom to show their affection so openly, even in front of John.

"That truly is remarkable." Undeterred, John asked, "Tell me everything."

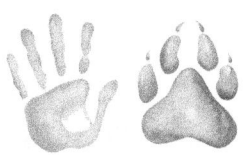

The hour's drive to the convention center passed quickly while Katey and her pack wove the whole story for John and Noah, from the night she and Logan met up to her training as a loup-garou. No one seemed willing to talk about the fight with Erik, and neither Katey or Logan mentioned the more scandalous moments they shared alone together. Darren and Dustin jumped in with little details of their own, including pieces of her own story that she hadn't been aware of because she wasn't there to see it.

Through it all, John and Noah, and even Forrest, were captivated and interrupted only to ask clarifying questions or make comments on the more outrageous parts of the story, like when Katey lost control the morning after she turned because of the hunger suppressant pills.

By the time they arrived at the convention center, John gave a gentle look to Katey. "The journey hasn't been easy for you thus far, but I assure you we'll do everything we can to make it smoother going forward."

What was that supposed to mean? Was something coming that was going to make everything that much harder? Or was that just what he told every other loup-garou that he helped to train over the centuries?

Noah pulled up in front of the building to let the gang out into the snow-covered streets before taking the car to the parking garage. Katey was shocked when her feet sank down to her ankles in a deep layer of snow and ice.

She squeaked in surprise and grabbed onto Logan's arm so she didn't fall, her heels gliding on ice just below the surface of the snow.

"Never walked in snow before, right?"

"Never," she replied. "How do I do this without breaking something?" Katey looked all around her feet as if the answer would magically appear on the puckered surface of the snow.

"Just wade through it, like this." Dustin proceeded to kick clumps of snow out of his way with his polished black dress shoes, creating a jagged path up to the stairs that led to the front door. The others trudged on ahead of them.

With Logan's solid frame as support, Katey tried that for a few steps, but shivered at the way the snow slid across her exposed feet and numbed her toes. Changing her approach, Katey picked up her feet and stomped her way up to the steps instead, so her skin came into minimal contact with the bitter snow.

Down the street, a huge Malamute barked so viciously that Katey jumped and clung tighter to Logan. The owner tugged back on the leash as the husky snapped and snarled at the pack standing on the steps of the convention center.

"Cool it, mutt. We're not in your territory," Logan mumbled, guiding Katey along to join the rest.

"I've never seen a dog so angry before." Katey scrunched her shoulders up as a gust of wind chilled the skin on her neck. Wearing her hair up might have been more convenient and faster to prepare, but foolish in cold weather.

"It happens. We have that effect on animals sometimes. They either cower in fear or get aggressive." Logan gestured his head toward the dog and its frantic owner. "That dog's warning us to get away from his human."

"How can you tell the dog's trying to say that?" she asked as they joined the others just outside the glass doors.

Logan turned a wondered look to her. "Couldn't you understand him?"

She shook her head. "All I heard was the barking."

Dustin opened the door for his alpha, while Forrest held open the opposite door for John. But both alphas looked at her in mild alarm.

Judging by their reactions, Katey knew this must not have been a good sign. "I'm supposed to understand dog-speak, aren't I?"

Dustin shrugged. "Well, not like in translated words, but more of the general idea. It's like how body language and the tone mean something specific."

"Perhaps that ability will manifest in time," John offered, though he gave an unreadable look to Darren that may have said something otherwise.

She breathed a sigh of relief as they entered the building. At least she wasn't missing what she should have already had, like everything else that was starting to disappear on her. Her wolf had decided to do a repeat performance and abandon her again. Only her heightened senses remained, and even they didn't feel quite so strong as they had days ago.

As they made their way through the lobby of the convention center, following the signs that pointed them toward the charity event, Katey held onto Logan's arm and found herself on the lookout for Erik. She continued to look over her shoulder, testing the air for his signature body spray and cigarette smoke combo scent. All she could smell was the gourmet meal that awaited them, but she noticed a particular lack of sensory input beyond that. There was the musty scent of the carpet and the overpowering perfume of the ladies they passed, but nothing more.

"I have to warn you," Katey told the guys, "I don't know the first thing about how to behave at something like this."

Logan put his hand over hers in a reassuring way. "That's all right. Just don't throw food at anyone and you'll be fine."

"At least put your napkin on your lap instead of trying to stuff it down your collar," Dustin muttered to her as they turned down various halls.

"Are you referring to my behavior last year?" Logan asked, a note of sarcasm playing in the question.

Dustin barked a laugh. "I actually forgot about that. Just follow our lead and don't look at what your boyfriend does."

Katey's face went hot when he called Logan her boyfriend. "Is that the story we're going with?"

Darren and Logan exchanged looks, and the latter nodded. "For now, yeah. Less complicated that way."

"I like less complicated." Katey held onto his arm a little tighter, savoring how solid he was.

Ahead, a crowd had formed around the ballroom doors. Katey could hear the din of voices from inside and the light clatter of dishes and glasses.

A man stood at the entrance, shaking hands and smiling professionally at all who passed through, occasionally chatting up a few of the guests he may have personally known. He was loup-garou, she was sure of it, and was glad to feel the tingling sensation in the back of her skull as they approached. Though, it wasn't as intense as she had felt before.

He wore a clean-pressed and expensive-looking suit with his dark russet brown hair gelled back. His beard was neatly trimmed and gave him a rugged, but sophisticated look that made Katey stare a little longer than she should have. Sapphire blue eyes regarded each guest with respect and he carried himself like a royal through the light conversation.

Logan leaned over to whisper in her ear. "That's Todd Rice."

Katey slid him a dubious look. "No way. Not the same Todd Rice that owns like, a dozen companies."

"The same. He's one of the richest loups-garous in the world. This is his charity luncheon. He founded the Global Association for the Conservation of Wolves."

Katey's jaw dropped as they came to the front of the reception line. If loups-garous could infiltrate the economic system, like Todd Rise, and the entertainment industry, like Rodney Bator, and education system, as Darren had, then where else were they hiding?

John and Todd acknowledged each other with a firm hand-shake, the same he had given everyone else. Their voices dropped as they spoke.

"It's good to see you here, John," Todd said in a husky voice. Katey could also detect a tinge of a deep southern accent in the cadence of his words that made her wonder where exactly he was from. It wasn't quite the same flavor of southern as Ben.

"It's good to see you, too." John turned to his entourage, which now included Noah. "May I present Darren Dubose, Dustin Keith, his grandson Logan, my son Noah, and the newest member to our family, Katey McCoy."

Katey started when John introduced her as a member of his family. Many foster families had introduced her like that during her first few weeks with them, but came to regret it all too soon.

Todd's intense eyes fell on Katey and she lost all comprehension of the human language. Instead, she gave him a weak smile and shyly stepped closer to Logan.

"It's a pleasure to meet you, Katey. As well as you, Darren," he addressed the alpha. "I recognize your name from the list of consistent contributors. You've donated a hefty sum over the years. It's a privilege to finally meet you."

The two loups-garous shook hands and Darren grinned. "I could say the same. Your organization has done great work."

Todd shrugged as if it were nothing. "I'm just doing what I can to help." He extended his hand to present the ballroom to them. "Please, enjoy your lunch. I'll be giving my opening speech shortly."

Katey followed the others into the ballroom and leaned up to kiss Logan on the cheek.

"What was that for?" he asked with a furtive smile.

"Because you're prettier than he is."

Logan chuckled as they made their way toward the front of the ballroom and the set of tables closest to the stage.

They passed by tables covered in white cloth, finished with a full place setting for six. Each setting boasted a full complement of silverware, dishware, and glassware that Katey would have expected from a five-star restaurant. Sitting in the center of each of the tables was a stunning centerpiece featuring quail feathers, antlers, tree trunk discs, and sprigs of pine branches to give the event a wildlife feel.

Katey marveled at the grand décor of the ballroom, festooned in everything that reminded her of the forest. The lights had been filtered to mimic the waning light of a sunset and the walls were trimmed in tapestries of flora and fauna characteristic of the dense wildernesses where the wild wolves ran free.

She breathed in the approaching aroma of lunch and her stomach rumbled in response, but still her wolf did not stir. It would have alarmed her, but another sight set her on edge that trumped anything else on her mind.

Sitting at a table not far from the front of the stage, were two loups-garous. One was older, somewhere between Darren and Dustin's age, judging by the way his black beard showed off bits of silver and deep crows-feet at the corner of his eyes. There was a harsh look of pride about him, coupled with the severe set of his mouth as he watched the crowds around him.

The other loup-garou was all too familiar, and even in a suit and tie, she recognized him in a heartbeat.

Erik spotted their pack and stood from his seat. The older loup-garou also stood as John approached, but neither rougarou put off an intimidating energy that would suggest hostility toward the alpha. Now standing, she saw the older rougarou was a tall man and formidable in size. He could easily fight any of them and probably win with one arm tied behind his back.

Darren and Dustin looked behind them to Katey and Logan with a cautionary look as if to tell them not to get involved. They listened, but Erik did not. He slipped away from the table and made his way toward Logan, Katey, and Forrest.

Logan guided Katey to stand with her alpha while he moved on a path to intercept Erik, but she wasn't about to leave Logan alone and chased after him, Forrest close at her heels.

"Well, look what the cat dragged in," Erik commented, sneering at the bunch.

"I could say the same for you," Logan replied with a snarl. The two stopped in front of each other, distrust blazing in their eyes.

"Who uses that line anymore?" Katey stood just beside Logan, showing that they were a team. Neither of them acknowledged her arrival on the scene.

From the edge of their table, she heard John's voice of authority. "Logan, remember what we spoke about this morning."

Still, he did not back down. Katey was about to step in, but Forrest beat her to it. The red headed loup-garou came between them and gently shoved Logan aside. Her heart hammered in her throat as she watched the two loups-garous she cared about face down Erik.

"This isn't the time or the place," Forrest told them. She had never seen Forrest get in a fight, or even show the least bit of anger, but now, he proved he was the son of an alpha. He needed no dominance to make himself be seen and heard.

"What are you afraid of?" Erik asked. "Why not give these humans a taste of what the real wild is like?"

Katey saw Erik's eyes turn a menacing gold.

"Erik," the older rougarou growled, his voice deeper and huskier than Katey had ever heard from any man before. It was as if thunder had been personified in a single man. She shrank back as his own brand of dominance added to the mix and hammered against her chest.

Forrest turned to the rougarou who killed his cousin almost a century ago and shot him a deadly glare, but did not raise a hand against him, even when Erik came well within striking range.

The older rougarou stormed toward them and grabbed Erik by the shoulder. Erik let out a low snarl, but resigned to the discipline of his elder and eased away.

"You'll have to excuse him," he said. "It was a long journey."

Katey stayed close behind Logan, her eyes fixed on the stranger.

John joined them and offered out his hand. "I am glad you're here with us."

The rougarou looked between John's face and the hand he had been offered in friendship. There was a moment of hesitance, and then he shook the great alpha's hand. He then greeted Noah in the same fashion and nodded his acknowledgement.

"I'm sure you haven't met Katey yet," John said, motioning to her with an air of respect. "Katey, this is Gregory Jennings, Erik's father."

Gregory turned to her with dark, almost black eyes, but he would neither nod nor offer out his hand. To be under his gaze set her teeth on edge. She could see the resemblance, though they seemed to be far different in temperament. Gregory at least seemed to be able to govern himself.

"Erik has told me about you," was all he said, then looked to Logan and Forrest. "It's been a long time. I trust you both are well."

Neither Logan nor Forrest moved, and Katey wondered if Gregory was in Chicago with Erik when everything went to hell in a handbasket.

"I wasn't aware you knew Logan or Forrest," John remarked, brows pinched.

"We met briefly in Chicago once upon a time." Gregory gave a forced smile, then gave a stern, nonverbal command to his son.

Erik quickly retreated to their table, in such a submissive way that startled Katey.

"We should take our seats," Gregory said, then turned without ceremony back to the table. John, Noah, and Forrest went with him.

"Why doesn't he sit with us?" Katey asked Logan, a spike of worry stabbing her guts at how Forrest had to sit across the table from Erik.

"Fixed seating arrangements," Logan mumbled as he guided her to their own reserved seats with Darren and Dustin.

Also at their table were a couple of guests that Katey could only recognize as human. The older and younger woman looked to be related, possibly mother and daughter, and casually chatted with the two loups-garous. The women's ears dripped with diamonds and their bodies were clad in stylish dresses that hugged their curves and sparkled in the tinted lights. The cut of the dresses showed off too much soft flesh for Katey's tastes. But, Dustin seemed particularly interested in the younger lady as he leaned forward over the table to hear her better.

Logan pulled out the chair for Katey beside the elder woman.

"Ladies, may I introduce my nephew, Logan, and his girlfriend, Katey. They insisted on seeing Alaska in its most brutal season."

They politely reciprocated their greetings. Darren seemed an expert in putting on a good show.

"It may be the most brutal season, Mr. Dubose, but it is one of the most beautiful," the elder lady remarked, her eyes sparkling with interest. She looked old enough to be Katey's grandmother.

"Very true," he relented with a smile. "This is Mrs. Rockshire and her daughter, Jenna. They've come all the way from New York to attend the luncheon."

"Oh, anything for Mr. Rice," Mrs. Rockshire crooned. "He's one of our most esteemed members at the country club and I'm crossing my fingers that Jenna will catch his attention one day."

Katey looked to Jenna who was far more entranced by Dustin's green eyes than their conversation. She was a pretty woman, but something told Katey that she had no idea who or what Mr. Todd Rice truly was. If she did, Mrs. Rockshire might not have been trying so hard to play matchmaker with the billionaire.

Looking around, Mrs. Rockshire was not alone in her wealthy lifestyle. It looked like all of North America's elite were present at the event and Katey's pack was out of place, especially Logan with his slightly longer hair and atypical facial hair style that gave him a rock star look.

She wondered who out of the room actually cared about the endangered wolves and who was there to show their allegiance to Todd Rice. But, if they were paying members of the association and contributed to the cause, did it really matter? Did the end goal of saving endangered wolves justify the shallow and self-righteous intentions behind their donations?

Logan was distracted, his eyes attentive on the far table where John and the others looked to be engaged in civil discussion. Several times, she had to squeeze Logan's hand under the table in order to bring him back from whatever deep thoughts kept him miles away, while Darren and Mrs. Rockshire talked about the different sights and socialite clubs of New York.

It bothered her that, all of the sudden, she couldn't hear or understand whatever the alphas were saying across the room. She heard their voices, but through the din of the crowd that waited for the luncheon to begin, she couldn't make out any full words or phrases.

That stunning realization froze the breath in her lungs and heart thump heavy against her ribs. First her wolf went dormant, the lack of urgency to eat, and now she began to lose some of her loup-garou senses. By all the signs, she did seem to be fading. How long would it take before she was completely human again, if that was even possible?

Of course, she refused to mention any of her fears to Logan. If her wolf would have responded to her call, then maybe the answer lied within her the whole time. However, as before, she got nothing but crickets, and it terrified her to be so alone in her body all of the sudden.

Katey began to feel herself spiral into uncertainty. She had risked her life, risked rejection and death for this chance to be part of Logan's world and in just one day, it looked to be slipping away from her. What would her pack do if she reverted back to her mortal, flawed self? What would John think? What would Logan do?

If it turned out that she would never be full loup-garou, would he abandon her? Sure, he might still love her imperfect human self, but would they even have a future together? Logan would carry on after she died and find someone else.

Her heart and stomach lurched at the thought of Logan in the arms of another woman and the blackness fell over her so suddenly that Katey wondered if she would ever climb out. She hadn't felt this dark since before Logan came into her life.

"Are you all right, dear?" Mrs. Rockshire asked in her withered New England accent.

Katey looked up, brows arched as she was thrown out of her black thoughts and back in the ballroom. All at the table but Dustin and Jenna looked at her with concern in their eyes. Logan probably couldn't sense a thing through their bond, because she couldn't sense anything on her end. He'd have no clue that she was about to lose her mind.

Without a hint of hesitation, Katey slipped back into her old habit and donned her mask. Somehow, her loup-garou spirit couldn't hold up the human defenses anymore. It was as if the mask itself fought against her, and she knew no one was fooled.

She smiled and nodded. "Yeah, I'm fine. I just need to use the restroom. Excuse me."

A speaker came up to the podium on the stage and tapped the microphone as Katey stood to make a hasty retreat. If she was going to have a breakdown, she didn't need to let it out in front of Logan and the others.

Logan grabbed her wrist to keep her in place, but she refused to meet his gaze. She twisted her wrist and pulled against his thumb, releasing his hold on her far too easily. Her heels tapped loudly against the hardwood floor of the ballroom as the speaker presented Todd Rice.

Katey let it all fade away and hurried past the tables to exit the room before anyone could see the tears that leaked from the corners of her eyes.

Todd Rice took the stage to thunderous applause from his prestigious guests. He smiled and waved for them to be silent and began his speech, but Logan's focus was elsewhere. It had only been half a minute since Katey left his side and he could barely contain the drive to bolt out of his seat and run after her.

He had felt her sadness build over the last hour alone as they drove from the lodge to the civic center. Like before, when she was human, he knew that something was not right, and their bond hummed with some dark, foreboding emotion he couldn't name. Without blatantly asking, there was no way for him to understand why. There were no hints, no warning in anything she had done or said that morning.

"Thank you for coming," Todd began. "As you know, The Global Association for the Conservation of Wolves has dedicated the last eight years to educating our communities and funding wildlife preserves across North America and Europe. It's my pleasure to share some statistics with you on how instrumental your donation dollars have been to these efforts..."

As Todd talked numbers, Logan looked once more to the far table where John, Gregory, and their kin sat. They quietly listened to the speech, but Erik was just as disinterested in the luncheon as he was. Logan tagged along for Darren's sake, but he would have gladly stayed behind at the lodge to spend time with Katey, knowing that the Jennings would be in attendance. Perhaps if they were back in their suite, curled up in front of the fire, she wouldn't be feeling such overpowering, inexplicable grief.

Suddenly, Erik smoothly slid out of his chair and made his way toward the exit without hardly a sound. Logan was sure he was the only one to notice, but as he rose to follow the rougarou, Darren forced him back down with a heavy hand on his shoulder.

Logan stifled a growl. Darren turned his attention away from Todd and looked at Erik as he exited the ballroom. With a subtle nudge, he got Dustin to tear his eyes away from Jenna and jerked his head in command to follow the rougarou.

Without protest, the beta stood and made his way out without nary a turning of the heads from the humans around them. About the same time, Logan glanced toward John's table and saw Gregory rise from his seat as well to follow Dustin out the doors.

Katey leaned against the wall around the corner from the ballroom. The civic center wasn't at all crowded in this part of the building, though she could hear the rumble of feet above her on the second floor and booming laughter from down the hall in other rooms that had been booked that day.

She swallowed hard and closed her eyes, willing the anxiety to leave before it consumed her completely. There were only a few minutes to compose herself before she had to go back and face the questioning eyes of her pack. Katey knew they could probably sense her disquiet, but would she have the strength to lie to them one more time and assure them that she was fine?

Another tear warmed the skin on her cheek as she remembered the immense kindness they had given her over the last few weeks. They had been nothing but supportive and she caused more trouble than they deserved.

Waste of time. Not worth it. A burden. Don't belong.

It would have been better if she never came with them to Alaska at all and found someone to stay with until they came back. But it went even further than that. Once more, like when she tried to join them for dinner at the barbeque restaurant, she felt out of place. She didn't belong with them. This was all a mistake. She was a mistake.

She wrapped her arms around her middle, willing the pain of doubt and regret to go away. She'd had a taste of what it was like to be special, to be unique. As a loup-garou, she could do things no ordinary girl could do and she wanted to be one of a kind, not just to Logan, but to her new pack and the whole loup-garou society. She wanted to be somebody, and it was turning out that she was a nobody all along and she shouldn't have even tried to be something she could never be.

The memories came back to her, seen through the eyes of a human that hated herself and her entire life. Logan had always been her lighthouse to guide her safely to shore. He was the beacon when everything else was dark and lost. He loved her as a human and if she turned human again, he would still love her. He always saw her as perfect, even before she turned, just like in his sketches. Katey had to hold on to that irrefutable truth or she would lose her mind. Even if the whole world came crashing down, and she wasn't loup-garou anymore, Logan would still be there.

With a deep, shuddering breath, she composed herself one more time. When she opened her eyes and turned to make her way back toward the ballroom, Katey felt herself pinned back to the wall, sharp claws digging into her shoulder and firm body pressed into hers until she almost couldn't breathe. Brown eyes locked on hers and Katey would have let out a beastly cry if she thought she could get away with it. Pain seared through her flesh and warm blood oozed from the puncture wounds, staining the front of her blouse.

"Where you goin' in such a hurry?" Erik's hot breath hit her face like a blast of toxic fumes.

"Let me go or I'll scream." Katey bared her teeth as if she were ready to snap and bite his throat.

Erik made a fake sound of disappointment. "Aw, I'm really hurt."

"When are you going to take the hint that I don't want you?"

His face went hard and glared. "Just because you got in the way the other night doesn't mean that he won you."

"You forfeited."

"Yes, but he hasn't made his claim on you. If he knew any better, he should have taken you that night."

"Just because he hasn't, doesn't mean he won't," Katey countered. "And you cheated that night. You put him in that shoulder hold to make him lose control."

His eyes narrowed. "I broke no rules."

"Except the rule of good sportsmanship. You knew that if he changed, it would cause a panic and endanger everyone's safety. You're nothing but a fraud and you couldn't win in a fight against Logan on fair terms, no matter what you were fighting for."

Erik's eyes glowed a devilish gold and his claws sunk deeper into her skin. She whimpered and tried to pry his hand away, but he wouldn't budge.

His strong grip found the nerve Darren had told her about, the same one that Erik had used against Logan in the match. Her body flooded with fire, coursing through her veins like a poison. Muscles quivered and her bones began to ache under the strain of the pull on her wolf.

He leaned in close until she could see every definition of his golden irises. "There's going to be a day when you regret every word you just said. Logan doesn't deserve you. A strong female needs a strong male and you know I'm the one who can give you what you need."

Katey growled in her throat and spat in Erik's eye. "You have no idea what I need."

Yet, inadvertently, Erik had given her exactly that. Her wolf awakened within her and roared at their attacker. Her senses exploded, as if the dial had been turned to the max after being set on mute for too long. She could hear Todd's speech and the rustling of clothing from down the hall. Exotic perfumes, expensive colognes, and the metallic scent of blood on her shoulder mingled in her nose in an astringent odor. She not only could smell their lunch, but snacks in the vending machine several hallways away.

Her own eyes flashed gold and once more, she felt loup-garou. But at what cost? How long could she hold up under his grip before she'd crumble or fall unconscious as the pain intensified.

A presence came close. Another loup-garou.

"Erik!" the thunderous voice shouted, blaring in her ears.

Gregory's command held just enough sway for his son to let Katey go. Like a dog with his tail tucked between his legs, he fled to his father's side.

She sniffled back the urge to cry as the pain slowly died away. Her senses and the wolf remained on alert as her hand put pressure on the wounds in her shoulder, waiting for her body to heal. When she looked back, Gregory and Erik were gone but she knew they hadn't returned to the ballroom.

Within seconds, Dustin came barreling around the corner. "Are you okay?" His gaze darted from her golden eyes to her soiled shirt.

"Erik cornered me again."

Dustin took her hand away from her shoulder and without asking consent, pulled back the collar of her blouse to reveal where Erik's claws left their mark. All that was left were the streaks of blood. All healed, but the evidence remained far too obvious.

"What did he want?" he asked as he shrugged off his jacket and slipped it around her shoulders in some attempt to hide the blood and holes. It did, but the garment practically swallowed her, six sizes too big for her frame.

She shook her head. "Just me. He seems to think that I'm still up for grabs, even after what happened at the match."

With a sigh, he gave her another once-over and gestured to her eyes. "You might want to take care of that."

She squeezed her eyes shut, though she never wanted her eyes to be another color ever again. At least then she would know that the loup-garou spirit was not dead in her yet. To feel so much and sense everything was a welcome thing.

For whatever reason, her abilities decided to go dormant, but when Erik rekindled that part of her soul, they were activated. But, how long would these effects last? Another week? A day? What could she do to make the change more permanent, more stable?

Then, it hit her. The nerve in her shoulder, when stimulated, could bring on an involuntary shift. That was what woke up her wolf and revived her abilities. She needed to shift, and she couldn't afford to wait until it was her natural time of the month.

She looked up to Dustin who seemed to take notice of her revelation. "I need to shift."

He blinked rapidly and pressed his fingers between his brow as if he had just been struck with a headache. "I'm sorry, I think you just said, 'I need to shift'?"

"Yeah. I need to shift. I... I can't explain all of it now, but can we make that happen? Can John help? There's plenty of woods around here and—"

Dustin moved his hands as if he were trying to pat down a fire. "Hold up. Hold up. I think you and Darren need to talk first, okay?" He glanced down at her blouse and how well his jacket covered her. "Do you think you can sit through lunch?"

Katey didn't want to, but if she had no choice, she would. She nodded and let herself be led back toward the ballroom, knowing she'd have a ton of explaining to do for the pack. But now, at least she had a plan. She had some solution for how to prevent the fading. She did belong, and she'd prove it.

CHAPTER 16

O nce they were back in the privacy of their room, Logan slid Dustin's jacket from Katey's shoulders. It was the dozenth time he had seen the dried blood and the torn holes in her shirt, but each time inspired a new, hot rage. He let out another curse under his breath, mad enough to run out the door and track down Erik in that very moment.

"Next time I see him, I'm going to skin him alive."

"You'll have to wait in line." Katey pulled off the jacket the rest of the way and laid it across Dustin's bed. "I'm going to take a quick shower to wash all this off and then I have to talk to Darren."

Yes, she did, about more than one thing. She had dropped the bomb in the van on the way back to the resort that she wanted to try and shift. Everyone was more startled than shocked by her declaration, given that she knew nothing about what was supposed to happen in a matter of hours. If she wanted to attempt a willful shift, she had to know the risks. If Darren hadn't already called dibs on explaining the process to her, he would have tried, but would likely stumble through it.

He glanced out the curtained window of their room. The sun was close to setting, typical for a midafternoon winter in Alaska. Thankfully, the usual aches of the shift were still hours away, leaving them plenty of time to discuss the future and take that trip into town.

When he looked back to Katey, her back was turned to him, but by the way her arms moved and how her head was slightly ducked, he knew what she was doing. His feet wouldn't move, and he couldn't tear his eyes away from the scene. His blood raced and mind went completely blank, except for the single expectant thought of what he might see if he stuck around.

Katey peeked over her shoulder and lifted a brow. "A little privacy?"

Logan's head cocked to the side as if he didn't understand what she said. It was only when she made that shooing motion with her hand that his brain kicked back into gear and he realized what he had been doing.

"Oh, right. Sorry." Logan's face scrunched with shame. "I'll be downstairs." He turned quickly to flee the room, heat creeping up his neck. He needed to talk to Darren anyway and while Katey was occupied upstairs, this was his chance.

Darren had taken a seat on the sofa in front of the fire, his jacket shed and tie loose around his neck with his hands laced behind his head. John was still in full formal wear, lounging in one of the armchairs next to the hearth.

He could hear Ben and Blake chatting in the game room, setting up the pieces for another chess game. Dustin had dressed down so far that all his shirt buttons were unfastened to display his bare chest and core as he stood in the kitchen, leaning against the counter with his hands propped behind him.

The sound of drawers opening and closing came from one of the suites and he could only assume that Noah was changing clothes completely.

"Is she all right?" Darren asked as Logan sat down next to him.

Logan pulled at the knot in his tie and unfastened the top button. "As far as I can tell."

"Why did she get up and leave like that in the first place?" Dustin asked from the kitchen.

His grandfather didn't have a knack for being serious when it was needed, but when the well-being of the pack was called into question, he came to his senses.

Logan leaned back against the plush cushion. "I felt her sadness, but she hasn't given me any clue as to why or what happened. Whatever it was, it's gone now."

Just then, the suite door opened and John's middle sons, Aiden and Liam, entered. Their clothes were saturated with the scent of feminine perfume, beer, and sweat.

"About time you two showed back up," Ben bantered from the game room.

Liam walked into the room, pounded on his chest, and held his arms out in a gesture that Logan recognized amongst brawlers.

It was an open invitation to fight, but he knew better, neither loup-garou would take his offer. Not even Logan would dare to challenge a burly man like Liam, unless he wanted his spine snapped in two. By the amused look on Liam's face, the challenge was not serious anyway.

Aiden chuckled and stood behind the couch, leaning on the polished log frame. "Well, look at all of you in your suits. How was the luncheon?"

John folded his hands over his stomach. "If you came, you would have known."

Logan didn't have to look over his shoulder to know that Aiden rolled his eyes.

"Hey, Aiden" Dustin barked from the kitchen. "Did you bring any of your craft brew?"

"Sure. I've got two six-packs in the fridge."

"Sweet." Dustin turned and pulled out two glass beer bottles from the shelf. "I need to see how much you'd charge to ship some of this gold down to Florida every once and a while."

Aiden scoffed. "For you, a thousand dollars."

Darren chuckled as Dustin's jaw dropped. "That ain't right, boyo," he complained in his thick Irish brogue. "I got as much right to this lovely stuff as any of your other customers."

"You can't even get drunk," Logan remarked. "Why bother drinking?"

Dustin pointed a finger at his grandson. "Just because you're a teetotaler doesn't mean I have to be."

He used his teeth to pop off the cap and offered the unopened beer to Aiden, who gladly took it and made his way to the game room to join the others.

Noah came out of the room he shared with two of his brothers, wearing a pair of sweats and a shirt that hugged his body in a way that would have made Logan nervous if Katey was present to see him. He jerked his head in greeting to Aiden and Liam just before he disappeared into the other room and sat down in the armchair across from his father.

"Did you mention tonight to her?" Dustin asked Logan after taking a swig of the beer.

He shook his head. "I haven't mentioned anything."

"So why the sudden desire to learn how to shift at will?" John asked.

Logan sensed the unease in his alpha next to him. He noticed the way Darren's jaw worked, his molars grinding as he deliberated some secret thought.

"Perhaps this has something to do with her attitude towards training," Darren mused, glancing to Dustin. "She seems adamant to prove herself."

"Prove herself?" Noah questioned with a note of interest.

Logan nodded. "She's told me about wanting to prove that she can handle this new life and control her wolf. She's been way harder on herself when she slips up or makes a mistake."

Dustin moved around the kitchen island to get closer to the group. "She's been determined from the first day of training. Remember how excited she was when she finally got the hang of running at top speed?"

"She doesn't need to shift in order to prove herself to us," Noah said with a shrug.

Darren narrowed his eyes on Noah. "That's not the impression I got last night or this morning. What changed?"

Noah and John exchanged looks, as if in a muted conference on the matter.

"I said that I couldn't sense a strong wolf within her," John began. "After she returned from her altercation with Erik, I could feel her wolf from across the room. I've never felt so strong a presence since... well, at least a few centuries. Nothing in recent memory."

Logan perked up at this. "So, you think there's a chance she'd be able to shift on her own?"

"Maybe, but if she does, she'll need extra attention and care." John looked to Darren. "Have you discussed breaking with her?"

The very word, breaking, sent an electric shock through Logan, every nerve set ablaze.

Dustin, too, started at the mention of it. "Breaking? For a willful shift?"

Darren nodded. "Yes, especially for her first willful shift into her loup-garou form. I planned to mention it when we had our talk."

"Such a breaking will be... challenging, to say the least," John pondered, a grave look about him that didn't settle Logan's momentary panic.

"Who will be there for it?" Noah asked. "Do you need help?"

The offer of any assistance from Noah snapped Logan back to the present. His lips twitched as if he'd growl at the very idea of

Noah helping with Katey's breaking, but out of respect for John and Darren, he stayed quiet.

"I think Darren and I will be able to handle it," John replied. "Where do you intend to have the talk with her?"

Darren shifted uncomfortably. "I hoped to find some quiet place in the resort, or perhaps the room upstairs." He paused and looked to Logan. "If that's all right with you."

Logan blinked curiously at his alpha. Darren deferred to him as if Katey were already his mate and the alpha needed permission to be alone with her. Perhaps his pack knew that Katey was unlikely to turn down the proposal, should the situation require it.

"Fine with me. I'll go up after she's out of the shower to let her know you'll be coming to her."

Darren nodded, then smacked the back of his hand against Logan's thigh in warning. "You have a few hours before sunset," the alpha reminded, changing the subject. "How are you feeling?"

Logan took a moment to reflect. Past the anxiety of how Katey would take all Darren would have to say to her, he felt fine. Though, that panic seemed all-consuming at the moment, so much that even if he felt his wolf stir and push against his human skin, he'd likely not even notice.

He took a calming breath. "I'm alright. After you two are done talking, can I take Katey out?" he asked, looking to the two alphas. "We'll be back before everyone leaves."

The alphas looked to one another for a long moment, as if silently communicating on some telepathic line that Logan couldn't link to. All he knew was that he needed to get Katey alone, away from the pack and away from everything that would hold them back this evening. If he could get her alone, maybe she would open up about what bothered her at the luncheon, and he could simultaneously discover her feelings on the shift, the breaking, and the preliminary mating bond business.

John was the first to nod his consent. "Do what you need to do."

Upstairs, the running water stopped and he heard the curtain rings grind against the rod as Katey stepped out of the shower. Logan stood to go to her.

Katey wrapped the robe around her and cinched the belt tight to keep it all in place. Outside the bathroom, she heard the bedroom door open and voices downstairs that she purposefully tuned out so their conversation would be private. She took a moment to drink in Logan's masculine scent that lingered in the room, thankful that she could detect it through the clouds of steam.

Foolishly, she didn't bring any of her fresh clothes into the bathroom with her. The bathroom door was still locked, but she couldn't stay there forever. She'd have to step out, naked beneath her robe that only reached down to her mid-thigh.

She unlocked the door and released the steam from the bathroom. The cold air of the hotel room hit her legs and chilled her damp hair that spiraled in loose waves down her back. Logan stood by the window with his back to her.

Logan still wore his crisp, white dress shirt, tucked into his black slacks, his thumbs hooked in his pockets in that casual way she loved. Her lips curled together as she admired the way the fabric outlined his hard, strong body and trim waist.

She moved closer, fully aware of just how precarious this situation was, and how quickly it could evolve into something else. Logan's head turned ever so slightly in her direction, but he still wouldn't look at her, as if he already knew she wasn't wearing anything under her robe.

So close, she reached out and let her fingers crease paths down the contours of his back. He shuddered beneath her touch and stiffened, his quick intake of breath just barely audible in the stillness of the bedroom. Katey grinned, loving how she could so easily set him off.

When her fingers gripped a fold in his shirt and pulled the edges free from his pants, he finally turned and grabbed her wrists, trapping her in a gentle, but firm hold. Once blue eyes were now a fiery red. His gaze took her in, and she heard the subtle uptick in his heartbeat.

Katey smiled up at him, feeling a piece of her wolf coming forward to embolden her in the moment. "What? Suddenly shy about going shirtless?"

She perceived the slightest loosening of his grip, and she easily twisted her hands free and upward to begin unfastening his buttons. She did so, slowly, letting her fingertips brush the smooth skin of his chest and abs as she went. Once his shirt was completely undone, she bit her bottom lip, appreciating the pure masculinity of his body as she had before.

Heat pooled low in her belly and sparks shot down her core, following the fire of want he had kindled in her.

Logan's lowered hands flexed as if he didn't know what to do all of the sudden. Katey stepped into his space, giving him the permission he needed. Arms encircled her waist and his powerful grip took hold of the plush belt of the robe. Her palms flattened against his chest, and she let herself fall into his embrace.

They froze in a breathless moment, Katey's pulse thrumming through her body so violently she thought she would burst.

Then, Logan let go of the belt. His forehead touched hers, his jaw muscles jumping as if he were fighting a battle she couldn't understand.

"Katey... I can't... I won't."

The complete sorrow in the whispered words startled her enough to pull back, questions in her stare.

His throat worked and he brisky shook his head. "I know it's old fashioned, but... I don't want that part of you too soon."

Katey relaxed. He wasn't rejecting her. He was rejecting sex. "It doesn't have to go that far."

Before he could protest, she reached up and slid off his shirt to drop it to the floor, not unlike the way she took off his jacket that night she was willing to take things that far.

Only this time, he didn't stop her. His mouth came down on hers with fierce need that sent a shock between her legs. A hot wetness came seconds before their passion doubled, the kiss deepening. Logan backed her up until the back of her knees hit the edge of the mattress and she fell. Her wet hair left a damp circle in the comforter beneath her head.

A flash of a draft on her stomach inspired a brief second of panic, but Logan's body crushed her into the mattress, hiding whatever nudity may have slipped out.

She sighed against his mouth as the feel of skin to skin made her want to take it all back. For a moment, she wanted more than making out, more than heavy petting and kissing. She wanted it all, every bit of him, or as much as he was willing to give. Their tongues teased and played, as hands explored in safe, tame ways that Katey hated. Every inch of her needed to be touched, needed to be caressed, just as her own hands worshiped the shape of Logan like she would never get this opportunity again.

He kissed down her jaw, to her neck, shoulder, then the shard of flesh just below her throat between the flaps of her robe. One leg hooked around his hip, her back arching against the rush of sensation. The building ache was too much. Thoughtless, her hands slipped to his leather belt. The tap of metal as she undid the buckle might as well have been the bell that signaled the end of a round in a fight match.

Logan grabbed her wrists again and pinned them at the level of her shoulders, denying her the right to take what she wanted. A low, guttural growl rumbled in his chest. It was meant to be a warning, but Katey shivered with the completely opposite feeling.

"Please." The plea came out raspy, laced with unrequited need.

His mouth returned to hers for one last, subdued kiss to wind them down from the incredible high of ecstasy.

"No. Not yet."

Katey accepted that her body and its wanton needs would not be satisfied. Not that day anyway. Part of her wanted to force it, to use her loup-garou strength and make Logan change his mind. But that wouldn't have been fair, even less fair than reining back their desire for each other before they were properly mated.

They stayed that way, Logan on top of her, motionless as the red in their eyes swirled away and a tinge of embarrassment displaced all the urgency of moments before. At least someone had their head on straight.

"Darren said he would come up here to talk to you... might want to get dressed."

The thought that their alpha might smell what almost happened in the room made her face go hot.

Logan eased off of her, hands blindly adjusting her robe to cover her up again, his blue eyes stayed fixed on hers.

"Are we okay?" Katey asked, fear stealing her voice.

Logan kissed her one more time, full of love but devoid of lust. "Yes, we are."

Katey pressed the heel of her palm between her eyes. "I'm so sorry... I lost it there for a minute."

He bent down and kissed her knuckles. "Remember how I said everything would feel so much more extreme as a loup-garou? That includes this." He gave her a disarming smile. "At least you didn't use claws this time."

Katey chortled a short laugh and then took a deep breath that moved her whole diaphragm.

Logan stood and she listened to his movement around the room as he picked up his shirt and went to put on another. She knew he wouldn't look her way, not as long as she lay sprawled across the mattress, so vulnerable and available.

"When you're done talking with Darren, we can leave for town."

Somehow, this shift back into "business as usual" after such a passionate moment didn't feel as awkward as Katey thought it would be. Her body still tingled with the afterglow of almost going too far, but her mind settled back into a sane flow of thought. Soon, she reviewed what she would say to Darren, and how it would change things between her and Logan. She remembered that he couldn't shift at will, and hadn't considered how her desire to learn how to do just that could have wounded him. If she tried, and succeeded, how would he feel?

Part of her wanted to trust that if it bothered him, he would say something, but Logan had never been the type to offer up his feelings without provocation.

Katey sat up and looked at his backside as he slipped on a black t-shirt that hugged his figure. "Are you sure we're okay? Does my wanting to shift upset you?"

Logan almost looked over his shoulder, but quickly corrected himself and stayed facing the wall. "Not at all... I want to say it's only natural, but... honestly, it's not." He ended with a tiny laugh. "I don't know any loup-garou who actually wanted to be loup-garou as badly as you do."

She didn't know whether to take that as a compliment or not, but she would speak her truth. "It's only because I want to be with you, to make this easier for both of us."

Silence fell, but Katey felt a wealth of emotion in their bond. Fear and happiness blended until the two seemed inseparable, creating a whole new sensation unto itself. Was that the wrong thing to admit?

Logan bowed his head and she watched his hand grip the back of his neck. "I don't know what to say to that."

Katey smiled. "Say, 'I love you, too.' Because that's what I meant."

He chuckled. "Yeah, I love you, too."

The rooms in the suite may have been soundproof, but they didn't block scents. Darren stood by the door, arms folded, waiting impatiently for Katey and Logan to stop... He tried not to think about it, or assume the worst, but his protective nature overrode any resistance to managing their love life.

The moment Logan exited the room, dressed in a clean shirt and jeans, Darren grabbed him by the elbow and spun him away from the doorway.

He didn't need to say a word for Logan to know exactly what he needed to know. "Nothing happened," he insisted. "I swear."

Darren searched his face for the lie, but didn't find it. He released his packmate with a light push toward the stairs. Logan strode away and went downstairs to endure the lude commentary from John's sons. With a sigh and shake of his head, Darren entered the bedroom.

Katey sat upon one of the beds, fully clothed and hair hanging in damp waves down her back and over her shoulders.

He had to address the obvious before going any further. "Either Logan is very good at lying or you two have more control than any teenager on the planet."

Katey's face went red, then ghostly white. "You heard us?"

Darren tapped his nose. "Smelled." He saw Katey squirm. "So, I'll ask you just once... have you two—"

"No!" She answered quickly, eyes round. "In Logan's defense, he has way more control than I do."

Even if Logan could manage a lie, Katey couldn't. Her tells were still too strong. She told the truth, however hard it was for her to admit. That gave him some consolation. It may have only been a matter of time before the two consummated their relationship, but he hoped it would be within the bounds of mating, or marriage, whichever came first. At this rate, they might need one or the other just to eliminate the temptation. Most loups-garous clung to the traditional ways of courtship, though many others, like Dustin or Aiden, held looser ideas on what was permissible.

Darren settled himself on the opposite bed and faced her. "You both need to be very, very careful around unmated loups-garous with that. Pheromones can drive a man crazy if he lets it." He took a breath. "Which leads me into what you need to know about what is going to happen tonight."

Katey's face pinched with confusion. She likely thought this conversation was solely about shifting.

"These gatherings are a chance for loups-garous to meet and socialize, and part of that involves groups of us going out to shift together on select nights. Tonight, we planned to shift with several other packs who owe their lives and allegiance to John. They, like myself, trained with John in France when we were young. We didn't bother telling you about this part of the trip because we were going to leave you behind with the other women. Your desire to shift changes that."

Katey straightened. "I can come with you?"

Darren held up a hand. "There are some things you need to know first. We can bring you along, but only on the condition that you and Logan come to some agreement on your relationship."

At that, Katey clasped her hands in her lap, waiting.

"Like in our human forms, unmated men can tell when they're around an available female. Dustin already told you that. The same likely applies in our loup-garou forms, but there has never been a female loup-garou so we don't know what may happen if you shift around us. Feral instincts may take over. It would be in everyone's best interest if you and Logan formed the preliminary mating bond, so that all will know you belong to him. You know what the preliminary mating bond is, right?"

"It's like being engaged." The sparkle of eagerness in her eyes confirmed what they all suspected. She knew far more than she needed to already and hoped for much more.

"It's more than that. It's a spiritual tethering between your souls. Once it's formed, it can't be broken. It's not like a pack bond, which can be formed and reformed at will. Mating with a loup-garou is for life. The next step to solidify the bond is a mating ceremony, which isn't possible right now anyway, but—"

"Why not?" she snapped.

Darren paused and tried to disregard her tone. "It involves the loup-garou to shift at will in front of their intended mate, along with some symbolic ritual. Neither of you can shift at will for that ceremony, but it is possible for you two to form the preliminary mating bond first, for the sake of tonight. But, that is only if you want to try to shift."

Katey nodded slowly in understanding. "So, if I want to shift tonight, Logan and I have to get engaged."

"Simplified, yes."

"Was that all?"

Her calmness at the notion was encouraging, but Darren wasn't done. "No. If you succeed in your shift, certain actions must be taken to secure the safety of yourself and everyone at the gathering. When a loup-garou shifts for the first time, they can be wild, unruly. It's the responsibility of their alpha to bring them under control. We call it breaking, like breaking a wild horse. If a loup-garou is not broken, they can go on a rampage. That's why John's mission to take in orphaned loups-garous was so important in an Era when people believed in magic and monsters. It made sure our secret was kept safe and prevented massacres. One rogue loup-garou could ruin it for everyone, so breaking is necessary. It brings a loup-garou to submission under an alpha."

Katey stared, unblinking, but he knew she comprehended what he meant. She could shift, but she would also have to be broken. He didn't want to scare her with their theory that she would be a challenge to break. That part wasn't important.

"Will I... Will I be conscious through it?"

"No. One moment, you'll be in the shift, and at some point you'll black out from the pain and wake up in the morning. It'll take many years before you gain consciousness during a shift."

That seemed to comfort her anxiety and she gave another faint nod of acknowledgement.

"What we told you the other night is not an exaggeration. The shift will be extremely painful. That pain is often what keeps young loups-garous from learning the skill. The other is their reluctance to trust their wolf. A willful shift is a joining of souls, a handing off the baton, so to speak. Many are too resistant to let the wolf take control, so it takes longer for them to learn. Given how eager you are, it may come naturally to you, or it may not."

"Is that why Logan can't shift at will?"

Darren grimaced. "Likely. It's no news that he hates his wolf, hates what he is. Tonight is his normal night to shift, eliminating the complication of having to force a shift upon him."

"So, if I don't shift tonight, he wouldn't stay behind with me?"

"No. But don't let that sway your decision."

Katey's gaze fell to the carpet. "I assume he knows all of this?"

"He does. He mentioned you two were going out. I encourage you both to discuss this thoroughly and make the best decision that fits for you... Mating is serious. It's not like marriage. Marriage is just a piece of paper. Mating is permanent."

Katey's mouth curled into a soft smile. "Permanent."

Darren sat back, studying her reaction. Anyone so young may have been intimidated by the idea. She had so much life ahead of her. To tie herself to someone so soon should have made her change her mind about shifting that night. Instead, she looked ready to go form the preliminary mating bond with Logan right then and there.

But, Katey wasn't like any other girl. She had a rough past. She was the first female loup-garou. Perhaps it was foolish to think she would be like any other teenage girl. She was strong, driven, stubborn, and she knew what she wanted.

Every doubt as to her ability to shift at will, vanished. Darren knew then that she would shock them all.

CHAPTER 17

Logan led Katey out of the lodge and offered his arm to her. Katey took it with a grin and they began walking in the freshly fallen snow down the road that led into town. They could have taken the bus, but the call of the outdoors was too tempting for either of them to pass up.

With her plush white jacket keeping out the cold, Katey felt she could tolerate the weather a little more. Her body didn't seem to register the harsh, biting winds as keenly as they had the day before when they stepped out of the airport. With her loup-garou senses returning, perhaps she would fare better on the long trek into town. Logan wore his usual leather jacket, considerably underdressed compared to her, bundled up with gloves and the stocking hat.

"Be careful how you step. The road underneath may be frozen," Logan warned.

Katey never had to wade through snow before and had to inwardly remark that it was easier than walking in sand on the beach, but still challenging. Some ice crystals melted through her shoes to dampen her socks and the hem of her jeans.

At first, both were silent, each absorbed in their own thoughts. All around, she could hear birds and woodland creatures that could brave such freezing temperatures. The further they got from the resort, the more distant the sounds of civilization became. No car engines, no conversations. It was a welcome reprieve. It was a fair walk to the bookstore Logan mentioned in the elevator on their way to the lobby. She didn't feel thrilled with the idea, but it was Logan's birthday and if he wanted to browse the bookshelves, she would be with him.

Even in the peace of winter, Katey wondered many things. When would Logan propose? If he decided to drop down on one knee in the bookstore, would she be disappointed? Proposing in front of a bunch of dusty books didn't seem romantic, but how much did that matter to her? How much would it matter if it meant they could be together forever?

Then, he had talked about them grabbing a bite to eat before going back to the resort. She could already feel her cheeks flush at the thought of a dozen or more people in a restaurant applauding after she said yes. Logan knew that she didn't like to be the center of attention, so perhaps he wouldn't go that route.

What if he proposed there in the forest? Katey wouldn't complain, but would it be on the way to town or on the way back to the lodge? And what did the bonding entail? Did they even know how to link themselves on that spiritual level? Would it happen in a moment too brief for her to even recognize?

No matter how he asked, Katey knew she would say yes. Not just because it would open the opportunity for her to shift that night with the other loups-garous, but because this was what she wanted, what they wanted, from the beginning. They wanted to belong to one another, to always have each other in their lives. It's what drove nearly every decision thus far, and nothing would change that.

She wanted to trust his timing, but part of her wanted to drag him among the trees and propose marriage herself just to get it over with. The wait was agonizing.

Katey breathed deeply and relished the fresh scent of the earth, an unblemished wilderness of pine and spruce. The wolf inside her basked in the glory of it, but strangely enough didn't beg for release as it had before when she gave herself to the pull of nature.

"Why did you lie to me?" Logan asked, his voice dropping and thick with emotion.

She knew exactly what he was talking about and she had desperately hoped that it would have never come up in conversation. But, they had to be beyond secrets.

"I was afraid of what you'd think."

"If you're not feeling well, you need to tell someone. If it was hunger or—"

"No," she cut him off. "It wasn't about anything physical. I mean, not really." Katey squeezed his arm, hoping that feeling his presence would help her form the right words. "I was scared that... that it was fading."

"Fading? What was fading?"

His gaze was on her, burning through her like a hot iron rod, but she would not take her eyes off the snow bank they trudged through. "Whatever it is that makes me loup-garou. I thought it was fading, but I didn't want to worry you."

Logan stopped her and her heart might as well have fallen dead in the snow. He turned her by the shoulders so she would have no choice but to face him. "When did this start happening?"

With her chin bowed low, nearly touching her chest, she replied, "Sometime yesterday. Or maybe the night before. I don't really know. It just kind of snuck up on me."

His thumbs caressed her cheeks and she looked up to meet his troubled gaze. "You should have told someone." Through their pack bond, she could sense his fear. She didn't want to make him think that what he had brought into creation could be snuffed out so easily.

"I tried outside the airport, but you sounded like you didn't want to hear it."

Logan leaned his forehead against hers, probably battling the impulse to feel guilty for the harsh words he had spoken. "I didn't mean to come across that way, Katey."

Her hands gripped his jacket sleeve. "It's okay, though. It's better now."

His brows furrowed. "Better?"

She nodded. "Yeah. At first, I just didn't feel my wolf, and then I started to lose a lot of my senses. Now, I can hear and smell just as I did before, like the morning after you turned me. Erik putting me in that shoulder grab woke up my wolf somehow."

Logan seemed relieved as he kissed her lips, but she could tell that he was anything but fine. He might have been wondering why her abilities faltered and she had been wondering the same, but was nowhere close to an explanation. She was sure that not even John or Darren could explain what had happened to her.

They started back on the path and he clung to her a little tighter. "Please, don't hesitate to talk to me. I don't care if I'm going to get furious and kill someone. I need you to tell me if something's wrong."

Katey's steps slowed at his exaggeration. At least, she hoped it was an exaggeration. "Darren told me about Chicago."

It was a simple sentence, comprised of simple words that even a child could articulate. Yet, the impact was far greater and she could sense Logan's reaction. He took a deep, pained breath and his gaze lowered to the path.

"That was a long time ago. I'm not the same person I was before... I'm not proud of what I did to those men in Chicago. I could have handled my grief better. I know that now. Being a loup-garou, you have time to think about your mistakes and what you could have done instead."

It made Katey speculate as to what mistakes she would make, or what mistakes she had already made that would haunt her for centuries.

"I understand that you were angry at Erik for what he did."

"Angry doesn't begin to describe what I felt." A biting edge scoured his words. "I could understand hunters killing us. I understand why I killed my parents. But what Erik and his gang did was beyond brutality. He gunned down my friend and dozens of other loups-garous. It wasn't just a hit to intimidate. They had silver bullets. He intended to kill them. All for some stupid scheme to do what? Take over a city? He only wanted power and would do anything to get it."

Katey pressed herself into his side, their steps in sync with one another, incapable of finding the words that would make the pain go away. If he hadn't healed in nearly a century, it was likely she couldn't do or say anything to mend the wounds.

Logan looked to the sky as a colorful bird swept through the air between the trees. "But I haven't killed since then. I never felt the need, never felt that consuming rage... until Erik came back into my life... our lives."

That was a small consolation to Katey, but it didn't erase his sins. He repented, that was certain, and Katey had come to terms with the fact that she loved a murderer. Yet, how many loups-garous back in the lodge could honestly say they had never killed a human or fellow loup-garou in cold blood? Killing was part of them, part of who they were as predators, and though Katey hated the idea, she knew that one day killing would be something that she had to do and whether it was avoidable or not was indeterminate.

"I'm sure we will live too long, but I almost want to make you promise not to kill again."

He shook his head. "If Erik or another rougarou attacks me, I won't hesitate to kill. If a hunter threatens the safety of the pack, I'll do what's necessary. If a vampire ever came into our territory with the intention to harm us, I'd do the same. Above all, if anyone tried to hurt you, I'd do everything in my power to keep you safe. That's the only thing I can promise you."

And in the moment, Katey knew that was all she could ask. She hopped up and kissed the bottom side of his tense jaw and felt the tautness ease away.

"Let's talk about something nicer," she offered cheerfully.

Logan laughed. "Please."

"About tonight... Darren told me what has to happen if I want to try and shift." Katey didn't expect Logan to go stony on her, especially under the subject of mating, but it was as if he had thrown up a shield to keep her out all of the sudden. "You don't want to talk about it."

As if realizing what he had done, Logan blinked hard and sighed. "It's not that... I just feel like I've led you on, and I didn't even realize it."

Katey dipped her chin. "You mean about the mating ceremony? Since you can't shift at will."

"Yeah. I was so caught up in making sure that mating was a possibility... that I forgot it wasn't possible, even if you were loup-garou."

She laced her fingers in his. "Don't say that. It can be possible... If you want to, that is."

A wisp of frosty air escaped Logan's parted lips. "At this point, I don't know if it's a matter of wanting to... I've been trying for so long to shift outside of my cycle, and the only times I've ever come close were when I didn't want it to happen."

"Like the night of the fight?"

"Yeah... And no matter how the shift starts, it always ends the same. I've never been able to hold onto my own consciousness. Every single time, the wolf takes over completely, and I don't remember a damn thing. Loups-garous only a quarter my age can retain control. It's not just shifting at will, it's being able to control my own loup-garou body for the ceremony itself... My point is, I feel so guilty for letting you think this could happen, and... it can't."

Katey's heart would have broken if her own stubbornness hadn't gotten in the way. She grabbed Logan by his jacket and turned him to face her, determination blazing in her eyes. "It can happen. We've come way too far for it not to. Whatever it is that keeps you from shifting on your own and maintaining control, we can work it out. We have plenty of time."

Logan stared down at her, defeat so etched in the lines of his face that Katey wondered if she had to say it louder, so it'd get through to him. She almost died for him, so they would have a chance. The fact that he had been trying for a century to shift voluntarily meant nothing to her. She was here now, he had a better reason to learn, to try again.

"But, can you wait for me?" he asked, voice a near whisper between them.

Katey gripped his jacket tighter. "I know I made a big stink about waiting before, but that was when I thought you wouldn't even love me until then... You say you love me now, before I'm fully trained and able to make out without tearing you up." She took heart in his little laugh. "And I can love you before you can shift at will. We can love each other before officially mating, and that's enough."

Logan's hands reached up and cupped hers, warming her fingers. "Are you absolutely sure you want to do this?"

Katey grinned. "Apart from becoming a loup-garou, I don't think I've ever been so sure about anything."

Was this the moment? Was this when they would form the preliminary mating bond? Or was there more to it than just an outward declaration?

Logan tried to smile and brought her hand to his lips to kiss, but nothing spectacular happened. No fireworks, no angelic music, fanfare of any kind. Nothing stirred with her wolf, besides the usual whenever Logan touched her, and nothing changed in her bond. No preliminary mating bond yet, but her wishes had been made known, and they still had hours to go.

The rest of the way into town, Logan explained what the true mating ceremony entailed. It wasn't unlike a human wedding, but with a little loup-garou ritual thrown in the mix. They would stand before friends and packmates and say their vows. In front of the officiate, usually the eldest loup-garou who knew the right words like John, they would cut their hands and mix their blood before the wounds healed up. Then, they would wrap themselves in a fur cloak to signify their union. In the usual ceremony, the groom would shift into his loup-garou form and look upon his wife for the first time, and she was to show no fear in front of him. Their acceptance of one another would be made through some sort of body language, often touching his paw to her hand or touching foreheads. For Katey and Logan, they would likely both shift.

The very idea of it sounded romantic, even though Katey was one of the least romantic people. Still, she couldn't help but smile to herself while they browsed the bookstore whenever she thought about how their mating ceremony would look and feel. She had never seen Logan in his loup-garou form, but she would bet anything he was all black, just like he was in her dream so long ago.

Then, while they sat through dinner at a little steakhouse not far from the bookshop, she wondered how she would look. If what Logan had told her before was true, she'd be all black as well. New loups-garous were always black, and their pelts took on color as they aged. Yet, in her dream, she was completely white. Maybe for female loups-garous, it'd be different.

All the while, Logan shared with her stories from gatherings past, and the second-hand stories passed down to Logan about when the packs would shift together. Many of them entailed some humorous hunting mishap or playful antics amongst the loups-garous. Katey listened and smiled so much that her cheeks hurt. Being loup-garou wasn't just about belonging to a single pack, but being a member of a wider family. It was the thought she had so long ago when she first heard about Alaska, and similar stories told between the guys, but now, she understood more fully. Despite the initial shock of her very existence, every loup-garou she encountered had been kind and accepting of her.

With every fiber of her being, she hoped it would last.

Logan paid the bill and left a generous tip for their server. Outside, night had settled in completely, blanketing Alaska in a sea of black with brilliant arrays of bright stars, so much brighter than back home. Sun had set early that afternoon, and Darren told them before they left the resort that they needed to be back before seven o'clock in time to catch a van that would take them to Denali National Park.

Logan assisted Katey into her coat. "You want to take the long way around back to the resort?"

"What's the long way?" Katey asked with a flirty lilt as they began walking in the direction of the wilderness that buffered the resort from the town.

"It's a little off the beaten path through the woods. It goes around a lake and leads right back to the resort. It's probably twice as long as the way we came, but it's more scenic."

Katey took his arm once more and gave him a warm smile. "Why not?"

He smiled back and led her through a particular cluster of trees whose branches were laden in thick patches of snow. The way was less than convenient. Logan seemed at home in the forest, moving gracefully through the thick foliage. Katey was trying to be just as agile, but felt awkward trying to step through the packed snow and not slip on hidden rocks or slabs of ice along the ground. Seeing her struggle, Logan assisted her through the rough parts and swept aside low-lying branches so she could pass through.

Fully immersed in the wilderness, Katey's wolf reawakened and it was a struggle to keep her eyes their usual brilliant green instead of reverting to gold.

"It's so perfect out here."

"You haven't even seen the best part." Logan took her hand and helped her to stand erect after they passed under a fallen tree propped against another. "It's hard to find places like this that haven't been touched by man."

With the growing threat of expansion into these wilderness-es, Katey could easily believe it. There was a reason Todd Rice and other wildlife activists lobbied for the protection of nature so adamantly. If humans continued their progress, building new towns and deforesting these beautiful landscapes, there wouldn't be a place for loups-garous to run free.

All at once, Katey began to wonder about the future of loups-garous. They had survived for centuries all over the globe, but how long could they keep their secret? There have been threats of hunters and vampires, but what about the threat of those who have no idea they exist? Where would they go then? It was completely possible that they couldn't hide forever in a world with no allies.

"There's something I've been thinking about. What's the big deal about vampires? Why are they a threat to us?"

Logan regarded her, a puzzled look in his eye as if he couldn't understand such a question. "Well, because they are. They've always wanted to kill us."

"But why? Forgive my train of thought, but I was just thinking about how vampires are just as supernatural as us, so why don't we get along?"

Logan sighed and they continued to trek down the path that weaved through the dark trees. "For as long as anyone can remember, loups-garous and vampires have never gotten along. They've been trying to kill off our kind for centuries. They even have scientists researching our biology, coming up with new and creative ways to kill us. Fights between packs and covens break out all the time. We have teams that go in and clean up the messes and so far, we've been able to keep the feud a secret."

Something in Katey wasn't settled with such a vague answer. "There has to be a reason for all that hatred."

"I don't know," he replied with a shrug. "Maybe something happened centuries ago."

"Do we hate them?"

"We only hate them because they hate us."

They came to a towering boulder, but instead of going around, Logan leapt through the air and propelled himself over the obstacle as if it were a waist-high fence. Katey, slightly unsettled by the height, tried at a running start but with the snow impeding her movements, she barely crested over the tip.

With a shriek, she came tumbling down and landed in a bed of fresh snow. Logan helped her up as she giggled off her blunder. He brushed off loose snow from her shoulder and arms while she cleaned off the other parts of her body that he might have been too hesitant to touch yet, especially after that episode in the suite.

Logan smiled and gave her a quick kiss before they continued on the path. "Looks like you didn't get enough air that time."

"I blame these short legs."

As they continued on, Katey's thoughts wandered back to the subject of vampires.

She couldn't fathom how two people could despise each other for no apparent reason. Prejudice was a thing that existed in the world, and when one looked back far enough, it came down to a difference of skin color, religion, or nationality. One side justified that they were better and that the other was less-than. Wars, slavery, genocide, all came down to an "us versus them" attitude. Katey never understood it. They all bleed the same color and breathed the same air. Those common factors alone should have helped them to be civil with one another and set aside their differences. But, humans valued the acquisition of land, money or power over peace. Weren't loups-garous, who lived for centuries, supposed to be above stuff like that?

"Hasn't anyone ever tried to stop the fighting?" Katey asked.

Logan, once more, seemed confused by her question, but humored her with an answer. "I'm sure they have, but if they did, it didn't seem to work."

Katey paused in thought. "So, all those myths about werewolves and vampires being archenemies are completely true? Not just Hollywood?"

"They are."

"Do you think the fighting will ever stop?"

"Probably when one of the species is completely wiped out. There's no telling how long that will take."

Katey thought for a moment again, letting it all sink in. "How do you even kill a loup-garou? I know the thing about the silver bullets and all, but what else?"

"The way I've heard it explained is that silver has a certain property in it that when we touch it in its purest form, it can burn our skin and flesh like acid. We heal once the silver is not touching us. So, a silver bullet would kill if it's lodged in the right spots, and we can't get it out in time. Vamps have invented a bullet that carries liquid silver. I've never seen its effects, but the silver gets into the bloodstream and burns the loup-garou alive."

Katey wrinkled her nose at the thought of dying in such an agonizing, inhumane way.

"Other ways would be beheading. And we can't regenerate severed limbs. I know a few loups-garous who are missing arms and legs. Fire would kill us if we let it consume our bodies for long enough, but it's a slow process. Starvation can kill us, of course, or oxygen deprivation for long enough. But if someone runs through me with a sword or shoots me in the head with a lead bullet, I'll heal. It may take a while, depending on the severity of the injury, but I'd live."

Katey thought on that for a while. Loups-garous were not the immortal, invincible beings she had once believed. They had weaknesses, despite their incredible bodies and ability to heal. Perhaps Katey had taken it for granted, but now, the idea of hunters and vampires who were hell-bent on killing them seemed much more terrifying now. Regular humans, not so much.

Soon enough, they arrived at the lake, but it was completely frozen over, a complete sheet of ice that reflected the moonlight as harshly as the snowbanks around it. A wooden dock stretched out several yards toward the middle of the lake.

The ground all the way to the shore was covered in fresh powder, smooth, and untouched by any other visitors, human or animal. On the other side of the lake, its shore was lined with dense trees, but beyond that was a gorgeous scape of snowcapped mountains.

Katey smiled and her wolf glowed. Never had she seen something like this in real life. Places like this only ever existed in books and on TV. This was the kind of place her wolf had yearned for and Katey sensed its need to run and be free, just as she had felt it in Florida the other morning on the back porch.

She hardly noticed Logan walk toward the edge of the lake and tap the icy surface with his heavy boot.

"What are you doing?" Katey asked as she tried to follow, wading through the thick snow.

"I'm testing it."

"For what?"

"To skate on, of course."

"Skate?" she exclaimed. "We don't have any skates." Her wolf bucked at the strangeness of it. Why skate when they could run along the shore?

"We don't need any skates," Logan said as he put some weight on the ice. Katey heard no cracking or splitting. The ice must have been incredibly thick and so frozen that it might as well have been as solid and stable as concrete.

Logan carefully stepped out with his other foot on the ice and glanced back at her, holding out his hands to show that it could be done. Then, he pushed himself off and was instantly sliding across the ice like a pro.

Katey shook her head in disbelief as he performed figure eights and little spins here and there, all in his slick-bottomed boots. It defied physics, but Logan was just as graceful on ice as he was in the forest.

"Come on, it's easy!" he shouted back to her from the middle of the lake.

"I've never skated before!"

He glided stylishly back over to her and offered out his hands. "Let me help."

Katey had to use every ounce of trust she had for the man to place her hands willingly in his and step out onto the ice. Her feet wobbled and slipped a little at first, wanting to slide out from underneath her at every little twitch of her muscles.

All the while, she could almost hear her wolf rebuke her and say that loups-garous were not made for ice skating. But, if Logan could, then she would certainly try. Her wolf thought she had gone mad.

She managed to get about a foot from the snowy shore when her right foot decided to skew to the left, crossing over her other foot and causing her to do half a turn and fall on her backside. Logan came crashing down on the ice with her.

They laughed at first and were soon on their feet again. After a while, they began to make more progress. She could launch herself off, but could only travel a couple of feet before falling again. She didn't worry about broken bones or bruises at all since she could heal quickly, but she did worry about ruining Logan's fun on the ice. However, his encouraging smile and semi-helpful instruction settled those fears. This little jaunt was as much for her as it was for him.

After her fifth attempt to skate like he did, Katey remained sitting on her behind near the middle of the lake, watching him skate circles around her with an entertained grin.

"I don't think I'm meant for skating," she admitted.

He just chuckled. "Give it one more try."

Katey pushed herself up to a standing position fine enough. Then Logan maneuvered behind her and gave her a firm shove. Katey moved forward toward the shore at a decent speed, and then she tried to push off with one foot to go faster. She thought she would lose her balance, but then regained it by shoving off with the other foot. She did this until she was just about to the shore, and then got brave.

She tried to pivot her body enough to make herself turn, but that only twisted her into sliding sideways toward the shore instead of away from it. Katey tried to stop herself, but it was too late and she fell headlong into the bank, disappearing into the layers upon layers of frost and snow. She couldn't help but laugh at herself and how she should have listened to her wolf from the start.

Logan skated over and extended his hand out to help her up. Katey took it, but tugged as hard as she could, making him lose his balance completely and he fell forward into the snow next to her. They both laughed at themselves and gazed up at the Alaskan sky.

Katey marveled at its effortless beauty. She had never taken the time to look at the sky, not until she met Logan. And just like that night in the graveyard, what felt so long ago, Katey came upon an earth-shattering revelation.

Looking up at the sky just then made her contemplate how much time she had wasted on things that didn't matter. It was then that she began to realize what really did matter. Logan mattered. She mattered. The wolf inside her mattered and how it was all connected to the world around them.

She remembered when she had sat on the patio back home and felt the pull to be part of the nature around her. In that moment, she realized that she really was a part of it. They all were. Everything around them had this special link that humans couldn't see, but loups-garous could. No matter how far a loup-garou was disconnected from the woods, from nature, no matter how much they denied it, it was still part of them, just like the wolf was. She could feel the pull. She could feel it deep within her and she knew it was real.

Katey closed her eyes and basked in this wondrous revelation as the edges of her lips twitched into a smile that she couldn't explain.

She was drawn from her thoughts when Logan suddenly rolled to hover half of his body over her, his hands holding him up so he could gaze down with his stunning blue eyes. Katey could see his irises seem to crystalize a much deeper hue of blue and his face edged ever closer toward hers.

A kiss was surely on its way, but Katey was too excited and restless for a kiss, even his.

She grabbed a handful of snow and chucked it into his face with a giggle. Completely surprised, he rolled off of her as she scrambled to her feet and trotted a few strides away, waiting for retaliation. Her wolf was ready to play, just like she saw the pack play that day when she saw them in their wolf forms for the first time. Snow stuck to his facial hair and dropped from his nose.

"You're going to pay for that!" he threatened with a smile as he raised himself up from the snowbank.

Katey stooped down to gather a nice chunk of snow from the ground and rolled it between her hands. "You have to catch me first!"

Logan had just stood up to brush himself off when she hurled the snowball, nailing him right in the chest. He gave a grunt and looked at her in disbelief.

Katey laughed impishly and jogged a little farther away as she saw him forming his own ammunition. They pitched ball after ball at each other, dodging what they could and enduring the ones they didn't see coming. They ran all along the shore of the lake, rolling and ducking from the other's rounds of snowballs.

She escaped into the trees at full speed, taunting Logan as she went. It seemed to work as she hid behind a large pine tree. Then, all went quiet. All she heard were bird calls in the distance. No more snow crunching under his heavy boots or Logan's laughter. Through her own pounding heartbeat, she couldn't listen for his. She peeked around the tree and saw nothing out by the lake and the endlessly disheveled snow from their game. She sniffed the air, trying to find his scent again.

She did and when she looked above her, she had just enough time to shield her neck and chest before a huge pile of snow dumped down on her from an obliging tree branch that Logan had twisted in his hands.

Katey laughed and shook off whatever icy snow hadn't fallen down the back of her shirt as Logan jumped down to land in front of her. He pinned Katey to the tree, pressing his body against hers, both of them panting for air.

"Gotcha," he proclaimed victoriously.

Katey giggled and watched his face get covered in more snow that had been loosened by his fall back to the forest floor. Logan shook his head briskly to get the snow out of his hair and turned his bright smile back to Katey as she tried to hold in her infectious string of giggles. He wrapped his arms loosely around her waist and leaned his forehead against hers as they locked eyes.

"Are you really happy with me, Katey?"

Katey laughed at the silly question. Didn't Logan know that he was her whole world now? "I've never been happier in my life."

Logan lowered his hands to rest on her hips beneath her coat as she curled her fingers around his strong arms. "I know we haven't known each other long and just the past week alone has been hard on you... But I want to make up for it all. I want to make up for everything that has ever made you sad or unhappy. I want you to have everything you ever wanted. Family, a home... unconditional love."

Katey felt her cheeks grow hot and red as she blushed, knowing this had to be the moment she had been waiting for.

"I've loved you since the first moment I met you. I knew you were the only person I wanted to spend every day for the rest of my life with... Even if that's a thousand years or only a couple of days... I want to make you this happy for the rest of eternity..." Logan paused, his voice shaky as he took a deep breath. "Katey, will you be my mate?"

She may not have been one for romance, but no words had ever sounded sweeter. Tears of joy pushed at the corners of her eyes. All at once, nothing mattered but this exact moment in time, cloaked in the Alaskan winter night, with Logan holding her and sharing his warmth.

"I will. I always will." Katey could barely contain her grin.

Logan's face split in a similar grin and his eyes sparkled brighter than any star in the heavens.

He raised his hand up to her cheek, gently wrapping his fingers around the nape of her neck, and pulled her face up to meet his. His lips were warm and soft against hers like velvet. Katey wrapped her arms around his neck, one set of fingers combing through his dark hair below his hair tie.

Logan pinned her to the tree, their bodies flush against each other, sending thrilling shockwaves throughout her body. The kiss deepened, lips parting and tongues flicking and rolling together. She savored his taste, sweet and intoxicating.

But this kiss was not the same as the others they had shared before. This was different, as her wolf came forward to experience it with her. For a brief instant, their wolf spirits finally touched, and Katey could feel something spark in her soul.

She shared a pack bond with each of the men she had come to trust. Darren's bond was distinctly strong, as the alpha and fatherly figure that guided her. Dustin's bond hummed with the same vibrancy that marked his personality. Ben's bond was subtle, but undeniable as she felt a kinship with him since they had both been turned by the bite and not by birth.

But, Logan's bond was special. Like a golden chord that linked their spirits, it outshined the rest, connecting them so thoroughly that her emotions were his, and vice-versa. As their wolves touched, the bond became stronger, as if the gold chord was now coated in an indestructible metal and galvanized to ensure it could never be broken. Their bond flared red-hot and burned within her soul and then slowly cooled to produce something that no man, vampire, or loup-garou could undo. The first stage of their mating was complete as her wolf retreated into the recesses of her soul to let her enjoy the rest of their kiss.

Logan's other hand fell back to her hips, fingering the edge of her blouse just enough to allow access underneath. Katey could feel his fingertips graze just above the edges of her jeans along her skin. Her body shivered under his touch and craved more. Her legs felt like they would have fallen out from underneath her, buckling against the crackling fireworks that coursed through her limbs. As if he sensed her weakness, the hand behind her neck slipped beneath her, quickly guiding her legs over his hips, her weight completely supported against the tree and by one powerful arm. She felt something hard pressed against the center of her heat beneath her jeans, and knew that she wasn't the only one ready for more than heavy petting and kissing.

His rough hand stroked along her flesh as their breathing became heavy and turned into clouds of mist around their faces. A flash of cold air drifted against her skin as her shirt slowly lifted. Logan's thumbs brushed along her rib cage, feeling its way higher up her body.

In the heat of the moment, Katey lost all sense of herself, letting her fingers get tangled in his hair, gripping his head to hers, needing his touch and caresses more than air. She knew where this could go, but she didn't care. If he wanted it, then she wanted it, too. They were as good as engaged. Maybe that was enough to make him forget his reluctance to take her before they were officially mated.

Logan broke away from kissing her lips and let his mouth slide along her jaw and down to her sensitive neck, sending skitters down through her spine and straight between her thighs. After a while, she didn't even feel the cold, only tightness in her core like a coiled spring and the ache a little lower that only he could release. When she detected the gentle grinding motion against the place that ached the most, she gasped and he pulled her tighter against him with her legs.

He let out a satisfied growl deep from within his throat that hummed against her skin just as his hand found the edge of her bra. Almost reflexively, Katey returned the same growl mixed with a whine of desire and her eyes rolled into the back of her head as her back arched to the flood of feelings that consumed her. The smell of both their arousals swirled around them, fogging her brain to the point there was only one thought in her mind.

His hand completely cupped her when another feeling interrupted them.

Logan's phone buzzed in his pocket. He growled again, but this time in frustration. He slowly pulled back from her neck, slid his hand out of her shirt to retrieve his phone. Katey forced her eyes open to check the screen on his phone. It was Darren.

Logan pressed the answer button, even though he looked mad enough to smash the phone against the tree. "Yes?" His voice came out hoarse with aggravation. Katey could hear Darren's angry words on the other end.

"Where are you two? We're about to leave."

"We're near the lake. We'll be there in a minute," He abruptly ended the call and shoved the phone in his back pocket. He turned his attention back to Katey and was about to finish what he'd started, but she put a hand on his chest to hold him back. That momentary break helped to clear her head enough to think straight. Having sex in the snow may not be that enjoyable for her first time.

"We do need to get going," Katey said breathlessly with a pang of remorse.

Both pairs of glowing red eyes stared at each other, knowing that what she said was true.

He took a deep breath to calm himself and nodded. "You're right."

He helped her to get her feet back under her, and wrapped her in a tight hug until both of them came down from the lustful high.

"That's twice in one day," Katey murmured. "You think we'll ever make it to the wedding night?"

Logan laughed and buried his face against her shoulder. "Maybe we shouldn't let ourselves be too alone again."

Katey hugged him tighter and let herself drown in his scent. Even though they nearly crossed that line one more time, she grinned as she felt their fresh preliminary mating bond harden even further. Now, every loup-garou at the gathering would know who she belonged to. All that was left was to prove that she belonged amongst them, too.

CHAPTER 18

When Logan and Katey finally arrived at the lodge, their pack, along with John's, waited outside near the drop-off lane, ready to go. The passenger van they had ridden to the conference center rumbled to life as steam spouted out the tail pipe.

Everyone possessed a look of anxiety and Katey couldn't tell if it was about the fact that they arrived back far later than expected, or if they were eager to see if Katey would be joining them.

No words needed to be spoken as they approached the covered walkway. They would all feel the preliminary mating bond and know that she was certainly going to try to shift with them. The group showed mixed feelings. Some excited, some hesitant.

A slow grin crept across Dustin's face. "I see someone said yes."

Darren leveled a serious look at Katey. "And you're sure you don't want to stay behind?"

Katey shook her head, proud and confident, despite knowing exactly what would come. "I'm sure. I'm ready to try."

Ben, who filed into the van with the other Croxens, gave her a skeptical look, but said nothing.

Her alpha nodded. "All right." He looked to Logan. "How are you doing?"

It was then Katey remembered Ben's description of the coming shift and she turned to Logan, looking him over for all those signs of discomfort. Besides a thin sheen of sweat on his forehead, she saw nothing that would have suggested he was in pain just yet.

"I'll be fine for another half hour, I think."

It amazed Katey that he could time it that well, but perhaps after a century of shifting every month, she'd learn her own limits too.

"We'll be at the park before then. Let's go."

The rest of the pack loaded up and Katey saw John and Noah sitting beside one another in the front seats as they had been earlier that day. Noah passed a glance over his shoulder and seemed to pause, then turned back to the steering wheel.

"I see congratulations are in order," John said with a warm smile to Katey. "I hope you didn't do it just so you'd have the chance to shift tonight."

Katey had already checked herself long before that to make sure her priorities were straight. "No. That's just a nice perk."

Some of the Croxens in the backseat laughed and Logan laced his fingers with Katey's.

"Don't count your chickens before they hatch, little girl," said the burly Croxen brother. "You may come to regret that before the end of the night."

"Shut up, Liam," Noah barked from the driver's seat. "This is her choice. She knows what she's getting into."

Darren, who sat on the other side of Logan from her, leaned forward to meet her gaze. "We will be with you every step of the way, Katey. You won't be alone in this."

The severity of their words made her stomach twist. It was then she understood this wasn't just another step in her training. It wasn't like running from one point to another or jumping from tree to tree. This was a bigger, more challenging milestone. The closer they drew to the park, the more she began to realize this was really happening. There was no turning back, no chickening out at the last minute. She would change and run like a wolf for the first time.

Darren had said the shift would be painful, but how could she judge pain for a loup-garou? He had told her once that they still felt pain, but just not as intensely as humans did. At the time, she was still human and unable to comprehend how pain can be felt differently amongst species. She remembered breaking her arm during training and the fiery pain of the shoulder grab from earlier that day, but how would it compare to her entire body morphing into another form?

Under the suspicion that her loup-garou blood might be slowly fading without her conscious awareness, the change may be even more painful. Katey's heart nearly stopped when she thought about how the change may be too much for her and she could die, despite what she had been told. That was only if her healing abilities worked, but what if they chose to give out on her at the last minute? To have found a family and a lover so suddenly and lose them in one evening due to her own defectiveness was not what she had in mind.

Through their bond, Logan likely sensed her unease and slipped his arm around her shoulder to comfort her unspoken fears. Katey leaned into him, taking what peace she could glean from his nearness. She wouldn't have it for much longer.

As they passed signs for the park entrance, John turned in his seat to face her. "Okay, Katey, this is how it's going to work. Darren and I don't want you to be around everyone when you shift, just as a precaution. We're going to pull you away from everyone and guide you through the shift. Once you've shifted, Darren will initiate the breaking, and then we'll take you to everyone else. This may be awkward, but you will be naked once you shift back in the morning and we have a robe in that duffle bag for you. If you can't manage a willful shift tonight, we'll take you back to the lodge because you shouldn't be around us in your human form."

Katey nodded and took a few deep breaths to try and calm her nerves again. Even the wolf in her was pacing, growing impatient. She told herself over and over that not shifting was not an option. She was strong enough. She could do this. She had to.

They arrived at the security gate to the park, and Logan suddenly jerked and grunted, his face contorted as if he were in pain. Katey could suddenly sense the urgency of his coming shift radiating off of him like an aura. His wolf side must have been pushing against his human skin, demanding release. He tried to hide it and control his facial muscles from twisting with agony, but every muscle in his body tensed as if he was in the midst of a seizure.

Instead of shying away from his pain, Katey snuggled closer and tried to give him the same comfort he so willingly gave her moments before. His jaw clenched tighter, but his breaths came a little steadier. Her touch and affection wasn't enough to block out the pain, but maybe it could distract him long enough.

Darren passed him a sympathetic look. "Just hold it in, Logan. We're almost there."

When they eased into the park's parking area, Logan suddenly pulled away from Katey. He reached into his jacket pocket and pulled out the blue bandana she remembered from the first night they met at the cemetery. With shaky hands, he loosely wrapped it around her wrist. It smelt so distinctly of him that she nuzzled her nose into the piece of cloth and deeply inhaled his scent.

"No matter what happens tonight, know that I will be thinking of you... Wear this for good luck."

The van rolled to a stop and Katey leaned up to kiss him, much to the amusement of the Croxens in the back. The kiss had to be brief, but she savored the taste of him one last time before they had to part ways.

As soon as they parked, Logan was the first to be let out because of his urgent state. Katey exited last after John's sons, but couldn't see Logan anywhere in the waning light of the snowy forest.

His absence was keenly felt, not only by her, but by her wolf. They had both grown so used to having him around that it was torturous to be without him for too long. But, their bond was still strong and she could somehow sense how far away he was as he put more distance between the two of them to join the other loups-garous in the forest.

It was for her own safety, but somehow she wished that he could have been there to see her change for the first time. She so desperately wanted to see him beam with pride when he saw that his efforts to make her loup-garou had not been in vain. That moment would have to wait until the morning when they were back at the resort and sleeping off a long night in front of the warm fireplace. At least, that's the sort of picturesque morning she envisioned. Who knew what would really happen.

She watched the crowd of loups-garous depart from their vehicles, most of them wearing just sweatpants or gym shorts in the frigid cold and walking through the dense foliage to the gathering place as they talked amongst one another in lighthearted tones. Some of them seemed anxious, but others were ecstatic and running about to find their friends before disappearing through the trees. There had to be at least sixty, maybe seventy of them. But Katey sensed something far different. There was a heaviness about the crowd, like a thunderstorm descending over a faraway hill.

She spotted Forrest arrive with another pack that included Parker and a few others of the Devian pack. Some she knew from their introduction at school, others she didn't. They waved and she shyly waved back as they continued on to disappear into the darkness.

There was nothing too serious about this gathering except for Katey and the miracle she had brought to their community. She was the only female there and everyone knew it. Many turned their heads to regard her with a curious look, as if they didn't understand why she was there when all the other women were back at the lodge.

Aiden, Liam, and Blake gave her encouraging looks before they shed their shirts and ran to join the others. Noah approached her after stepping out of the vehicle and placed a light hand on her shoulder.

"Good luck tonight, Katey," he said with a nod. "I'll see you out there."

Without another word, he also slipped his shirt over his head to toss it into the vehicle and hurried to catch up with his brothers.

Darren and John came up beside Katey and led her a little farther in another direction, away from everyone else. The two alphas didn't speak, but Katey mostly listened to the excited conversations in the distance. Some spoke about her and others reunited with old friends, but everyone seemed happy and almost cheerful, despite that heavy air she sensed before. They may have been happy to see everyone, but who would be happy about an agonizing, painful shift?

They walked through the woods until they reached a small, deserted clearing in the trees. Oddly enough, Katey couldn't hear any other noises in the forest besides the loups-garous. It was like the entire world slipped into reverent silence as soon as the loups-garous walked in. Even nature showed respect for the beasts. The stars sparkled brilliantly against the black night and Katey's superb night vision allowed her to see every detail of her surroundings as clearly as if they were in the daytime.

John and Darren watched the sky and patiently waited. For what, Katey didn't know.

Katey hugged herself around her stomach and tried to wish away the storm of feeling that threatened to conquer her. Darren placed a firm but comforting hand on her shoulder, keeping his eye on the full moon above that washed the world in its bluish gray ethereal glow. His gesture was one of caring intent and Katey didn't shy from it.

She tried to hold onto the fact that the guys were there to help, that they wouldn't let anything bad happen to her and perhaps it wouldn't be as terrible as what she thought. Darren said himself that she would black out eventually. Maybe she'd miss most of the pain.

Then, all grew still. The voices at the gathering place shushed and the only sounds she could hear were her own heavy, shaky breaths and the pulsing heartbeats of the men beside her. Katey tried to inhale deeply through her nose, but her breaths came out shivering between her lips, pluming into mist.

A gut-wrenching scream split the night air. Katey jumped and almost fell over if she didn't have Darren steadying her. She recognized the scream. It was the same kind of scream that Logan belted out when Erik had him in the shoulder hold during their fight. She felt hot tears sting in her eyes and spill down her cheeks, suffering along with Logan, and she couldn't do anything about it. This was the natural course for them. Pain was expected and endured.

The scream gradually turned into a mighty roar, which was then joined by many more from the gathering. Screams, roars, growls, and yelps erupted like an explosion, shattering her heart like it were glass and the pieces fell into the crisp snow at her feet. Terror and sorrow pierced her soul, empathizing with their agony.

Through the pack bond, she could feel Logan, Dustin, and Ben changing into their loup-garou forms probably miles away from where she currently stood. Even the wolf within her whined and whimpered for her packmates, wishing she could ease their torment somehow.

Which scream belonged to Forrest? Or Noah? Would Liam, a mighty man in his human form, scream in such pain?

John and Darren didn't seem to be bothered by their cries. Such sounds had become part of their life, their loup-garou life. It was the nature of the beast. Nothing could be done for the pain but to accept it. After a few disturbing moments, the screams and roars subsided and turned into the occasional grunt or sort of excited barking as loups-garous met each other in their truest forms.

The two men stood on either side of her and waited a little longer while the others at the gathering became too distracted with each other to care about anyone else nearby.

John turned to Katey "Are you ready?"

She gave him a nervous laugh and shook her head. "Not anymore." How could she possibly be ready for what she just vicariously experienced through her pack members?

Darren gave her shoulder a reassuring squeeze. "It's best you get it over with as soon as you can. If you continue to be nervous about it, you'll never be ready and when your other half comes out it'll hurt that much more."

John stepped in front of Katey. "First, you need to clear your mind of all other thoughts and distractions. The wolf will only come forward if you willingly accept and welcome it. If you harbor any fear or uncertainty, it will sense that and refuse to come."

Darren gave her a gentle push to drive her to the snow-covered ground, her clothes growing moist as the ice crystals melted beneath her.

Katey nodded and closed her eyes to do just as John instructed. It was harder than anticipated. After a couple of moments, she shook her head in dismay. "I can't, I'm too nervous." She wasn't afraid to be candid with them. They probably demanded it. If she felt anything amiss, they would want to know.

"You can do this, Katey. If it helps, look up at the moon. Focus on it," Darren advised.

Katey looked up at the full, bright moon. Wisps of translucent clouds just barely concealed it, but it was still very visible. After several moments of intense concentration, not only was she looking at it, but her wolf was as well.

She gazed, almost longingly, letting it overwhelm her vision. The loup-garou golden hue spiraled over her green irises. Gradually, she could feel the wolf inside push forward, testing the ground it treaded upon with a certain hesitancy as if it had never been this close to becoming unleashed before. Katey knew better. That wolf had taken control a few times already. Only now, she would have to take over her body as well.

"Good, now just relax and feel the wolf inside, focus on that feeling of release. Surrender to it." John's voice sounded so far away.

She tried harder to focus, taking deep breaths, but the wolf presence within her stayed strangely distant as she continued to gaze at the moon. Her ears were filled with the gentle beating of her heart. The wolf was just on the cusp of its journey to the surface, but was suddenly too shy to take the next step. It was as if it could sense Katey's uneasiness, just like John said, and it inspired a skittishness in the wolf as well.

Then, Katey began to feel warm inside, starting in her gut and slowly spreading through her to battle against the frigid Alaskan winter. She wasn't sure if that was the feeling she was supposed to have, but she didn't fight it. Katey began to feel the heat turn hot like lava, burning and searing her muscles. She knew this feeling. This was right. It blazed through her blood and Katey winced, her golden eyes still fixed on the moon. It was the same sensation she felt when Erik gripped her shoulder and the wolf became a little bolder. The change was coming soon.

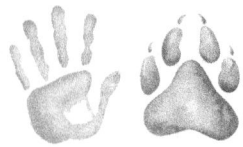

The black wolf padded about the clearing, its piercing blue eyes darting between his fellow wolves, but none of them could help him. None could tell him what was wrong, but they could all feel it with him and were just as concerned as he was.

Something's missing. It's aching.

What is it? Have to find it. Where is it?

Something's missing. Something's lost.

Have to find it. Must find it. Must stop the pain.

His massive paws dug into the earth beneath the layers of snow, clawing into the soil, readying himself for the hunt ahead.

CHAPTER 19

"That's it. Just focus on that feeling, don't fight it," Darren's voice coaxed to her from the sidelines as the pain became steadily more intense.

Katey gritted her teeth and clenched her hands into tight fists, digging her nails into her palms. Blood trickled from her skin from the sheer force of her grip, but this pain was nothing compared to what pulsated through every bone and muscle in her body.

"It burns," Katey groaned as the pain deepened to her very soul.

John's voice became a low rumble beside her, like she was under water. "I know, but don't resist it. You're doing fine."

Katey could feel her vision narrowing. The burning became so great she could have sworn she was on fire, inside and out.

Then, in the darkened gloom, Katey heard a lonely howl coming from the gathering place. One more joined it, and then it became a chorus of wolf howls singing into the night. Katey blinked and the burning began to ebb away.

John gripped her arm. "No, Katey, focus. Call back your wolf. You almost had it. Ignore them."

It was too late, the heat had dissipated and her mind flooded with thoughts, emotions, and instinct. The howls danced about her ears, reverberating in her head until that was all she could hear. She could almost pick out Logan's in the bunch, even though she had never heard it before. It was mournful and searching. Katey had to answer him. She could never leave him, not even tonight when it mattered most.

She threw back her head and poured her soul into the best howl she could muster. Whether it was Katey that howled or her other half that refused to come out, she didn't know. Maybe it was both. Her howl was long and melodious, answering Logan's.

Darren cursed under his breath and John pulled Katey to her feet as soon as she had let her head drop from the howl.

All went silent and still for a pregnant moment as they waited for the aftermath of her mistake.

Her head was spinning and ears ringing, her body half numb from the downpour of pain she had endured. When she turned her green eyes to John and Darren, she saw the mixtures of frustration and anxiety written on their faces.

She looked toward the trees in the direction of the gathering and could hear the soft padding of footsteps approaching, crunching through the snow as they went. They heard her howl and were coming to answer it with their company.

"Katey, run as fast as you can, deep into the park," John explained. "Don't look back and get as far from here as you can. Wade through every body of water you can find, cover your tracks and hide... If you can manage to get to one of the vehicles after that, do so and go back to the lodge. We keep the keys in the cup holders. Go!"

He turned Katey around and shoved her in the opposite way from where the others were coming.

She stood there a little dumbfounded at first before Darren barked the same orders, "Go! We'll do our best to hold them off." The fire in his eyes told her he was far from joking.

There was no time to recreate what they had been working so hard to accomplish that night and if the others stumbled upon her human form, there was no telling how they would react, especially the new loups-garous.

Katey bolted for the tree line. She didn't look back, but she could hear Darren and John shedding their clothes and shifting with fewer screams than she had heard from the others.

She jumped, vaulted, climbed, and ran as fast as her legs could carry her through the thicket, using every bit of her training to propel her onward.

The grunts and growls, yips, and barks came up from behind her, hunting her down. The soft walk they started with earlier had accelerated into a run and it sounded like the whole gathering was after her. From what Katey remembered of watching documentaries about wolf packs, they could track their prey for days, traveling endless miles for the chance at a meal. How far would they chase Katey?

Katey pushed herself to run faster, letting her loup-garou speed carry her away from danger, marking her scent on one tree but then running in the other direction. The deep snow wasn't helping at all, so she tried to jump onto as many protruding rocks and fallen logs as she could find. Katey prayed she would come upon a river or a creek that wasn't frozen over. She had no idea which direction she was going or how far she had run. All she knew was that she had to keep going until she couldn't hear them anymore.

The wolf inside her pleaded with her to slow down, to turn and face them. Katey refused to listen.

When she finally came to a creek with a swift current, she splashed downstream, hopped out, and began running again. The icy water felt like needles jamming into her skin, but she had to keep running.

Katey got the idea to toss off her jacket to help distract her hunters. It was a serious sacrifice because she truly loved the white fabrics and furs, and what the jacket represented. It was a gift from her alpha. But, as a human, she would be no match for a dozen or more packs of loups-garous. They could always get another jacket, if she lived to see the morning.

Katey shrugged it off her shoulders and threw it in one direction while she ran in the other. Discarding the jacket proved to be a bad decision. Her body temperature dropped as she ran into the cold wind with nothing to block it out but her blouse. The water around her ankles and shins turned to ice that clung to her pant legs and numbed her skin.

She could see her breath coming out in heaps of mist around her cheeks and just barely taste the metallic tinge of blood in her mouth as the cold air made the back of her throat raw. It felt like she had been running for hours before she finally began to slow down and stumble to a stop. It was hard to hear anything else over her heavy panting, or feel anything but the little pinprick shocks through her nerves.

She came to a dead end. A sheer rockface blocked her way, towering above her with no visible handholds to help her get up to the top. She looked to both her left and right, but there seemed no end to it and no quick way to get around.

Katey closed her mouth and tried to listen for any sign of her pursuers. At first, she could only hear the sounds of the forest. Night birds twittered in the trees and she could hear other animals in the distance that she didn't identify as the loups-garous. If the animals were still around, perhaps that meant they weren't close by.

She thought she was safe. Her knees wobbled and buckled underneath her, dropping into the freshly fallen snow and she resumed her attempt to catch her breath, with tears streaming down her cheeks that froze into tiny ice crystals.

She had come so close. So close, and once more tripping over the starting line. If Logan hadn't howled and broke her concentration, she would be in her loup-garou form by now and everything would have been fine. Now, she didn't even know where she was or how far she had run. She was completely lost. New hot tears brimmed at her eyelids.

Wishing the cold would devour her, she cried into the snow, ignoring the slowly disintegrating pieces of her heart. She would have rather died than face Logan and the others the next morning and their disapproving gazes. She would have preferred a slow, numbing death in this arctic wasteland than hear them say, "We thought so. We knew all along she wouldn't really shift. What a waste of time."

Suddenly, another howl broke through the air. Katey's head shot up and she looked behind her from where the howl rang out. It was Logan, howling for her again, she knew it. This time, she bit her chapped lips together to resist the urge to answer his call. Instead, she let it spur her into action, knowing that they were gaining on her.

Katey pushed herself up and looked around for any other way she could go. If she followed the rockface, she might lose much more time and probably just get caught a lot quicker than if she went forward. She judged the size of the cliff and trotted back a couple of paces, remembering her training lesson on jumping. It was a long shot to think that she would make the ledge, but she had to try.

She started at a run toward the rock and jumped as high as she could, but only made it about half way up the side. Her thick loup-garou claws scratched and raked at the stone for a good hold as she slid down to the bottom, but she only managed to break a couple of her claws and rip her jeans.

Katey glanced around again and saw a nearby tree that had just enough branches for her to climb up. She could hear the pack's grunting and paws breaking the surface of the snow, heading straight for her. She was running out of time.

Katey pounced onto the trunk and shimmied up the first branch like Darren had taught her, hauling herself up to climb to the next. The bark rubbed and scratched against her exposed palms and tore her blouse a bit, but she kept climbing as high as she could, fear pushing her to keep going until she ran out of branches.

Then, the tree began to shake and shudder. A loup-garou rammed his body into the tree trunk again as claws dug into the wood. Menacing growls rumbled from below and she knew that they had found her.

Katey didn't dare look at her attackers or guess their numbers, but glanced toward the rock face and found she was about even with the ledge. It was now or never. She balanced herself on the limb and leapt.

Her lower half hit the edge of the cliff, and she kicked and clawed for stability, her upper body deep in snow. Ahead of Katey, she saw a bit of a thick root sticking out from the ground. She reached over to grab it. Her fingertips just barely touched the top of the root before she could feel the icy ground sliding her elbow back over the rocky edge. She tried to catch the ledge again, but dropped away from the cliff.

Katey fell fast, cold air whishing past her ears. After what was only seconds, but felt like hours, her body crashed into the earth, the snow a partial break to her fall. The air knocked out of her lungs, she lay there for a long moment until she felt she could move again, body jarred and bruised by the impact. All around her, she could hear growls and the snapping of massive jaws. Katey raised her eyes for the first time to meet the loups-garous that were supposed to be her new family, her heart about to explode with terror.

They were everything she had imagined. They looked wolf-like, covered in fur with long ears and muzzles, mouth full of sharp fangs, and glaring eyes of all different colors, not just gold. But their body structure was much more human-like with a chest, abs, hips, arms, and shoulders like a human. The only exception was that they were massive, towering beasts, twice the size of a normal man, and the bone structure of their hind legs resembled that of the canine species. Their hands had the full skeletal form of a human hand with the addition of razor-sharp claws at the tips and rough pads along the palm and underside of their fingers.

Just on all fours, they were taller than Katey was standing. They all ranged in color from black to brown, red, blonde, a few silvers, and multi-colored pelts gleamed in the moonlight. They were stunning creatures and if she had the luxury of being awestruck by them, Katey would have been.

The loups-garous stalked forward, most of them with curiosity blazing in their eyes. The group closest to her were mostly dark-furred, therefore young, and seemed to eye her as if she were prey. The ones further back, those older and likely in control of themselves, looked on cautiously, monitoring the situation and trying to make sense of it. They were the ones her life depended on. They would be the ones to save her, and yet they hung back from the scene.

She wondered which one was Logan, but she didn't have to look far. The loup-garou right in front of her had Logan's familiar, striking blue eyes and pelt that was black along the top of his body, but had a tannish blonde coat along his bottom muzzle and his entire underside. Her pack bond confirmed that this was her lover, the man she had grown so attached to over the last few weeks. The man who walked away and stole her breath with him. He was beautiful, even as a monster.

Logan led the pack of younger loups-garous, baring his pearly white fangs at Katey and face wrinkled into a snarl as he padded closer. He wasn't the only one growling. Katey scrambled to back herself up against the rockface, waiting for one of the older loups-garous to jump in.

If only she could shift right now and save herself, then they would see that she wasn't prey, but one of them. However, the wolf inside was dormant and Katey was too stricken with horror to take the time to coax her out. She stared into the blue eyes of the man that she adored, wishing there was some way to make him see, to make him remember her.

As he padded forward, suddenly, he stopped and stared at her. There was a hint of something human in his eyes, but it was fleeting. His lips slipped over his teeth and he lowered his head further to the ground, his ears erect and shoulders tense, ready to pounce, but hesitating.

Katey shook her head slowly, as if it would somehow communicate with him. If she knew how to speak through her bond, she would have tried that. All she could do was try to impart the love she still felt for him, the love that was supposed to break through every barrier.

From out of nowhere, three massive bodies of silver and gray fur blocked her vision. Their hind ends revealed that loups-garous did indeed have tails. The loups-garous stood up, looming over the hunting party. They let out booming roars at her assailants and the younger loups-garous cowered in their presence, as her defenders let forth their waves of dominance. Even Katey pressed herself against the solid rock behind her to escape the immense power of the alphas.

Some took little steps backwards with their tails between their legs and ears folded back against their heads, a show of submission. Some didn't move, but gazes jumped between Katey and the alphas.

Logan snapped at one of the silver loups-garous and growled back, his ears flattened against his head and crouched low, but not in a submissive stance that she was used to seeing. This was a challenge.

The silver one he'd snapped at came on top of him and bit at his neck to put him back in line. Katey stared in shock at the scene and how quickly it all happened. If she blinked too many times, she would have missed it. She noticed the eyes of the silver one was a friendly and deep brown that she recognized in Darren. The other must have been John, but she couldn't identify the third that had darker distinctive markings in his fur.

Logan writhed under Darren's jaws and yelped for mercy. The alpha released him and lowered himself onto all fours, snarling at his packmate.

In that moment, the alphas had claimed her under their protection and none were foolhardy enough to challenge their authority. The younger loups-garous lopped away to join their packs closer to the treeline. Only then did they receive some bit of punishment from their elders in the forms of growls, shoves, or bites.

The clearing fell into silence, the hunt over, and the crisis finally averted.

Katey sank down into the snow, relieved and exhausted. Logan padded off to the side with his tail between his legs to retreat from his alpha's wrath, but she could feel his eyes watching her every movement.

Darren turned back around to Katey and gently nudged his head against hers. To have such an immense creature so close to her was unsettling at first, but knowing who they were was a comfort.

"Thank you," Katey whispered breathlessly to Darren and John.

The third loup-garou turned to regard her with dark blue eyes. For a moment, she suspected it to be Noah. The longer she stared, the more convinced she became. He sulked away and nipped at a few loups-garous that were venturing too close into her space, mostly out of curiosity than in search for a meal.

Darren gave a guttural grunt in Logan's direction. Katey looked up and watched as her fiancé timidly shuffled through the snow to where they sat. He kept a safe distance both from her and his alpha.

She wanted to retreat into Darren's warm fur, but before she could, his huge paws pushed her toward Logan like she was a puppy that needed to meet the older dog of the family.

Logan stopped a few feet from her with his huge loup-garou frame and shadow overwhelming her, shielding her from the moonlight. They locked gazes and his gorgeous eyes, so full of emotion and wonder, mesmerized Katey. There was no sign of recognition in them, only aloofness like he didn't care to be near her after the thrashing he endured from his alpha, yet there was an indication of interest.

Katey offered out her hand, knowing that dogs needed to sniff a stranger before getting to know them. Logan glanced to her hand, but didn't react.

"Logan," she whispered.

His eyes lit up only faintly and he padded a step closer to her hand.

"It's me... Katey."

His ears perked up inquisitively as if to hear more of what she had to say. Katey had an idea and quickly untied the bandana that he'd given her earlier and offered it out to him. He seemed intrigued, sniffed it and then snorted, shaking his head like he didn't like the smell at all. Katey withdrew it and held it in her lap as a painful lump developed in her throat.

If he couldn't even recognize himself, how could she expect him to recognize her? Somehow, she had hoped that their love would bridge through the unfamiliarity, but that was clearly too much to ask.

Katey glanced back up to Darren who guarded her from behind and saw him shake his head, as if to tell her that it wasn't going to work. She felt more tears sting her eyes and sobbed into the bandana.

Logan stepped a little closer and laid himself down on his stomach sinking into the cold snow. It was almost as if he could sense her sadness, perhaps through their bond. He laid his hefty head in her lap to comfort Katey. He may not have remembered who she was, but there was nothing to stop them from building a relationship right now.

Katey unveiled her face from the bandana she gripped, then cautiously lifted her hand and weaved her fingers through his fur, feeling the coarse fibers on top and the silky strands underneath. It felt just like Ben's fur when she petted him for the first time in his wolf form in their backyard.

One long, lupine arm stretched out over her shins while the other trapped her from behind. By now Darren had walked off to greet the others, seeing that there was no more hostility between them.

Her hand glided over his thick mane and Katey could once again feel their bond. The aching loneliness that settled over her when Logan walked away was gone and she felt just a little whole again, now that they were together. His warmth was a balm to her aching heart and the emotional turmoil that had sent her spiraling out of control moments before was fading into the past.

Somehow, she thought Logan felt the same. The rippling muscles under his skin relaxed under her soothing caresses and his eyes drooped shut as if he'd fall asleep at any moment.

As they sat there together, tears drying on her cheeks and Logan trying to console her in the only way he could, Katey began to wonder if this evening was going to get any easier. At least now she didn't have to worry about being killed. She still didn't want to face everyone in the morning, but perhaps there was time and hope that she could change later. Both John and Darren were there, and they could guard her from the pack. They could start over again. There might have been hope. But, for the time being, Katey wanted to rest and be with Logan.

In a daring move, Katey leaned down and slipped her arms around Logan's thick neck and hugged him, wiping her icy tears against his black fur. He didn't seem to mind, and she thought she could feel his arms edge in a little around her as well. It wasn't a hug, but it was close enough.

A few silent moments passed, then every loup-garou in the clearing perked up their ears, and raised themselves up onto their hind legs to sniff the air. Something wasn't right. Even Katey could feel a hint of it.

Logan broke from her embrace and stood up like the others, straddling his two powerful hind legs on either side of her, his tail swishing against her hair. Katey looked around frantically. She didn't smell anything, but that didn't mean that nothing lurked in the shadows of the woods. The air seemed to electrify, and she knew, just like they did, that something was approaching.

A bellowing growl emanated from the group as they looked around with alert and searching eyes. Then, the wind shifted in her direction and Katey could smell something that was like a mix of sulfur masked by a cheap imitation of pine scent. The smell was repulsive, and she covered her nose to keep from gagging.

"What's happening?"

Darren slowly walked over to them and in his loup-garou grunting noise language tried to tell her something urgently.

Katey was about to let him know that she didn't understand when she heard something like pellet guns firing from all directions. One by one, she saw loups-garous fall down to the snow with tranquilizer darts lodged deep in their fur. Whatever could take out a loup-garou must have been some high-powered doses. By the continued beating of their hearts, she knew they weren't dead, only knocked out.

Katey tried to crawl out from underneath Logan, but he quickly pounced on top of her and trapped her between his four legs, roaring up at the hidden attackers, guarding her from any impending darts.

She shrank low under Logan's body and watched as some tried to escape, but were met by a wall of black-clad assassins.

They were surrounded, but by who?

She peered up into the treetops and saw more shooters aiming down at them. All the shooters were shrouded in black cloaks, hats, and masks, making them into shadows against the snow.

Several loups-garous spotted their attackers and climbed the trees. Some shooters were ripped from their perches and mauled, while others managed to shoot the beasts before they could get that far.

Katey heard a soft thud just before Logan's heavy body began to sway and quiver above her. He'd been hit. Before he toppled to the snow, she maneuvered out from under him and saw the tranquilizer dart in his arm. Katey took a firm hold on it and managed to yank it out, but it was too late and Logan was unconscious.

He was still breathing, heart still beating, but his eyes were closed as if in a deep sleep. At least he was alive. The dart resembled something of a thick hospital needle, half-filled with a dingy yellow liquid that reeked of something herbal and powerful.

She threw it aside and screamed at the shooters to stop. She stayed by Logan's body and waved her hands to get their attention. It was likely that they didn't know she was even there, their sole focus was on the loups-garous.

After a few frightful seconds, Katey succeeded. They didn't shoot, but their guns swiveled in her direction.

By now, Darren and almost all the other loups-garous lay in the snow, shot, but still alive. Katey gawked in disbelief at the sight of formidable beasts defeated before an enemy that ambushed them.

She stood up and began screaming at the shooters about the injustice of what they had done, but before she could get much out, she received a hard knock to the back of her skull and all went black.

Logan's bandana slipped from her fingertips and fluttered down to the snow.

CHAPTER 20

Harsh awareness bashed through the wall of unconsciousness. The soundless, feelingless void slowly swelled and filled with scents and noise, rousing Logan from his shift-induced coma. The cold came first, bitter and unrelenting. Then the earthy, moldy smell of damp stone and mortar. Sweat, warm bodies, and the subtle whiff of blood and death told him something wasn't quite right. Voices raised in anger and concern broke against the ring of nothingness in his ears, a second clue.

Then, like the boom of an atomic bomb, it hit him. Katey wasn't with him. She was far away, so far out of reach that their mating bond strained over the distance. His wolf exploded in rage and Logan's eyes popped open.

He lay prone on a stone floor, naked, and surrounded by loups-garous. Firelight danced across their bodies, casting undulating shadows. It wasn't enough light for him to distinguish one face from another until his dark vision adjusted. Then he saw that the other loups-garous, probably about twenty or thirty in the tight space, were all dressed in the same gray sweatpants, and the walls and ceiling were made of the same stone beneath him.

Logan's tired and stiff muscles protested as he pushed himself up. A hand landed on his shoulder, and he reflexively shoved it off.

"Hey, settle down." Ben's familiar voice brought Logan back to himself.

A second later, Darren came to his side, brown eyes inspecting him. "Are you all right?"

"Katey.... Where's Katey?" Logan's hoarse, crackled voice was fraught with the panic he and his wolf shared.

"We don't know. She's not among us." Logan tried to burst to his feet, but Darren held him down. "Logan, listen to me. Reach through your bond with her. You know she's alive if you can still feel her. She's not hurt."

Darren was right. Just on the edge of their bond, he could feel her heartbeat, strong and steady.

"Then where is she?" Logan felt the cold wash of gold over his eyes.

"Just be glad she ain't in here with us." Ben handed him an identical pair of sweatpants that everyone else wore.

Logan took the clothes and looked around one more time. "Where is here?"

Darren's mouth dipped in a deep frown. "We were ambushed last night by vamps. They could have killed us, but they didn't. They knocked us out with tranquilizers and brought us here. All we can tell is the vamps are nearby, and this is some sort of prison."

Logan slipped on the pants to hide his nakedness and keep out some of the cold. "Was Katey in the ambush?"

Darren nodded. "Yes, but she was in her human form. It's unlikely the vamps know what she is, otherwise she might be in here with us."

Logan froze, his heart nearly stopped. Disappointment added to the roiling emotions in his chest. "She couldn't shift."

"She came close," Darren replied gently as if to console him.

"If it wasn't for you," Ben added, "she might have pulled it off."

Darren then went on to explain what happened the night before, how Katey had been so close to shifting but his howl and the impromptu hunt interrupted her efforts. If it hadn't been for Darren, John, and Noah, the hunt may have ended differently. But, the last moments before the ambush encouraged him that not all had devolved into chaos. They made some connection, but Logan remembered none of it.

"It's likely that the vamps have her." Darren helped Logan to his feet. "The fact that she is unharmed and alive is good."

That wasn't any comfort, but Logan could do nothing about it. As long as Katey was alive, there was hope enough.

"Dustin?" he asked, eyes jumping between the dimly lit faces around him.

"In the next cell over. As far as I can tell, we're all here."

Logan went quiet, listening to the worried voices of the other loups-garous in the prison. They all shared one common concern.

"Food?" He pinned Darren with a serious look.

He shook his head. "A man came a little while ago and distributed some meat to us, but he won't be back for a while."

"They're probably gonna starve us just for the fun of it," Ben muttered with contempt.

No food in close quarters. No loup-garou liked to be caged, especially a hungry one. It was a recipe for disaster, and the vamps weren't so dumb not to know that.

"Has anyone tried to get out yet?"

Darren looked in one direction, presumably toward their only exit from the prison cell. "The bars are silver."

Logan hissed a curse and leaned to get a look at the metal bars beyond the wall of loups-garous mulling around the cell. He noticed how none of them were willing to venture too close to the silver.

"How did they know where to find us?" Logan asked. "Didn't they do a sweep of the park before the gathering?"

Darren sighed. "I don't know. I suppose we all took for granted that Alaska was safe. Maybe this was bound to happen, after hosting the gathering for so many years in the same place."

"Nope." Dustin's raised voice from the other side of the stone wall drew their attention.

They came closer to the corner their two cells shared.

"What do you know?" Darren asked his beta.

"You guys were still out when we got here, but we weren't the first prisoners. Gregory and Erik are in the far cell."

Logan's lips pulled in a snarl, and he tested the air. There were too many loups-garous to pick out the rougarous.

"They weren't with us last night," Darren replied with a note of confusion.

"Nope. They told the vamps where we were. Or, more specifically, Erik did."

Logan was too angry to listen to the rest of the story, how Gregory confessed his son's scheme to get rid of his enemies and weaken the strength of the loups-garous in Crestucky so the rougarous could take over. It was Chicago all over again, except this time, the plan backfired, and the Jennings were caught in the dragnet.

"I hope his father has dealt with him," Darren growled, his own wolfish eyes gleaming bright.

"Oh, yeah," Dustin laughed. "Got a worse beating than we gave Logan last week. I'm surprised he's still breathing."

Served him right. If they didn't make it out alive, Logan was satisfied that Erik would finally get what he deserved too.

Their only hope was Katey. If the vamps hadn't killed her and didn't know what she was, there was a good chance she could put herself in the ideal place to help them. Just how, he had no idea, but Katey would find a way. He trusted his future mate, trusted her strength, and that she wouldn't rest until they were together again.

The soft crackle of a fire and the strong rotten scent of sulfur pulled Katey out of her deep sleep. When she began to stir, she realized she was lying on a soft mattress. Her hands slid across the smooth, silky sheets as she grunted and cracked open her eyes.

Her first sight was of a thick red velvet canopy, accented with golden fringe along the edges of the fabric and the gentle glow of amber flames flickering against the ceiling and walls.

She turned her head and took in the ornately decorated bedroom. It looked like something out of a medieval castle. Rich colors, carvings, and gold embellishments trimmed everything, capturing the light from the fireplace. Katey glanced down to her clothes and saw she was still wearing her torn jeans and blouse.

She painstakingly sat up only to find that she wasn't alone. In a luxurious wingback armchair near the fireplace, sat a man she didn't recognize at first. He seemed to pay no mind to her presence as he stared into the fire, holding a goblet of some sort of red liquid just inches from his pale lips. His facial features were familiar, but she couldn't quite figure out why. His eyes were a deep, rich blue that almost seemed to glow in the darkness, like polished marbles reflecting the flames.

Dark blonde hair, even longer than Katey's, draped over his chest, reminding her of a lion's mane, soft and thick. Beneath a

black vest, he wore a white dress shirt, the first few buttons undone to reveal a pale chest and sleeves rolled to his elbows to show
the thick, ropy muscles of his forearms. His legs were crossed at
the knees and his free arm rested casually on the padded arm of
the chair.

Overall, he projected an aura of masculinity and dignity, but
there was an undercurrent of danger about him that Katey
couldn't ignore. He was good looking with strikingly handsome
features, like she would expect to see on a model, with his hollow
cheeks and defined brow.

But this man was the source of the sulfuric stench, and blood
filled his glass. Vampire.

"Who are you?" Katey asked, her voice throaty and trembling.

The man turned to her with his mystifying eyes and grinned a
toothy smile. "You're finally awake."

Again, his voice sounded so foreign, yet so familiar at the same
time, like a vague memory of someone she had met long ago. She
could see the long fangs bared in his grin. The sight of them sent
her wolf into high alert, though Katey didn't feel quite the same.

"Who are you?" Katey repeated more demandingly.

He put down his goblet on a small round table next to the chair
and stood up in one smooth, graceful move. "You don't recognize
me?" He held out his arms to allow a better look. Her mind frantically searched for the answer, but she couldn't place a name to his
face.

"You look familiar, but..."

"Maybe this will help you remember." He began to hum a tune
and waltzed with an invisible partner around the room to the edge
of the bed.

When the realization finally hit her, she gasped. "Martel!"

He was the president of the ballroom dance club from high
school so many years back. He was the one who encouraged her to
pursue dancing, along with Lily. But he certainly was not a vampire
back then and he didn't look this way when they first met.

Martel chuckled and held out his hand to Katey. "The one and
only."

She looked to his pale skin and was tempted to take it, if nothing
else than for the sake of who Martel used to be. She remembered
all of their long conversations and the humorous glint in his eyes
that were so devoid of feeling now. There was a time when she

thought his eyes were insanely gorgeous. Now, there was something new in them, like he had been marked by an evil she couldn't understand or name.

Her mind seemed to pull against her instinct to hate him, but she shook her head. "But you're..." She couldn't bring herself to say it.

"I'm a vampire. Yes, I know." He clasped his hands behind his back and he lost a bit of his bravado at the admission. "I suppose you're wondering how."

Katey nodded and waited, not trusting her voice to stay steady.

Martel took a stabilizing breath. "Well, you were just a freshman when I graduated, and we fell out of touch, so I can't expect you to know what happened to my mom. She... She had a lot of issues. Drugs, guys... I didn't let on at school, but... there were just a lot of days when I didn't exactly want to go home."

His tight-lipped smile told Katey he didn't want pity, just like she never wanted pity for being a foster kid. "I had no idea."

"No one did. I wanted it that way... A few months after graduation, I moved away. I finally got out of that little town and didn't want to look back. Got a call in the middle of my first semester of college that my mom had blown her brains out." He shrugged and looked away. "Probably couldn't handle daily living without me there to clean up her messes."

Again, Katey knew that plot already. She bit her lips together and patiently waited, trying to make sense of how the guy who always seemed so happy and positive at school could have had so much going on at home.

"Her suicide messed me up for a while, and I fell in with the wrong crowd. My grades slipped, finances were running low because I couldn't keep a job... It was a dark time I'm not proud of." Martel lifted his gaze, a glint of something brazen in his eyes. "Then, I met a guy. He called himself Raven. I thought it was pretty cheesy, but he had an offer for me. He could make me forget the pain. So, I took him up on his offer, thinking maybe it was some sort of new drug. Little did I know..." He gestured to his chest as if to make his point.

Katey looked away, horrified that such a friend could have fallen prey to such a terrible fate. She couldn't believe, out of all the things she had guessed what could have happened to him, that this was it. Looking at him now, she could tell that he had accepted what he was and somehow, it suited him well. The confidence he carried in his body posture was enough to tell her that he actually liked being what he was.

"Oh, it's not such a bad deal, really. I became Raven's apprentice after that. Dropped out of college, obviously. I get to have nice clothes, wonderful accommodations, and all the food I could want."

She cringed at what his idea of food could be.

Panic rose within her as she remembered what happened before she had blacked out. The loups-garous had fallen in the snow, unmoving, defeated.

She reached out through the pack bond and knew that they were still alive and somewhere close by, but for all her powerful senses, she couldn't find them. The stench of sulfur was too strong and the stone walls muffled much of the noise outside of the bedchamber.

"What happened to Logan?" Katey turned desperate eyes to Martel and gripped the fabric of the sheets between her hands to keep herself from bolting off the bed to search for her fiancé herself.

Martel's smile faded and confusion pinched his eyebrows together. "Who?"

A ball of fury spiraled in her chest. "The loups-garous! The werewolves! Where are they? What did you do with them?"

On the borderline of hysterics, Katey pushed herself off the bed and charged at Martel as if she was ready to fight him if he didn't give her what she wanted. She didn't care if she couldn't shift and he was a vampire, she would beat the truth out of him with a spoon if she had to.

Martel placed his cold hands on her shoulders to keep her at bay. "Calm down, they can't hurt you now. They're down in the basement in their cages,"

"Cages?" Katey breathed. "They were never going to hurt me! Take me to them right now!" She swatted away his hands and glared at him, being careful to not let her golden eyes gleam through or any hint of dominance leak out. It was clear he didn't know what she was, otherwise she'd be in a cage too.

"I have no authority to do that. I can try to see about getting you down there, maybe tomorrow night."

"Tomorrow night? How long have we been here? Where is here?" Katey glanced out the barred window just behind Martel, but it was nothing but black past the frosted edges of the panes.

"We're about a hundred miles from the Canadian border. We brought the beasts in last night by trucks. It's now just a little past sundown... I had kind of hoped we'd spend some time this evening catching up. It's been a long time, and I want to hear how you've been."

Katey slowly sat herself back down on the bed, her throat constricting. The last thing she wanted to do was sit down and have a casual chat, even if it was with Martel.

"Besides," he continued, "The human food around here isn't that great, and there are few places for private conversations. I thought we'd go down into town for dinner, if you're feeling up for it."

Katey glowered up to him. "Do I have a choice?" She wasn't sure what was truth or fiction, but the movies did not always paint vampires in the best of lights. Manipulative, cunning, selfish. How much of that poisoned Martel to become someone she didn't know anymore?

His expression turned a bit wounded, and she regretted her biting words. "If you don't want to, I won't make you... But I'd like to spend time with you. You're the first person from my old life that I've seen in years. Humor me?"

Katey thought for a moment, then met his gaze. "If I go with you, can you give me your word that you'll make sure I can go see the werewolves?" Katey thought it best to refer to them by their species rather than by names. Perhaps if he thought she was too attached to them, then he might second guess his intentions to keep her safe.

"I can try." Martel gave her a humble bow of his head.

"Then, I'll go... Can I get a change of clothes?" Katey asked, pinching a bit of her dirty blouse that had torn in a few places while she had been chased by the younger, confused loups-garous.

"Sure... Helga!" he hollered at the door, causing Katey to jump a little at his booming voice.

She had never heard him yell before, not even as a human. Martel had always been the temperate sort, never raising his voice or his hand against anyone.

A little girl, probably not more than thirteen years old, entered the room dressed in a maid's outfit. She kept her head down and hands folded neatly in front of her with her shiny ebony hair braided into a bun behind her head.

"Find something for Katey to wear for going out. Take her clothes and get them washed and mended." He turned to Katey and gave her a soft, closed-lipped smile as if conscious of the way his fangs showed any other way. "I'll be waiting downstairs."

With that, Martel left the room, leaving Katey and Helga alone. Helga didn't smell of sulfur, so Katey knew she was human.

The frightened Helga hustled to the wardrobe in the corner of the room and sifted through the clothes. Katey stood up, her legs weak from the new weight that had been placed on her shoulders. The temptation to picture her friends in cages was strong, but she couldn't think of that now.

She came up beside Helga and peered at the contents of the wardrobe. Everything was fancy and regal with full skirts and strapless tops. Nothing looked remotely comfortable.

"Aren't there a decent pair of jeans? Or even just a skirt?"

The poor girl trembled as if she'd be struck or reprimanded for something she had done. Unless she personally burned every pair of jeans, Katey wouldn't do anything to her. But, after serving the vampires, maybe it was out of habit. Fear radiated off of the little girl and filled the room with the potent, peppery odor. Katey's wolf did not glory in the scent, but whimpered and sympathized.

"Relax, I'm not one of them. I won't hurt you."

Though Katey was completely untrained, she tried to do what alphas did, and projected her dominance to comfort rather than control Helga.

Helga let out a tight breath and shaking hands flitted over the fabrics until she came upon a long, silky black skirt and blouse that looked more like it belonged on a medieval barmaid than someone going out for dinner. The canvas-like fabric was wrinkled, sleeves loose and billowy, with a drawstring collar that was purposefully wide to hang off the shoulders. It would have looked better underneath a leather corset.

Helga held up the outfit and Katey made a face. "Like the skirt, not the blouse."

Katey took charge and turned to the wardrobe to have another look. Soon, she came across a beige, silky, long-sleeved buttoned blouse with a plunging neckline. It would show way too much

skin for her comfort, but it was better than the Renaissance
Faire outfit.

She took the new outfit combination, undressed and threw
her old clothes on the foot of the bed. To her astonishment, the
skirt and blouse fit perfectly, fitting to her figure as if it were
made for her. She walked up to the full-length mirror standing
in the corner of the room next to the wardrobe and inspected
her reflection for the first time. Katey's face puckered in a
deep frown. Her hair was a tangled mess. No wonder Martel
may have thought she was in danger from the loups-garous.
Though it was completely true, it looked like she had been
chased through the Alaskan wilderness.

"Is something wrong, miss?" Helga asked as she presented
Katey with a pair of heels to match the skirt.

There was plenty wrong. She was in an unfamiliar place, one
of her former childhood friends was a freakin' vampire, and her
future mate was locked away in a cage somewhere, probably
wondering if she was even alive. Nothing was right, but she
couldn't tell anyone that. Until she could free her pack and all
the other loups-garous trapped below her, Katey would have
to play the part that they all expected of her.

"Do you have a brush or something so I can fix this?" Katey
slipped her fingers into the tangles and pulled to make her
point.

Helga then pointed out a small vanity on the other side of the
room. "Would you like me to do your hair, miss?"

"No, I can do it myself."

Katey sat at the vanity and strapped on the heels. A brush,
hair clips, and a perfume bottle sat upon the vanity top, along
with an elegant jewelry box. This definitely wasn't Martel's
room. By the clothes and the vanity, it had to belong to another
woman, but who? Where was she now?

While she tried to fix the disaster that was her hair, her mind
drifted. How did the vampires sneak up on them so suddenly
and manage to overtake them with those darts? What poison
could have taken down a loup-garou so easily? And above all,
why didn't the vampires just kill them? It would have made
much more sense, but they were being held in the bowels of
the castle and alive. For what purpose?

"How did you get tangled up with this bunch?"

"My parents are dead, miss. I didn't have anywhere to go so I came to work here. My uncle tends the gardens. My whole time consists of serving the vampire lords and their guests."

Katey's heart bled for Helga. To have no family besides her uncle who was bound in the same servitude as she was, no friends, no means of supporting herself, and forced to work for a race that drank blood to survive, all of it was too great a burden for any little girl to bear. Hopefully, they had no plans to make her dinner one day if she ever proved to be useless. Then again, did vampires do that sort of thing? By Helga's reflexive timidity, she doubted that the vampire lords were that benevolent.

"Can you tell me exactly where I am?" Katey glanced at Helga in the mirror, who stood some distance behind her, waiting for orders.

"We're on a high mountain overlooking my hometown." There was a hint of pain in her voice as if she didn't want to be here either. "Unfortunately, it's far away from any big city. The vampires set up here for that reason."

"Is this Martel's castle?"

Helga giggled and shook her head. "No, miss. It's Michael and Yaverik's. They're the vampire lords of this region."

That wasn't comforting. "How many vampires are here?"

"We're in the middle of the Winter Solstice celebration, so it's hard to say. We have many guests from across the country staying with us right now."

That was even less comforting. She was surrounded. She had hoped maybe only five vamps at the most lived here. Now she realized how surrounded she truly was. A gathering of this many vampires and the ambush on the loups-garous was no coincidence. Something was coming and she had to stop it somehow, but there was too little information to go on.

"I'm assuming this is a big castle?"

"Yes, miss. You'll have a good view of it from the bottom of the mountain. We have a beautiful courtyard, too, if you get to see it during the day."

Katey considered the perfume, and wondered if her nose was too sensitive for it. After a tiny spritz, she figured that's all she could handle. The scent resembled something like lavender or orchids and Katey liked the subtle feminine touch it gave her. It was familiar too, but she couldn't place exactly where from.

"Have you seen the werewolves in the basement?"

A chord had been struck in the little girl and Katey heard Helga swallow hard. "I caught a glimpse of them when they were being brought in, miss, but nothing more. I'm not allowed in the basement."

Katey's heartbeat quickened. "Did you see someone specific? He was a younger man, dark hair with blonde streaks and a bit of facial hair around his jaw? What about an older man with a bit of a graying beard? How about one that's young, but with reddish hair?"

Her questions came at Helga too rapidly. All the girl could do was shake her head.

"I'm sorry, miss, I didn't get a good look at them like that."

Katey let out a heavy sigh and her shoulders slumped. She wouldn't know if Logan and the others were safe until later, but patience was never something she possessed.

With one last look in the mirror, Katey knew there was little else she could do to make herself look decent. Then again, why would she care about that? It was just Martel, a vampire, and also an old friend. She had Logan, so why would she want to look good for Martel? She shook her head to rid herself of that feeling, and stood to join Helga by the door.

The halls were carpeted with more red and the grandeur she had admired in the bed chamber seemed to carry into the décor for the rest of the castle. Ancient tapestries and sconces lined the walls. They passed door after door that led into unknown chambers and Katey heard whispered conversations behind each one. The stench of vampire was everywhere, an ever-present odor that singed her nostrils.

The foyer boasted high raftered ceilings with extravagant golden carvings in the corners of the hall that trailed down along the walls in intricate scrollwork. The floor was paved in marble tiles and gleamed in the golden light from the torches throughout the foyer. She saw only three sets of doors leading out of the room. One led to a dining hall packed with vampire guests, while the other opened up into a ballroom where she could hear humans bustling around and talking amongst themselves about decorations. The third massive door led outside, etched with old world designs and straight across the long foyer floor from the grand staircase.

They hadn't passed by a single vampire until they descended the grand marble stairs down to the main foyer. They were pale, just as ashen as Martel, and held their heads high as if they were the true royalty in the world. Some dressed in formal gowns and suits, while others were clothed more humbly in slacks and polos. The women were stunningly beautiful and the men were handsome, but more sophisticatedly handsome like Martel.

A few were followed closely by humans who kept their heads bowed and eyes cast to the floor. Were these servants like Helga, or did they serve some other purpose?

What struck her odd was that some didn't exude the same haughtiness like Martel. Others actually met her stare and nodded their greeting before walking past, showing her some deference despite not being a vampire at all. But there were plenty of sneers to outweigh the kind smiles she received, too.

It was different from the roguish good looks of the loups-garous. The vamps had a regal quality to their appearances, while the loups-garous featured more of the dashing essence of adventurers and warriors. These people looked like they had never worked a day in their lives.

It was then that she realized she couldn't read their emotions in the same way that she could for humans or loups-garous. It was as if they blocked her out, her mind hitting a brick wall in an effort to figure them out. Either that, or there was nothing there for her to find but a soulless shell of a creature so different from herself and her pack. It troubled her to know that she wouldn't be able to gauge their reactions and motives so easily. At least she could tell which were friendly and which to avoid.

As they approached Martel at the bottom of the stairs, Helga took her leave with a little curtsey and walked off.

Martel grinned and gave her a once-over. "How did I know you wouldn't wear any of the dresses?"

Katey shrugged. "Not much has changed. I still don't like getting that dressed up."

"Well, you look exquisite anyway."

Katey's lips parted a bit at the oddness of the remark. It sounded so strange coming from Martel. He seemed to add flair to the word that sent her mind reeling. Did he mean that, or was he saying it just to be nice?

He offered his arm, but Katey kindly refused it. "Let's just get this over with."

She had to remind herself that was a means to an end, just like the date with Erik had been. Going out with Martel would gain her access to her pack. That was all she wanted and much to her dismay, she had to play along.

Again, Martel looked injured at her remark, but relented to her attitude and led her toward the massive oak doors that led outside. Snow flurries greeted them with a cold gust of wind. Katey could feel the chill climb up her legs from under her skirt and squeezed them together in hopes to keep herself warm. Now she regretted not grabbing a jacket or wrap before leaving the bedroom. She remembered seeing a white fur shawl. It may not have gone with her outfit, but it would have kept out some of the chill.

"I have a spare jacket in the car. It's in the backseat," he said, as if reading her thoughts.

Martel ushered Katey to a slick black sports car parked not too far from the high stone steps that led down from the front doors. A valet was present who, despite the cold, was not dressed warmly in his bright red attendant uniform. He held open the car door to let Katey slide into the passenger seat. As soon as the door was shut behind her, she blindly reached into the back and swept her arm along the seat and floorboards to find the jacket. Her hand brushed a bit of leather and she snatched it up.

Martel was given the keys and got into the driver's seat just as she slid her arms through the sleeves that were far too big for her. He started up the car and launched off at a dangerous speed down the snowy mountainside. Katey braced herself and even with her seat belt securely fastened, she was jostled on her side of the car due to the bumpy road and hairpin turns.

"Sorry about the rough roads. I don't like going to town too often because of it."

Katey gave him a sidelong glance and wondered if he really could read her mind, or perhaps he was just more observant than she gave him credit for.

At the bottom of the mountain, once they were driving on smooth blacktop, Martel turned to Katey, a wrinkle between his brows. "You seem pretty calm about all this."

"What do you mean?" Katey loosened her grip on the leather seats and hoped she didn't leave a mark in the fabric.

"I mean, I'm a vampire. You just walked past a bunch of vampires, and you don't seem to be bothered at all. What gives?"

Katey realized that her behavior must have been highly suspicious, as if the news that bloodsucking monsters existed wasn't news to her at all. After learning about werewolves, not much was bound to surprise her anymore.

She shrugged. "I guess... It just doesn't bother me."

"Why not?" There was a hint of puzzlement in his words.

"Because I know you won't do anything to me and neither will anyone else."

"How can you be so sure?" His voice dropped deeper and Katey looked back to him with a cool expression.

"I know you better than that. The Martel I knew in school wasn't cruel, and you wouldn't let anyone hurt me."

He turned his icy stare out the windshield. "The Martel you knew is long dead."

Katey watched him for a moment, examining his hard, bitter countenance. "You may be a vampire now, but people don't change that easily."

He gave a mirthless laugh. "You don't have a clue. Turning into... what I am... it's not like a haircut or a makeover. It changes everything. You don't know me anymore."

In a way, he didn't know her anymore. And she did know what that was like. Katey underwent her own transformation, and it was hard to imagine what she was like before she turned loup-garou, even though it had been less than a week. Nothing was the same. Nothing would ever be the same.

CHAPTER 21

They soon arrived in the town that Helga had spoken of earlier. The streets were fairly empty, with few cars and nearly no pedestrians out. Perhaps they all knew a coven of vampires lived not too far away and knew better than to walk out alone at night. The town was small, but reminded her of the Old World villages of Europe in its architecture and layout. In this remote part of Alaska, it seemed bizarre. Maybe, if vampires could live as long as loups-garous, a vampire built up this town to make it look like their old home in Germany or Italy. The addition of a castle up in the mountains only completed the vision.

During the entire trip through the town, Katey couldn't stop thinking about Logan, her pack, and the other loups-garous that were trapped. She wondered what was going to happen to them, and if any had been injured during the ambush. They were alive, that much she could tell, but if they were harmed and miserable, that was another thing. If she played her cards right and buttered up Martel, she could milk him for answers. The idea of kissing up to him made her blood run cold, but it was for her pack. For them, she would endure anything.

Martel pulled up in front of a quaint French restaurant. Like the town near the resort, their storefronts were decked out in Christmas lights and garland to inspire a festive mood. Through the windows, she could see several customers seated at tables draped in white cloth and decorated with little flower vases and votive candles. Even from inside the car, she could hear the faint notes of Parisian music that played over the speakers in the restaurant, and smelled the savory aroma of food she likely couldn't eat and could probably never afford by herself. It was the sort of place a husband

and wife would go for their anniversary, and it made Katey's lonely heart ache for Logan all the more.

As Martel assisted Katey out of the car, she noticed that his hand was colder than the air that swirled around them, and she quickly withdrew from the shock of it. She remembered when his touch used to be so warm when they had danced during club meetings. It was another reminder that he wasn't quite the man that he once was, but Katey wasn't going to give up so easily. There had to be something left of the human she knew.

He noted her surprise and he withdrew his hand with a look of apology. Katey wondered if his bashfulness was a show, or if any part about this evening was genuine. She wished that it was, but what Logan told her the day before kept repeating on loop in her mind. They were supposed to be enemies. Vampires made it their mission to kill loups-garous. Her desire to find humanity in him warred against this learned instinct to revile everything Martel had become, and she couldn't make up her mind.

They entered the restaurant and all eyes turned to Martel. Fear exploded in the air, suffocating the pleasant scent of the rich food until Katey began to feel a little queasy. Expressions varied across the dining room. Some weren't shy about showing their fear. One couple, who had likely been done with their meal for a while anyway, stood and abruptly walked out. Others quickly turned away, afraid to make eye contact, though she heard their whispered words of panic to their companions.

It made her wonder what kind of fear the occupants of the castle had inspired in the townspeople to make them so submissive.

"Popular one, aren't you?" Katey mumbled with a cocked eyebrow as she shed his leather jacket.

Martel let out a long breath, but said nothing as they waited for a hostess to seat them.

The young woman who had been manning the hostess station before they walked in, had retreated somewhere else in the restaurant. Instead, an older man in a suit and tie approached, likely the manager. He greeted Martel with a feigned friendliness that he might have given naturally to any other customer. Like everyone else, he was terrified of the vampire.

"Good evening, sir. What can I do for you and your lady?"

Katey didn't quite like the idea of being called his lady and wanted to correct him, but Martel was too quick to answer.

"A table for two, please."

The manager grabbed two leather-clad menus from the station and nodded. "Absolutely. Right this way."

He led them to a booth in the far corner of the restaurant, well away from the other patrons. Katey slid across the vinyl seat and eyed the intricate place settings, complete with wine glasses and cloth napkins. A quick glance inside the menu revealed no prices next to the entrees and appetizers, a sign that everything must have been incredibly expensive.

"What can I get you two to drink?"

The moment the words came out of the manager's mouth, Katey could tell he instantly regretted it and blanched a perfect shade of white.

"Water," Martel answered without hesitance.

"Same for me."

The manager visibly relaxed, tense muscles releasing. "Of course. I'll be right back with those waters."

Martel didn't even bother to look at his menu, while Katey tried to make sense of the cursive French across the pages. She wondered why the manager even bothered to give Martel a menu. Perhaps, just like asking for their drink orders, it was pure muscle memory, and had little to do with the fact that a vampire had entered his restaurant and he had to act like it was business as usual.

"Can you even read this?" Katey asked, tilting the menu toward him.

He smirked. "A little. We spent a winter in France last year. What are you in the mood for?"

Katey shifted uneasily. "Is there a steak somewhere on here?"

Martel finally picked up his menu and browsed. "They have one."

"I'll take that. Rare. No sides, if that's even an option."

"I think everything is a-la-cart, so yes, I guess you can just get the steak by itself."

The way Martel regarded her made her squirm. Had she given herself away so easily?

Quick to take the focus off of her, she folded the menu and squared her shoulders. "So, you can't eat anything here, can you?"

He shrugged. "I probably could, but it's not as appetizing as... other things."

Her eyes narrowed. "I sincerely hope you don't plan to make a meal out of me."

Martel laughed, the same laugh she remembered from all those years ago. "No, I don't. That was one of my first lessons. Never drink from someone of the opposite sex."

Katey's head tilted. "Because...?"

If it were possible, a hint of color rose in Martel's cheeks. "Well, I guess we could, but it normally ends with the blood donor in a precarious state."

She gave him a sassy look. "You're going to have to be really straight with me. I don't read between the lines that well."

Again, he smirked. "Always the blunt one." He leaned forward and lowered his voice to a private conversation level. "If I were to bite you and drink your blood right now, you'd get so turned on that you'd be begging we go someplace private so I could ravage you."

That was too straight. Katey's empty stomach dropped. "Vampire bites are an aphrodisiac. Good to know. Good thing you're not going to do that then."

"Unless you wanted me to," he said with a sly glint in his leer.

Katey rolled her eyes. "I may have had a crush on you when I was a freshman, but a whole lot has changed. Including that."

Martel seemed to brighten at her confession, and he sat back in his seat. "You had a crush on me?"

She held up her pinched thumb and forefinger. "Just a tiny one."

Once more, he laughed and leaned against the back of his booth. "Oh, come on. You can tell me the truth. You were in love with me, right?"

Katey wagged her head. "In your dreams."

"You did. In my dreams anyway. I had a little crush on you too."

Katey grinned. "Liar."

"Not lying. You were cute and all shy, but dancing really made you come out of your shell. It was nice to watch."

This conversation was going too far too fast. Katey started it, but wouldn't encourage this trail of banter any further.

Martel never broke away his solid eye contact with her as he pulled out a pack of cigarettes and lighter from his coat pocket. With one flick of the lighter, he lit up the end and took a drag.

"I don't think you should be smoking in here," Katey said, her nose wrinkling and throat closing up in response to the acrid smoke.

"No sign on the door says I can't."

"I'm asking that you put it out for my sake. It bothers me."

Martel eyed her curiously, then put out the cigarette in his own palm, twisting the lit end into his skin. He tossed the butt of it onto the floor. He didn't even flinch as the burn wound healed up quickly.

Katey lifted a brow. "Is that supposed to impress me?"

"No. They didn't have an ashtray out."

The manager came back shortly with their glasses of water and Martel ordered for her, the name of the steak dish rolling off his tongue so fluently she would have guessed he spoke French on a regular basis.

As soon as the manager left to put in the order, Katey greedily grabbed for her drink. She drank it earnestly, hardly realizing how thirsty she had become until that moment. Not only that, but subtle hunter pangs made her belly tender and achy. She could appreciate this little sign that her loup-garou nature was still there, still strong. Her wolf continued to seethe inside, wishing to escape the company of the vampire, but it was better than feeling nothing from her spiritual partner.

It reminded her of what she had left behind at the castle. That one single through snapped her back to reality. Shame crept up her neck that from the minute she walked into the restaurant, she let herself forget about Logan and the pack. Being with Martel had distracted her from the pain in her bond with Logan, and how the distance wrapped her heart in barbed wire.

"You seem very far away... Something on your mind?" Martel folded his arms over the table, blue eyes fixed on her.

Katey looked up to him, realizing that now was the perfect time to probe for answers. "I'm thinking of the werewolves and what you intend to do with them."

He almost seemed confused by her question. "Why should you care?"

"Because I do... I don't like animals being caged without good reason."

He snickered. "That was another thing I liked about you. Always compassionate. We're going to make some sport of them. The night after tomorrow, the last day of the winter solstice, we'll be letting them loose on the mountain, but each of them will be fitted with a collar that will give off an electric shock if they try to leave the mountain perimeter. Forty-thousand volts to be exact. And since they will be contained nicely, we'll be packing our guns with some liquid silver bullets and killing them off one by one." A wicked grin split his face. "I can't wait to mount one of their heads over the fireplace in my room."

The lilting music continued to play over the speakers and diners kept on eating their meal, all while Katey's world slowed to a stop. How could this man, who had once been so kind and compassionate in high school, speak so placidly about murder?

"You're a monster." The words slipped out, as much out of shock as out of anger.

"Now, that's not fair," he said, pointing a finger at her. "They are, too."

"At least they don't hunt you down and murder you as if you were some animal." Her words were laced with venom, vicious and cold.

Martel peered at her with his hypnotic eyes and shook his head. "You have no idea, do you?"

"About what?" she spat.

Martel leaned back and looked away, irritated. "They must have brain-washed you or something, because they are not the innocent ones here."

"What are you talking about?"

He turned back to her, a rise of some rage in the set of his brows. "We have just as much right to kill them as they have to kill us. *They* are the beasts to be exterminated. Their kind are like mangy rabid dogs. They're uncontrollable, volatile. One rogue werewolf could easily take out this entire town if they wanted. They need to be taken out before they infect the world with their violence."

"I could say the same for you and your kind. At least the werewolves don't need to drain the life out of people to survive."

Martel's lips broke into an unexpected smile. "You can't win this argument, Katey. I remember you from school, always arguing and making your opinions heard. You can't convince me to see this your way when you don't even know anything about me or my kind."

Katey's face wrinkled into a snarl and she leaned in closer. "Those werewolves have families, wives and children, who are waiting for them to come home and you're just going to kill them in cold blood over some stupid righteous ideology for no reason but to exterminate something you think is a problem? I'd say you and your own kind are the problem, frightening the human population and feeding off them like parasites. At least the werewolves moderate their hunting or buy meat from the store. What could you possibly do except steal blood from innocent victims?"

Her fiery speech may have been coming too close to giving her away. No one would defend a loup-garou so adamantly, unless she had something to gain from their existence, whether it was her own family or lover, which Martel knew nothing about.

His eyes went hard and penetrating. "That just goes to show how much you don't know, Katey. But, why bother trying to explain my side if you're determined to misunderstand me?"

That struck Katey a little harder than she was willing to show. She had always thought herself an open-minded person, accepting of others no matter who they were. Yet, here she was, calling Martel out on things she only assumed or what little Logan could tell her.

She sat back. "Fine. I'm listening."

Martel didn't seem convinced, but he decided to humor her anyway. "First, let me set one thing straight. Yes, we drink blood. Yes, it has to come from a live vein. But, those we take blood from are not victims. At least, not always. There are a lot of vampires, Raven included, that don't draw a line, but I do... I try. We have what are called blood servants. They agree to give us their blood in exchange for money, for companionship, protection, whatever. We can have one or more than one, but they are never unwilling."

His words, so thick with emotion, made Katey listen that more intently. He spoke as if he struggled with this aspect of his new life as a vampire, as if he had done things or seen things he wished he could undo.

"That being said, you'll still see a lot of stuff while you're at the castle that will make you uncomfortable, but you have to understand that the actions of a few don't reflect the whole. We're not all like Raven, and I try everyday not to be like him, but it's a lot harder because he's the one who turned me. It's complicated, but just trust that I'm not the guy who's going to run out and steal a kid off the street as if they were a snack of something, okay?"

He paused and she gave a tiny nod of understanding.

"Secondly, this 'righteous ideology' you say I have is grounded in historical fact. Werewolves have always been the problem, and I'll be the first one to say vampires haven't all been saints either, but the body count is seriously slanted against them. This war has been going on for ages, and if we and the hunters don't take out the werewolves, no one else will."

At this, Katey couldn't stay silent. "Haven't you even thought to reassess what is going on in the world? Werewolves aren't running a muck anymore. They're settled in packs. They have alphas to control them now. I mean, there are still werewolves that eat humans, but—"

Martel pointed at her. "And they're the problem."

"Then only target them," she pleaded. "Take them all on a case-by-case basis. The werewolves you imprison right now are not that way. If you just talk to them—"

"There's no reasoning with a beast."

Katey's face went hot. "Will you listen to me? Not all werewolves are the problem."

"And neither are all vampires."

Her mouth opened to come back with another point, but her brain snagged on that. What he just told her about some vampires not feeding off unwilling victims, might as well have been the exact same as what she just told him too. There were bad apples amongst the batches, but that didn't mean they could arbitrarily throw out the whole bushel.

He had stumped her, and all she could do was sit back and match his fierce stare with her own.

Soon, the manager came hurrying forward with a hot plate and rare, juicy steak, fresh off the grill. That seemed incredibly quick turnaround service for the kitchen, but what were the chances that they all knew the steak was for the table with the vampire guest?

Despite her gnawing hunger, Katey picked up her fork and knife and began gingerly eating away at her meal, careful not to ruin her skirt or blouse with the drippings from the steak.

"I suppose you're happy in your new life, then?" she asked.

A bit of some dark emotion passed over his face, but was instantly gone. "As happy as I can be, I guess."

"Do you ever miss Crestucky?" Katey slid a slice of steak between her teeth.

There was a faraway look in his eye as he replied, "Sometimes, I do. I miss the simplicity of smalltown life. But, my masters give me a level of freedom that I would have never had otherwise."

"The ballroom dance club kind of fell apart after you left."

Martel's gaze finally dropped, and his lips tightened into a white line.

"I'll admit that I missed you, too," she continued as she cut into her steak. "I wondered how you were doing and even tried to look you up online a few times, but I could never find you. I guess I know why now."

"Yaverik and Michael said that I needed to sever all ties with the outside world. No distractions or reminders of my old life."

Those names had been mentioned that night already, and she was sure she'd have to meet them eventually. Katey paused and watched how the grief and regret darkened his countenance. "Did you ever miss me?" It was a dangerous question, but one that had plagued her thoughts ever since he left that summer after graduation.

He met her gaze and a small spark of the human she once knew shined through. "Every day."

A chill swept down her back. There was too much emotion behind those words for there to be anything but truth in them. Martel, as a vampire, did not scare her, but his honesty did.

"I bet you never thought you'd see me again, huh?" she said, stuffing her mouth once more to hide how she really felt.

Martel smiled. "Never... Are you still dancing?"

Katey nodded and told him how she and Lily started working part time at the ballroom dance studio. "I would never have had the courage to apply if it wasn't for you pushing me to go after something I happened to actually be good at."

Martel's smile widened and he looked away, his fingernails tapping rhythmically on the table. "I thought you were too headstrong to take anyone's advice."

She shrugged. "Lily can also be pretty persuasive."

He laughed, the corners of his eyes crinkling. "How is she? Still bouncy as ever, I imagine?"

Katey gladly told him all about Lily and everything new that was in Crestucky. With each story she told and each piece of news she recounted, Katey could see a little more of the old Martel come back. His masters may have beaten the smalltown out of him, but she could tell that he still longed to go back home. Perhaps one day, he would.

If he did, what would she do? If he was an enemy of her pack, they would expect her to show him the same kind of welcome that any loup-garou would. Martel would be chased off or killed. Nothing else would satisfy them.

Her disposition smoothed out the more she ate, and she hoped that it would last her a good while. She didn't know where her next meal would come from.

While Martel laughed at one of her funnier stories regarding a particular sophomore Spanish teacher, Katey leaned her elbows on the table. "Something I don't get is, why didn't you tell someone about your mom? If she was doing drugs and making home a living hell for you, why not tell someone? You could have gotten help."

Martel scoffed. "There was no way I was going to let them put me in some foster system. I know what Mary did to you."

Katey sat back, slightly thrown by his statement. "It wasn't that bad."

"Don't lie, Katey. I can tell when humans are lying. Their heart-beats are a dead giveaway."

"A foster home would have been better than living a nightmare. I know what that can be like too."

He shrugged. "Maybe you're right. Maybe you're not. But, it's in the past now, and I'm better off. Honestly, if I hadn't crossed paths with Raven, I might have ended up just like my mom in the end. A druggy without a home or family. What kind of a life would that be?"

"And being a blood-sucking creature of the night is better? Blood might as well be like your drugs. Only you can't go into rehab or you'd die, right?"

Martel's expression hardened. "Believe me, this is better than the path I was already walking down in college. You didn't know me during that time, and I'm glad for it. You wouldn't have recognized that version of me."

"I barely recognized this version of you."

He flashed her his fangs in a sardonic grin. "Still heaps better than I was."

Katey held up her fork and knife. "Agree to disagree?"

Martel huffed a laugh and nodded. "Fine."

"I bet you miss all these little arguments," she said proudly, taking the last bite of her steak.

A sparkle of amusement made her breath hitch a bit. "Definitely."

Had she just been flirting? The thought inspired even more shame, again. Martel had an uncanny way of making the whole world disappear, even when they knew each other as humans. Part of her mourned the way things could have been between them, but her wolf couldn't agree with her. Her pack bond couldn't agree with her.

Martel was a vampire and she was a loup-garou, to be mated to another loup-garou who had swept her off her feet and stolen her heart. Yet, in this restaurant, Martel reminded her of life before Logan, before loups-garous and the complicated world of the paranormal. She tread into dangerous territory when she let herself get carried away by his old charm and the memory of days they could never have back.

All at once, she felt as if she had betrayed Logan, betrayed her pack, and all the other loups-garous who counted on her for freedom. Here she was, eating her fill, when it was completely possible that the loups-garous were being starved in the dungeon. All that hungry rage bottled up was bound to explode into chaos. She determined that even if she couldn't find a way out for them immediately, she'd help them to at least last another day.

CHAPTER 22

They hardly exchanged a word as they rode back to the castle. The road was just as rough going up as it was going down the mountain, but Martel seemed to be an expert at maneuvering through the snowy climate on the steep slopes. Katey stared out the window, gazing at the night sky. The full moon had risen high above, but it was not as golden as the night before.

When the two arrived back at the castle, Martel took Katey by the arm and walked her inside, as the poor shivering valet took the keys to the car and drove it around to some hidden garage in the mountain.

As they made their way up the stairs, Katey turned to the vampire. "Now can I see the werewolves?" she asked, despising that she needed permission to see her pack at all.

Martel pulled a face and took a sharp breath in. "Well, it's not really my call. I need to ask Yaverik or Michael. Yaverik probably won't agree to it, and Michael won't be around until tomorrow night for the solstice celebration."

Katey balled her hands into tight fists and wanted to lash out in a violent rage against her old friend. Even if she managed to land a right hook into that pretty face of his, she'd have to find some way of explaining the strength behind the punch. "You knew that all along, didn't you?"

He gave her a feign look of regret. "Sorry. I did enjoy dinner, though. It was good to spend some time with you."

Her jaw tightened, and she hated to admit it, but a small part of that outing was enjoyable. Yet, her indignation at being lied to had overwhelmed any reciprocation of that sentiment.

If she couldn't get what she wanted from Martel, then she'd find a way to see the loups-garous her own way.

The main foyer was a little more vacant than when they had left, but Katey's nose was assaulted by the odious scent of sulfur that seemed to fill the whole castle. There was also a horrible, putrid smell coming from the dining hall off to the left of them. The doors were cracked to let out the stench of fresh blood and rotting flesh, as well as the bouncing tune of drunken laughter. The vamps must have been feeding, but were these the vampires that leaned more to Raven's way of thinking, or Martel's?

Katey was disgusted and turned quickly toward the stairs to escape the distasteful scene.

Martel paused at the foot of the stairs as he tried to follow after her, and she saw the entranced look in his eyes as he stared toward the dining hall doors. The whites of his eyes began to gradually turn black and the irises deepened into a crimson red color, giving him a wicked gaze. Katey may not have known much about the vampire anatomy, but if it was anything like that of a loup-garou, then he was certainly feeling something right now and she didn't want to get in the way of it.

"Go on," she said. "I can show myself to my room."

She turned to make her way up the stairs.

"Wait," Martel's deep voice commanded.

There was something in his demand that made Katey freeze in her tracks, as if her heels were glued to the floor. It was a tone that she had only ever heard out of Logan, and perhaps that was why she stopped. Nothing else made sense.

Martel came into her view, the whites of his eyes still blacked out from the hunger. Katey began to panic that perhaps he wanted to make a meal out of her, instead of a blood servant.

"Don't be afraid of me," he whispered, lifting a hand to graze the back of his fingers across her cheek.

She shuddered, but not from fear. "I'm not."

One corner of his mouth tilted up, and as he spoke she caught sight of one of his fangs. "Then you're braver than I am." He leaned closer, his breath engulfing her face. "I always wondered what a goodnight kiss would be like coming from you."

Before she could fully register what he said, she felt a wave of weird peace flood through her, so much that she didn't have the will to resist. There was no doubt that this new feeling was a trick of some sort of mesmerism. She had heard stories about vampires seducing their prey this way, and just like a frail human, she was falling for it. Or, was this some remnant of old feelings for Martel back when she was a freshman? At this point, she could barely tell the difference.

Their lips touched and Katey could taste his longing for her. She responded, hardly knowing why, kissing him back with a rush of feeling she had only ever reserved for Logan.

His arms wrapped sensuously around her waist as their lips played in tender, but hungry motions. Katey was under his spell, unable to move, think or speak without his consent. He wanted her to love him, to want him the way that he wanted her. But the preliminary mating bond between her and Logan was unbreakable and not even his magic could override it.

He finally released her from their kiss and grazed the back of his fingers down the center of her back.

"Sweet dreams, Katey," he whispered in her ear,

In one smooth release, he freed her from his sway and made his way toward the dining hall.

Katey snapped out of the trance and wiped her lips against the back of her arm in repulsion. She glared after him, willing to hate him for such an invasion of her privacy and free will. Yet, was it an invasion? Or had she simply let her guard down enough that he perceived an invitation? She watched him walk away and felt a stirring in her guts that scared her more than the vampires.

A soft tap of footsteps coming down the hallway from the foyer diverted her attention and she looked to see Helga, eyes swollen red and downcast as if she had been crying for hours.

Under an empathetic impulse, Katey got the blood servant's attention and held out her hand as a sign for Helga to follow quickly. She obeyed and ran as fast as her little black loafers could carry her, holding back the urge to sniffle and whimper.

Katey grabbed her hand and almost dragged her up the stairs. When they found a secluded alcove, poor Helga burst into sobs, tears rolling down her face in torrents.

"Helga, what's wrong?" Katey placed her hands on the girl's jerking shoulders.

"It's just terrible, miss! Now I really have no one!" she cried, covering her babyface in her hands as she wept.

"What do you mean? What happened?"

Helga flung her arms out and wrapped them around Katey's waist, crying even harder. "They've killed my uncle!"

It took a minute for Katey to understand. The meal in the dining hall must have been Helga's uncle, and Katey felt nauseous at the very thought. Did Martel know the moment they walked past the doors? Would he willingly drink the blood of a murdered man? Was anything he said at dinner the truth? Or had he been playing the "tortured monster" card for her sake to gain sympathy?

She bowed her head and returned Helga's embrace. Her wolf urged her to comfort the girl, even though she wasn't pack or family. She patted Helga's convulsing back and tried to hush her sobs. She didn't care if Helga's tears and snot soiled the silky blouse.

Even though this girl didn't know what Katey was, she trusted her enough to be so vulnerable and seek shelter in her. Katey had to do something. She just didn't know what. She stroked her pretty dark braids until the girl began to calm down. Helga pulled back to look up into Katey's empathetic eyes.

"I'm sorry, miss... He was all I had." More sobs threatened to bubble up from her heaving chest.

Helga's tears held the last shred of her childhood. The girl was alone now, with no family or friends to help her continue in life. She had to grow up quickly, just like Katey did, to cope with her new situation, and heaven knew it wouldn't be easy.

"I know, I know. It'll all be okay," Katey said softly as she pulled out the handkerchief she spotted hanging from the girl's pocket. It had been used many times, judging by how worn the fabric looked. Helga used it to wipe away the tears she blew her nose rather loudly.

Helga straightened out her wrinkled shirt and stuffed her hanky away. "You've been so kind to me, miss. Is there anything I could do for you?"

Katey bit her lips together in thought. This girl was going through hell, but all Katey could think of at that moment was getting to Logan and her pack. She had to make sure they were safe and fed.

"I'd like you to help me with something very important," Katey asked, her quick mind hard at work and developing a new plan. "Can you show me where the kitchen is?"

Helga nodded and led her out the door, down a few twisting and turning halls, passing by several other vampires who were coming from the dining hall, giggling and laughing like drunkards. They took no notice of the two humans, two high from their meal to care.

They came to a darker hallway with a wooden door with no carvings or ornamentation like the others. "The guests of the castle don't use this kitchen, but the blood servants do. It has real food." Helga opened the door to a primitive style kitchen and dining area.

The kitchen looked like it was straight out of a eighteenth or nineteenth century nobleman's manor with a woodburning stove and oven and raw wood countertops. Some modern appliances like a refrigerator, coffeemaker, and microwave stuck out like a sore thumb. It just seemed wrong to have stainless steel next to seriously old wooden cabinetry.

Katey immediately went to the fridge and peaked inside. She saw the typical groceries and was pleased to see the fridge was well stocked, but there was nothing in there that could satisfy the hunger of dozens of loups-garous.

"Do you have anything meatier like a whole chicken or ham or lamb legs or something?" she asked Helga who stood patiently in the doorway.

She tilted her head at the question. "May I ask why, miss?"

"Don't tell anyone, but I want to feed the loups-garous."

"They were just fed this past evening, miss. Ralph took a bucket of raw meat down to them."

Katey shook her head in dismay. "That's not near enough for them to survive on. If they starve, they're going to get real mean, real quick."

After a moment of thought, Helga hurriedly walked across the kitchen and pushed on a small stone in the wall that blended in with the other stones seamlessly. Like a scene from a mystery movie, a hidden door swung outwards into the kitchen. A fluorescent light flickered to life inside and Helga disappeared into the walk-in refrigerator. Katey's senses went wild as she detected the hint of meat that drifted out from the room.

The maid returned with a five-gallon bucket full of raw meat. Katey wanted to kiss the girl as she waddled over carrying the bucket in her two little hands.

"Will this help, miss?" she asked with a big smile.

"Yes, it will help tons! How much more is left in there?" Katey motioned to the secret storeroom as she took the load.

"At least three more buckets worth."

But, how much would the pack need between now and when they finally escaped? It wasn't nearly enough to sustain them, if Katey couldn't come up with a plan quick enough. Some may even lose themselves in the hunger before they had a chance to escape.

"Do they get fed every evening?" Katey asked.

"One bucket per day, miss... Are these loups-garous your friends?"

Katey gave her a sweet smile. "Yeah... They're very good friends." She would have said they were family, but she wasn't sure if that would incriminate her.

Helga smiled and nodded in understanding. "You're a good friend, miss."

"You can call me Katey."

"Okay... Katey."

Katey reasoned that she could only take two buckets. The third one would be left behind for the next evening feed. The guy named Ralph in charge of their feeding, wouldn't grow suspicious at the missing meat. With luck, more could be requested, but Katey hoped by then the loups-garous would be free. She carried both buckets since Helga could scarcely manage one, and they left the blood servants' kitchen.

By the time they made their way to the basement, more of the vampires had left the feast in the dining hall. Katey and Helga slipped around corners and took servant passages to make their way across the castle without notice.

They came to a thick metal door, securely fastened shut by a padlock. The sensation that traveled along her spine affirmed that the pack was just behind that door.

Katey cursed when she saw the lock and examined it. "Do you know where the key is?"

"Only Ralph and the lords have a key and all of them are indisposed. Ralph is the head caretaker of the castle. He sleeps at night to avoid the guests and cleans up after them during the day."

Katey sighed. "Do you have another padlock?"

"I'm sure Ralph does."

"When you see Ralph next, let him know that the basement door will need a new lock by the time the vamps wake up tomorrow evening."

"What will you do?" the girl asked, looking between her new friend and the impassable door.

"Don't worry about that. I'm going to find a way in, but I need you to cover for me. Tell Martel not to bother me. Make up some excuse like I had a headache or something."

The little girl nodded and smiled sweetly as she turned to leave the corridor, though Katey sensed the wealth of questions that she refused to ask.

She took deep breaths and tried to focus all her energy into destroying the steel lock. Katey cupped her hands around it and used her loup-garou strength. There was a low metallic pop as it broke in half, and she quietly set the pieces on the floor.

Katey readied herself for what she might find behind the door. She wasn't sure if they would all be in their loup-garou forms or their human forms, naked or clothed, happy to see her or resentful. But making an appearance with the food would hopefully brighten their spirits.

She kicked open the door, her hands full with the bucket and basket. The room was nearly pitch black with the exception of fire-lit sconces along the walls and a narrow window at the very top of the far wall that allowed in just enough moonlight. It took a while for her loup-garou senses to adjust to the dim light.

Martel had lied. The loups-garous weren't in cages. They were in prison cells, locked behind thick bars that glinted in the firelight. Three cells, separated by stone walls, were packed with loups-garous. Golden eyes turned to her, nearly iridescent in the dark. By the restless shifting, sounds of sickness, growling, and low, biting conversations, she knew the hunger had already gotten the better of many of them. The metallic scent of blood, fear, mold, and dampness stung her nostrils, suffocating Katey at first until she could get her bearings. Through it all, her bond with Logan shivered to life.

She descended the slick stone stairs after closing the door behind her, the moisture on each step threatened to make her slip in her heels. Now she wished she had changed clothes first. As she drew closer, she noticed the loups-garous were all shirtless, but wore identical sweatpants that the vampires must have provided to cover their nakedness. That courtesy alone surprised her.

They looked to her, eyes full of despair, hunger, and anger. Many recognized her instantly and edged closer to the bars. Others were too far gone to care who she was, apart from the fact that she brought food.

She wanted to hate herself for not being with them behind the bars. There was no reason that she should have been saved from their fate, since she was truly one of them.

Katey looked around hastily for a guard and saw none. The vampires must have had a ridiculous amount of confidence that these simple metal bars would be enough to keep the wolves in their cages. And it seemed to work because no loup-garou ventured within three feet of the bars themselves.

"Logan!" Katey called out as she scooped a handful of meat into her palm and approached one of the cells.

"Katey?" The voice was faint, but unmistakable.

She looked to her left and saw Logan pushing through some other loups-garous to get near the bars. They gave him a hard time, shoving him back and snarling. Logan struggled against them until he came to the front and met Katey, tears of relief welling up in her eyes.

Dirt stains covered his smooth skin and his hair glinted with natural oils and sweat. Otherwise, Logan looked to be unharmed. The closer she came to the mass of bodies, she could feel a heat radiating from the cells that fought against the bone numbing cold of the northern winter that seeped through the stones.

"Don't touch the bars!" he warned.

But it was too late.

In her eagerness, Katey had wrapped her free hand around the icy metal. Nothing happened. Katey recoiled her hand and touched it again with her fingertips to test it. Still nothing.

Logan stared in bitter awe. "It's silver. It should burn you."

Katey now understood why the loups-garous kept their distance from the bars. The vampires were clever, but that was not why more tears spilled down Katey's cheeks.

She hadn't come into contact with silver before to know exactly how it was supposed to feel, or if this was a new development. Maybe that weakness would manifest later? Or maybe her loup-garou self was fading again.

Katey let out a shrill whine and looked up to Logan with sad, pleading eyes.

He edged closer to the bars, but would not risk a touch. "Darren told me how you weren't able to shift."

"I'm so sorry, Logan. I wanted to. I wanted to so badly. I'll try again once we get out of here,"

Her words did nothing to soothe his dejected spirits. His golden eyes brimmed with so much emotion that she couldn't begin to comprehend it fully.

"How is everyone? Is everyone okay?" Katey offered out the meat to him through the silver bars. If there was one advantage to her handicap, it was that she could get close so no one else would have to risk a burn.

Other loups-garous who had been watching the situation surged forward to snatch at the food in her hand. Before they could, another loup-garou rushed forward, turned his back to Katey and let out a loud but unmistakable warning growl to the others. Dominance detonated from the alpha, whom she now recognized as Darren, and the other loups-garous in the cell, including Logan stumbled backwards. The hungrier of the loups-garous crouched as if they would challenge him, but otherwise didn't move.

The loups-garous in the other cells grew excited and tried to get Katey's attention so they could get meat as well. Disoriented and a little frightened by the mounting chaos, Katey wasn't sure what to do.

Darren turned and gave a grateful nod to her before taking the meat from her hands. He looked ill and grouchy, but otherwise sane and in full control of his faculties. "We'll ration this out fairly," he announced.

With Logan's help, meat was passed out equally to the loups-garous in their cell. The recipients took what they were given and hurried away to devour it before anyone else had a chance to steal it.

"The pack is well," Darren told Katey as they continued to distribute the meat. "Dustin's in the next cell over with John and Ben is with us. Most of us have been able to control ourselves, but some of the younger loups-garous have needed counseling."

Katey felt her heart would break and she had no words. She should have come sooner. She should have brought the third bucket. When she had nearly emptied the first bucket, Darren directed her to go to the next cell.

John met her at the bars and gave her an appreciative smile. He appeared just as civil as he would have if he were fully fed, but she could still detect an sharp edge in him that only meat could dull. They began handing out food to those that came to her a little bit at a time. She made sure she reached all the way through the bars, pressing her body against the silver.

"Where's Dustin?"

"I'm here, Katey Kat," came the familiar voice of her beta. She smiled weakly as she saw him totter up and take a bit of meat from her hands. He began passing it out as Logan had done. Dark circles hung under his eyes, just like the others, but had a more sickly look about him.

"How are you holding up?" Katey asked sympathetically.

"I'm doing fine. I'm glad to see you're okay though. We got worried when we didn't find you among the ranks in here."

It was then she spotted a shock of red hair moving from the back of the cell. "Forrest!"

He staggered forward and took a bit of food from John, his body hunched and shivering.

"What's wrong with him?"

Parker, the flirty Devian loup-garou that she met at school, came forward and took his packmate by the shoulders. "The tranquilizer darts hit him hard. I think he took three when he was trying to protect us during the ambush. He's still a bit shaken up from it, but he'll live."

Katey's lips quivered. With her free hand, she reached out for Forrest's arms. He let out a low growl until they locked eyes, and it was as if he had snapped out of a dream. The growl died in his throat and his mouth struggled to form the words.

"Don't worry," she whispered. "You're going to have one hell of a story to tell Lily when we get home."

There wasn't a flicker of recognition or understanding in his face, as if he hadn't heard a word she said. Parker guided him away and back into the crowd as Katey's heart squeezed with grief for her friend.

Katey looked back to Dustin. "I wish I was in there with everyone. I'd rather be in there than out here with these vamps."

"Have they hurt you? Ouch!" Katey heard Logan cry out after the faint noise of sizzling flesh.

John took what was in her hand and she rushed over just in time to see Logan stagger back from the bars, holding his burnt shoulder. It soon healed and Katey breathed a sigh of relief, glad that it wouldn't be a serious injury.

"No, they haven't hurt me. They have no idea I'm one of you... Or at least halfway... I feel so awful about last night, Logan," Katey said, burying her face in her hands out of embarrassment, ignoring the fact that her hands were wet with residue from the meat.

"It's all right. You'll try again..." Logan's voice trailed off, struggling to hold back the disappointment in his tone. "I wonder why they haven't caught onto you yet."

"Probably because they don't smell it on her," Darren said, joining them near the bars.

"What do you mean?" Katey asked.

"When a loup-garou shifts for the first time, that guarantees all the other perks, including a very distinctive scent that vampires can pick up on. Since you haven't shifted, you don't have that scent yet. We can still tell what you are, but they can't. And I agree with Logan. You were very close to shifting the other night. We can try again. This time, without the distractions." He shot a look at Logan.

"What about the silver?" she asked. "Is that weakness going to come along after I shift, too?"

She saw the answer in his eyes. No, she was supposed to be burned by the silver as easily as any of them but she was immune.

"Keep giving out the meat," Darren said, gesturing to the adjacent cell.

Katey obeyed and continued distributing food to John and Dustin before moving into the third cell. John's sons were near the front and elected to pass out the meat to their cellmates. But beyond, she spotted a memorable head of dark hair and dark eyes to match.

Gregory stepped forward, tall and defiant amongst the other loups-garous. He hadn't been with them the night before.

"What are you doing in there?" Katey exclaimed.

The rougarou's lips pulled into a snarl. "Watch your tone, pup. I'm in no mood for your attitude."

He snatched the meat Noah offered him and turned away to shoulder his way through the mass of bodies.

Katey looked to Noah for an answer.

"His son's the reason we're in here. He told the vamps where we'd be shifting and arranged the ambush. Something about taking over your town, I think. Erik's in here too." He jerked his thumb toward the back cell wall, but she couldn't see anyone.

Finally, she had someone to blame. Before, she had the suspicion that the loups-garous were just in the wrong place at the wrong time. Now, she knew it was planned and coordinated. How could they have been betrayed by one of their own kind to their most hated enemy?

Rage swelled within her, but she couldn't hold onto it somehow. The old Katey would have crawled through the bars and tore him apart for what he had done to them all. This wasn't only an attack on her or Logan, but on her pack and the loup-garou community as a whole. This was no minor offense, and yet, her hands were too slippery to hang onto a grudge.

Katey leveled a serious look at Noah. "Make sure Erik gets some meat."

Noah gave her a wry look. "He hasn't woken up since before we got here. His father gave him a pretty tough beating. I can't guarantee I'll be able to hoard anything for too long, but I'll try."

Liam snorted. "That's only if he'll stay conscious long enough after we get our turn with him."

Katey glared at the massive loup-garou. "He's suffered enough. Everyone deserves to eat, even him."

That shocked enough of the loups-garous into pausing during their scant meals, but not for too long.

Soon, both buckets were empty, scraped clean and the last of it was stuck under her fingernails. They were a long shot from satisfied, but it would have to do until they devised a way out of the castle and were far away from the vamps. Her chest ached as she looked to the loups-garous, wishing with every cell in her body that she could somehow save them from this torture.

Katey returned to Logan's cell and saw him patiently sitting on the floor. Darren stood not far off, and she finally saw Ben leaning against the stone wall, eyes closed and head tilted back as if he were asleep.

"This was a brave thing you did, Katey," Darren said.

"I wish I could do more..." Her voice faltered and she swallowed hard, willing herself not to cry.

"You're doing what you can." Logan's eyes told how much he wished that he could have gotten closer to hold her.

Katey examined the bars that separated them, judged the space, and edged closer with a probing thought. She slipped her arm through, then her shoulder and sucked in her diaphragm, as she tried to squeeze herself between the smooth metal. It was slightly painful, and she was pretty sure she had dislocated a joint somewhere, but she managed to slide through and tumbled into Logan's arms.

They embraced each other tightly, the first hug they had shared in what seemed like an eternity. Katey buried her face into his soft skin and savored the feeling of completeness that only he could give. The fact that his skin was grimy, and slick didn't detract from the absolute bliss of hearing his heartbeat strong against her ear.

"I missed you," he whispered into her hair. She could almost taste the relief in his words.

"I missed you, too. I couldn't stop thinking about you and everyone here the whole night."

Logan took her face in his hands and gave her a firm but loving kiss. When he pulled back, there was a slight look of confusion, but he said nothing. Maybe he tasted Martel on her lips and her cheeks reddened with shame.

"What happened to you?" he asked, still holding her in his strong, but dirty arms.

"They knocked me out when they were shooting at everyone last night. I woke up in a room in the castle and I... It's going to sound so weird, but one of my old friends from school was there in the room. Martel. He was the president of the ballroom dance club at the school and encouraged me to pursue dancing. He was sitting in a chair by the fireplace in the room I woke up in."

Darren took a step toward them and crouched down to meet their gazes. "Martel? I remember him. He had a class with me his junior year."

Katey related the whole story of Martel's turning into a vamp, how he was in the room, and everything he had told her. When

Katey went into detail about going out to dinner with him, Katey could see the anger rise in Logan's golden eyes.

"You went out on a date with him?" he growled.

"I didn't consider it a date. It was a bribe. He promised to get permission for me to come down here if I went out with him, but I don't think he ever intended to make good on that promise."

There was no way Katey would tell him about all the little things they talked about during dinner. Any mention of that kiss would surely send Logan into a savage rage and they couldn't afford that. Not here. Not now.

Logan seemed to calm down and pulled her back to encase her in his arms again. "As long as you're safe now. How did you manage to find us and bring food, too?"

Katey then told them about how Helga helped her find the kitchen and the door to the dungeon. "I wish I could do something for that girl. She can't stay here much longer, and there's every chance that they'll eventually kill her just like they killed her uncle."

"I don't know what we can do if we're still in here."

"Has anyone thought of shifting and busting out?"

"Yes," replied Darren. "We did, but reasoned that it was too risky. There's not much room to shift in here and there's no guarantee that we could take down those bars, even in our loup-garou forms. If a loup-garou is under enough pain and starvation, they could become vicious and then we would all be in danger."

Katey shuddered at the thought of the kind of damage a loup-garou could do when provoked. "I thought of trying to shift, but I figured that would cause more problems than solving them."

"And you'd be perfectly right, too. Don't do the stupid thing," Dustin called out from the next cell over.

"Did they tell you what they intend to do?" Logan asked.

Katey almost didn't want to tell him, but his eyes pleaded for her to say it, no matter what it was. The whole dungeon had been drawn into a hush to listen to what she had to say.

"They're going to put shock collars on you, turn you all loose on the mountain and hunt everyone down with those liquid silver bullets you told me about... They're going to kill you."

Everyone who heard her had their own reactions, but no one seemed surprised.

She looked up to the window at the other end of the room and saw sunlight just beginning to chase away the night. The vampires would be going to sleep soon. Katey buried her head in Logan's chest, feeling more tears pressing at her eyelids. He held her tighter and petted her back to soothe her. She didn't know how much longer they would have together like this and she intended to cherish every moment while she could.

"Are you tired?" he asked.

Katey gave him a little nod, finally realizing how fatigued she had become over the last hour or so. The adrenaline of trying to find them and help them wore off.

Logan led her deeper into the cell toward a far corner. Together, they sat against the cool wall, Katey nestled between his legs and head on his chest. She took the time to slip off the heels and tossed them aside. The flood was wet and chilly, but she didn't care. Logan wrapped his strong arms around her, shielding her from the chilly air.

"You can rest as long as you need to. I'm right here. Nothing's going to take you away from me."

Katey burrowed against him, readily believing his words. She became vaguely aware that Ben and Darren had settled around them, facing the crowd of loups-garous in the cell as if guarding them. It was completely possible that it'd only be a matter of hours before their hunger returned, but she wasn't afraid of them. Not while she still felt her wolf inside of her and Logan was there to protect her.

The rest of the world melted away as she lay there with him. The other loups-garous weren't there, and the vamps upstairs weren't there. Nothing else existed but Logan and her. As Katey drifted away, she remembered her last thought being that she couldn't wait to fall asleep in his arms every night and wake up to him holding her every morning once they were mated.

CHAPTER 23

L ogan refused to move since Katey fell asleep in his arms. Not the ache in his muscles nor the return of the burning hunger could make him budge. She stirred occasionally, but never woke. As long as she dreamed, Logan wouldn't risk disturbing her.

As time passed, the noxious odor of vampire faded from Katey's skin and clothes. Once it did, his wolf quit squirming and writhing in disgust. If it was even remotely possible, he would have tracked down this Martel and strangled the bastard. Katey belonged to Logan. The vampire had no right to touch her, to kiss her. He knew that's what the vamp had done, but he also knew from the stories that vamps could manipulate their victims. It wasn't Katey's fault, so he wouldn't blame her. But he could imagine all the ways he'd kill Martel when they got out of here.

Sunlight through the dungeon window faded to a sunset orange, then gray twilight. The vamps would rise soon. Most of the loups-garous curled up on the stone floor to get some sleep, their internal clocks thoroughly messed up. It was only late afternoon as darkness fell in this part of the country. This time of the year was ideal for the bloodsuckers, with more hours of night than day.

Either way, sleep would help the loups-garous forget their hunger, and kill time before their next meal came down the stairs.

That moment came soon after full night settled in, plunging the dungeon in silvery moonlight, the lanterns having died hours ago. The heavy metal door swung open and the scents of two humans came down the stairs. He recognized one as the scrawny older man with a gray beard who brought them food before. The second was young, a girl, and she reeked of fear and vampire, though he could tell she was fully human. She had just spent so much time with the vamps that the stench was all over her.

But it was the smell of meat that destroyed the tentative peace in the dungeon. Loups-garous ignored the silver and lunged at the bars to reach for the food in a greedy frenzy. Odors of burnt flesh and blood mingled with sweat and desperation. The older loups-garous who knew better tried to throw back their pack-mates before they caused greater harm to themselves. Hunger led to weakness, and weakness slowed their healing abilities. Prolonged exposure to the silver could poison their blood and then it was only a matter of time before the loup-garou was dead.

Darren and Ben were among those who tried to maintain order, and Katey was finally thrown from her sleep by the shouts, roars, and growls of the loups-garous in the three cells.

She blinked hard and grabbed for Logan as if he were a lifeline. "What's happening?"

Logan brought in his legs around her and tightened his embrace. "Someone's here. They brought food."

Katey watched the chaos unfold, but none of the fear in the cold, dank air came from her.

"Katey? Miss Katey?" The timid, shrill voice of the human girl floated over the din.

Logan glanced to her, knowing his eyes hadn't changed from the hungry gold since before she came to the dungeon. Katey straightened in his hold as if readying to stand. Desperate, Logan tried to pull her back to his chest. She didn't resist, but turned a look to him that asked for release. He gave a sharp shake of his head, his wolf closer to the surface than he liked. Neither of them were willing to let her go.

Darren came to them and squatted. "Who is she?"

"Helga," Katey answered. "She helped me to get the meat and get down here."

The alpha nodded. "Stay here."

He strode away, passed the loups-garous that frantically devoured the bits of meat the old man had tossed through the bars. They were too hungry to care if the meat landed on the floor or in the tiny puddles of standing water that formed in the divots in the stone. Ben came through with two palms full of meat, presumably for his pack.

Darren walked up to the bars, but Logan and Katey remained out of sight past the churning mass of loups-garous bodies. "Who are you looking for?"

"Ka... Katey."

"Why do you want her?"

The old man said, "Martel has been asking for her. She's been invited to join the Lords and Ladies for the Solstice Celebration."

Logan growled at the mention of the vamp and his grip cinched possessively. He didn't take the meat Ben offered to him. He couldn't risk loosening his hold, even for food.

"Why?"

"How should I know?" the man asked roughly. "She needs to come back with us. If they catch her down here, a lot of people will be punished."

Everyone who helped Katey, including Helga, might be killed. Too absorbed by his wolf and the need to keep his to-be mate with him, Logan didn't care. The world could burn. He didn't want to let go.

Darren told them to wait, then returned to his packmates. "She needs to go."

Logan snarled, ready to fight his alpha over this. "No. Mine." The growl of his voice only bothered Darren. Katey didn't flinch.

Carefully wielded dominance wove its way past Katey and strangled Logan to make him obey. Hunger and silver hadn't made Darren the least bit sloppy.

Under the pressure of his alpha, Logan smothered his growl and slackened his arms, but not willingly.

"I promise I'll come back," Katey whispered. "I'll figure out a way to get everyone out."

They shared a hasty, but meaningful parting kiss, before Katey allowed herself to be led away by Darren toward the cell door.

With great effort, Logan ignored the food Ben tried to push in his face, then forced himself to his feet, feeling every tender and strained muscle protest in the task. He limped toward the bars as his strength came back, all too slowly, and watched Katey follow the two humans up the stairs. The empty bucket swung from the old man's hand, and the girl in the maid's outfit kept her gaze down.

At the top of the stairs, Katey looked back and met his sorrowful stare with her own. He felt her pain through their bond, and both he and his wolf lamented the growing distance between them. The shutting of the dungeon door was like the dropping of a guillotine over his heart.

Numb and broken, Logan stood on shaky feet, feeling like only half a person without Katey.

That parting had to be the absolute worst Katey had ever experienced. She could hardly breathe, and each step away from the dungeon door tightened the noose of misery around her neck. Her blood screamed for his presence, her skin ached for his touch. How could she possibly walk away like this and survive?

She and Helga returned to the room she had dressed in the night before. Once the door was closed, Helga turned to her, terror etched in the taunt lines of her face. "Martel is so angry. I tried to tell him that you weren't ready for company, but he kept on insisting to see you. I'm sorry, Katey. I tried, I really did."

Katey, tired and heartbroken for her mate, shook her head. "It's all right. I probably shouldn't have stayed down there all night, but I..." She let her voice trail off, unable to confess it.

"They're more than friends, aren't they?"

She gave a sad smile. "They are. They're family. My fiancé is down there and I..." She took a fortifying breath and squared her shoulders. "I have to find a way to get them out, but I can't do anything just yet... What's this solstice thing?"

Helga seemed sympathetic and she folded her hands on her white apron. "It's an annual celebration of the longest night of the year. The vampires gather and exchange gifts."

"Like Christmas?"

She shrugged. "Somewhat. The grand hall is decorated like Christmas, but it's not Christmas."

Katey considered that for a moment and wondered if the myths about the vampires' weakness to symbols of Christianity held some level of truth. "Well, I need to get cleaned up first."

Helga pointed to a basin of water set on the vanity with a towel. "The water may not be as warm as it was when I brought it in."

Katey then made work of removing the dirty shirt and blouse from the night. She dipped the towel in the tepid water and rubbed at her skin, washing away the grim of the dungeon and Logan's scent. It was then she realized that she forgot the shoes in the dungeon and hoped that no one would notice they were missing.

"The celebration is very formal. You'll need to wear a dress."

Katey rolled her eyes and stood in her underwear by the vanity, wiping down her legs. "Fantastic. What are my choices?"

Helga went to the wardrobe, considered the selection, then pulled out a gold silk gown with a voluminous full skirt. It had no straps to conceal her shoulders and the cut of it looked to be too form-fitting to Katey's liking. She turned it down. Another dress was offered, one that was a faint pink hue and the fabric was so sheer that she could nearly see through it. Katey shook her head. Everything the maid pulled out did not seem remotely appealing.

"Why don't I take a look?" Katey saw a robe lying across the foot of the canopy bed and slipped into it before joining Helga by the wardrobe.

Katey dug through the drawers, praying she would find a pair of jeans or even slacks. This thing may have been a formal affair, but that didn't mean she'd cooperate and dress like a princess.

In the midst of her search, the bedroom door opened. A woman stood in the entrance and with her came a chilling rush of air that sent goosebumps crawling across Katey's flesh.

A revealing and seductive black dress hugged the woman's thin body like it was painted on her skin. Her blonde, almost white, hair was pulled back into a stylish up-do. Black eyes rimmed in purple eyeshadow held a sort of laughing quality. Such eyes didn't look like they belonged to a night-stalking creature, but her pale skin and the smell of death on her were unmistakable clues to her identity.

Her high and protruding cheekbones made her look more like a model or member of royalty. Even the way she walked made Katey think of a queen. This woman commanded respect and affection just by breathing. Yet, she was not overly intimidating.

"What are you two girls doing in here?" she asked sweetly, showing off her pearly white fangs. Even her voice held a note of playfulness.

Helga dropped her gaze and stepped into the shadows while Katey turned to face the vampire.

"I'm trying to find something to wear for the solstice thing. Doesn't anyone wear jeans around here?"

Katey's wolf prompted her not to submit, not to show fear. Her witty remark was her way of commanding the situation, to show that she had a mouth and she wasn't afraid to use it. Whether that would endear her to the woman or get her killed, time would tell.

"Don't you like any of these gowns?" The vampire waved her elegant hand toward the wardrobe.

Katey crossed her arms. "I'm definitely not the kind to wear big princess ball gowns, and I won't wear one tonight."

The woman's laughing eyes sparkled with amusement and her smile widened. "Well, in that case, we'll have to figure out something else, won't we? Martel won't be kept waiting forever."

"Did he send you?"

The woman chuckled, a mature and throaty sound. "Oh, I'm terrible! I take for granted that just about everyone knows who I am. My name is Julia. Martel sent me to check on you and Helga. Or, more or less to make sure you were actually here." Her dark eyes darted across the room to the pile of dirty clothes by the vanity. "Take an afternoon stroll through the garden?"

Katey wondered just how keen their senses were, if she could smell the loup-garou on the clothes. "Yes. Ralph was showing me around."

Julia laced her fingers together in front of her. "Ralph is very kind..." She looked thoughtfully at Katey. "I think I have a dress that might satisfy you. Come with me."

The vampire turned toward the door and waited as Katey weighed her options within the span of a few seconds. She looked to Helga, who emitted no fear. Perhaps Julia was one who could be trusted, if Helga didn't feel too cowed by her presence. Nothing about her seemed threatening or menacing. Katey made the tentative decision to trust her and gave a little goodbye wave to Helga before following Julia into the hall. The vampire walked so smoothly and gracefully that, if Katey didn't know anything else about her, would have suggested she was something other than human.

Julia brought Katey to what she assumed was her own room, which was similar to the one she had been given, but everything was draped in black and gold instead of red and gold. The vampire hurried to her own wardrobe to sift through the garments. At first, every dress looked the same; black evening gowns with slits up to the hips.

Then, to Katey's surprise, Julia pulled out a stunning sky-blue dress with straps that came just off the shoulders. The hem of the dress reached to the floor with a modest slit up the side, accompanied by intricately woven bead designs along the bodice and jeweled appliques scattered along the skirt. Katey marveled at the dress's beauty and couldn't help but want to try it on.

"With your hair and complexion, this gown will look absolutely gorgeous on you."

Once the vampire had deftly cinched Katey into the dress and slipped on matching blue heels, she noticed how snug it was around the midsection. They stood together in front of the vanity mirror and to Katey's astonishment, she could see Julia completely. So, the myth about vampires having no reflection was a complete farce.

Katey tugged at the shoulder straps, willing them to sit higher. Other than her mild self-conscious picking at the fabric, the dress was a perfect fit, and it did show off her features well, just as Julia had said it would.

Julia beamed in the mirror, looking ten times more beautiful than before, if that was even possible. "You look wonderful."

Then, as suddenly as the joyful expression was there, it was gone and replaced by a dark look, as if a thought had entered her mind that terrified her.

"What is it?" Katey asked.

Julia blinked, her dark lashes fluttering wildly. "It's nothing." Her mouth tried to pull into a fake smile. "You just reminded me of someone who used to wear that dress."

"It's not yours?" Katey pinched at the loose fabric around her hips.

With a sigh, Julia crossed her skinny arms over her stomach. "No. It belonged to a friend of mine, but it's been years since I've thought about her. Funny how little things can bring up memories like that."

Katey couldn't read the vampire's emotions as well as she could a human's, but there was something haunting Julia about this friend. Whatever it was, Katey wasn't so sure she wanted to know.

"Now, we just have to do something with your hair to show off that pretty neck of yours."

Katey shuddered. "Can't I just wear it down? I'm more comfortable with it down." That was a partial lie. For ballroom dance, she always preferred her hair up and away from her neck. It helped to stay cool and hair wouldn't fly in her face with every twirl. But the idea of showing off her neck to a castle full of vampires was not a comforting thought. It'd be like presenting a buffet to a starving dog.

Julia giggled and flipped her hand at the thought. "Nonsense. We'll curl it at least. Come, sit down." She pulled out the vanity chair as she took an iron rod from a bucket of hot coals on the tabletop. It was like something out of the dark ages, but Katey sat down in front of the mirror and allowed Julia to wrap portions of Katey's hair around the hot metal to style it. It was then she realized that certain parts of the castle must not have been fitted with modern electricity. Fireplaces and lantern sconces lit every room and corridor.

Katey watched as Julia's quick and nimble hands styled her hair almost flawlessly with minimal fixes or mistakes. She had definitely done this many times before. It took Julia mere moments to get Katey's hair completely curled and pinned up in such a way that the delicate skin on her neck was exposed. Katey had to inwardly acknowledge that she looked better than she thought she would.

Without Katey's consent, Julia patted some powder on her face, neck, and shoulders making her look pale, though not as pale as a vampire. The look was completed by some blush on Katey's cheeks and the most striking earth-toned combination eye shadow design she'd ever seen, making her green eyes even more stunning than they already were.

When all was done, Katey stared dumbfounded at her image in the mirror. "I look like an actress or something." She tilted her head to get a good look at both sides of her face.

"Martel is just going to eat you up when he sees you," Julia exclaimed excitedly.

Katey looked to her with brows arched high.

Julia laughed. "Oh, I don't mean literally, dear. I'm saying that he's going to adore how you look. No, ma'am. You are a guest of Martel's, so no one will ever consider it. We have our own blood servants for that sort of thing. Even though you do smell scrumptious." Julia giggled once more at what she thought was something universally humorous.

Her enthusiasm reminded Katey of Lily back home. A pang of homesickness made her hate the girl in the mirror. It wasn't the real her and this wasn't where she belonged. This wasn't her world.

"Something wrong?"

Katey stood up from the chair, the fabric of the skirt rustling with her movements. "Nothing, just feeling a little homesick... Why is Martel inviting me to this solstice celebration?"

Julia shrugged her slender shoulders. "Probably because he likes you. You're a very beautiful girl. I wouldn't be surprised if quite a few gentle-vamps in the castle ask to dance with you." She gave Katey a reassuring look and motioned toward the door. "Let's go. We don't want Martel stomping his scrawny ass up here yelling for you again."

They shared a little laugh the way friends might, and left the room. The idea of catching the eye of any male vampire didn't put her at ease. Seeing Martel again and experiencing the rush that he brought with him was disconcerting enough.

Julia led Katey down to the main foyer and turned to the double doors across from the dining hall. Her sense of smell might have been fading, but the sulfuric stench that wafted from the ballroom was distinctive enough for her to know that it was packed with vampires, all eager for the festivities to begin.

Martel was waiting for Katey at the door, looking sharp in his finely pressed tuxedo. It wasn't unlike the one he wore to prom for his senior year. The ballroom dance club put on an exposition that ended rather badly, with students crowding the dancers and ruining the performance, despite the best efforts of the chaperones.

She did her best to calm and control herself against the urge to flee. Memories, again, came barreling through her mind, pushing out the reminder that this was not her old friend. This was a vampire, a man she wasn't supposed to like. Yet, she did. The butterflies in her stomach from her freshman year came back with vengeful force and she knew her wolf was not pleased with her.

A gentle but distinct ache grew low in her belly as Martel turned to her and smiled. "You look absolutely gorgeous, Katey. Thank you for helping her, Julia."

"My pleasure." Julia cast a furtive glance to Martel, and then slipped into the ballroom.

Martel turned to Katey with eyes that she could only describe as predatory, but attractive in a powerful way. She blushed a deep red under his gaze and didn't have the sense to run from him as she had wanted to just seconds ago.

He took her hand in one suave sweep and bent down low to kiss the back of it. Katey remained speechless as her pulse quickened. His face lingered along her skin and he breathed deeply, a subtle reminder that she was a little lower on the food chain than he was.

When he came up from the kiss, he asked, "Where did you run off to?"

It took her a minute to remember her lie from before. "I wanted to see the gardens. Helga introduced me to Ralph and I got a tour before sundown."

Martel peered at her for a moment and then seemed to accept the fib. "Did you like the gardens?"

She donned a smile. "I did."

"Wasn't too cold for you?"

The breath in her lungs froze. She completely forgot that the castle was on the side of a mountain, covered in snow. Was the garden in a greenhouse or some courtyard sheltered from the elements? She had to stay the course.

"No, not at all. You know I always preferred the cold weather anyway."

Martel made a thoughtful sound in the back of his throat. She realized they were still holding hands when Martel escorted her into the ballroom.

The hall was elaborately decorated in rich crimson and gold tapestries. Fresh garland and holly stretched across the lengths of the room on all sides. As she drew closer, the stink of vamp was overpowered by fragrances of cinnamon, pine, and many other smells that reminded Katey of the holiday season.

The ladies were outfitted in evening dresses or ball gowns like hers. Most held glasses of blood in their hands and were cooling themselves with paper fans while they gossiped and chatted with one another. The men were decked out in tuxedos and suits as she had seen them in the day before. A band was set up in the corner of the ballroom, playing classical tunes over the multitude of voices in conversation.

The main centerpiece of the room was an enormous, festooned Christmas tree, complete with all the trimmings one would expect.

The tree sparkled with lights, littered with an array of ornaments, and topped with a bright glittering star at its peak. It was a dazzling display and Katey had never seen its equal before, not even in movies. She was so taken by the decorations that she almost completely forgot that Martel was watching her.

"What do you think?"

"It's beautiful!" Katey replied with a genuine grin as she let her eyes roam back over the elegant details of the hall.

It was certainly a world apart from the one she had grown up in, or the one Logan opened up to her. Although, loups-garous cleaned up nicely, as she discovered from the benefit luncheon in Alaska, such a scene was not their style. Their gathering wasn't a ball or fancy dinner. It was a return to nature.

The vampires had a culture of their own, filled with propriety and elegance that Katey could never be part of. She looked the part of a human who might belong there, but her wolf spirit told another story.

"I want to introduce you to some very important people here at the castle." He offered his arm to Katey, and she took it without a second thought. He led her through the crowd, which graciously parted ways for him and his human companion. She noticed their appraising gazes, and didn't know if it was because of the way she was dressed or because she looked like their next meal.

He directed Katey toward one side of the room where three men stood in casual conversation. All were vampires, of course, but two of them emitted a commanding aura that stuck out to her. These were the equivalents of alphas.

One was young, but still older than Martel by a couple of years from the looks of it. Though, if they aged liked loups-garous, there was no telling how old he was. He had spiky black hair and dark eyes to match while his bony facial structure seemed similar to Julia's. Perhaps they were related.

Another was taller, older, and held himself with more confidence. Even with his cold, mocking blue eyes, he seemed to know he was a cut above the rest. His hair was just as black as his younger counterpart and slicked back against his head, caked on with gel to make it stiff and shiny in the candlelight. Something in her, however, waved a red flag, telling her that this vampire was more dangerous than he appeared.

Katey got the exact opposite impression from the third vampire. The last man was much older, with a graying beard, but gentler in demeanor, and had rich brown eyes that reminded Katey of Darren's. They were soft and caring, full of feeling. His short silver hair was combed back behind his ears with a posture that proclaimed self-assurance, but not arrogance. She remembered that Martel mentioned he may have been more sympathetic to her need to see the loups-garous, but he had only just arrived that day. She wondered if he could be incorporated into her hopes to bust them out, but perhaps that was wishful thinking so soon before getting to know him. He could hate the loups-garous just as much as any of them.

This vampire, unlike the others, she knew could be trusted somehow. Not only that, but there was a familiarity about him that she couldn't exactly place in her memory. It was as if seeing him for the first time had brought back an ambiguous image from her past that she couldn't make out.

Everything seemed to have become blurry to Katey in such a short time. Her affections, her validity as a loup-garou, her loyalty, and memories were called into question, and she was lost in the chaos of it all. The only force that grounded her was the wolf that silently observed and gave unsolicited commentary. She watched them, studied and kept her claws gripped tight to the solid foundation that Katey was loup-garou. She did not belong here. For once, she wanted to hold onto that soul-wrenching sadness that came with being separated from Logan. It reminded her of what she truly needed.

"Katey, I'd like you to meet Raven, Lord Yaverik, and Lord Michael," Martel gestured to the individuals he spoke of. All three bowed their heads and Katey attempted a curtsey. She smiled only to the elder gentleman who seemed to be eyeing her with peculiar interest. She didn't want to believe that this vampire could be responsible for the imprisonment of her pack, and she would show absolutely no respect to the vamp that turned Martel. "Gentlemen, this is Katey."

Lord Yaverik, the cold, derisive one, bowed his head. "Welcome to our party, Miss Katey. Martel has told me much about you." He took her hand in his and kissed the back of it as Martel had. But, his touch was chilling and unpleasant as if she had just been touched by death itself.

"I hope all of it was good," Katey replied cordially, masking her nervousness.

"Just that you are the most beautiful woman he's ever seen and that's one of the only reasons you were not our lunch the other evening," Raven, the spikey-haired one, stated with a dry sense of humor that Katey couldn't laugh at.

Martel gave a threatening hiss.

"Now, boys, none of that. This is a celebration. No fighting tonight." Lord Yaverik gestured to the happy crowd of vampires.

Katey glanced around once more at the ballroom and finally realized how many vampires were there. There had to be close to a couple of hundred, if not more, bustling around the expansive ballroom. She was surrounded.

"So, do you all celebrate Christmas the same as we do?" Katey inquired, purposefully pushing back her anxiety just so she could portray some semblance of normal.

"In a way, but we don't call it Christmas," Lord Michael replied kindly, his voice heavily laden with an Italian accent. "It's the winter solstice to us and it lasts for a few weeks. Tomorrow is the last night."

"When we're all going to hunt down those dogs as a last revel before the year is out." Raven fired a pretend gun at an invisible target just over her shoulder. Katey could feel her blood boil just from the mention of their hunt. "Oh, sorry, I forgot Martel said you were a dog lover."

"That's enough, Raven," Lord Yaverik barked. "As long as Miss Katey is a guest of ours, we will respect her as such. You have been taught better manners than that."

Here earlier assessment of Lord Yaverik being an alpha was affirmed in this little exchange, but Lord Michael had yet to show his dominance. Maybe he didn't need to.

She could feel Lord Michael's gaze trained upon her and something told her that he knew something more than he let on. She also knew Martel watched her with piqued interest, but she tried to ignore it, despite her fluttering nerves. If she faltered now, her cover could be blown and any hope of helping her pack escape would be lost. She determined that she was here to gather information and make a plan, not get caught up in the festivities.

The lightheaded sensation of hunger rushed upon her so suddenly she visibly winced and wrinkled her face in pain. She took a deep breath and tried to hold the hunger at bay for just a little longer. Once she regained a bit of her composure, she turned back to the group and immediately met the compassionate eyes of Lord Michael.

"Miss Katey, you look ill. I hope our presence isn't bothering you." His deep voice soothed a bit of her dizziness somehow.

Katey forced a smile. "No, it's not bothering me... I'm just a little hungry."

Lord Yaverik appeared sheepish. "My apologies. Someone should have made sure that you ate with the rest of the blood servants earlier this evening. I'll have one of my servants take you to the dining hall. They'll serve you whatever you'd like and we'll be here when you're finished. We still have some time before the gift exchange begins."

CHAPTER 24

Lord Yaverik waved over one of his servants to accompany Katey to the dining hall and gave explicit instructions that whatever she asked for, she could have. Of course, he didn't know that she already knew what kind of food she had to choose from in the blood servants' kitchen.

As she was led away, Martel remained with the others. Lord Michael's eyes were still fixed upon Katey until she disappeared into the foyer. Now, more than ever, she wished she could have read the vampire lord to understand why he stared so intently and why he seemed set apart from the rest. There was a thread of authority about him that told her he carried weight within the community, but if that were so, why didn't he dominate the conversation as Lord Yaverik did?

In the dining hall, one long table occupied the center of the room, able to host at least twenty guests with complete table settings and several candelabras down the length to provide light for the diners. The décor and design of the dining room and ballroom matched almost perfectly, from the cut of the crown mold to the distinct coloration of the marble slab floor. She could still smell the hint of blood from the meal the vampires shared the night before and sighed when she thought of Helga's poor uncle who had become the main course.

The servant seated Katey near the middle of the empty table and asked what she would like.

"This is going to sound weird," she began, "but all I want is a tall glass of water and a plate of sandwich meat or whatever other kind of meat you have available. It doesn't have to be warm."

The servant bowed and hurried off to fetch her meal without so much as a suspicious look. If he had worked for the vampires for long enough, perhaps he was accustomed to strange requests.

As soon as the servant walked out of the dining hall, Katey rested her elbows on the table and buried her face in her arms, uncaring if she messed up her makeup in the process. The hunger was taking hold faster than she had expected. It'd been almost a whole day since she had eaten and the wolf within her grew restless. She wished that she could have been immune to the hunger like she was before when her loup-garou blood faded for a day or two.

Katey began to perspire as every pore of her body cried out for relief from the intense nausea that swept over her. Her vision blurred and she held on tightly to her humanity, pushing back the wolf with promises that food was on the way.

Just moments later, Katey heard frightened squeaks, shuffling feet, and manic chuckling burst through the dining hall doors. Her head shot up and through her dizziness, she saw three vampire boys, who didn't look much older than herself, dragging Helga into the dining hall and toward a shadowy corner. One held her legs and half carried her, while one held her mouth and around her torso. The other smacked his lips like a psychotic monster, ready to devour their meal.

Helga's frantic eyes fell on Katey and her arms reached out for help as the boys set her down and detained her against the wall. The girl put up a good fight, but the vampire's incredible strength couldn't be matched by a mere human.

She remembered what Martel told her, about vampires taking blood from someone of the opposite sex. This wasn't just taking blood, this was to take something else from Helga.

Katey burst up from her seat and charged toward the boys, fire in her eyes and rage boiling through her veins. It didn't matter whether she lashed out from hunger or righteous anger. They were about to harm the maid she had grown so attached to, an unwilling victim to their thirst. These boys would feel her fury if it was the last thing she did in human form before her wolf would make an untimely appearance.

"What do you think you're doing?" Katey roared. She hoped to possibly frighten them into submission without resorting to forceful violence. Along the way down the length of the table, she grabbed a sharpened dinner knife from a place setting.

The three vampires looked at her with hungry, crimson eyes, irritated that some other human girl interrupted their unauthorized snack. They didn't know what a threat Katey could be when she was hungry, too.

"Fuck off! We saw her first!" The vampire grabbed Helga's wrist and pulled back her sleeve to expose her fair, unblemished skin.

"Oh, look! She has a knife. I'm really scared!" another mocked, imitating fright. He then let out a rowdy laugh as he pulled back Helga's ruffled collar.

Katey growled deep in her throat and flung the knife toward the adolescents. The blade soared through the air and nailed the mocking boy's fedora hat. The sharp tip pinned the hat to the wall behind him.

Now she had their attention.

They looked to her as Katey snatched up another knife from the table and rapidly closed the distance.

"Let that girl go or I won't miss next time."

Their eyes drifted over her shoulder to something behind her and genuine fear flickered in their faces. They slowly let go of the terrified Helga and fled out of the dining room doors in such a flash that Katey could feel the rush of air blow past her, but only saw the blur of their bodies as they left.

She dropped the knife back to the table and hurried to Helga's side as she whimpered and collapsed to the floor, gaping at the same thing that had frightened the boys away.

Katey finally had the sense to turn around and see what it was, though her first priority was to comfort Helga.

Lord Michael stood with his arms folded over his thick chest, watching them with a calm but calculating gaze. Katey wasn't frightened of him as the others were. They might have known him better, but Katey had a feeling she was in no danger from the vampire lord. If the boys ran at the sight of him, then Lord Michael must not have approved of taking blood unwillingly from a human. Katey was on his side.

She turned her attention back to Helga and looked her over for any bitemarks. "Are you okay?"

The girl nodded urgently, and tendrils of hair that had escaped from her bun fluttered around her cheeks. Katey helped the trembling girl to her feet.

"You threatened those boys pretty boldly," Lord Michael commented as he soundlessly walked forward to meet them.

Katey looked over her shoulder as she supported Helga up by her forearms. "I'm not afraid of them, and I don't mean any disrespect, but I'm not afraid of you either. I know what they were going to do to her. I wasn't about to stand by and let that happen."

Katey had no idea where such audacity came from all of the sudden, but Lord Michael seemed to be impressed by it. He gave her a pleased smirk and then issued a dismissive wave to Helga. The maid hurried from the dining hall as fast as she could carry herself, still shaking and on the verge of breaking down into sobs.

Once she was gone, Katey felt another wave of faintness swamp over her, the adrenaline fading from her system in one bitter rush. She braced herself on the back of one of the chairs and took deep breaths through her mouth.

Lord Michael peered curiously at her. "Are you well?"

She caught the note of sincerity in his tone and pressed her fingers between her eyes to will away the pounding headache. "I'm just really hungry."

A moment of silence passed, and she wondered why Lord Michael was still standing there. She could feel his eyes focused attentively upon her, studying her with unnerving concentration. Was he waiting for something? Did he see through her brushoffs and lies?

Not a moment too soon, the servant entered with a glass of water and a plate piled high with slices of deli meats. He set the plate down at a setting between Katey and Lord Michael, forcing her to venture closer to the vampire. She dropped into the chair and inhaled the delicious aroma before taking the deli meats and rolling them together so she could get as much of the meat into her mouth as possible.

Lord Michael eyed her choice of food questioningly and took a deep breath, his chest expanding under his arms. "Come with me, Katey... You can bring your food with you."

She felt a hot flash of anxiety skitter down her back as the meat chased away the worst of her hunger pains. Did he suspect something?

Lord Michael turned on the balls of his feet and made his way out of the dining room. Katey swiftly grabbed her plate and glass of water, and followed him.

Katey obeyed him out of respect rather than fear of punishment if she disobeyed. Out of all the vampires she had met, she felt like she could trust him, but there wasn't a single point in their brief acquaintanceship that would have given her cause to believe that. All she knew was the aura he put off, and even if she were human, she would have been able to detect that credibility.

They traveled out into the foyer, up the stairs, and toward another wing of the castle that she hadn't explored yet. The rest of the castle seemed deserted since every guest and servant was down in the ballroom. He led Katey to a large oak door and held it open for her to walk into a large library with bookcases lining the walls on all sides. Katey saw absolutely no windows, but a few kerosene lanterns cast amber glows from side tables scattered amongst velvet armchairs and sofas.

The room was warm, filled with the aroma of old parchment, leather, and dust. It reminded her of the old bookstore that she and Logan visited the other day. The memory sent a pang of loneliness to her heart, wishing that she were with Logan in that moment instead of Lord Michael.

The low-pile burgundy carpet muffled their footsteps as they crossed the floor to a pair of armchairs near the center of the room.

Lord Michael motioned to one of the plush wingback chairs. "Take a seat."

They were completely alone in the library, and she had a feeling that as long as Lord Michael wanted it that way, it would stay that way.

Katey clumsily sat herself down, grappling with the fluffy skirt of her gown and set her plate and glass on the end table next to her. Lord Michael twitched his finger at an adjacent armchair and it slid itself closer so the vampire lord could ease himself down without having to drag the chair forward himself.

She froze in amazement as he gingerly lowered himself into the chair, as if he had done nothing out of the ordinary. It shouldn't have been surprising that a vampire could have such power over inanimate objects. She saw them do that in some movies. It proved she still had a lot to learn.

Lord Michael settled himself into the chair and laced his fingers over his lap before turning his stare to Katey. He gave her a reassuring smile. "Please, eat if you need to."

She didn't have to be told twice and shoveled the meat into her mouth again, but with a little more decorum that she had before. She didn't want to risk dropping any on the carpet or upholstery. Slowly, the last of the dizziness faded away and the wolf within was put to rest once more. She took a long swig of the water and set the glass down before looking up to Lord Michael again. His gaze never wavered, as if reading her thoughts or seeing something peculiar that interested him.

"Why have you been staring at me like that?" Katey asked, unafraid to offend her host, despite his obvious power.

Lord Michael smiled and shook his head. "You remind me of someone... Especially in that dress," Sadness feathering his words. That was the second person tonight who had said she reminded them of someone because of this dress.

Normally, Katey would not have taken the bait, but the heaviness in his countenance prompted her to ask, "Who?"

"My daughter..." His voice seemed to drift into the air and swirl between them.

She blinked and felt her full stomach turn hard.

"Oh, don't worry," he added quickly. "I know that you aren't her. It's just you two are... very much alike. You both have a fiery spirit and a similar face." Lord Michael's gaze lowered to the floor for the first time since they came in, and the easy smile faded from his lips.

Katey couldn't help but notice that it was the identical look that Julia gave when she made a comment about how the dress reminded her of an old friend. It was possible that Michael's daughter and Julia's friend were the same woman.

"What happened to her?"

"She was killed eighteen years ago." The words seemed to take on a life of their own and inundated the room with its own haunting energy that gave Katey chills.

"I'm sorry," she mumbled, wishing she hadn't asked.

"It is all right... Does anyone else know?" Lord Michael looked back up to Katey with fresh determination.

"Know what?" Katey gulped and a cold sweat began to form at the nape of her neck.

"That you're not human?"

Her heart fell to the floor between her shoes. She expected guards to come barging into the library to cart her down to the dungeon. But no one came and the silence between them stretched for a hard moment as Katey neither agreed nor refuted his statement.

"Don't worry. Your secret is safe with me," Michael continued. "A person is a person, no matter their race or species." Katey let out a breath of relief that she had a vamp on her side for once. "This little feud is the most foolish thing I have known, and I can't wait for the day when it ends." The disdain in his voice was keenly felt.

It occurred to Katey that perhaps he would be unbiased enough to know more about the war between the vampires and loups-garous than anyone else. It was clear he knew something and didn't agree with whatever had caused it. He did look to be the eldest out of both races that she had seen besides John. In fact, he looked much older than the great alpha, boasting deeper lines in his forehead and around his eyes.

Katey leaned closer. "Do you know how the feud started?"

"Just how every feud starts," Michael began, leaning back in his chair. "Close to four thousand years ago, a werewolf killed a vampire."

Katey wanted to groan in disappointment. So, it was the loups-garous that started the feud.

"Of course, the werewolf didn't know what he was doing," Michael said with a shrug of his shoulders. "He was a new pup, and the vampire shouldn't have been anywhere near that region in the first place because it was a restricted area for vampires.

"Back then, the two species lived in harmony, but had specific territory agreements and neither were to cross those boundary lines. There was only one place where both races co-existed and that was the city of Arnathia. The vamp was found dead on were-wolf ground, so it was supposedly the vamp's fault in the first place, but the whole dilemma centered around the identity of the vamp. He was a diplomat, an important political figure. He had great influence over a new territory agreement.

"The piece of land was discovered by the vampires, but rumor had it that the werewolves were going to be given an unequal share of the land in this new territory compared to the vampires and they weren't happy with that. The conspiracy was that the werewolf knew perfectly well what he was doing, wasn't alone, and they were the ones that crossed the lines to kidnap the vamp and murder him before the treaty could be agreed upon. They said the vamp was the one who made the proposal about the uneven distribution of the land.

"Of course, this is insanity because the treaty stated that both species would get an equal portion of land and the other werewolves on the council showed no hesitance to the pact in the first place. I, personally, think it was all a big misunderstanding fueled by distrust, and it was nothing more than an accident but, the only one who witnessed the murder was the werewolf that allegedly did it and he was too young to remember anything during his time in his wolf skin. Up to that point, tension had already been mounting between the two races and a break was inevitable."

Michael saw her entranced expression and chuckled. "I'm sorry if this is a little long winded and confusing. After the accident, both sides took up their weapons and declared war against the other. All peaceful relations dissolved. A millennium of peace between the vampires and werewolves was shattered and both sides became vindictive to one another, claiming that they were in the right and the other was wrong and deserved death for their transgressions.

"When I was a young lad, I witnessed the horrors of the war. From what my father told me of the early days, the werewolves were simply on the defensive against the vampires, killing when needed and protecting their families. What tipped them over the edge was when the vamps systematically began killing off the female werewolves."

Katey gasped and held out her hand for the old vampire to pause. "Wait! There were females?"

He nodded gravely. "Yes, there were. The vampires, in their search for retribution against the injustice done to them, completely wiped out the females and crippled the werewolf population. Now, as I'm sure you know, only the male gender of the species can be born as a werewolf, and no female can be changed because of their biology. When the werewolves lost their women, they fought back with just as much unforgiving fervor as the vampires did."

Katey shook her head in disbelief. All this time, she had thought there had never been another female. The fact was that they had simply been killed off thousands of years ago and the knowledge of why had been lost, just as easily as the reason for why the feud started in the first place. She was not the first female loup-garou in history, but she was the first one for ages and a light of hope for their race.

"It's a tragedy, pure and simple," he said with a wave of his hand. "The world may have been a very different place with less conflict, murders, war, and chaos... It sickens me to think how both sides are completely opposed to making peace with one another and it's been going on for so long." Michael finished his speech and veiled his hand over his eyes.

Katey couldn't believe there was such a long, drawn out history of loups-garous and vampires hating each other. "But what can be done to stop it? If both sides don't want to even try to make peace, then how will the fighting ever stop?"

Michael looked up to Katey and stroked his beard. "The only way is for her to step forward and fulfill the prophecy."

"What prophecy?"

Michael took a deep breath once more and closed his eyes. "Long ago, a prophecy was made concerning the unrest between the two species. The prophecy said that the product of the two species would come forward, incarnating the spirit of peace, and settle all disputes between werewolves and vampires and there would be armistice."

Ancient civilizations, a pointless war, and age-old prophecy. Katey couldn't believe that this was truly happening. It was like something out of a tropey novel.

"How do you know all this?"

A guarded smile crawled across his face. "I met the spirit centuries ago and she told me. She appeared to a few others and myself one night in Russia. She was beautiful. She was the spirit of a princess during the height of peace between the two species."

Totally engrossed, Katey hardly realized she was on the edge of her seat. "So, this princess is the same thing as the spirit of peace?"

"Yes. She, herself, was a product of a vampire queen and a werewolf king of the old civilization. She was neither werewolf, nor vampire, but a half breed that shared the positive traits of both her parents. Prejudice raged among certain members of the council, and she was assassinated. They were afraid of her power and what she might become. Instead of it bringing about even more hatred, she became revered as a spirit of peace. One tradition was to welcome her spirit into the hall at the beginning of each council meeting and let her have influence over whatever decision they made."

This went beyond culture, packs, and covens. This was an intricate history that had been lost except by those who somehow knew, like Lord Michael.

"But you said the one who would fulfill the prophecy is a 'she'. How do you know it's a girl?"

The vampire shifted in his chair and crossed his legs with a grunt. "About a century ago, there was hope that the prophecy would be fulfilled... My daughter, a vampire, fell in love with a werewolf... Such an affair would have been considered so unnatural, but it was fated love. They didn't even know about the prophecy. I supported my daughter, knowing the union could result in peace for everyone. I arranged for their clandestine meetings, I covered for her when she was missing, all with the thought in my mind that my daughter and her lover could somehow bring this feud to an end..."

Katey waited as she watched Michael's eyes glaze over. "But, what happened? You said she died. Something must have happened."

"Something did happen... She conceived. We had to keep it a secret. I made arrangements for them to escape to the mountains in the states where they could hide until the child came of age to understand the responsibility and come forward to make peace... It was shortly after the child was born when it happened. It was a baby girl. A beautiful child, the most beautiful I'd ever seen... And I'm not just saying that because she is my granddaughter," he said with a short chuckle.

"My blood servant at the time traveled with me, and a midwife to help her with the delivery. There were no complications. A perfect birth." Michael smiled nostalgically. "I remember my granddaughter's first laugh was like music. The child was neither werewolf nor vampire, I could tell. She was human, but she had a special spark in her." His words echoed something all the loups-garous tried to tell her and her heartbeat quickened.

"I could sense that spark would sway one way or the other if she was bitten. Therefore, she could change into werewolf or vampire if she was bitten, regardless of her gender, and wouldn't reject the change. It was a short while after she was born when my daughter and her husband were found. I had connections, but they couldn't hold off the search for long. A band of assassins sent by the vampire council led the ambush upon their home in the mountains. They captured both my daughter and her husband and put them on trial for their transgression against the natural order of relations between vampires and werewolves. My daughter endured the sight of her lover being experimented on with the new invention of the liquid silver and she was burned alive in the sun."

A moment of silence passed between them in reverence for his daughter and her lover for their bravery against insurmountable opposition. Even though it was many years ago, Katey could still sense the pain and sorrow within the old vampire. "What happened to the baby?" she asked, almost in a whisper.

Michael sighed heavily. "I was there when my daughter and her husband were taken. When I got word that the assassins were coming, I wanted to steal them away somewhere else so my family would be safe. But, my daughter refused to leave. Instead, she led me into a hidden cellar in their home and gave me the child. She made me promise to take care of her..." Michael blinked hard as her last words reverberated in his mind. He opened his eyes once more, keeping his stare steady upon the captivated Katey.

"Moments later, I heard the assassins storm in and take them away. I waited until it was close to sunrise before coming out of the cellar... I had no idea of what to do with a child. I was, and am still, too old to take care of one. I knew if I took the child back with me then questions would be raised and the child would be killed. I would have been, too, for treason against our race, just as my daughter was. They would have called the child an abomination. I couldn't allow that.

"So, I took the child and gave her to my blood servant and the midwife. I gave instructions to take the child as far from any vampires as she could. I think she had relatives in the southern states and took her there to be cared for. That was the last I've seen of her... She would be eighteen now." Michael smiled to himself, probably remembering his granddaughter with a bittersweet fondness. "She is the key to peace between the species... I only wish there was some way I could find her."

"Haven't you tried?"

Michael nodded. "Oh, yes. I tried many times, knowing that she would come of age soon. I could only find the grave of the midwife and blood servant. The reports said that they died in a car accident after they took my granddaughter and that an infant was found with them. My granddaughter was put into the foster care system, but the records are so confidential for the safety of the child that I couldn't find anything useful.

"I don't even know the child's last name. My daughter named her Katherine, after her grandmother, but I have no idea if that name was kept when she was put into the foster care system since we had no documentation of her birth. There were thousands of Katherines in the southern states that matched her age, but unless I went to every single one, it was unlikely I would find her. Not only that, but I couldn't be away from my duties as a vampire elder for long before they began asking questions. There were other ways I could find her, ways that only a vampire is capable of. I can track the essence of an individual almost across the country, but her essence has either been masked somehow, or she is no longer alive."

Katey leaned back in her seat as her mind raced. Was it all coincidence?

"I'm sorry if I've bored you."

"No, no," she stammered. "Not at all. It's fascinating to think that..." Katey debated on how much she could tell him. What would have been a surprise and what else did he know? If he knew that she wasn't human, and if his story had anything remotely to do with her, she should have come clean about everything. But, there was still a bit of hesitance in her, as if she wanted to see how the rest of this was going to play out before showing all her cards. "I've wanted to know about the werewolf history for a while, so it's interesting to learn."

Michael nodded. "I just wanted to make sure you were going to be comfortable here for however long you will be staying with us. I didn't intend to ramble as I did. Is there anything I can do for you?"

His voice sounded far away as her heart beat a little louder in her ears. She took a stuttered breath before opening her mouth. "Well, I'm not looking forward to tomorrow. My fiancé is down in the dungeon along with many of my friends and his pack. I don't want to see them murdered.... Is there anything you can do to stop it?" Katey looked to the vampire lord with pleading eyes.

There were a million other things she could have asked, but they were not going to help her in freeing Logan and the others. The pressing issue at hand was to escape this castle and she knew that Michael was the one who could assist her.

"I've tried to convince Lord Yaverik that this whole affair was a bad idea, that those werewolves have family and friends that will catch onto what we've done. A massacre like this would surely spark another conflict that we don't need. My compassionate tendency toward the werewolves is exactly why I am not in charge, as I once was a century ago. Yaverik, though a gentleman, is an adamant warmonger. He only laughed in my face and told me that a conflict is what he wants. There are many things about the way he runs this castle that unnerve me. His disregard for human lives, his blatant cruelness to the blood servants, all of it. It's not the way I taught him, but I hold little sway as his mentor anymore."

"Can't you overrule him? You're older."

"No, he's the head vampire lord of this castle now. I'm only secondary, despite my age. My daughter's sin has crippled much of my influence in the covens and with the council. In this region, there is no one above him. We have a high council in Romania, but they've become so lazy and complacent that it wouldn't matter if we told them about this or not."

Katey's head swam with the severity of the whole tragedy that they seemed to be stuck in the middle of. "Well, this sucks!" she exclaimed, feeling herself drown in the hopelessness of the situation.

"I concur."

"Can you help me free them? There has to be some way!"

Michael grimaced. "I want to help, I really do. I did my best by petitioning them to have food and clothing. If it were completely up to Yaverik, those werewolves would be naked and ripping each other to shreds from starvation."

Katey was thankful for Michael's generosity. "I appreciate your effort, but we have to get them out... Do you have a key to the cells at all?"

The vampire lord shook his head. "Yaverik is the only one that has a key to the cell locks."

"Is there any way you can steal the key?" Katey's face twisted in desperation.

He turned pensive, his mind tracing through a plot. "I could but it would be very tricky."

"Are you at least willing to help me?"

That was the key question. If Michael didn't want to help, there was no amount of convincing that would make him agree to a plan. But if he did, if he wanted to save the loups-garous just as much as he said he did, then Katey might have found their ticket out of the castle.

Michael looked up into her eyes and he must have seen that Katey was completely and totally serious. She would do anything, up to sacrificing her own life if needed, to free the loups-garous. When one is given something to live for, they're also given something to die for. He, of anyone in this castle, should have understood that concept. It's what his daughter did.

He nodded. "Yes, I will... The best time would be just before sunrise. I'll think on it and confer with you when I have a plan in mind."

CHAPTER 25

Lord Michael stiffly lifted himself up from the chair. "I believe we will be missed downstairs soon."

Katey, her head still spinning with everything the vampire told her, rose to follow him out, but stopped him just short of the door.

"How did you know what I was?"

He looked back to Katey with wise, warm eyes. "I don't know what you are, but you certainly aren't human."

Katey tilted her head, silently requesting an explanation.

"I know you're not human," he said with a sly grin, "because you don't smell like a human, you don't smell like a vampire or a werewolf, yet you smell unique. Almost like you're a species all your own that I can't recognize. Don't be alarmed though because no one else here has their senses as honed as well as mine. I'm sure no one can notice. I could probably reach into your memories and find out what you are, but if it were important, I'm sure you would tell me, yes?"

She blinked and looked away, glad that he chose to be discreet, but troubled that she had to lie to the one person who would have deserved to know the truth. She nodded.

They walked into the hallway, leaving the library. Even though their conversation was over, his words lingered with Katey the whole way back to the ballroom.

The irony of Katey looking like his daughter, his granddaughter being named Katherine, which was her full name, being from the South where his granddaughter was put up into the foster care system, her never knowing her real parents and above all, her being able to change into the first female loup-garou in centuries coincided so well with his story that it was borderline freaky.

Could Katey have been the one mentioned in the prophecy that would bring peace and order between the two species? Was the spirit within her the spirit of the half breed princess? All signs pointed to a "yes", but Katey didn't want to believe it. She was a nobody, an orphan that wasn't anything special until Logan turned her. How could she be the fulfillment of some age-old prophecy?

Then again, what if Lord Michael had been lying. What if he did probe her memories like he said that he could? Firstly, if she knew vampires could do that, she wouldn't have put herself in so many precarious situations where her mind could be harvested for information. She had no doubt that he could reach into her mind and read her thoughts somehow. If he could make a chair move and Martel could make her stand perfectly still while he kissed her, then there was no telling how far the vampire psychic abilities could go.

But, what if he was telling the truth all along? If she was the savior of the loups-garous, what did that mean? What was she supposed to do? And how could she be expected to save the future of two warring races when she couldn't even save her fiancé and pack?

As soon as they walked through the ballroom doors, an eager Martel greeted her. His smile was infectious and she tried to silence her thundering heart at seeing the excited sparkle in his eyes.

Almost everyone had taken their seats in chairs around the room or lounged on the floor by the Christmas tree in the far corner. The roar of voices had lowered to a dull murmur. It must have been time for the gift exchange, but Katey's thoughts were far from festive.

Martel took her hand and pulled her away from Lord Michael. "Katey, come with me. I saved us a spot near the tree."

Katey looked back to see Lord Michael join Yaverik on the far wall as he monitored the activity of the ballroom. If her suspicions were true, then the old vampire might have been her only known relative on this earth.

She and Martel wandered through the crowd until they came to a pair of empty chairs near the tree. Katey took her seat beside him and let her eyes skim over the many pale faces around her. A hundred questions, new and disturbing, flitted in and out of her mind so quickly it made Katey dizzy. How many would have known her mother? She spotted Julia in the crowd and wondered how long she and her mother had been friends. Who was there for her execution? Who knew about Michael's pacifist and sympathizing tendencies to the loups-garous? Who experimented on her father with the liquid silver bullets? Were the assassins that hunted them down here in this very room?

It was then she remembered her chronic dreams. The cabin. The blood. The woman with the blonde hair and white gown. Had those been memories? How could she have remembered something like that as a baby? Was that why Lord Michael's voice and accent was so comforting? Because he hid her from the assassins that came to arrest her parents?

And if that dream was also something of a memory, what did that mean for her other dreams? Were they premonitions of the future? The past? Had they been guiding her to this destiny all along? She thought of that dream she had of the pack before she knew what they were, and how they ran together as wolves. Then what was that giant black loup-garou that ended her dream? What did it all mean?

She swallowed hard and bit down on her lips to keep herself from slipping into a panic attack. If she let herself slip into such hysteria, then she'd never make it until dawn when Michael promised to help them escape.

Several volunteers sifted through the hundreds of gifts laid out under the tree, calling out names and tossing them to their respective owners. Once the first few gifts were passed out, the racket of paper ripping, joyful glees, and general merriment resumed.

Martel had received several gifts, mostly from other ladies who watched him with hopeful gazes. He gave his cordial thanks and set them aside with perfect impartiality, much to the dismay of the ladies, who waited for a flicker of interest.

It was amusing for a little while to see someone open their gift and either squeal in delight or laugh at the gag inside. On more than a few occasions, she let her eyes slide a glance toward Lord Michael across the room, observing the way he interacted with the other vampires.

No one would have known that he was somewhat of a defector, the way he laughed and socialized with the others. If any vampire could read memories, wouldn't they have known that he had helped his daughter escape and elope with a loup-garou? Or were they only able to read the feeble minds of a human? Or maybe Lord Michael was just powerful enough to block out any psychic invasion?

As the gift exchange drew to a close, the vampires scattered, carrying their goods to the edges of the ballroom, where they set their presents down and retreated back toward the center to continue mingling. Numerous blood servants, including Helga, who looked to have recovered from the attack earlier, came out to the floor to clear away the wrapping paper and trash while others took the chairs and pushed them toward the walls to get them out of the way.

All the while, the band tuned up their instruments.

"What now?" Katey asked.

"Time for more dancing. The night is still young!" He gave her a wide grin as he led her away from the center of the hall to take their seats and gifts out of the way of those gathering together to dance.

He must have seen her eyes light up with the thought of dancing. If there were any good dancers out of this bunch, it would be them. Katey remembered waltzing with him on her first day in the ballroom dance club. She was so nervous and constantly stared at her feet, but he asked her to dance and they learned the basic box waltz pattern together.

As Katey watched couples pair up for the first sets, she began to wonder which dance they would do first. No doubt it would be something traditional, and her mind rotated through all the possibilities.

Katey didn't notice that Martel had momentarily walked away and came back with an oblong shaped box wrapped in beautiful shiny green paper and a golden bow.

She glanced down to the gift and her heart rose in her throat. "Whose is that?"

"Yours," he purred.

She blinked in surprise that she would receive a gift at all from anyone, let alone him. Katey smoothly took the box from his hands and carefully unwrapped the gift, being careful not to make a mess of shredded paper that the servants would have to clean up. Upon opening it, she was met with a pristine rose in full bloom.

Katey was never one for romance and simple gifts like these usually made her want to roll her eyes. Gifts like roses, chocolates, and teddy bears shouldn't have been the go-to for any man. Thought was what mattered, not clichés.

But as she stared at the soft, silky petals of the rose, she smiled at its simple beauty. A rose meant many things. To some, it was just a flower. To others, it was a symbol of love and devotion. To Katey, it was a gift and in this wintery world of vampires, loups-garous, and mysteries, this rose seemed to pull her back from all the desperate and disquieting thoughts. For a moment, she forgot about it all.

She lifted the single rose from its tissue bed and brought it to her lips to take a deep whiff of its pleasing aroma.

"I thought a girl as beautiful as you deserved to be reminded of what she outshines," Martel whispered intimately.

She looked up to Martel, wondering what exactly she was feeling. This gift and the peace it brought to her mind, combined with their passionate kiss from the night before, stirred something within her that was kind of exciting in a dangerous way.

This pull of affection she felt for Martel came all too easy, resurrected from a life she had left behind when Logan turned her. One side, the side that neglected to remember her mating bond, enjoyed the rush of it. The other side of her screamed that she should run, slap him, anything to break the spell that he cast over her. Because, that's what it had to be. A spell, an enchantment, a trick of the mind. What else could make her forget Logan and everything they shared so quickly?

Katey didn't want to return the flower back to its case, afraid that if she let go of it, the chaos would charge back in and take away that peace.

"Katey," Martel began shakily, taking her free hand in his. "Even in school, I knew you were special. I had thought about asking you out, but there was such an age difference that I didn't want you to get scared and turn me down. But now that we're older, the difference doesn't matter so much."

She held back the urge to laugh. If age ever played a factor in whom she loved, then she wouldn't have adored Logan so much, but Martel didn't know that.

"You are an amazing girl, and any man would be blessed to have you. I would be even more grateful if you would be mine. I know I haven't exactly put the best foot forward, and a lot has happened since we last saw one another. I am a different man than I was.

That can never change. But when I'm with you, I feel like... like I'm human again, just a little."

Katey bowed her head and closed her eyes, wishing Martel would stop. Even if she wanted to be his, even if she had a crush on him as a freshman in high school, they could never return to the way things were. He was not the first one to give such a speech. He was a few weeks too late to claim her heart, if that's what he wanted.

She braced herself, hoping she would have the heart to say what she needed to. "Martel, I don't know if I can just ignore everything that's happened to me over the last few years. And I can't ignore what you are. I don't have a problem being your friend, but I can't see us in the way that you do."

When she lifted her gaze, she saw the brokenness in Martel's eyes and she wished that she could have taken away his pain. Short of accepting him, there was little she could do, but accepting his request for a deeper relationship was completely out of the question.

Martel forced a smile, and she could tell it took probably all the strength he had. "Then we can be friends."

She absolutely hated how she had to throw him into the "friend zone" like that, but he would never understand. His hatred of the loups-garous was too deep, too consuming. There was no use in telling him that she was already taken by one. To his knowledge, it wouldn't have mattered in the end, but he didn't know that her mate would not die the following night.

"You have dozens of women here who would throw themselves at your feet. Why not go dance with them?"

The vampire huffed. "Do you know how long I've been waiting to dance with you again? I'm not leaving your side."

The band began to play a light, swaying melody that flowed sinuously through the ballroom, cutting through their conversation. The music took on a life of its own and twisted its way around Katey's mind. She watched the couples begin to twirl, skirts billowing out from their legs as they stepped and swayed like elegant sprites to the rhythm of their own world.

In the excitement of the rose, the music, and the beautiful people dancing, Katey began to lose herself and the wolf slipped away into the darkness.

All of the sudden, Katey was glad to be right where she was at that moment with Martel. The knowledge that her fiancé was below her in a prison cell and that his death sentence was scheduled for the following night, was a distant concept. The idea that she could bring peace between vampires and loups-garous was a faraway nightmare. The feeling of homesickness and loneliness was little more than a memory as she saw Martel gracefully bow and offer out his hand to her. She felt herself drowning in the murky forgetfulness that crept upon her mind and heart.

Katey took his hand without hesitation and set the rose aside.

Martel led her to the dance floor, guiding her through the moving bodies with ease. They waited for the beat and began their graceful spin. All around, skirts whirled and brushed by each other, but never collided. Everyone knew where everyone else was and each couple was in sync with their part in this grand display that seemed to require no rehearsal.

Martel held Katey with perfect posture and she did her best to hold her own as they traveled across the dance floor. He spun her, dipped her, and led her in moves that even Katey had never learned. The smile on her face couldn't be willed away and the building ecstasy within her shined through every graceful move.

"You seem happy." The corners of Martel's eyes crinkled in a smile.

Katey giggled. "You know what? I am."

"See, it's not so bad to be with me."

The dress, the makeup, and her companion all made her feel like the belle of the ball, though there were plenty of other vampire ladies present that might have surpassed her in looks and refinement.

So many sensations moved within her that she could feel it overflow within her soul and swell to unimaginable depths. Her blood raced with each turn and her spirit soared with the music. Katey couldn't remember a time when she felt like this, not even when she danced with Logan did she feel this free.

Then, all of the sudden, Katey could contain her delight no longer. She lost control of herself. As Martel sent her into a final dip, Katey threw back her head and released a great, loud... howl.

In that moment, time stood still as her wolf song must have echoed through the entire castle. Martel raised Katey up from the dip, brows furrowed and lips parted in utter confusion.

She lowered her head as the final notes of her howl faded. Every-one in the ballroom grew deathly silent and motionless, all staring at her with shock and contempt. Even the band had abruptly stopped their music on a sour note.

Katey's eyes darted around to all the glaring vampires and up to Martel who had released her suddenly and backed away from her. His blue eyes looked her up and down as if she had transformed into something detestable and otherworldly. It was then that she realized her own eyes were a bright, glowing loup-garou gold.

She turned her frightened gaze to Michael and Yaverik. Michael didn't move but donned a wistful expression, as if all the puzzle pieces finally came together for him. Yaverik slowly rose to his feet, borderline furious as his face contorted with rage.

With her heart pounding and chest heaving as she tried to catch her breath, she looked to Martel again and wordlessly pleaded for asylum. He would not give it. His words of love and devotion from before became meaningless now. He knew the truth. They all knew the truth.

A few pregnant seconds passed, and then every one of the loups-garous below her feet returned her howl and sent shudders through the ballroom. It was as if they were in the room with her and their power surged through her soul. It quickened her loup-garou blood and she could feel her inner wolf stir with a renewed vigor since the night she almost changed. She longed to be with her pack.

It wasn't hard to make her next decision.

She ran.

Katey bolted out of the ballroom doors at lightning speed, knocking over stunned vampires in her way. When she reached the stairs, she kicked the heels off, and sent them flying across the marble floor. She ran as fast as she knew how down the halls and corridors, tears streaming down her face.

She made her way to the dungeon doors. The loup-garou howl still rang in her ears as she took the lock in one hand and ripped it off with one quick tug. She didn't want to be anywhere else but with her pack. No one else could comfort her at a time like this when she couldn't tell what was real or a fantasy anymore. She was probably bound to end up in a cage anyway after that episode and it would save the vampires the trouble of dragging her into the cell.

Katey hurried into the dungeon, slammed the door shut behind her, and flew down the stairs so fast she didn't even think her feet hit the stone.

Every pair of golden eyes turned to her. Some charged forward, drawing dangerously close to the silver. Others continued to stay at a safe distance and watched it all unfold. But beneath it all, the atmosphere of the place was thick with mounting tension, as if one wrong move or word would send every loup-garou over the edge into a wild and uncontrollable hysteria.

Darren came daring close to the silver bars to meet her. "Katey! What happened?"

She grabbed the bars and pressed her body against the metal that would not burn her, willing to get closer to her pack and pull on their bond for strength and stop the wave of sobbing. "I'm sorry, Darren. I'm so sorry! I should have told them the truth. I'm so sorry!" Katey gripped the bars tightly between her trembling hands. She fell onto the damp floor, ruining the precious fabric of her dress as cold, filthy water seeped through to chill her skin.

Darren crouched down, ready to console her in whatever way he could while the silver separated them. Tears streamed down her powdered cheeks, leaving streaks of spoiled makeup.

"Wait, just calm down. What happened? Why are you dressed like that?"

"Katey?" Logan's choked voice called from amongst the pack inside the cell. He sounded weak and disoriented. Had he degraded that fast since she left just a few hours ago?

Her head shot up to see her fiancé step forward, scrutinizing her appearance. Her guts knotted together knowing what he saw, a girl who had allowed herself to step into a place she never belonged.

She wanted to crumble with the shame of it all. He didn't know what she had felt, what she had thought, how she had betrayed him.

Nonetheless, he ran to Darren's side and squatted down with him, still keeping a safe distance from the harmful silver. Katey reached out her hand beseechingly, hoping that he would take it despite everything he knew and didn't know yet.

He did, but it was a weak and unsure grip. The hunger must have been taking a harder toll on him. Dark circles hung under his eyes and after she took a quick look at the others, she knew they had all reached their limit. Haggard and tired faces turned to her for an answer or some comfort that they would escape this terrible place soon.

"They were doing a gift exchange. Martel gave me a rose and we were dancing, and I was just getting so excited that it just came out. I feel so embarrassed about everything."

"Embarrassed that you howled and showed who you really are?" His words came out in a growl. "Embarrassed that you're one of us?"

Logan's words were like knives in her chest.

"No, not like that!" Katey implored, feeling more tears stinging at the corners of her eyes.

"Well, that's sure how it sounds," Logan dropped her hand like it would sting him, and snarled bitterly.

"I was confused, Logan! I didn't know what I was doing!" Katey reached out to him as he slipped just past her fingertips. "I was in the middle of the room, and everyone was staring, and Martel looked so disgusted with me."

Fury radiated from his body and she had never felt such dominance hit her before. She couldn't breathe, couldn't think, and curled against herself for shelter from his rage. For once, she was glad that the silver separated them, but it didn't keep her from needing his love and understanding.

"Why does it matter what Martel thinks of you? Why should you care what any of them think of you? Do they matter more to you than we do? Your own pack? Me?" Logan regarded her as if she were one of them. "After all we did for you, after all I went through to make you part of this pack, you're willing to throw it all away for what? A rose? A stupid dance? I thought you were different, that you had sense and could be grateful. We didn't have to take you in. We didn't have to give two shits about you, but we did, and this is how you repay us? You were supposed to be figuring out a way to get us out of here and you're wasting your time at some fucking party!"

Logan turned and stormed away into the mass of loups-garous that began to glare at her. They agreed with Logan, and she could already hear them whisper about her in all three cells.

Katey bowed her head in disgrace. He was right and she knew it. He was completely right. She had let them all down, she betrayed their trust, and ultimately dishonored herself as a loup-garou and as his potential mate.

She sat back and pulled up her knees against her chest.

How could she have allowed herself to be wooed by a vampire? How could she have allowed herself to be distracted for one moment, a precious moment, when she could have been working to free her new family? Instead, she let herself forget who she was and where she belonged.

Knowing that Logan was on the verge of disowning her was the worst imaginable punishment she could have ever felt. Forget Darren, John, or even Michael. If Logan despised her, she had nothing, was nothing. It was like her heart had been ripped from her chest and trampled on, ground into the unforgiving stone and left to bleed out in agony. She fully expected him to sever the preliminary mating bond in that moment, but it stayed intact, alive and feeding her the tidal wave of emotions.

Darren was the only one that didn't leave her and continued to look upon her with sympathy. "Don't mind Logan. He's been that way for a while now... It's just the hunger talking. He'll be better once he's eaten something."

Katey shook her head, droplets of tears dripping from her chin. "No, he's totally right. I was so obsessed with putting on a good show for everyone, dressing up and acting right to hide what I was, but I should have just confessed it from the beginning. I should have been down here with you the whole time... He's probably never going to forgive me."

"Katey, listen to me. You are part of this pack. We care about you, and nothing you've done tonight changes that. Just give him time... There isn't much between now and tomorrow night, but if we can find a way out of this, then there will be more time."

That reminded Katey of her conversation with Michael. She related the whole meeting in the library to Darren, everything including the prophecy but excluding the details of Michael's daughter and granddaughter. Then she told him about how Michael agreed to help, but hadn't come up with a solid plan yet. All she knew is it had to be done around sunrise when the vamps couldn't follow them into the dawn.

By now, John, Ben, and Dustin had made an appearance and squatted near the bars of their respective cells.

"You did very well, Katey," John said. "I don't know how much I'd trust this vamp, but it's worth a shot."

"He knew I wasn't human from the very moment I met him and he didn't seem bothered at all by it. He didn't even look surprised when I howled, but since everyone else was, that means he was keeping it a secret."

"He knew you were loup-garou?" Darren asked.

"Well, not exactly. He said he knew I wasn't human, but he couldn't tell what I was. He said it was like I was a species all my own... Makes me feel worse that I'm not officially... anything. I'd rather be all of something than a little of two or three different things."

The way she put it made her think of the prophecy and Michael's granddaughter being born from a vampire and a loup-garou. Katey still wasn't sure if she wanted to believe she was the one to bring peace. The way she felt right now, she wasn't sure she could bring peace to herself, let alone two feuding races.

Darren let out a long, tired breath. "Well, then maybe he can be trusted... But I'm not going to put all my eggs into one basket."

"Come through the bars like you did last night before the vamps come down," John urged. "We'll keep you safe."

Katey began to pull and tug at her hair to let it all down when she heard something tumble out. It fell to the stone with a little metallic tap, and she looked down to see a hairpin. She picked it up and began to wonder.

She raised herself up onto her knees and began tinkering with the hairpin inside the lock. She had no clue how to crack open a lock with a hairpin, but it was worth a shot. The pack watched her and some other loups-garous who had been paying attention came closer to the bars.

Then, they all heard it.

A click.

Katey froze. She gently released the hairpin from the lock and gave the bars a good tug.

It opened.

Who would have thought that having her hair up in that crazy style would have been such an advantage after all? It shouldn't have been that easy.

Suddenly, the dungeon door flew open and the odious stench of sulfur filled the cold air.

CHAPTER 26

Katey knew a vampire had just entered the dungeon. She looked at Darren, eyes wide with fear. She slowly shut the cell door without a sound and casually dropped the hairpin on the floor in front of him.

Darren's eyes followed the pin to the stone and nodded in understanding.

The vamp rushed down the stairs, his shoes beating against the stone as he went. A communal growl erupted from the loups-garous as the enemy approached.

"There's the little she-wolf!" Yaverik's voice boomed. Katey spun around and glared at him with fierce, golden eyes. "You're coming with me, young lady."

He marched forward, grabbed Katey by her arm, digging his sharp nails into her flesh. She cried out in pain, and then heard the dull thud of flesh against metal behind her, followed by a sizzling noise.

"Let her go, you bloodsucking son of a bitch!"

Katey looked back to see Logan snarling out more nasty curses and insults, his hands firmly wrapped around the silver bars with wisps of smoke seeping from his grasp. Katey smelled his flesh slowly burn and blood dripped down his hands and wrists. His gold eyes blazed with fury as his face distorted into a beastly scowl, ignoring the pain.

"Logan, let go of the bars!" Darren tried to pull Logan away from the silver but not even the alpha's strength could make him budge.

Many loups-garous followed Logan's example, and many rammed themselves against the bars, burning their shoulders and arms in their attempt to escape. All who were strong enough exploded in a thunderous roar against Yaverik. The deafening noise made the very rock and stones of the dungeon tremble and crack under the force of their hatred and rage.

Tears welled in Katey's eyes as Yaverik blatantly ignored the prisoners and hauled her up the stone steps, causing her dress to tear along the hem.

Pandemonium ensued and the growls of the loups-garous didn't cease once Yaverik slammed the door shut. Katey could hear them, even as she was pulled down the hall.

"Where are you taking me?" Katey asked, stumbling over the dress and her feet as he yanked her down corridors, taking turn after winding turn.

"Back to your room. Out of respect for Martel, I won't have you stay in the basement, but that doesn't mean you won't suffer their fate."

"You're going to hunt me down like the rest of them?"

Yaverik gave an ominous chuckle. "No, I have something much better in store for you."

Michael appeared in front of them, his glare searing with indignation. "Yaverik! What are you doing?"

Katey turned to the man that might have been her grandfather and gave him a beseeching look. If anyone could save her from the vampire, it was him.

"I'm going to lock her away in her room until after the solstice. Then I'm going to have our scientists take a look at her. I have no idea how she got past our noses and how a female could be a beast in the first place, but I intend to find out."

They had arrived at her room and Yaverik fumbled with his keys to find the right one. Katey tugged against his hold, but he was just as strong as she was and she was more likely to wrench her shoulder out of joint if she continued to struggle.

Michael took her other arm to try and pull her away from Yaverik. "This is insanity! The girl has done nothing wrong!"

"She is a werewolf and living. That's plenty wrong!" Yaverik hissed at Michael as he threw open her bedroom door and tossed Katey inside. She crumbled to the floor with a cry and glanced up just in time to see Yaverik's hateful sneer. The door was slammed shut and Katey could hear the key turn to lock it tight.

Yaverik turned and marched down the hall away from Katey's chamber. Michael followed closely behind, still incredulous as to what had just unfolded in the past hour. He witnessed something he never thought he'd see in his lifetime. Discovering that Katey was a loup-garou gave him more joy than any man should have been allowed. Could she be who he suspected? It was too good to be true that his granddaughter, after eighteen years of separation, would fall so easily into his lap. If he were not under the watchful eyes of so many other vampires who knew his past, he would have shown much more emotion to her great reveal. Equally, if he wasn't careful in how he addressed this issue with Yaverik, he would be unable to help Katey or her friends.

"Mark my words, Yaverik, this will not end well. You made these plans for the lupo-manneros without my consent. If you had consulted me prior to my arrival, I would have cautioned you against it."

"If you fear the council punishing us, don't be. I already have their permission for tomorrow night."

Michael's lips parted with disbelief. "How could the council have agreed to this heinous act?"

Yaverik laughed. "You know as well as I do that the council is just as blindly patriotic for our kind as any of us. Having some more dogs put down is a welcome request to them."

The older vampire shook his head. "I can't let you go through with this! I don't care what the council says."

Yaverik stopped and turned to his old mentor with a glare. "You're alone in your beliefs, old man. No one is siding with you on this."

Michael jammed a finger behind him, toward his daughter's old bedchamber where Katey was locked away. "At least have mercy on the girl. Let her go back and grieve with the other women who will lose their loved ones. Let her go home."

His former apprentice let out a wicked laugh. "Go home? She has no home. After we murder her pack, she will have nowhere to go. Besides, aren't you the least bit curious why she's a werewolf? I know as well as you do that the females of her species were wiped out long ago. It shouldn't be possible."

If Yaverik knew what Katey meant to the world, she would not be allowed to live past the solstice. "That doesn't give you the right to dissect her."

Yaverik stepped closer, his voice dropping. "She shouldn't even exist. She might be an anomaly, a freak of nature, but we owe it to our predecessors to finish the job they started."

Michael wanted to reach him. He had to make his apprentice understand. They had spent centuries together, learning from one another, and the last decade alone had brought a change in Yaverik that was unpleasant. His ruthless character had intensified, unrestrained by the limits of authority. He was free to do and say as he wished now, but Michael couldn't abide by it.

He stepped closer. "But, you also know that she could be the key to ending this war," he whispered. "You remember what we found in the ruins of Arnathia. I told you about when the spirit came to me. It's our responsibility to make sure she completes her mission."

Yaverik's face twisted into a devilish grin. The mentor's words had fallen on ears that had become deaf to reason. "And that's another reason to kill her."

"What could this possibly resolve for you? To what end?"

A maddening look came in Yaverik's eye, a glimmer of insanity shining through. "I will not rest until every piece is in the perfect place. The Beast shall rise again, mark my words."

He knew exactly what Yaverik spoke of. The Beast from the days of the war, the indestructible monster more powerful than vampires and werewolves combined. It was put down once before, but legend said it took more than a legion of their army to contain him. The spirit of such a beast still roamed the earth, looking for a host to possess and bring about a reign of terror and destruction for vampires, werewolves, and humans alike. There would be no stopping it a second time, unless Katey could be given the chance.

"You've lost your mind," Michael mumbled.

"No," Yaverik uttered softly. "I have a vision."

The younger vampire turned and walked away, leaving a horror-stricken Michael behind to mull over all his young apprentice had said.

Darkness engulfed Katey's room, but with her loup-garou vision she could still make out silhouettes of her surroundings. She pushed herself up off the floor and staggered toward the door. She could hear the vampires argue all the way down the hall and listened until their voices faded away into silence. She couldn't believe she was so close to setting them all free. The hairpin trick was a stroke of dumb luck, but if they could have just had a little more time, perhaps they would all be in the snow right now and running for safety.

Katey shrieked in anger, picked up a vase that sat on the end table by the fire, and pitched it across the room. It shattered against the far wall and pieces scattered along the rough hardwood floors.

She took a deep breath to simmer down and shimmied out of the dress to change into the clothes she had worn the other night when she first arrived. The clothes had been washed and mended since then. She wanted to be ready to leave and hoped that her pack would come to rescue her when they attempted their escape. Darren would know what to do with the pin and he could get them all out without a key.

Katey hated to feel so helpless, trapped in the room and unable to help. She heard and smelled the approach of two vampires that took sentry posts just outside her door, making escape for her even more difficult.

She threw back the thick crimson curtains so she could see the sunrise when it came in several hours. Outside, snow swirled around the mountain, sputtering against her windowpane.

She dragged herself over to the bed and collapsed on her back. She stared up at the canopy as she tried to clear her head of all the thoughts that pressed in and threatened to devour her. She had to believe that they would make it out of this.

Even if the pack did manage to escape, there was no guarantee that they would come and get her, or if they would make it out of the castle alive. The vampires had enough ammunition and firepower to take down the pack, and many of the loups-garous, especially the young ones, would be far too weak to shift and defend themselves.

Katey's future was still unsure, and with so many uncertainties about what would happen come morning light, she wondered how she would get any sleep.

Her thoughts turned to Logan and how angry he was before she left the dungeon. She didn't want to let his words cut her so deeply, but they did. Katey knew what was happening when she spent time with Martel and she didn't guard herself the way she should have. She let herself be caught up in old memories and feelings. In essence, she cheated on Logan, and she despised herself for it. How could she have done that to him? How could she have gotten so lost so quickly?

She wasn't sure if Logan would ever forgive her, if he would even want to mate with her if they got out of this alive. If he wanted to end it, she couldn't blame him. After all they had been through, she betrayed his trust and dashed his love aside as if it were nothing.

Yet, if he didn't care anymore, if he hated her guts, then why would he have wrapped his hands around the silver bars and shouted at Yaverik the way he did? Shouldn't he have looked the other way and let her be dragged off without so much as a word of protest? Was that some glimmer of hope?

She rolled over and grabbed the pillow nearest her to squeeze it between her arms and legs, wishing it could have hugged back. Katey buried her nose in the silky fabric of the pillowcase and tried to fight the tears caught in her throat. She let sleep take her, hoping it would help to make this whole disaster seem farther away.

Down in the dungeon, Darren stood and stared intently at the silver cell door, the hairpin clutched in his hand. He was hesitant, especially after finding out that the cell door locked itself when Katey shut it earlier that night. Instinct told him to stay clear of the bars. It was comparable to the human reflex to hold their breath while being dunked underwater. But he knew that the survival of the pack and all the loups-garous depended on this. The sun was just about ready to rise, and their window of opportunity was fast approaching.

Not far behind him, Logan paced back and forth, a sneer permanently fixed on his face. He was furious at everything and everyone, just like the rest of them. The other loups-garous already fought amongst one another, quarreling bitterly over nothing. John and his sons tried their best to coach them to control their fiery impulses, but many were too far gone to listen.

The effects of hunger intensified with each passing hour, building upon their weakness and need to escape. No loup-garou wanted to be caged, and the minimal rations only increased the risk of all of them shifting into their loup-garou forms in the sheer need for survival. Once that happened, they were beyond saving. The beasts would take over and no one would be safe, not even the elders.

The alpha took a preparatory breath, reached out and tried to slip his shaking hand with the hairpin between the bars next to the lock, careful not to let his skin touch the silver. These bars, unlike the ones Katey managed to squeeze through, were closer together, as if they were designed to prevent this exact scenario. His fingers and the bulk of his hand made it through, but when he needed to bend his wrist, he bumped the metal. A light burn formed on the back of his wrist and he hissed out a curse.

He took a second to let it heal before easing forward again. At a certain point, the gap between skin and metal would be nearly unavoidable, his forearm too thick to go any further. Yet, he needed to angle his arm so he could push the tip of the pin into the locking mechanism. This, in comparison, was supposed to be the easy part and sweat already dripped down Darren's temples under the stress.

He gritted his teeth and knew he had to push himself beyond what was comfortable. In one quick move, he twisted his arm and jammed the pin into the lock, at the same time pressing his flesh into the silver. It had been years since he felt the sting of silver, but it was everything he remembered.

Blood seeped from his wound as he continued to rotate and probe the lock, waiting for that click and release of the mechanism they had heard earlier.

In the next cell over, Dustin called out, "You got it yet?"

Darren would have throttled the beta if they shared a cell. "No, damn it! This bloody fucking hurts!"

"Just feckin' push through it!"

"I'm trying!" Darren roared. Blood dripped from his elbow and dampened the floor around his feet.

Another moment passed with no success and the blinding pain of the silver against his arm nearly made him want to give up. He knew he couldn't and pressed on, despite the potential risk of irreversible damage to his muscles and nerves.

Finally, though his fingers trembled so violently he nearly lost hold of the pin, the tumblers fell into place. Logan, who had been standing close by, charged for the cell door. It swung open against his assault and banged against the bars with a resounding clang that rang in every loup-garou's ears. The sound of freedom.

The young loup-garou barreled out of the cell. Darren hurried out first to tend to his ward, followed closely by the others in the cell. Patches of Logan's skin were charred but began to steadily heal. Logan fell to his knees, snarling at the intense anguish of his burns across his shoulder and back.

Only then did Darren look down to his mangled arm. He swallowed hard at the shock of white bone surrounded by blackened, twitching flesh. Blood covered his arm to the point he couldn't see a speck of unblemished skin.

Darren's body began to shiver and he felt a rush of cold all through his limbs. The wound wasn't healing. Ben knelt beside him and Logan, but Darren had enough sense to shove the hairpin into his packmate's hand.

"Get the other cells unlocked," he ordered, voice hoarse from the pain.

Ben's eyes fell on his wound and shook his head before handing the pin to Logan to do the job instead. He reached down and ripped one of his pant legs at the knee. With great care and deftness of skill and experience, Ben wrapped Darren's arms and tied it off. There was little else he could do until his loup-garou healing could kick in.

"Try not to use that arm for a while," Ben told him. "Movin' it more will only make it take longer to heal."

The loups-garous from their cell stretched their limbs and began to check on their packmates in the remaining cells. Darren didn't rise from his knees and Ben dutifully stayed next to him. By now, Logan was with Dustin at the bars of the middle holding cell. By the sound of it, Dustin was losing patience with his grandson as he tried to explain how to pick the lock. Logan complained of his fingertips grazing the silver, making the task more difficult.

Suddenly, the dungeon door opened again and many of the loups-garous braced themselves for a battle, expecting a vampire to enter. However, it was Ralph and Helga, the two who had come looking for Katey the evening before. The loups-garous recognized them as the givers of food and gradually backed off, though Darren could sense the primal hunger urging them to attack instead. This was the least safe place for fragile humans.

The young girl gasped and gripped Ralph's arm for security at the sight of the beasts out of their cages. The two humans stood at the top of the stairs, nonplussed at the sight of the loose prisoners.

With the help of Ben, Darren stood and took on the role of mediator. Even injured, he could use his dominance to hold back the loups-garous who may have been willing to make a meal of the humans. He stepped forward and raised his hands as if to show he was unarmed, even though his golden eyes said otherwise.

"We're not going to hurt you," Darren assured them. "It's Helga, right?"

Helga nodded and managed to stutter, "Yes, sir."

"First, we need to know, is Katey safe? Do you know what that vampire did to her?"

Again, she nodded, her dark braids bouncing with the motion of her head. "Yes. Lord Yaverik locked her in her room. There are two guards at her door."

Darren glanced over his shoulder to Logan, who had stopped his work on the lock to listen. Dustin, impatient to be free, did what Darren had done, and his hand shot through the bars to grab the pin. Though he was burned in the same way, it didn't take him nearly as long to unlock the cell. His injury was hardly anything compared to Darren's. The beta was much more crafty with locks.

Helga and Ralph could only watch as more loups-garous flooded the dungeon floor. John joined in the defenses to make sure the humans were safe, standing close to Darren to hold them back with his dominance.

"Are the vamps asleep?" Darren asked.

Ralph answered this time. "Yes, all but a few. I'm sure you lot won't have any trouble taking them out though."

Dustin came to stand beside his alpha. "Do they have an armory? Do you know where they're keeping the silver bullets?"

Ralph nodded. "I can show you the way. I've been wanting to stick it to these bastards for years."

At least the humans were on their side. Darren looked down to the bloodied, makeshift bandage and grimaced. He wouldn't be much help in a fight, but there were plenty who could take up arms against the vampires. His pack's first priority was to get Katey out. Logan watched his alpha intently, waiting for the word to go rescue his mate. Darren gave his nod and the loup-garou bolted up the stairs, along with a stream of other loups-garous who were just as ready to leave this terrible place and see the sun again.

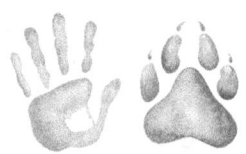

Katey bolted upright in bed when a great force slammed against the bedroom door. Shouts, hisses, and growls accompanied the telltale signs of a scuffle outside her door. A stampede of feet joined the mix and hope sparked in her chest.

She scuttled to her feet, acutely alert. Another bang and the sound of two heavy thuds in the corridor. She turned her head to the window and saw that dawn had finally come. The snowstorm had passed, and the brilliant sun peeked over the snowcapped mountains, melting the ice that had formed around her window frame.

One more bang did the trick and the door splintered under the weight of a loup-garou's shoulder. The fully changed beast crashed into the room and dropped to all fours. Katey recognized it as Ben with his pure golden eyes and black fur mixed with patches of silver on his chest and paws.

Katey cried for joy, ran up to him, and hugged around his thick mane, never happier to see anyone in her life. Ben let her embrace him for a second, then used his humanlike paw to push her toward the door where she saw the other loups-garous, some in their human forms and some in their full loup-garou forms, running down the hall at a slower speed than she would have expected. Logan stood by the door, waving for them to hurry up. There wasn't a hint of anger in his eyes as he hastily ushered her out of the bedchamber. The bodies of the two vampire guards lay in a heap in the corridor and she couldn't tell if they were dead or simply knocked out.

Just outside the door, Helga stood grinning with her slim shoulders squared in pride. Katey hugged her, suspecting that she had the blood servant to thank for them finding her room.

Logan placed his hand on the small of her back to guide her away. "Come on, we don't have much time. The vamps are sleeping, but with all this noise they won't be asleep for long."

He shepherded Katey into the hall and into the stream of fleeing loups-garous. She spotted Forrest and the Deviants, as well as John's sons in the mass of bodies. Who she didn't see was Erik, the one who got them into this mess in the first place. Either he had been left behind as a corpse in the dungeon, or his father made sure to prioritize his escape before any of the other loups-garous could take a shot at revenge against him. Darren and John, too, were nowhere in the crowd.

Ben rushed on ahead of them, while Helga stayed close by Katey and Logan as they hustled toward the main foyer.

"What's the plan or do you have one?" Katey asked.

"Darren and John are taking the elders and their packs out first. Ben, Dustin, and I are leading out the Deviants. Gregory has already started to lead out many of the others. You're going with Darren and John out first."

Katey turned to him with bold determination. "I'm not leaving until every last one of the loups-garous are out of this castle."

Logan pulled her aside in the corridor and glared, but his dominance wouldn't change her mind. "No, I won't have you stay here when you can leave."

Hardly knowing what possessed her to say it, she replied, "I'm not leaving you behind. I already left you once before and I won't do it again. Not ever... Everything you said was dead right and I know I don't deserve your forgiveness, but I can try to make up for my mistakes."

Logan let out a breath. "I said a lot of hurtful things that aren't true, but this isn't the time to talk it out... So I can't convince you to leave and save yourself?"

Katey lifted her chin. "Nope."

He rolled his golden eyes. "Fine. But the minute we're all free, I'm hauling your ass out of here and not letting you out of my sight."

"I wouldn't expect anything less."

He smirked. "I still love you."

"I still love you, too." Even though they were far from out of the woods, Katey kissed Logan on the cheek, a tame and acceptable place while they were still at odds with one another.

That, however, didn't satisfy Logan. He grabbed her around the waist and pulled her in for a deep, long kiss on the lips. It didn't hold that same passionate fire she loved, but it conveyed enough. Their mating bond ringed to life once more and revitalized the part of her that she thought might have been lost in the madness. She should have known that their love would transcend anything the world threw at them.

Logan released her mouth and looked as if he were ready to fall asleep on his feet, their heads bent together and relaxed in each other's embrace as if nothing were wrong with the world. Katey tapped his shoulder and he nodded.

"Right. Escape first."

They came to the stairs that led down to the grand foyer and continued to conduct the loups-garous to move faster. Light and drifts of snow poured through the two massive oak doors that remained propped open as more and more of the pack took off. Many shifted on their way out the door, knowing that it would be a lot faster and warmer to travel in the snow in their fur coats than on bare human feet. They left behind the shredded remains of their sweatpants, but some had enough sense to strip before their quick and painful shift in the cold.

Some who were too weak to shift, rode upon the backs of stronger loups-garous. Ben, even in his loup-garou form, managed to catch anyone who happened to slip on the ice as they made their way out the door.

Katey found Noah out of the crowd and grabbed him before he could make his way down the stairs. Helga was still by her side.

"Noah, take this girl with you and your pack back to the lodge. She needs a good home. Find her one!" Katey guided Helga into Noah's arms. He nodded and began to take her hand, but Helga shied away to run back to Katey.

The young girl wrapped her skinny, frail arms around Katey's torso and embraced her friend one last time. "Thank you, Miss Katey."

Katey returned the hug, and then let her hurry with Noah out into the snow. It was the least she could do for her. She saw that even Ralph staggered out into the wilderness with a small pack thrown over his shoulder and a set of sports car keys dangling from his fingers.

Dustin appeared from upstairs with a sack over his shoulder. Katey had thought he left long before.

"What's all that?" she asked as he slid down the banister with his heavy load.

"All the silver bullets their armory had in stock!" Dustin landed on the marble floor and ran out the doors to sling the sack down the side of the mountain. He returned inside, brushing his hands on the seat of his pants before standing by the door with Ben to make sure everyone exited safely.

It almost seemed too easy, until the last of the Deviants were about to make their way out. The two oak doors suddenly closed by themselves, throwing the foyer into pitch black darkness. By now, the remaining loups-garous were gathered in the foyer, none remained upstairs or in the dungeons. A chill fell upon the room that sent shockwaves up Katey's spine just seconds before the fresh scent of vampire hit her nose.

CHAPTER 27

Ben and Dustin tried to open the doors, but they wouldn't budge, no matter how hard they pushed their shoulders against the thick wood. Katey and Logan, as well as the others, rushed upon the doors and all joined in the effort to force them open, but no amount of inhuman strength even made them creak under their power.

Logan snarled toward the stairs, along with all the other loups-garous that could smell the vamps approaching.

Katey wrapped her hands around Logan's arm and clung to him as she saw Yaverik descend the grand staircase with angry red eyes. His small army fell in behind him on the steps with swords and daggers.

Dustin and Ben moved to stand in front of Logan, as he shielded Katey, pushing her behind him. Forrest was near the head of his pack beside his alpha and Gregory. Those who were older and experienced enough to shift quickly, did so, but many stayed in their human forms, fangs and claws extended for battle.

Katey saw Martel among the ranks of the vampires and they locked eyes. There was no more warmth or affection in his gaze when he looked at her, just the cold, calculating glare of a warrior. Katey no longer fit into his plan and it made her wonder if anything he ever said had been true.

Their army filled the stairs all the way to the bottom step with Yaverik in the lead. They were severely outnumbered, and she would have bet anything that the blades were edged with silver.

Yaverik chuckled and clapped his hands in a slow, rhythmic fashion. "Well done, you beasts. Well done... I won't bother asking how you all managed to escape. It doesn't matter now." He slowly drew out a long blade from the scabbard on his belt and tapped its tip on the marble floor. "Because you're not going anywhere."

The rest of his troops drew their swords and waited for the word. All eyes glowed red upon the loups-garous.

Before Katey knew it, both sides lunged at each other in a rush of blurred bodies and flashing sabers.

Silver blades clashed with teeth and fangs. Flesh was ripped and rivers of blood spilled over onto the cool tile. Logan pushed Katey even further behind him, nearly throwing her into the magically locked doors as Dustin and Ben slashed through any attackers that dared to come near her.

She winced at every whimper and blood-curdling scream that echoed through the halls. In front of her, she could see Logan's back heaving, as he must have been willing himself to shift so he could join the fight. Katey slipped around her defenders and grabbed a sword that had fallen from the hand of a dead vamp and returned to Logan's side. The pommel of the handle was wrapped in leather, deeming it safe for him to handle despite the toxic nature of the blade itself. No doubt, their weapons were silver by the way loup-garou flesh sizzled and burned under its touch.

"Take it!" She reasoned that fighting with a sword would have been much better than trying to shift and become uncontrollable; that was the last thing they needed. If he was going to fight at all, he would do so as a man and not a beast, even though Katey wanted to beg him not to. Holding a man back from a battle like this might as well have been like trying to push back a roaring typhoon with an umbrella.

Logan took it, gave her a kiss on the lips for good luck, and rushed into the fray, using the weapon masterfully against the vamps.

Katey watched with wide eyes as loup-garou and vamp alike tore each other to shreds. She saw that the loups-garous had a serious advantage in the way of size and strength, if they were in their loup-garou forms, but there were so many vamps in comparison to loups-garous that they seemed to match each other equally, the body count nearly equal as the moments passed.

The silver blades took a heavy toll on the loups-garous, but unless they were stabbed or mortally wounded, slices and cuts healed well enough to allow them to stay in the fight. Vampires, however, couldn't come back after their heads were separated from their bodies or their guts forcibly removed.

Katey felt silly just standing around doing nothing, so she grabbed another discarded sword from the corpse of a nearby vampire and stepped forward to partner with her loup-garou defenders.

But she found that she couldn't use it. It wasn't too heavy for her, but she didn't have the strength of will to wield it. The wolf inside her roared in fury at the sword and compelled Katey to drop it. The blade clanged loudly against the marble, the sound lost in the cacophony of battle in the foyer.

The inexplicable sensation of scorn for violence consumed her and she found that she simply didn't have the heart to inflict harm upon anyone. Katey couldn't understand why. She wanted to stand beside her man, help defend their pack, but she simply couldn't.

Katey scanned the fight for any sign of Michael, but she couldn't find him. She hoped that Yaverik hadn't done something to him. Glancing at the fearless vampire lord, she saw him hack through any loups-garous that dared to challenge him. This is what he wanted all along. A bloodbath.

Then Katey saw something that gave her greater cause for alarm. Out of the corner of her eye, she saw Martel and Logan stand face to face. Martel hissed viciously and Logan roared in return. It was as if the two knew exactly who the other was.

A loud cry rang out through the foyer. A vampire had been wounded and the two heavy doors lost a bit of the telekinetic tension that kept them shut tight. A sliver of sunlight pierced the foyer in half, telling them all that the way was clear for them to escape. Dustin and Ben took the chance and rammed their shoulders into the oak doors, allowing more sunlight to fall across the hall. The sun burned some of the vamps before they could dash to the safe shadows, and the opening was just wide enough for some loups-garous to run out single file into the snow. The injured ones were ushered out first and then more followed. Katey did her best to help them, unable to do much else. If they could just retreat into the sunlight, the vampires couldn't follow.

She then turned and anxiously watched from the sidelines as Martel and Logan sparred, coming nearly inches from dealing the deathblow to the other. She noticed Yaverik laying across the steps, gripping his bleeding knee as other vamps either fled or surrendered to the loups-garous that remained in the fight.

Dustin and Ben tried to pull Katey to the doors, but she tore away from their grip. The former growled at her and though she couldn't understand what he said, having shifted for the fight, she could tell that he wanted her to follow them out. There were only a few loups-garous left still battling in the foyer, their fallen comrades bleeding out on the floor or motionless in death.

"I'm not going anywhere without Logan!" Katey ran off toward the bottom of the stairs where Martel and Logan dueled. They fought passionately, each eager to see the other's corpse rotting on the floor.

Dustin, Ben, Gregory, Forrest and a few others remained in the foyer, picking off the last of the vampires when Logan sliced open Martel's fighting hand, causing him to drop his sword.

Logan was about to pierce Martel through the heart when Katey realized none of this was right. She wasn't sure if it was still the sway that Martel had over her, or her sudden need for peace in the middle of absolute chaos, but she knew this victory was tainted.

Katey ran up and stood defiantly between the two, interrupting another of Logan's matches. Logan's sword was held high above her while Martel cowered on the floor, shielding his head from the impending blow.

She placed her hands upon Logan's arms, willing them to lower in truce. "No, Logan. Not like this. You won. Leave him."

Logan snarled at her, but when she refused to stand down, he turned golden eyes to the disarmed Martel. The two warriors locked gazes and both of them seemed to reflect what Katey was feeling. With just a touch, Katey was able to calm Logan's vengeful spirit and he lowered his sword. Martel sat still, unwilling to move, lest the beast change his mind.

In that moment, Katey heard hurried footsteps from the adjoining stairs. Michael entered upon the gory aftermath. He looked at the carnage and shook his head in disbelief. The vampires sensed his presence and the fighting suddenly stopped as all eyes turned to the elderly lord.

"Michael, help us!" Yaverik's command stuttered as he slowly healed from his wounds.

Michael didn't move and glared at his former apprentice. The remaining loups-garous edged toward the ajar doors, but the vampires would not pursue or even get close to the sunlight.

"No, Yaverik. I will not fight." Michael turned to the vamp soldiers. "Let them go."

The vamps dropped their swords, slowly backing away from their opponents, though Katey could see that they thirsted for vengeance for their fallen brethren.

The loups-garous slowly backed away toward the door, their fangs bared in warning to any of the vamps. If they pursued, they would not hesitate to continue the slaughter. Some loups-garous who had been injured had recovered enough to make their way out into the snow to escape.

Katey tugged on Logan's arm. "Let's go."

He dropped his sword and begrudgingly obeyed. Martel didn't budge and continued to hold his injured hand, waiting for it to heal.

"How dare you give orders! You are not in charge here!" Yaverik screamed, limping up toward Michael, who stood tall and defiant. For a moment, Katey could see the flash of boldness that he must have not shown since before he fell from his prominent position as a high-ranking elder.

"A good leader has to know when he's beaten... and we have been beaten, Yaverik. How many more lives do you intend to sacrifice for your selfish pride?"

The floor was slick with the black blood of the vampires. Dismembered corpses littered the floor, loups-garous and vampires alike. Yaverik seethed like a madman in his forced surrender.

Katey looked over her shoulder to the two vampires on the stairs and she caught a glimpse of something from the corner of her eye.

Yaverik pulled out a pistol from his jacket and pointed it straight at Logan's back. He was the closest loup-garou, the closest target.

Katey didn't have a moment to think.

So many things happened in an instant, so fast that Katey could hardly take it all in.

"Yaverik, no!" Michael lunged for the pistol.

The loups-garous still present roared as Yaverik pulled the trigger.

Logan turned just in time to see Katey step behind him to intercept the bullet.

She could have sworn she saw it speed through the air and lodge itself deep in her chest.

At first, all she could feel was the pressure of the impact. Then the breathlessness came, as if she had been knocked in the chest with a hammer. Then finally, the searing, burning pain shot through her core, setting her nerves on fire.

Logan's hands gripped her shoulder as if to move her out of the way, but it was too late.

Katey blinked hard and tried to focus, but her mind went completely blank. Not a single thought was there, not about Logan, Martel, Yaverik, Michael, her pack or anyone else. The world just faded from her consciousness.

Her vision tunneled out and all she could see was the moon. The gorgeous, majestic moon consumed her mind's eye, bathing her in a brilliant golden hue.

Katey waited for death, but it didn't come. She thought she would feel cold, but instead she felt hot. Insanely hot. Her blood boiled beneath her skin. It grew hotter and hotter until that's all she could feel and nothing else. Her heart pounded in her ears and from there, she remembered nearly nothing.

She no longer controlled her body, but the wolf inside her came forward to take the reins.

Her eyes popped open to reveal pure white. No pupil, no irises, just pure white like the snowy ground outside the castle.

Everyone was blown back to the walls of the foyer or up the stairs by an unseen force. Katey remained standing in the middle of the room, exactly where she was when Yaverik shot her. The force that pushed everyone back slammed the doors shut, blocking escape and plunging them into a darkness that didn't last long.

A brilliant light released from Katey's body. The others in the foyer shielded their eyes against the white, blinding light that obliterated every shadow and shattered the darkness around them, but did not disintegrate the vampires.

Slowly, the light receded back to Katey.

But, Katey no longer stood there. In her place was a magnificent, white loup-garou. She stood on her hind legs, towering above the others, white fur shimmering with an ethereal glow and a pair of emerald green eyes blazing.

Logan struggled to prop himself up on his elbows. Michael pulled himself onto the stair banister to gaze at the loup-garou. Even Yaverik was dumbfounded by her pure form. The once war-ring loups-garous and vampires stared in wonder at the white wolf.

The white wolf stood for a moment in all her regal glory and then threw her head back into the most melodious howl that had ever graced their ears. Out of her mouth poured a billowy mist that spread and collected in a dense, murky cloud along the high ceiling, drawing everyone's attention upward.

A scene began to form in the mist, like a smoky vision in a crystal ball. The first image was of a vamp walking through the woods, wearing the garb of the ancient civilization, Arnathia. The vamp looked to be inspecting his surroundings, his concentration unwavering.

Then, a large black bear emerged from the bushes. The bear lunged at the unsuspecting vampire in a blind rage. There was no sound as the spectators in the foyer watched the vampire struggle with the bear in the cloud, entranced by this scene from centuries past.

He was scratched, bitten, and nearly torn to shreds by the beast, unable to heal fast enough as the lifeblood drained from his body into the earth.

Just when it looked like the vampire was about to break free from the mighty bear's claws, he drew precariously close to a ledge that dropped down into a wide river below. He threw himself and the bear with him over the ledge and they plunged into the rapids.

The scene faded into another that followed a dark loup-garou in his full form padding alongside the very same river. The loup-garou sniffed the air when he turned toward the river's shore. There, floating face up was the vampire, alive but just barely.

The loup-garou hurried to investigate and seeing that it was a vampire, took what was left of his collar between his teeth and pulled him onto his side of the shore. The loup-garou took in the vampire's scent and noticed that he was badly wounded.

He looked confused at first, then saw the vamp's eyes slowly open to show that he held onto the last bit of life in him. The loup-garou whimpered and whined, nuzzling the vampire's cheek with compassion. There was nothing he could do.

The vampire's hand reached up and patted the loup-garou's furry neck and gave a weak smile. Then, all at once his eyes drifted shut and his hand dropped to the grass next to him. The loup-garou knew that the vamp was gone and let out a mournful howl to the heavens.

Then, the clouds dissipated and the scene was erased.

"The feud is over." The white loup-garou watched the assembly with her glowing eyes, surveying each of the creatures that stared at her. Her voice, more mature and feminine than Katey's, was perfectly clear and musical, echoing through the foyer like a tumbling chime. "No boundaries were crossed in hostility and no blood was shed by either wolf or vampire. Put aside your hatred and see the truth. We were born from the same bloodline from the dawn of creation. We are brothers and sisters in this life, a family by origin and by blood. There will be no more fighting."

Yaverik was the first to move, using the wall to help him stand in insolence against the white wolf. "I refuse!" His voice sounded so harsh and grating compared to the voice of the white wolf.

He aimed his pistol once more and fired his shot. Instead of hitting its target, the bullet stopped in midair, spinning wildly in place several inches from the tip of her muzzle.

The white wolf didn't even flinch. Yaverik's countenance fell as the bullet dropped to the floor with a resounding ping.

The loup-garou then slowly raised her white paw, lifting Yaverik from the floor without touching him. He struggled against the unseen forces that moved him, shouting for help from his friends, but none dared to move against the white wolf. Her paw turned upwards to show the perfectly white pads underneath and her arm bent toward her as if she were summoning Yaverik forward.

The hateful vampire levitated toward the loup-garou, fear-stricken by what she would do.

He stopped just inches from her, her piercing eyes burning a hole through his soul. "Your days of aggression are over, Yaverik. Yes, I know you and have seen your cruel deeds. There will be peace. You will come to accept that, as will everyone else from both races. If you cause any more unrest, justice will be dispensed upon you so fierce that you will wish for a slow and agonizing death instead of the punishment I would design for you. You have been granted a second chance. Do not waste it."

Yaverik's eyes widened with unparalleled terror.

The loup-garou's hand turned over once again with her palm facing down and she flicked her sharp nails toward the far wall. Yaverik went flying and landed heavily on the stairs with a grunt, falling unconscious.

The loup-garou's paw slowly lowered and she looked to Michael who still gripped the banister on the stairs, his knuckles white.

"A council of both vampires and werewolves will be formed with you as the head of the vampires. John Croxen will serve as head for the wolves, because I have seen his heart and know it is pure. Only assign those who love peace and harmony to this council. They are to decide upon territories for each race and settle disputes among their kind, just as it was in the ancient days."

Michael smiled at the order and nodded proudly to accept his appointment.

The loup-garou then closed her eyes and the same blinding light radiated from her once more. When the light withdrew again, Katey had returned in her human form, fully clothed with the bullet still embedded in her chest.

Katey could feel herself pulled back to consciousness.

The scorching pain and all the sensations, both good and bad, returned to her in a swift rush.

Her legs gave out from beneath her and she crumbled to the floor.

Everyone's cries seemed far away to her ears. Logan rushed to her side to catch her as she fell. Her eyes were still closed but she could feel him cradle her in his arms.

The excruciating pain rattled her body, so much that she couldn't distinguish where exactly she hurt the most. Every muscle and nerve shrieked out in utter agony. The sound of her own heartbeat throbbed in her ears and pounded against her temples, telling her that despite everything, she was still alive. But for how long?

Logan's voice pierced the cloud of muffled noises. "Katey! Katey, can you hear me? Stay with me!"

She cracked open her eyes, expending so much strength to keep them open. She glanced around and saw Logan, Dustin, Ben, and Michael all had rushed to her aid.

She could feel a warm, heavy liquid seeping onto her shirt and pants. The expected cold she thought she would feel with death, gushed over her. Blood drained from her face and her body was given to tremors.

Logan shook her, urging her to keep her eyes open, even though they felt like they weighed a thousand pounds.

"We need to get the bullet out!" Dustin's lips moved in time with the words, but she barely understood them until seconds later as her mind caught up with the moment.

Michael gave an order to a vampire to go into their infirmary to get necessary tools for extracting the bullet.

Katey blinked hard as she tried to hang onto that spark of life she still had left. She could barely breathe, but she knew she had to say something before she left. Katey turned her face up to Logan, whose cheeks were stained with tears as he kept trying to coax her to stay awake.

She reached up and touched his warm cheeks with her fingertips. She gathered her last breath together and uttered those words she reserved for him and only him. No one else ever deserved these words as much as he did.

"I love you, Logan."

He took her hand and pressed it against his flushed skin, his hands trembling. "I love you, too. Please stay with me." Sobs choked in his throat.

Katey gave him a weak smile and let her eyes close one last time. She was ready for this, even if he wasn't.

Just as darkness took her and she could feel her consciousness slip away, Katey heard a chorus of mournful howls that echoed through her mind. She would never forget their sad and grief-stricken tune. She realized then that she would be missed.

CHAPTER 28

I t's been said that people see their whole life flash before their eyes just before they die. For Katey, that wasn't true. She saw the highlights that forever branded the memories in her mind. They were the moments of her life that meant the most.

She saw the time when a strange lady had given her a piece of candy for being a well-behaved child when she was only three, and when she was placed with her first foster family. Katey wouldn't have given these events a second thought a week ago, but the excitement and happiness that she felt when they first occurred was rekindled and filled her soul with warmth as her body went cold with death. Some things were even beyond her remembrance, like the blurry images of Michael handing her over to the midwife when she was a baby.

Katey relived the moment when she first met Logan. Love and joy burst within her silent heart as she saw everything that had happened over the last few weeks. She thought of everything, from their first date in the cemetery, seeing him for the first time in the school hallway, and learning who the teachers really were.

She remembered the pain of Logan turning her and saving her from Mary's totaled car just before it burst into flames. She recalled the thrilling times when they danced at the studio and when she played paintball with him and the guys. She recalled saving him from Erik at the fight, lying with him in his bed that night, playing on the ice back at the lake, their first kiss, and his proposal. Every scene that ever meant anything to her concerning Logan, replayed in her mind in exact detail, as if she were there all over again. He was that much more handsome, the feelings that much stronger, and the pain of separation that much greater.

In the last scene, Katey saw Logan smiling down to her with immeasurable tenderness. She wished she could have looked at that face for the rest of eternity, but it soon faded into white and disappeared.

Then, all she could see was a bleached void and there was no feeling in her body. She looked down and saw she wore the same outfit that she had just died in, but there was no blood or hole in her chest where the bullet had entered.

She looked around in the pure white, but saw nothing and no one at first. Katey wondered where she was, if this was some form of heaven. There was no floor, and no clouds either, just whiteness in all directions and no shadows.

Ahead of her, almost blended perfectly with the white void, was a wolf, pelt as spotless and pure as snow. It watched her with bright golden eyes full of intelligence and wisdom. With his presence came the subtle scents of earth and sea, of wilderness and adventure. Something in her recognized the wolf as male and incredibly old, though she couldn't figure out why. She took a step toward him, testing the distance between them. He calmly turned and she was able to grasp just how large it was.

With slow, careful steps, he walked away from Katey with the silent expectancy that she would follow. She did, and soon, the wolf faded into the void like a puff of smoke.

In his place stood two people, mere figures against the blaring white backdrop. She could distinguish they were a man and a woman. The latter wore a glimmering white gown, and the former wore darker, more casual clothes.

The longer she stared at them, the more she came to realize exactly who they were. Katey had seen the woman so many times in her dreams, and she smiled at her so lovingly, like a mother should. The man with the tanned complexion and squared jaw, she suspected to be her father. His long, dark brown hair was tied at the nape of his neck and piercing green eyes locked with hers in a moment of surreal bliss. Those same eyes stared back at her whenever she looked at her own reflection in the mirror.

When she saw that they weren't getting farther away the closer she came, Katey bolted into a run. Both met her with open arms, and they embraced for the first time since they were parted by fate eighteen years ago.

Katey didn't cry, but her heart felt it would burst with happiness, feeling a wholeness she had never experienced before. It was like her soul was complete once more, having finally acquired that one thing that she felt was missing in her life. Not even Logan could have filled this hole in her heart left by the parents she never knew.

"We are so proud of you, Katey," her mother said softly into Katey's hair. Her voice was musical and gentle, angelic in every way.

"We knew you would do great things," her father added. His wise voice was deep and rumbled against her ear.

Katey pulled back from their hugs to look at them together. "I wish things could have been different."

Her father smiled down on her. "If they were, then you wouldn't have grown up into the amazing young woman that you are." He placed a tender hand upon her cheek. "Things happen for a reason, and you grew up fine despite everything, not because of it."

"And we still watched you grow from a distance." Her mother cradled Katey's other cheek in her warm hand and petted it soothingly with her thumb.

She gave her mother's hand a squeeze and grinned. "I'm just glad we can be together now."

Both of them donned looks of dismay, as if they knew something that they didn't want to confess so soon. Her father's eyes lowered and her mother looked to him for strength.

Panic gripped her chest. "What? Can't we be together now?"

Her father hugged her tightly, his strong loup-garou arms wrapping around her. "It's not your time yet."

"But I just died! I got shot! How can it still not be my time? I want to stay with you!" Katey gripped his shirt and refused to let go, loving the fatherly embrace that she had gone without her whole life. She didn't want the loneliness to return, not now that she knew what she had been lacking all along.

"There are so many more things waiting for you," her mother began. "You have more people who are going to turn to you for guidance. You have a new responsibility now to werewolves and vampires all over the world."

Katey balked at the injustice of it. What more could she possibly do? What more was there to fulfill? Her life was over and now that she knew exactly who she was, Katey was satisfied to stay in the white void for eternity as long as she could be with her parents.

But even in death, the wolf within her was very much alive. With a guiding nudge, she told Katey that her parents were right. It was not her time and there were many more years yet to live before she could be released from her new responsibilities. She resigned to the unfairness and nodded.

Katey pulled back from her father with tears at the creases of her eyes. "How much time do we have left?"

"Not much. They're calling you back right now."

Logan's voice could be faintly heard in the distance, calling out for Katey to return to the living.

"But always know," her father said, "that we love you very much and are proud of you beyond what words can express. We wish you could be here with us, too, but we know you're needed. This just gives you more chances to honor us and make us even more proud of you than we already are."

They hugged one last time, knowing it would be a long, indeterminate amount of time before they would see each other again. She held tightly to her vampire mother and her loup-garou father, proud to be their child.

"Never forget," her mother told her, "that love is what binds us together for eternity."

Her words echoed in Katey's ears as the whiteness faded to black.

In the place of her voice, Katey could hear Logan call out her name in the darkness, drawing her back to consciousness. His voice gradually became louder and louder until it sounded like he was screaming in her ear.

Pain rushed back, and it was almost too much to bear. She felt Logan's arms wrapped tightly around her and many voices were mingled in with his. She heard Dustin shout for the vampire who had run off to get medical tools, Ben trying to tell Logan that she was gone, and Logan denying him over and over.

Katey could even hear the whispers of other vampires and loups-garous as they discussed the vision they had seen in the ceiling produced by a white wolf. She didn't know what they were talking about.

Her senses exploded, and she became acutely aware of every detail down to the breath of everyone in the room and the trace of the metal from Yaverik's gun. Her ears ached with how loud they perceived the heartbeats of those around her.

Then, she felt something peculiar, a watery coolness dropped into her chest where the bullet had buried itself. It filtered past the warm blood and dispersed through her veins, filling her with an airy lightness that shattered the pain and chill of death. Katey began to feel warm again and strength returned to her muscles.

Then Katey's lungs expanded with air. Her heartbeat thundered to life. Her eyes shot open wide and her mouth gaped to gasp for oxygen. Logan was hunched over her, his golden eyes reddened from crying. Dustin and Ben looked down on her in amazement, both had changed back into their human forms.

"She's breathin'!" Ben cried out. Almost everyone in the foyer ran to where Katey lay. Her fingers groped in the vacant space for Logan.

He gripped her hand tightly and pressed it against his wet lips. She could feel the remnants of cold tears. Michael appeared in her field of vision, and she watched him breathe a prayer of thanks to a deity she didn't recognize.

Every breath Katey inhaled was rasping, her body starved for air with such intensity that she began to hyperventilate. The pain ebbed away, but she felt exhausted and fatigued beyond imagination. Every muscle in her body felt strained, as if stretched beyond their limits and then snapped back into place, and she could hardly move. There was a new level of perception with her wolf spirit, like the bond was even stronger now, if that were possible. She could have sworn that she felt it breathing with her, giving her life.

The vampire arrived back with the medical kit, but when he came in with his long tweezers to extract the bullet, he found that the wound had completely closed and healed perfectly, leaving no scar.

"Where's the bullet? There's no hole here," he exclaimed.

Katey thought she had felt something cold slide down her side. She reached under her shirt and touched something that stung her fingertips. She recoiled her hand and hissed at the unexpected burn.

Before she had a chance to touch it again, the vamp reached through and pulled out the silver bullet, coated with her blood.

Katey stared at it and realized that the silver had burned her skin. Somehow, the change was complete, and she was full loup-garou. If her chest didn't feel as if a heavy weight were pressing down on her, she would have laughed in hysterics.

"It was silver, it should have killed her," the vampire marveled, examining the bullet to make sure it really was silver.

Logan pulled Katey up tighter, cradling her against him. A new and unfamiliar sense came that alarmed her. She knew that Logan was overjoyed because she could feel it in her own body and through their bond. The racing heart, the pulsing adrenaline through his veins, she experienced all of it, but she knew that it wasn't her own elation. It was solely his. This wasn't the same as before when she caught little samples of his feelings. She felt it with full and unabridged force.

"Give her some room, Logan!" Ben admonished.

Dustin seconded him and laid her flat onto the cold marble floor. Katey closed her eyes, her mouth still hung open so as to allow the air to flow freely through.

"We've got to get her to the resort's infirmary," Dustin said. "They'll have the right resources to take care of her." He looked at Michael. "How far are we from where you found us?"

"Nearly three hundred miles," the old vampire replied. "It would take days to trek over the mountains."

Dustin shook his head. "Not if we shift and run."

Logan's hold on her hand clenched tighter. "I'll carry her on my back myself if I have to."

"It'd be easier to have her ride on one of us," Ben added. "We can last longer than you can. Darren and the others must be a fair distance away by now."

"Perhaps we could fly her across?" Michael smartly suggested. "We have a helicopter."

"I think your people have done enough for one day," spat one of the loups-garous who had been badly wounded in the fight.

"I'd like you to take what help I can give, please?" the old vampire pleaded. "She's my granddaughter after all."

Everyone's eyes went wide in shock and disbelief.

"What?" Dustin shouted.

Michael chuckled. "I can explain it all on the way there. The helicopter is out on its landing dock. It has special tinted glass that can enable me to accompany you."

"I know how to pilot," Forrest chimed in.

Logan swiftly lifted Katey up into his arms and started to carry her toward the stairs. The rest of the pack quickly followed after them, knowing that there was no time to lose.

"You're going to be okay, Katey," Logan whispered sweetly, kissing her forehead. Katey leaned against his shoulder and let herself drift into a deep and restful sleep.

It took three days for the loups-garous who escaped the vampires to arrive back to the resort. The fanfare of relieved families and friends welcoming their men home, and the mourning for those that died in the battle consumed everyone's attention. All but Logan's pack.

"And then, this bright light filled the whole room!" Dustin waved his hands animatedly as he and Ben tried their best to explain everything that happened to Darren.

Their alpha sat on a cot in the resort infirmary and let another medically trained loup-garou properly bandage his arm. Logan shivered at the sight of the half-healed wound caused by the silver cage bars. The frigid cold of Alaskan winter and biting hunger that persisted during the long trek over the mountains had somehow interrupted the healing process. Dark circles hung under Darren's eyes, and he knew the alpha was in dire need of sleep and a hefty meal, not a story.

Katey had drifted in and out of consciousness, waking just for a bit of meat and water before slipping away again. Still, Logan never moved from her bedside. Not even now while Dustin and Ben took turns telling the tale about Katey and the fight with the vampires. Logan cupped her hand, absently stroking his thumb over her skin.

They came to the part where Katey shifted and Logan watched his alpha's face. Darren's brows lifted as much as they could, given his fatigue.

"White? Completely white?"

Dustin nodded excitedly. "I've never seen a loup-garou old enough to get that kind of white."

They continued to describe the vision Katey created and her little speech about peace and the formation of a new council.

Ben added, "The old vamp told us on the way back that she's some sorta... avatar for a spirit of a princess from thousands of years ago."

That old vampire hadn't made an appearance since he left with his helicopter. However, Logan had a feeling he wasn't too far away. Katey, as impossible as it seemed, was his grand-daughter. She had vampire blood in her, a half breed. It shamed him to remember all the hateful things he said about vampires, but perhaps that was the point. She embodied both races, and there was no room for prejudice anymore.

Darren's stare fell on his sleeping packmate. "Good God... That must have been why we all felt something special in her."

"And why she could survive the bite," Dustin said. "Michael said she could have been turned either way without trouble. It turns out she's not the first ever female loup-garou either."

They shared what few details the vampire told them on the short helicopter ride. They talked about Arnathia, the ancient civilization where vamps and loups-garous lived in harmo-ny. The concept still sounded strange and unnatural. In time, maybe the reverse would be true.

The loup-garou medic finished bandaging Darren's arm, and left the infirmary, though Logan could sense he wanted to stick around to hear the rest. Now, the pack was alone. The loups-garous who were insanely weak chose to convalesce in their own rooms with their own packs and families. But Logan, Darren, Dustin, and Ben couldn't fathom being anywhere else but with Katey.

Darren shifted and adjusted the edge of the gauzy wrapping. "And John is supposed to be in charge of the loups-garous on this new council?"

Dustin nodded. "The vamp said he would find John and catch up with him once everyone's had time to recover."

"We should probably get somethin' to eat." Ben stood. "Want me to bring up some plates from the restaurant?"

Logan noticed how he didn't suggest that they leave the infirmary, but that they would eat there, so Katey wouldn't be left alone. She may not have been conscious, but no one wanted her to wake up by herself. If Logan could help it, she never would again.

Darren gave his consent and Ben left. His brown eyes watched Katey, thoughtful and amazed. "Nothing will ever be the same, will it?"

Dustin huffed a laugh. "Nothing's been the same since Katey walked into our lives."

Logan turned back to his future mate, once more sending her a wordless sentiment of love through their bond. She may have been asleep, but maybe she could feel it. For the third time since they met, he almost lost her to death. He had turned her to avoid such a fate, and even being a loup-garou didn't save her from the silver bullet. Now, knowing just how important she was to their race, he wondered if anything could keep her safe. If she kept jumping in front of bullets, Logan was already set up for failure in protecting her.

He studied her beautiful face, relaxed in a deep sleep. Logan couldn't help but feel lost. What would they do now? How would she change after knowing who she was? Would she change? Would he?

No, this changed nothing for Logan. He still loved her more than air. Nothing she did, nothing she said or turned into would ever weaken his need for her. He couldn't forget everything they had been through, everything they shared. She was his, and for the rest of his life, he belonged to her.

The next time Katey pulled herself from sleep, she felt much more rested and conscious. All the times before, she could barely make sense of her surroundings or utter anything above a couple of pleas for water or food. She knew she was back at the resort, and that she was safe in the infirmary, but little else.

The fatigue she had felt before passing out was gone, and in its place was the common soreness from lying in bed for too long. She took a deep breath, thankful for the air in her lungs. After such an intimate experience with death, she realized all too suddenly that life was not a gift to be wasted.

She knew she wasn't alone in the infirmary. Her spine and skull tingled with the presence of loups-garous. As her senses returned, she could hear conversations above and below her in the other rooms of the resort, but the infirmary was silent. The expansive window on the far wall was dark, telling her that night had come, but that didn't mean much in Alaska. It could have been three o'clock in the morning or six o'clock in the evening, and it would still look pitch-black outside. A few of the overhead lights illuminated the other side of the clinic, but her part of the room was dark, probably so she could sleep more soundly.

Cots lined the walls with carts of medicines and other medical supplies stationed between them. All but four beds were empty. Her packmates occupied three, all sleeping soundly nearby with blankets draped over their bodies. She had never seen them sleep before and cracked a smile at this weird, intimate scene of her pack. Darren was among them and that part of their pack bond became reinforced by his nearness. Besides some white bandage on his forearm, he looked well and fed. He must have returned to the resort with the other loups-garous recently, because he wasn't in the infirmary the last time she woke up.

She turned her head and her eyes fell on Logan, who sat next to her cot in the same place he had been every single time she awoke before, holding her hand firmly in his. His body was bent over the edge of the bed so he could rest his head on his folded arms. There was a peace and fullness to his face that gave him a healthier glow. He must have eaten well and was now dressed in his usual jeans and black shirt that stretched across his muscled back.

The corners of her mouth tilted up and she stroked the back of his hand, watching him sleep. Their mating bond was strong, probably stronger than it had been before she died and came back to life. She recalled how he had consumed her final dying moments. In that white void, he was what she remembered with the most fondness.

Logan was her whole world and happiness. That was why she took the bullet for him. Her love for him went beyond the clearly defined line between life and death. If given the chance, she would sacrifice herself for him all over again. He was worth it.

A familiar scent drifted through the clinic. She turned toward the window and saw a shadowy figure take a step forward into the light.

"You look to be doing very well," Michael said softly, almost in a whisper as he approached her cot. If any loup-garou knew he was here, they might not have been so tolerant to his presence, despite everything that he had done for Katey and her pack. Part of her wondered if his psychic powers kept the rest of her pack sound asleep as they talked.

"Thanks to you." Her voice was weak and cracked.

"Me?" He stood beside her cot and clasped his hands behind his back.

"You offered the helicopter."

Michael smiled. "It was the least I could do after what Yaverik did."

Katey reached out and took his hand. His grip was warm, just as her mother's had been, but not like Martel's or Yaverik's. "And for telling me about... who I am. At least I had a fair warning."

They both chuckled a bit, but both knew that it was true. Katey was the one from the prophecy. There was no doubt about it now and everyone who had witnessed her transformation now had the duty to spread the word across the world. There was to be an armistice and a new council was to be created to orchestrate that peacetime. Katey didn't remember any of that immediately, but her dreams during her recovery got her up to speed. She suspected she had the hybrid princess spirit to thank for that.

"So, I guess that means we're related." Katey's mouth twisted awkwardly at the thought. She also remembered the flashback in the void of when Michael entrusted her to the midwife after her parents were taken. If there was any doubt as to her family ties, they had been shattered in that instant.

"It does... I'm glad to have finally found you. You did your mother proud."

Katey's thoughts ran back to when she had passed to the other side and got to see her parents for the first time. She couldn't help but smile at the vision of her mother, and knowing that she had never really left. Her mother had appeared to her in that chronic dream for so long, a constant presence, even if it was only in the dreamworld. "I know... She's beautiful."

"You saw her?" A string of excitement stitched through his voice.

Katey turned to him and nodded an affirmative. "And my father... They were both there... She says hello."

She saw a wealth of pain and gratitude in his eyes, and just like with Logan's joy, she felt it in her own soul. She wasn't the only one who had been separated from her family for eighteen years. Not only were they bound by blood, but by a common grief that they could share.

"I'm glad I got to see them."

"I am, too... Oh, I almost forgot." Michael reached into his inner coat pocket and pulled out a red rose. It appeared to be a little crushed from the ride it took in his coat on the way there. "Martel told me to give this back to you."

Katey carefully took it from his hands and sniffed the petals like she had the other night. It still smelled just as sweet as it had then, but it no longer held the same meaning somehow. Hearing Martel's name and learning that after everything, he still wanted her to keep the gift, Katey felt next to nothing. His spell over her had been broken in light of all that had happened. That, in itself, was an immense relief.

"Are you going to stay?" Katey asked Michael, hoping that he would. He was the only living blood family she had left and she wanted to hear all about her parents. Not only that, but he was the only one who might have known more about the prophecy and the spirit of peace. He could tell her everything that she needed to know, and she had so many questions.

"Alas, I have been given orders." Michael smiled proudly.

Katey nodded her understanding, knowing that the spirit of the princess had given him the assignment to go recreate a joint council of loups-garous and vampires. It'd be a difficult task, but the spirit knew he would be perfect for the job. After all, they were familiar with one another.

She was sure there would be opposition. Vampires and loups-garous alike would be too absorbed in their hatred to put down their weapons. But with time, Michael and John would do whatever was necessary for the sake of peace.

"I will be in touch. Now that I have found you, I won't lose you again." He planted a tender kiss on the crown of her head, and turned to walk back toward the window.

Katey glanced down at Logan and remembered their inevitable mating. She turned back to let Michael know, but he had disappeared as if into thin air, leaving no trace of his vampire scent.

Something told Katey that they would speak again, very soon. When that time came, she would ask all of her questions and tell him about what few plans she had for her own future. In the meantime, she had a life to live and training to continue with her pack.

Her stiffened muscles protested as she tried to sit herself up and place the rose on the side table next to her bed.

The movement must have awoken Logan. He dragged in a deep breath and looked up to Katey, his blue eyes bright and glistening in the dimmed lights.

"Hey," she greeted with a smile. It was the first time she spoke directly to him since they arrived at the resort.

"Hey." He kissed the back of her hand, all the love in his heart pouring from his lips.

Katey gripped his fingers tighter and smiled. "So, that was a little crazy, huh?"

Logan chuckled and sat himself up onto the cot, still holding her hand between his. "Yes, it was... I thought I lost you."

"You did, at least for a couple of minutes."

Katey then proceeded to tell him about meeting her parents in the void.

"I'm glad you got to see them, but I'm gladder that you didn't stay with them."

They were silent for a moment, as they gazed into each other's eyes, simply happy to be together again and out of immediate danger. After all that had happened, it was the simple things that made the moments worthwhile. Just to hear his heart pumping strong, feeling his pulse in her hand, and knowing that he was alive. There was no rush in this moment, no expectations, no one waiting on them, no one trying to hurt them, no one pushing them in one direction or the other. Right here, they could just exist and breathe the same air, and Katey wanted more of these slow, intimate moments.

"I shifted," Katey finally said, her words woven with awe and delight.

"Yes, you did... You look so beautiful in white."

The two loups-garous whom she wanted to prove herself to hadn't been there to see her shift, but there would be plenty more chances to show them. Logan saw and that was enough for her.

"So, what all happened after I passed out? Is everyone okay?" She glanced toward Darren and his injured arm. She could detect the scent of old blood and some healing salve beneath the bandages.

Logan related to her how they took the vampire's helicopter up and over the mountains to the lodge. Himself, Katey, Dustin, Ben, and Michael were the ones who took the flight. Jacob, the alpha of the Deviants, was put in charge of getting the remnants of his pack over the mountain on foot. Gregory went off on his own, presumably to meet up with his son, whom Logan confirmed was still alive, much to his dismay.

He told Katey about how they had met Michael and that he had related the entire story of her parents, about the war, the prophecy, and brought them up to speed on everything involving what they had witnessed back at the castle.

He told her that when they had all arrived, the families of the loups-garous were waiting at the resort, worried sick for their loved ones. Darren, John, and Forrest arrived with their charges earlier that day. Apart from some loups-garous who needed a good meal, all were well and recovering.

"A few Deviants were killed in the fight. Several were injured that managed to make it out, but their wounds healed slowly."

The battle in the castle had been a massacre of loups-garous and vampires. She remembered the blood and carnage so vividly and knew that it would take a long time to erase such images from her mind. It would have been naïve to think that they would all escape unscathed, but somehow, she wished that the death toll hadn't been so high. She wanted to believe that this whole fiasco wasn't her fault, but she couldn't wish away the nagging guilt that if she had perhaps done something different, all of this could have been prevented.

Then again, perhaps this all happened for a reason, just like her father said. If they hadn't been captured, she would have never found Michael and the feud might not have been resolved.

All she could do was carry on, mourn those who had given their lives, and learn from their mistakes. An era of peace was dawning and if Katey had anything to do with it, no more blood would be shed. But, like Logan had said so long ago, death was part of their lives. Violence might not be avoidable.

"Will you two shut up?" Dustin's crackled voice broke through the quiet of the infirmary. "Some of us are trying to sleep."

Katey held in a giggle as Logan flipped him the bird with a teasing sneer.

Dustin's complaint apparently roused Darren enough for him to crack open his warm brown eyes and look at his two packmates. With great effort, he forced himself to sit up and pushed back his blanket.

"How's the arm?" Logan asked, jerking his chin at the alpha's injury.

He tested it and winced when his fingers found a tender spot. "Still raw." Darren looked to Katey and gave her a tired smile. "How are you feeling?"

"Much better."

"They told me you shifted. How does it feel to be a full loup-garou now?"

Katey took a deep breath and shook her head. "Honestly, I was so worried that I didn't belong anywhere. Not with humans or loups-garous. Before I shifted, the loup-garou part of me was fading away and I was scared that I'd be human again. Now that I know beyond a doubt that I am loup-garou, it's a relief. It's like I know who I am now."

Part of the way through her speech, Ben sat up from his cot, hair disheveled and bleary eyed. "We didn't know you felt like that."

Katey grimaced, remembering the days spent in mental anguish as she wrestled with the thought of whether she was loup-garou or not. Those days were behind her and there was nothing to stop her from excelling as a true member of their pack.

"After I didn't shift and how I wasn't getting burned by the silver, I felt like I wasn't really a part of the pack."

Logan pressed the back of her fingers to his lips and shook his head. He was the only one who knew her fears, after that day they walked into town and discussed it.

"No matter what would have happened," Darren said, "you would have always belonged here with us. You were one of the pack even before you changed."

Dustin sat up, apparently giving up on sleep. "And that makes you family."

She never knew they accepted her so unconditionally as a human. Darren had mentioned it a few times before, but it never quite hit her the way it had now, after everything that had happened.

All she could do was utter a soft thank you.

She gazed up into Logan's rich blue eyes, and remembered when she had seen his face in her first moments of death. She thought he had never looked more handsome, and she would never forget the loving sparkle in his eyes. Katey wouldn't forget any of their faces. When she died again, she knew she would relive this moment.

This was the moment when Katey finally realized where her home had always been.

AFTERWORD

Dear Reader,

Ready to find out what happens to Katey, Logan and the whole pack? It's going to be interesting, I can tell you that. Follow the loup-garou pack into the next book, Beast Within, to see what kind of new threat they must overcome in their effort to bring peace between the races.

If you're interested in learning more about these characters' backstories, also check out The Legacy Series. Each books follows a certain character from the Loup-Garou Series. Find out how Ben got turned during the Civil War, or how Katey's parents met at a lighthouse in Oregon.

In the meantime, I invite you to check out my social media sites for more updates and sneak peeks into my progress. You can find me at my blog, www.moonstruckwriting.wordpress.com.

Happy Reading!
Sheritta Bitikofer

About the Author

Sheritta Bitikofer is an author of paranormal and historical fiction. She lives for the deep, engaging stories that enthrall readers from cover to cover. As a wife and mother of eclectic tastes, she can be found roaming Civil War battlefields, haunting her local coffeeshop, or relaxing with a plate of chili cheese fries.

Follow her for upcoming novel releases
www.sherittabitikofer.com

Also by Sheritta Bitikofer

Bewitching Darkness
Bewitching Hearts
<u>Wolves in the Open</u>
Highland Howls
Silver Screen
Mourning Moon
<u>The Decimus Trilogy</u>
The Beast of Verona
Amber Ashes
Saving the Beast
<u>Redemption Duet</u>
The Rose
The Lion
<u>Standalones</u>
Escape
Clouds
Passions
By The Book

www.ingramcontent.com/pod-product-compliance
Lightning Source LLC
Chambersburg PA
CBHW072258020726
47501CB00002B/310